Studying Crime in Fiction

The primary aim of *Studying Crime in Fiction: An Introduction* is to introduce the emerging cross-disciplinary area of study that combines the fields of crime fiction studies and criminology. The study of crime fiction as a genre has a long history within literary studies, and is becoming increasingly prominent in twenty-first-century scholarship. Less attention, however, has been paid to the ways in which elements of criminology, or the systematic study of crime and criminal behaviour from a wide range of perspectives, have influenced the production and reception of crime narratives. Similarly, not enough attention has been paid to the ways in which crime fiction as a genre can inform and enliven the study of criminology. Written largely for undergraduate and graduate students, but also for scholars of crime fiction and criminology interested in thinking across disciplinary boundaries, *Studying Crime in Fiction: An Introduction* provides full coverage of the backgrounds of the related fields of crime fiction studies and criminology, and explores the many ways they are reciprocally illuminating.

The four main chapters in Section 1 (Orient You) familiarize readers with the history and contours of the broad fields within which *Studying Crime in Fiction: An Introduction* operates. It introduces the history of crime and criminology, as well the history of crime fiction and the academic field dedicated to its study. In its final chapter it looks at the ways these areas of study can be conceptually interrelated. Section 2 of the book (Equip You) is dedicated to examining aspects of criminological theory in relation to various forms of crime fiction. It highlights a range of the most relevant theories, paradigms, and problematics of criminology that appear in, shed light on, or can be effectively illuminated through reference to crime fiction. Its five chapters deal with the definition of crime; explanations for crime and criminal behaviour; investigations into crime; the experience of crime; and, finally, punishments for crime. All of these areas are examined alongside examples of crime fiction drawn from across the genre's history. Section 3 (Enable You) presents six case studies. Each of these reads a work of crime fiction alongside one or more criminological approaches. Each case study is supplemented with a set of questions addressing issues central to the study of crime in fiction.

Eric Sandberg completed his PhD at the University of Edinburgh, and has held positions at universities in Turkey, Japan, and Finland. He is currently Associate Professor at City University of Hong Kong, and also holds a docentship at the University of Oulu, Finland. His research interests range from modernism to the contemporary novel, with a particular focus on crime fiction, adaptation, and nostalgia studies. He has written and edited six books, and his work has appeared in numerous edited collections and journals.

Studying Crime in Fiction
An Introduction

Eric Sandberg

 Routledge
Taylor & Francis Group

NEW YORK AND LONDON

Designed cover image: © Getty

First published 2024
by Routledge
605 Third Avenue, New York, NY 10158

and by Routledge
4 Park Square, Milton Park, Abingdon, Oxon, OX14 4RN

Routledge is an imprint of the Taylor & Francis Group, an informa business

© 2024 Eric Sandberg

ISBN: 978-0-367-74210-2 (hbk)
ISBN: 978-0-367-74209-6 (pbk)
ISBN: 978-1-003-15658-1 (ebk)

DOI: 10.4324/9781003156581

Typeset in Sabon
by Newgen Publishing UK

Contents

Acknowledgements

This project was initiated by Professor Emeritus Fiona Peters of Bath Spa University, and acknowledgment of this fact is due. I of course bear responsibility for the final product; any errors or missteps are mine alone. I am grateful to Bryony Reece at Routledge for her support and patience, and to Hilary Wun who offered very useful research assistance. Ffion Davies has been a valuable interlocutor with regards to all aspects of crime fiction. Dr Simon Harrison of City University of Hong Kong has offered a model of intellectual curiosity and ambition, and even more importantly friendship, during the writing of this book. The same could be said of many of the academics around the world I have met and worked with over the past years, but I would like to mention Drs Lena Ahlin and Maria Frej of Kristianstad University, Drs Carlos Uxo Gonzalez, Stewart King, and Barbara Pezzotti of Monash University, Dr Rune Graulund of the University of Southern Denmark, Dr Collen Kennedy-Karpat of Bilkent University, Professor Thomas Leitch of the University of Delaware, and Professor Niklas Salmose of Linnaeus University, all of whom have been enormously helpful, and have made being an academic something closer to the dream of a scholarly community than would otherwise have been the case. I would also like to acknowledge the invaluable support throughout my career of the late Professor Laura Marcus of Oxford University. Finally, Johanna Sandberg has not only kept me on track when I wandered or wondered or procrastinated, and provided invaluable editorial assistance, but has also been, along with The World's Greatest Detectives, my reading companion and my life companion—but what's the difference?

Introduction

On a lonely moor in England, a husband and wife masquerading as brother and sister scheme to frighten a man to death and inherit his estate by painting a huge dog's mouth with phosphorus to simulate an ancient legend; their plot is foiled by an eccentric genius and his loyal if dim-witted partner. On a train travelling between Istanbul and London, a man is killed by 12 people in revenge for the kidnapping and murder of a young child many years before; the crime is solved by a Belgian detective with prodigious mustachios coincidently travelling in the same carriage. In interwar Los Angeles, a private eye is hired by a wealthy old man to deal with a clumsy blackmail attempt; a convoluted string of murders ensues, leading the gumshoe back to the family mansion, and to his client's daughter, who has killed her sister's husband because he refused to sleep with her. In 1980s America, a woman is kidnapped by a man who wants to make a suit out of her skin; a young FBI agent develops a rapport with an imprisoned cannibalistic serial killer, and with his help cracks the case. In twenty-first-century Sweden, a disgraced journalist and a young, tattooed hacker team up to find a missing girl; they uncover a multi-generation history of abuse, torture, and serial murder in a family of wealthy industrialists. All of these stories will be familiar to many readers of crime fiction. Arthur Conan Doyle's *The Hound of the Baskervilles* (1902), Agatha Christie's *Murder on the Orient Express* (1934), Raymond Chandler's *The Big Sleep* (1939), Thomas Harris' *The Silence of the Lambs* (1988), and Stieg Larsson's *The Girl with the Dragon Tattoo* (2005) are all popular examples of a popular genre, and even in the truncated versions of their plots offered here they are readily recognizable.

But what do these novels, and the tales of crime and investigation they offer the reader, have in common? Their settings and characters are diverse, as are their formal structures. They all centre on or around a criminal act, but they do so in very different ways, perhaps because they are representatives of a number of different subgenres. There is no reason, we

DOI: 10.4324/9781003156581-1

might think, that an English Golden Age detective novel should have much in common with an early twenty-first century Scandinavian crime thriller, or a classic nineteenth-century mystery with a late twentieth-century American crime novel. But one thing these works share, despite their many differences, is their fictionality. These are stories that are openly implausible, relying on plots that may not be literally fantastic (although at times they certainly approach that condition), but are certainly unlikely. They make, in other words, little if any pretence of being realistic. People are murdered on trains in the real world, but they are not murdered by groups of irate citizens carrying out elaborate forms of vigilante justice.

It may seem tautological to point out the fictionality of crime fiction, but it is an important point for two main reasons. First, as Lucie Armitt argues in her study of fantasy proper, there is a clear and well-established hierarchy at work in the literary world: 'realism is certainly the type of fictional writing adopted most readily by the canon, seen as most fitting for serious or weighty subject matter'.[1] Crime fiction's lack of apparent connection to the real world, its overt fictionality, is part of the reason that it has long been relegated to the less prestigious corners of the literary world as a genre 'capable of offering entertainment, excitement, and even intellectual stimulation, but [...] separate from, and subordinate to, mainstream literary fiction'.[2] In terms of criticism, the idea of realism has frequently been used to justify crime fiction, as when W. H. Auden writes of Raymond Chandler that he 'is interested in writing, not detective stories, but serious studies of a criminal milieu [...] and his powerful but extremely depressing books should be read and judged, not as escape literature, but as works of art'.[3] The closer a work of crime fiction is to reality, in other words, the closer it is to literature. The veracity of this statement is, to put it mildly, doubtful, but it does reflect a widespread and persistent attitude towards the genre as a whole. Crime fiction is in many cases, and even in many of its forms, simply not realistic enough to matter.

The second reason that crime fiction's fictionality is important is that its lack of verisimilitude and facticity would seem to separate the genre from other discourses on crime, and specifically from the discourses of criminology. This is a field that draws inspiration from a wide range of very different contributing disciplines, including biology, cultural studies, education, forensics, history, politics, philosophy, psychology, sociology, and law.[4] While this is indeed a diverse set of specialities, they are all (with the possible and partial exception of cultural studies) directed towards reality and the understanding of the real world of real people in real places dealing with real problems. It might seem, then, that this book, based as it is on the conjunction of factual and fictional responses to crime, is likely to face a substantial problem in reconciling these fundamentally different approaches. I hope that the book itself will be able to allay this concern by indicating some of the ways our two longest lasting and most influential discourses on crime, criminology and crime fiction, can indeed be read alongside each other in ways that are interesting, engaging, and enlightening.

A great deal of work has already been done in this field, with scholars very effectively making the case for integrating the study of crime fiction and mainstream forms of criminology. Rafe McGregor, for example, contends in his recent monograph *Critical Criminology and Literary Criticism* that crime fiction (or what he calls 'criminological fiction') offers at least three main forms of 'criminological knowledge': 'phenomenological (representing what certain experiences are like), counterfactual (representing possible but non-existent situations), and mimetic (representing everyday reality in detail and with accuracy)'. All three of these forms of knowledge, McGregor argues, are in effect 'data that explains the causes of crime or harm and that can be used to improve policies, procedures, and practices aimed at the reduction of crime or harm'.[5] Crime fiction, in this view, has a role to play alongside traditional sources of criminological information (such as crime statistics, victim interviews, or public surveys) in providing valuable data to the criminological investigator. Similarly, in *Criminology, Deviance, and the Silver Screen: The Fictional Reality and the Criminological Imagination*, Jon Frauley makes the case for using fictional narratives (in his case, Hollywood cinema) as part of a 'craft-enterprise' approach to criminological theorizing: 'fictional worlds offer contained social realities that can be used to exemplify abstract concepts and can also operate as empirical referents to which our concepts and theories can be applied'.[6] This means that fiction can help to both clarify criminological concepts and to illustrate how these ideas can contribute to understanding crime.[7] Both of these approaches can be placed in the context of what can be described as cultural, critical, or creative criminology. These approaches 'supplement the often sterile and scientistic view of criminology—constantly searching for correlations, causality and background forces—with a more creative, cultural and critical or *Verstehen*-oriented [empathic] approach looking for human meaning-making, creativity, cultural processes and critical understandings'.[8] In other words, reading crime fiction can help develop a new, or at least improved, version of criminology.

This book is very much part of the movement towards a more culturally inclined criminology, introducing and exploring the ways reading crime fiction can shape and re-shape our thinking about criminal transgression, policing, justice and injustice, punishment and deterrence, and so on. But the process of illumination is, or should be, reciprocal. By this I mean that we should be able to understand crime fiction better by reading it alongside criminological theory. This is a genre of fiction that developed, after all, in an intimate relationship with real-world judicial structures. Consider the fact that the memoirs of Eugène Vidocq, a criminal-turned-policeman who played a key role in founding the criminal investigation bureau of the Paris police force (the *Sûreté*), were among the most popular and influential crime texts of the nineteenth century. These memoirs were presented to the reading public as factual, but this characterization is dubious. Vidocq himself quickly appeared in fictional guise in the work of other writers, such as Honoré de Balzac's Vautrin, who appears in several novels in *La Comédie humaine* (1830–1856), and Émile Gaboriau's Monsieur Lecoq, who was in turn an inspiration for Arthur Conan Doyle's Sherlock Holmes. Even today, some two centuries after crime fiction began to develop as a separate and readily identifiable genre, its relationship to the real world of crime, investigation, and punishment remains close. One notable recent example is David Simon's landmark television series *The Wire* (2002–2008), which was based on his own work as a Baltimore journalist on the crime beat, and on his writing partner Ed Burns' 20 years of experience as a Baltimore police officer.

To achieve its goal of introducing and extending this cross-disciplinary conversation, this book is presented in three main sections. The first, labelled 'Orient You', is introductory in intent. It offers a broad historical context, including chapters on the history of crime as a phenomenon, and criminology as a discipline that studies that phenomenon, as well as chapters on crime fiction as a literary genre, and crime fiction studies as a discipline that studies that genre. The section concludes with a chapter examining the linkages between the two fields. The second section of the book, 'Equip You', is intended to help develop an effective conceptual tool kit for thinking about criminology and crime fiction. It focuses on five separate areas in which criminology and crime fiction overlap in important ways: these chapters deal with the definition, motivation, investigation, experience, and punishment of crime. Each chapter draws on a relevant body of criminological theory and refers to a diverse range of crime fiction texts. Finally, the third section of the book, 'Enable You', offers six case studies, each focusing on a particular crime fiction text and reading it in relation to one or more criminological approaches. The goal of this section is to demonstrate how criminological readings of crime fiction can work.

Each of the case studies in the third part of the book concludes with a brief reflection on areas for further thought, study, and research, but I hope that *Studying Crime in Fiction: An Introduction* will as a whole perform a similar function. The whole set of questions that circulate around criminality, be they about the definition of criminal behaviour in relation to social and legal norms or broader economic structures, or explanations for crime's persistence across time and place, or debates over the best ways to reduce crime and its impact, are becoming more, not less, important as we move further into the twenty-first century. Similarly, crime is occupying an ever-greater cultural space, as it remains dominant in older forms of cultural production like the novel, and as it spreads into newer media like streaming television and video games. This fascination, this obsession, with crime is unlikely to diminish soon. There is abundant evidence that we live in a world under extraordinary environmental, economic, political, and cultural stress. These are problems that feed into not just crime itself, but into our definitions and responses to it. The better we are able to think about crime with all the tools at our disposal, including both the factual and the fictional, the better we will be able to face these challenges.

Notes

1 Lucie Armitt, *Fantasy Fiction: An Introduction* (New York: Continuum, 2005), 1.
2 Eric Sandberg, "Contemporary Crime Fiction, Cultural Prestige, and the Literary Field." *Crime Fiction Studies* 1, no. 1 (2020), 5.
3 W. H. Auden, "The Guilty Vicarage: Notes on the Detective Story, by an Addict." *Harpers* (May 1948), 408.
4 Rob White, "Criminology," in *The Wiley-Blackwell Encyclopedia of Social Theory*, edited by Bryan S. Turner (Oxford: Wiley Blackwell, 2017), 1.
5 Rafe McGregor, *Critical Criminology and Literary Criticism* (Bristol: Bristol University Press, 2021), 5.
6 Jon Frauley, *Criminology, Deviance, and the Silver Screen: The Fictional Reality and the Criminological Imagination* (New York: Palgrave Macmillan, 2010), 2.
7 Ibid., 13.
8 Michael Hviid Jacobsen, "Towards the Poetics of Crime: Contours of a Cultural, Critical and Creative Criminology," in *The Poetics of Crime: Understanding and Researching Crime and Deviance Through Creative Sources*, edited by Michael Hviid Jacobsen (Farnham: Ashgate, 2014), 3.

Section 1
Orient You

1   A History of Crime

In 1941, a 33,000-year-old calvaria—the upper portion of a human skull—was recovered from the Pestera Cioclovina cave in Southern Transylvania. The Cioclovina calvaria, as this fragment is known, is one of the oldest directly dated and well-preserved remains of a modern human ever found in Europe; it is also our oldest evidence of what the forensic scientist Elena F. Kranioti and her colleagues Dan Grigorescu and Katerina Harvati (a geologist and a paleoanthropologist) call 'fatal inter-personal violence among early Upper Paleolithic modern humans'.[1] The unlucky possessor of the Cioclovina calvaria was killed, the scientists' examination suggests, 'by a blow from a likely left-handed perpetrator facing the victim' that may have been 'a result of a one to one conflict or murder by one or more perpetrators'.[2] As the media were quick to note, this was the ultimate 'cold case closed',[3] providing direct evidence of a history of violence stretching far back into our past.

Yet describing the reconstructed event that led to the sudden and violent death of the Cioclovina man as murder raises important questions regarding the history of crime. While the evidence clearly indicates violence, there are many situations in which this would not be equated with crime in general or murder in particular. If, for example, the 'blow with a round, bat-like object'[4] that felled the victim was delivered in self-defence, we would be discussing a case of justifiable homicide; if it was delivered under a sudden impulse arising from emotional or situational stress it might be considered manslaughter. If, however, it was delivered during a conflict between two groups of palaeolithic hunter-gatherers competing over access to scarce natural resources in a challenging environment, we might describe Cioclovina man as a casualty rather than a victim. When we kill on behalf of our social group, we are soldiers rather than murderers, and our violence results in honour not opprobrium. In a less likely (or even ahistorical) but nonetheless imaginatively useful scenario, the killers could have been Neanderthals (who may have survived in isolated pockets

DOI: 10.4324/9781003156581-3

in Europe until roughly 35,000 years ago) rather than *Homo sapiens*. In this case, the violence would be inter- rather than intra-species, and would no more be considered murder than would a modern human killing, for instance, another primate. And given the fact that the Neanderthal were at this time probably subject to exterminatory pressures from migrating *Homo sapiens*, in this scenario the killing of Cioclovina man could be seen as an act of heroic resistance, not just justifiable but necessary.

In any case, in a palaeolithic context the question of the criminality or otherwise of the killing would be anachronistic. William Golding's extra-ordinary work of imaginative fiction *The Inheritors* (1955) deals with a conflict between Neanderthals and *Homo sapiens*. The main characters, the Neanderthals Lok and Fa, are horrified when they discover that an encroaching band of 'the new people' have killed two members of their small band and kidnapped two others.[5] But they do not interpret this almost complete destruction of their family as a crime. It is just something that happens, horrible and terrifying, but no different from the many other dangers they face in their precarious existence.

All of this is of course speculative, but it is a useful reminder that a his-tory of crime is not the same thing as a history of violence; while acts of violence have occurred, as Kranioti and her colleagues have demonstrated, for tens of thousands of years, and presumably much longer, these acts cannot be seen as crimes unless they are situated within a collective code of behaviour. The existence of crime, in other words, requires the exist-ence of law. These laws may not be—indeed for most of human history were not—written down or formally codified. But they would certainly have existed: any group that did not have prohibitions intended to protect itself from the disruptive violence of individuals would not have lasted long in an environment that favoured group cohesion and collaboration. Anthropologists and legal historians point out that preliterate societies vary tremendously in terms of the social norms, behavioural codes, and disciplinary processes which prefigure our own judicial processes and institutions,[6] but all such societies have them.[7]

One example of this sort of system is the concept of taboo. The term is of Polynesian origin, where it describes according to Franz Steiner's ground-breaking work, 'social mechanisms of obedience which have ritual significance' and 'specific and restrictive behaviour in dangerous situ-ations'.[8] Taboo is thus intended to protect both individuals and society as a whole. Following James Cook's voyages in the Pacific (1768–1779), the term entered wider circulation, and has proved extremely useful in describing a range of pre-legal, socio-religious ritual prohibitions (although as Sigmund Freud points out in *Totem and Taboo* [1913], it has analogues in many other linguistic traditions).[9] Golding's *The Inheritors* is again illu-minating here. The novel's last chapter focuses on the modern humans (the inheritors of the title) in the aftermath of their encounter with the Neanderthal. Tuami, a young man, is enraged by the group's older leader Marlan, 'hating him' and planning to 'use the ivory-point' of his dagger.[10] But even to 'watch Marlan's face and intending to kill him was daunting', and Tuami quickly abandons his murderous plan.[11] This reluctance stems from neither ethical doubt nor personal fear, but from the fact that the leader's life is wrapped in a protective mantel of customary reverence; it is taboo. Should Tuami ever work up the nerve to carry out his attack, it would be better thought of as social and ritual transgression than as a palaeolithic crime. Taboos, as Freud notes, 'themselves impose their own prohibitions; they are differentiated from moral prohibitions by failing to be included in a system which declares abstinences in general to be necessary and gives reasons for this necessity'.[12]

Crime in the Ancient World

In order to have crime proper, then, we need to have a system of laws. Our oldest extant legal codes emerge out of the Mesopotamian civilizations of the Middle East. The Code of Ur-Nammu, for example, is recorded on a fragmentary tablet (c. 2100 BCE) excavated from Nippur, a Summerian city located in present-day Iraq. The five laws that remain legible are concerned with witchcraft, the recovery of escaped slaves, and physical harm,[13] with a focus on financial compensation. If a man breaks another man's foot, he must pay '10 shekels of silver', while a severed nose is worth roughly four times as much.[14] The much more famous Code of Hammurabi, carved on a 2.25-metre stone stele (c. 1754 BCE), contains 282 laws dealing with commercial, domestic, and civil behaviour, as well as crime.

Three key points emerge out of an examination of the Code of Hammurabi. First, it tells us by inference what criminal acts people committed in ancient Mesopotamia. The history of criminal law is, as it were, the visible shadow cast by an invisible history of crime. The eighth law in the code, for example, stipulates that

> if a man has stolen an ox, or a sheep, or a donkey, or a pig, or a boat he shall pay thirty times its value if it belongs to a god or a temple and repay ten times its value if it belongs to a workman. If that thief does not have enough to pay he shall be killed.[15]

The existence of this law implies that the behaviour it proscribes was reasonably common, and even indicates the type of property most vulnerable to theft: domesticated animals and boats are both compact sites of highly portable value, which as the contemporary car thief can testify is an attractive combination. Second, the code is an explicit and detailed assertion of the state's sole authority to regulate deviant behaviour; private revenge or feuding is supplanted by the state's formal vengeance. Third, penalties and punishments are both clearly defined and linked to the social position of the perpetrator and the victim. This was, as Mitchel P. Roth writes, 'a rich man's law'.[16] The epilogue of the code claims that it was created 'so that the mighty might not exploit the weak, and so that the orphan and the widow may be treated properly'.[17] This is all good and well, but proper treatment here depends on social hierarchy. The last of the laws, for example, defines the assertion of individual freedom as a crime: 'if the slave has stated to his master, "You are not my master," his master shall prove that it is his slave and cut off his ear'.[18]

To find any sense of the injustice inherent in this sort of legally mandated hierarchical violence, we must look not to legal codes but to literature. In the *Epic of Gilgamesh*, which has survived in a version that is tradition-ally attributed to the Babylonian scribe Sîn-liqe-unninni (c. 1200–1100 BCE), we find the ancient city-state of Uruk (in approximately 2750 BCE) ruled over by the semi-divine King Gilgamesh. Gilgamesh is an impressive figure, 'surpassing all other kings, heroic in stature',[19] but he is also a tyrant who 'harries' the 'young men of Uruk without warrant' (likely meaning he uses them for forced labour) and 'lets no girl go free to her *bride[groom]*' (emphasis and brackets in original).[20] While Gilgamesh tells his officers, very much in the spirit of the Hammurabic Code, to 'judge the lawsuit of the weak',[21] he is himself above the law. However, his adventures with his companion Enkidu, during which they slay Humbaba, guardian of the forest, and the Bull of Heaven, are transgressive, and are divinely punished by Enkidu's death. This loss, and Gilgamesh's subsequent failed quest for immortality, can be read as asserting the existence of a sort of natural, universal law that applies to all people, no matter where they are located in the social order.

This discussion of crime and punishment on the banks of the Euphrates may seem excessively detailed. But Mesopotamian legal concepts had a lasting influence throughout the Near East, ancient Greece and Rome, and, eventually, much of the Western world.[22] In broad terms, we can describe the Code of Hammurabi as a prototypical statement of the law that can stand in for other well-known ancient attempts to formalize the boundaries governing the behaviour of individuals in society, like the Mosaic decalogue, a proto-legal document that prohibits specified behav-iour without assigning specific penalties (c. 1500–1200 BCE); the Athenian Code of Draco, the severity of which has left us the term 'draconian' (621–620 BCE); and the Roman Law of the Twelve Tables, which dealt with a wide set of behaviours including familial and economic relations (449 BCE). The last of these was supplanted by the Emperor Justinian's *Corpus Juris Civilis* (529–534 CE), a vast and elaborate complex of laws which has had a powerful influence throughout Europe from the Middle Ages into the modern era, and (via colonization) on the world as a whole.[23]

Like the Hammurabic Code, all of these sets of laws offer an indication of what a given society viewed as mandatory, permissible, and impermissible forms of behaviour, and thus by inference the many ways people transgressed these boundaries. The Code of Draco, for example, prohibited murder, but distinguished between premeditated, unpremeditated, and justifiable homicide.[24] The Twelve Tables stipulated financial recompense for lesser offences such as theft, but capital punishment for the incitement of a public enemy, while also attempting to regulate personal behaviour by, for example, banning marriage between members of different social classes.[25]

It is again to literature, however, that we must look for an imaginative expansion on, and response to, the cold tablets of the law; literature tells us not just what crime was, but how it was experienced, felt, and framed within a broader context. Sophocles' *Oedipus the King* (c. 429 BCE), for example, offers a sustained meditation on its protagonist's impulsive violence, exactly the type of behaviour ancient codes of law were concerned to regulate and channel into the hands of the state. By failing to control his rage during what was essentially a traffic dispute, Oedipus unleashes a sequence of events including patricide and incest that ultimately has grave consequences for himself and his whole community. Sophocles' *Antigone* (c. 441 BCE), on the other hand, deals with the misapplication of centralized legal authority. When Oedipus' daughter defies her uncle King Creon's command that her brother's corpse be left unburied as a punishment for his rebellion, she knowingly breaks an unjust and tyrannical law. Her subsequent death once more leads to serious consequences, in this case for Creon and his family. These two plays illustrate the Scylla and Charybdis of criminal law: it is necessary for any civilization above a certain developmental threshold to control violence and other forms of injustice that endanger the community, yet it is always in danger of becoming itself a force for injustice.

Crime in the Middle Ages

In a European context, the collapse of the Roman Empire and the advent of the Germanic kingdoms led to fundamental changes in conceptions of crime and legal procedures. The sixth-century CE Frankish Salic or Salian law, for example, was much less interested in family law, inheritance, and marriage than in establishing a set rate of fines for a wide range of often violent offenses.[26] In this it is not too distant in spirit from the Code of Hammurabi; also familiar is the graded scale of payments based on the social status of the victim of a crime. The *wergild*, or 'price of a man', was fixed at 200 pence for the murder of free man, but triple that for an associate of the King or a free woman of reproductive age; the cost for a murdered slave was only 100 pence.[27] Britain, before the Norman conquest of 1066, had a related justice system, with a system of fines supplemented by physical penalties. Guilt or innocence was determined by trial by ordeal, in which fire and water took the place of the Roman jury, or by the intercession of 'oath-helpers' who could attest to the accused's character and thus probable innocence. When Queen Uota (or Ota) of Carinthia was accused of adultery in 899 CE, she was able to clear herself of the charge with the help of an astonishing 72 oath-helpers.[28] This should make clear both the distinction between an oath-helper and a witness, and the way the definition of crime changes over time and place. Uota may or may not have 'yielded her body to a lustful and wicked union' as recorded in *The Annals of Fulda*,[29] but adultery has not been a crime in Austria (the present location of the Duchy of Carinthia) since 1997, or anywhere in Europe since 2006.

While we no longer view adultery as criminal, many medieval offenses would be both familiar and recognizable as criminal today. Physical assault and theft of various degrees of severity were common; so too were crimes of deceit, including forgery, the use of false weights and measures, and other fraudulent business practices. What would strike a contemporary observer as outlandish would not be the crimes committed, but the ways they were prosecuted and punished. While the Norman conquest introduced many familiar aspects of the modern legal system to Britain, other judicial practices such as trial by combat (which like other types of ordeal was intended to facilitate divine adjudication) are less familiar. When guilt had been determined, punishments were often ferocious, with both social penalties like the pillory and corporal chastisements such as mutilation and amputation. Recourse to execution (generally by hanging, but considerably more painful alternatives were available) was always possible, even for what we would today think of as minor crimes.

These increasingly severe punishments—and historians have associated the shift from a general reliance on the monetary penalties of the *wergild* tradition to corporal punishment with the emergence of the centralized, early modern state—were often a response to another familiar phenomenon: the sense that a particular society is being overwhelmed by crime.[30] An early example of this is the widespread judicial reform instituted by Henry II of England following the collapse of social and administrative order during the Anarchy (1135–1153 CE). In this case, it seems the increased scope of legal activity and the increased emphasis on punitive deterrence were justified by the reality of large-scale disorder and criminality.[31] Some centuries later, however, we find a similar judicial crackdown directed not at murders, kidnappers, and rapists, but against witches. This 'witch craze', which has been described as the ' "mother" of all moral panics',[32] saw somewhere between 200,000 and 500,000 people across Europe—the vast majority women—tortured and murdered over the course of roughly 150 years with the full sanction of the state.

Crime in the Modern World

The imprecision of the number of people who fell victim to the witch craze's sustained wave of judicial murder indicates one of the key problems in studying the pre-modern history of crime: records are scattered, imprecise, and unreliable. Much more information is available about crime and punishment in the modern era. Yet how to interpret the evidence remains hotly disputed. A key figure here is Roger Stone, who in 1983 used data provided by Ted Robert Gurr on murder rates (as a proxy for all types of violent crime) to challenge the notion of an idyllically peaceful English past which had been disrupted by the developments of modernity and its concomitant violence. Instead, he argued, there was a significant long-term trend of decreasing violence from the late medieval period to the present, attributable, he postulated, to a shift from feudal to bourgeois values.[33] Historical homicide rates indicate that medieval England was twice as violent as early modern England, which was in turn an astonishing five to ten times more violent than twentieth-century England.[34] Other historians took issue with this thesis, both in terms of Stone's interpretation of the data—counting indictments for murder is not the same thing as counting murders, and comparative data on population size and growth was necessarily unreliable—and, more importantly, in terms of his explanation for the phenomenon of decreased violence as a product of modernization and the rise of the middle class.[35]

However, broader, pan-European data seems to support Stone's theory of a 'massive decline in homicide rates over time'.[36] One recent study indicates that average European murder rates fell from 5.5 per 100,000 in the first half of the eighteenth century to 2.9 per 100,000 in the nineteenth century and 1.0 per 100,000 for the first decade of the twenty-first century—although these averages conceal considerable local variation.[37] This sort of argument has been advanced most publicly and influentially by Steven Pinker, who describes a profound change from the eighteenth century onwards as the increasing influence of Enlightenment values of reason, civility, and education have reined in the evolutionary predisposition of the male *Homo sapiens* towards violence.[38]

Yet resistance to this interpretation remains. Modernity has brought us not just a set of bourgeois values opposed to the blatant expression of physical aggression, but effective medical treatment and, especially in wealthy urban areas, rapid emergency services. Recent studies estimate that with equivalent access to medical care, the contemporary murder rate would not be lower, but twice as high as is suggested by the eighteenth-and nineteenth-century historical records.[39] In other words, a man knifed in a pub brawl in the mid-nineteenth century was much more likely to die than he would be if the same thing happened to him today, and what was a murder becomes an assault. The historical record in America also complicates the picture of a steady decline in criminal violence. Generally low homicide rates in the eighteenth and early nineteenth centuries were followed there by an upsurge that peaked in 1993 with a murder rate of 9.5 per 100,000[40] (a figure that fell, according to the FBI's latest figures, to 5.0 per 100,000 in 2019).[41] And expanding beyond Europe and America complicates the picture even further. Stephen Pinker would have little success selling his thesis of the great moderation to a resident of the Mexican border city of Ciudad Juárez, with its murder rate of 103.61 per 100,000 in 2023.[42] In other words, it would be 'unwise', as Richard McMahon writes, to rely on statistics alone 'to posit a fundamental shift in social and cultural practices of and attitudes towards violence'.[43]

This discussion of the (potential) transformations in the commission of crimes over time must be accompanied by two further observations. First, while it may be difficult to make generalizations regarding crime rates, we can certainly speak about changes in the social response to crimes, or, in other words, to the punishment half of Dostoevsky's famous binary. The second of these two transformations is often associated with the work of Michel Foucault, whose 1975 *Discipline and Punish: The Birth of the Prison* was hugely influential in conceptualizing the transformation in 'penal style' from a pre-Enlightenment system of public, exemplary, spectacular, creatively and fantastically violent justice directed against the body of the offender—'the gloomy festival of punishment'—to a modern regime of incarceration based on anonymity, collectivity, and regimentation.[44] The latter regime, Foucault argues, extends well beyond the walls of the prison proper to shape many of the institutions of modern society, from the school to the factory. While many critics have pointed out that Foucault's work is frequently empirically inaccurate, it is nonetheless important in identifying the fundamental shift towards the penitentiary as the standard response to crime and social deviance.[45] Society may or may not, as discussed earlier, have become safer and less violent over the past centuries, but its response to transgression has transformed in fundamental ways.

The second point that needs to be made in relation to a specifically modern history of crime is that by focussing on one type of crime—murder—as a proxy for crime in general, we may be obscuring many less spectacular crimes that are just as important in defining the modern era. Daniel Defoe's *Moll Flanders* (1722) sits very close to the beginning of the English tradition of the novel, and to the birth of modernity, and it is very much concerned with crime—but not murder. After a series of bigamous, incestuous, and fake marriages, the eponymous Flanders is thrown upon her wits in London, and becomes a practiced and effective thief and shop-lifter, part of the large-scale criminal industry involving thieves, fences, and the authorities lampooned in John Gay's contemporaneous *The Beggar's Opera* (1728). As Tammy Whitlock points out, while compara-tively little cultural attention is paid to the type of retail crime depicted so successfully by Defoe (as opposed to violent crime), its costs 'dwarf those of muggings and pub brawls'.[46] While theft has always been a reality, there is a close association between the rise of modern industrial, commercial, and consumer society and property crime. This is true both of the small scale but ubiquitous forms of petty larceny discussed by Whitlock—she estimates global annual losses at 30 billion dollars—and other forms of systematic economic crime.[47] White-collar crime seldom makes headlines in the same way as grisly murders or waves of street violence, and appears even less often in cultural representations of crime, yet its consequences are staggering. As Mary and Steven Ramirez write in *The Case for the Corporate Death Penalty: Restoring Law and Order on Wall Street*, the 2008 sub-prime mortgage crisis had by 2016 led to losses in excess of 15 trillion dollars, to say nothing of the ensuing human, social, and polit-ical damage.[48] While many banks involved in this epic fraud paid fines, few if any individuals faced criminal charges for the events leading up to the crisis, or have done so in the many financial scandals that have been uncovered in the subsequent decade.

One of the key features of this sort of large-scale, systematic white-collar crime is, as John Vervaele notes, that it is a global and globalized phenomenon.[49] To take a single example, the Libor Scandal (although the term scandal diminishes the seriousness of the crimes committed) involved up to 20 banks in the United States, the United Kingdom, the European Union, Canada, Japan, Switzerland, and elsewhere.[50] This sort of global-ization is a key feature of contemporary criminality. We live in a world defined by the flow of goods, services, people, and capital across national borders—the extent to which this is the case was amply illustrated by the disruption caused by the Covid-19 pandemic—and crime, too, is now in many ways a global phenomenon linked to the operations of corporate organizations (the mafias, triads, and cartels of organized crime) across national borders. From the illegal drug trade to human trafficking to wild-life smuggling, many of the definitive crimes of the twenty-first century are linked to globalization.

This may seem very far afield from the local, intimate violence embodied in the smashed palaeolithic skull with which this chapter's history of crime began. But even the most abstract, networked, and corporatized systems of criminal enterprise tend to resolve, at some point, somewhere, into bloody bodies. Each of the murders committed in Ciudad Juárez, for example, is individual and personal, but each is also inescapably connected to transnational flows of drugs and weapons, money and goods. This is a city shaped by free trade, by multinational factories and migrant labour, and by the economic ties that bind the nations and peoples of the earth together. And it is 'the most violent city in the world'.[51] Thus, while much has changed in the way we live and die since Cioclovina man met his untimely end, crime, despite its many faces, remains a constant.

Notes

1   Elena F. Kranioti, Dan Grigorescu, and Katerina Harvati, "State of the Art Forensic Techniques Reveal Evidence of Interpersonal Violence Ca. 30,000 Years Ago." *PLOS ONE* 14, no. 7 (2019), 2, https://doi.org/10.1371/journal.pone.0216718.
2   Ibid., 10.
3   Laura Geggel, "Cold Case Closed: Scientists Pin 33,000-Year-Old Murder on a Left-Handed Palco Killer." *Live Science*, July 3, 2019, www.livescience.com/65849-paleolithic-man-murdered.html.
4   Kranioti, et al., "State of the Art," 9.
5   William Golding, *The Inheritors* (London: Faber & Faber, 1961), 114.
6   Robert Redfield, "Primitive Law," *University of Cincinnati Law Review* 33, no. 1 (1964), 4.
7   E. Adamson Hoebel, *The Law of Primitive Man: A Study in Comparative Legal Dynamics* (Cambridge, MA: Harvard University Press, 2006), 4.
8   Franz Steiner, *Taboo* (Harmondsworth: Penguin, 1967), 20–21.
9   Sigmund Freud, *Totem and Taboo* (New York: Moffat, Yard and Company, 1919), 30.
10 Golding, *Inheritors*, 226.
11 Ibid.
12 Freud, *Totem and Taboo*, 31.
13 S. N. Kramer, "Ur-Nammu Law Code." *Orientalia* 23, no. 1 (1954), 42.
14 Ibid., 48.
15 M. E. J. Richardson, *Hammurabi's Laws: Text, Translation and Glossary* (London: Bloomsbury, 2005), 45.
16 Mitchel P. Roth, *An Eye for an Eye: A Global History of Crime and Punishment* (London: Reaktion Books, 2014), 26.
17 Richardson, *Hammurabi's Laws*, 121.
18 Ibid., 119.
19 *The Epic of Gilgamesh*, translated by Andrew George (New York: Penguin Books, 1999), I.29.
20 Ibid., I.67–68, I.77.
21 Ibid., III.209.
22 Israel Drapkin, *Crime and Punishment in the Ancient World* (Lexington, MA: Lexington Books, 1989), 31–32.
23 Frederick W. Dingledy, "The Corpus Juris Civilis: A Guide to its History and Use." *Legal Reference Services Quarterly* 35, no. 4 (2016), 255.

24 Walter Woodburn Hyde, "The Homicide Courts of Ancient Athens." *University of Pennsylvania Law Review and American Law Register* 66, no. 7/ 8 (1918), 334.

25 "The Twelve Tables," *The Avalon Project: Documents in Law, History and Diplomacy*, Lillian Goldman Law Library, Yale Law School, 2008, https://ava lon.law.yale.edu/ancient/twelve_tables.asp.

26 Roth, *Eye for an Eye*, 58.

27 Régine Le Jan, "Wergild," in *Encyclopedia of the Middle Ages*, edited by André Vauchez (Paris: James Clarke & Co., 2002), *Oxford Reference.com*.

28 Timothy Reuter, *Medieval Polities and Modern Mentalities*, edited by Janet L. Nelson (Cambridge: Cambridge University Press, 2006), 217.

29 Ibid.

30 Roth, *Eye for an Eye*, 110.

31 John Briggs, Christopher Harrison, Angus McInnes, and David Vincent, *Crime and Punishment in England: An Introductory History* (London: University College London Press, 1996), 6.

32 Erich Goode and Nachman Ben-Yehuda, *Moral Panics: The Social Construction of Deviance*, 2nd edition (Chichester: Wiley-Blackwell, 2009), 169, 178.

33 Lawrence Stone, "Interpersonal Violence in English Society 1300–1980." *Past & Present* 101, no. 1 (1983), 30.

34 Ibid., 25.

35 Paul Knepper, *Writing the History of Crime* (London: Bloomsbury, 2016), 38–39.

36 Lawrence Stone, "A Rejoinder." *Past & Present* 108, no. 1 (1985), 224.

37 Manuel Eisner, "From Swords to Words: Does Macro-Level Change in Self-Control Predict Long-Term Variation in Levels of Homicide?." *Crime and Justice* 43, no. 1 (2014), 80–81.

38 Steven Pinker, *The Better Angels of Our Nature: The Decline of Violence in History and its Causes* (London: Allen Lane, 2011).

39 Richard McMahon, "Histories of Interpersonal Violence in Europe and North America, 1700-Present," in *The Oxford Handbook of Crime and Criminal Justice*, edited by Michael Tonry (Oxford: Oxford University Press, 2019), 116.

40 Alfred Blumstein, "Some Trends in Homicide and Its Age-Crime Curves," in *Wiley Handbooks in Criminology and Criminal Justice: The Handbook of Homicide*, edited by Fiona Brookman, et al. (Chichester: Wiley-Blackwell, 2017), *Credo Reference.com*.

41 "Table 16: Number of Crimes per 100,000 Inhabitants by Population Group, 2019," *2019 Crime in the United States*, FBI: UCR, 2019, https://ucr.fbi.gov/ crime-in-the-u.s/2019/crime-in-the-u.s.-2019/tables/table-16.

42 "Ranking of the Most Dangerous Cities in the World in 2023, by Murder Rate per 100,000 Inhabitants," *Statista*, February 2023, www.statista.com/sta tistics/243797/ranking-of-the-most-dangerous-cities-in-the-world-by-murder-rate-per-capita/.

43 McMahon, "Histories of Interpersonal Violence," 120.

44 Michel Foucault, *Discipline and Punish: The Birth of The Prison*, translated by Alan Sheridan (New York: Vintage, 1995), 7–8.

45 Knepper, *Writing the History of Crime*, 147.

46 Tammy Whitlock, "Forms of Crime: Crime and Retail Theft," in *The Oxford Handbook of Crime and Criminal Justice*, edited by Michael Tonry (Oxford: Oxford University Press, 2019), 155.

47 Ibid., 165.

48 Mary Kreiner Ramirez and Steven A. Ramirez, *The Case for the Corporate Death Penalty: Restoring Law and Order on Wall Street* (New York: New York University Press, 2017), 3.

49 John Vervaele, "Forward," in *White Collar Crime: A Comparative Perspective*, edited by Katalin Ligeti and Stanislaw Tosza (London: Bloomsbury, 2018), v.

50 John R. Boatright, "London Interbank Offered Rate (LIBOR) Scandal," in *The Sage Encyclopedia of Business Ethics and Society*, edited by Robert W. Kolb, volume 1 (Thousand Oaks, CA: Sage Publications, 2018), 2116.

51 Charles Bowden, *Murder City: Ciudad Juárez and the Global Economy's New Killing Fields* (New York: Nation Books, 2010), 234.

2   A History of Criminology

Criminology, or the interdisciplinary study of crime from legal, psychological, sociological, and philosophical perspectives, is a relatively recent
field. Although the term itself is generally attributed to Raffaelle Garofalo
in his 1885 work *Criminologia*,[1] criminology's attempts to define crime
and criminal behaviour, classify its types, measure its levels of incidence,
understand its causes and, ultimately, prevent its occurrence have their
roots in the latter half of the eighteenth century. Of course, as was discussed
in Chapter 1, crime itself has a much longer history than this, and people
had dedicated a great deal of thought to it before the rise of criminology
as a formal discipline. However, those who considered crime and justice
in the pre-criminological era inevitably did so from a philosophical or religious or administrative perspective, rather than as an object of study in its
own right.[2] Paul Rock has described the various discourses on crime, its
causes, and its prevention produced by what he calls 'Ur-criminologists'
as an 'unorganized mass of allegation' by writers, religious figures, and
others who had, or claimed to have, expertise in crime, criminals, and their
punishment.[3] Yet despite this dismissive characterization, Rock acknowledges that these non-institutional thinkers not only developed what
persists as the 'common-sense' understanding of crime, but also frequently
anticipated many of the main tenets of academic criminology.[4] To take
a single example of this sort of proto-criminological discourse, consider
John Gay's 1728 *The Beggar's Opera*, which, as Vincenzo Ruggiero argues,
offers not just an entertainingly parodic melodrama but also a study of 'the
practice, the rationale and the structure of a criminal enterprise developing
common interests with agencies of social order', alongside a 'realistic analysis of how organized crime and the official establishment can exchange
services and perform a role of mutual enhancement and promotion'.[5] It
is, in other words, a sort of criminology with songs. Despite an apparent
clear-cut demarcation between pre- and post-criminological discourses, it
is possible to see the emergence of criminology as formalization rather

DOI: 10.4324/9781003156581-4

than innovation, as an instance of continuity and development rather than radical change.

Classical Criminology

With this proviso in mind, we can turn to the development of criminology from the mid-eighteenth century onwards. But here we immediately encounter another problem, for as Pieter Spierenburg points out a variety of 'founding fathers'—and they are all indeed men—have been proposed for the discipline, depending on both favoured criminological theories and national histories.[6] It is nonetheless possible to identify several central figures. Rock's discussion of the emergence of the discipline out of attempts to reform the criminal justice system in the late eighteenth century refers to a number of key works, including Cesare Beccaria's 1764 *On Crimes and Punishment*, John Howard's 1777 *The State of the Prisons in England and Wales*, Jeremy Bentham's 1791 *Panopticon; Or the Inspection House*, and Patrick Colquhoun's 1798 *Treatise on the Police of the Metropolis*.[7] While all of these are key writers in the history of criminology, Beccaria (1738–1794) is most often seen as a founding figure, due to that fact that he has been repeatedly designated as such by scholars, and also to the importance of his work to the development of the classical school of criminology.

The primary underpinning of classical criminology is the idea, or assumption, that individuals are independent actors, possessed of individual agency, who are able to exercise free will and make rational choices based on the information available to them. For Beccaria, this philosophical background, derived from Enlightenment thought, is perhaps less important than the pragmatic conclusions that can be drawn from it with regards to reforming a blood-thirsty, arbitrary, cruel, and ultimately ineffective criminal justice system. Beccaria's departure point is Jean-Jacques Rousseau's notion of the social contract that reciprocally binds the individual and the group: 'If every individual be bound to society, society is equally bound to him by a contract'.[8] If a member of a society breaks this contract through crime, he or she must be punished, but not in a way that would in turn break society's side of the agreement, by, for example, applying the same laws differently to different people or arbitrarily increasing the severity of the punishment. The goal of these punishments, and the 'principal aim of all good legislation', Beccaria argues (along the utilitarian lines developed by Jeremy Bentham), is to ensure 'the greatest happiness, or [...] the least unhappiness possible, to put it in terms of the total calculus of the goods and evils of life'.[9] Society's reaction to crime should be rationally planned, then, to benefit society as a whole through deterrence: 'It is better to prevent crimes than to punish them'.[10] This goal can be achieved by making society's response to crimes—its punishments—certain, or as close to inevitable as possible; lenient, or proportionate to the damage done to society; and swift, with as little time as possible elapsing between crime and punishment.[11] As Beccaria concludes,

> in order that punishment should not be an act of violence committed by one or many against a private citizen, it is essential that it be public, prompt, necessary, the minimum possible in the given circumstances, proportionate to the crimes, and established by the law.[12]

Beccaria's approach to crime rested on the assumption that criminals, like everyone else, were rational actors capable of evaluating alternatives (to commit a crime or not to commit a crime, and if to commit a crime, which crime to commit) and reaching valid, logical conclusions (it is better not to commit a crime, or if I do commit a crime it should be one with a relatively mild punishment). This view was central to the classical school of criminology that developed out of Beccaria's work in the late eighteenth and early nineteenth centuries and dominated criminological discourse and judicial practice in much of the Western world for the best part of a century.

Lombrosian Criminology

The first major challenge to this classical approach views the question of agency very differently, by emphasizing not individuals' capacity to make rational choices, but the extent to which behaviour is determined, or predetermined, by factors beyond their control. This may sound plausible, even intuitive—at the very least we all know that not all of our decisions are purely rational—but the first major proponent of this view, Cesare Lombroso (1835–1909), put forward a set of ideas that, while hugely influential, are now quite rightly seen as racist, sexist, and discriminatory. Yet despite the contempt in which many, if not all, of Lombroso's ideas are now held, his work represents an important development in the history of criminology.

In large part this is due to his pioneering insistence that the study of crime and criminals should be governed by scientific principles and methodologies. This positivist approach, developed out of the early nineteenth century philosopher Auguste Comte's insistence on the study of empirical data and quantifiable facts rather than abstract concepts, represents a genuine milestone in the study of crime. It is one thing to say, as Beccaria did, that swift, proportionate, and certain punishment deters criminal behaviour, but another thing to attempt to measure the effectiveness of this deterrence.

This sort of criminological measurement was exactly what Lombroso attempted, albeit in ways that strike us today (and indeed struck many of his contemporaries) as highly dubious. Lombroso noted in his 1878 work, *Criminal Man*, that current judicial practice (inspired by the classical school of criminology) with its focus on the nature of the crime was singularly ineffective, particularly in relation to high rates of recidivism.[13] Lombroso argued that this pattern of repeat offending was attributable to the fact that criminals 'are different from other people, with weak or diseased minds that can rarely be healed'—'most criminals', he claimed, 'really do lack free will'.[14] His explanation for this is highly deterministic, first linking biological traits and defects to intellectual failings and an inability to reason effectively, and then linking these differences and failings to a theory of evolution emphasizing the appearance of atavistic, regressive individuals whose less-evolved status inevitably leads them to commit crimes.

This theory was developed through and supported by a vast accumulation of evidence (though evidence of a problematic nature) including cranial and other bodily measurements, records of tattoos, and studies of handwriting, physiognomy, and studies of the size and shape of genitalia. Much of this material was eventually collected and displayed at Lombroso's Museum of Criminal Psychology at the University of Turin, established in 1899, which contained the skeletons of criminals, a scale model of the Eastern State Penitentiary in Philadelphia, portraits of criminals and epileptics, an international display of criminal types, cases of weapons, and much more.[15] The implication of all this accumulated data and the elaborate if shaky tower of theory built on top of it was, as Lombroso noted in the fifth and final edition of *Criminal Man* (1896–1897), that 'punishment is ineffective against born criminality', and that biological factors 'explain criminal behavior in 35 percent and possibly even 40 percent of all cases'.[16] In practical terms, this means that 'punishment should be proportional less to the gravity of the crime than to the dangerousness of the criminal'—a complete reversal of the Beccarian standard.[17] While there is much that is questionable, distasteful, and downright erroneous in the work of Lombroso and his many followers, he nonetheless represents an important shift away from the classical model of criminology towards a broader and more scientifically rooted understanding of crime and its causes. As Douglas Starr notes, 'by focusing on the criminal and not just the crime, he encouraged other scientists to study the roots of criminal psychology and urged authorities to consider prison reform'.[18]

The French School of Criminology

The same argument can be made—but without the reservations necessary when discussing Lombroso—with regards to the work of Alexandre Lacassagne (1843–1924) and other members of the 'French school', a group of scholars, doctors, and other professional criminologists active in the years around the turn of the century. Their work was opposed to the Lombrosian (or Italian) school of criminology, both theoretically, through a very different conceptualization of crime, and institutionally, through a series of International Congresses of Criminal Anthropology and the publication of the journal *Archives d'anthropologie criminelle*, both of which became sites for the contestation of Lombroso's ideas.[19]

Lacassagne, a medical doctor and professor at the University of Lyons, was a key figure in this movement, developing a theory that emphasized an individual's surroundings as an important factor in criminal behaviour: 'The social environment is the breeding ground of criminality; the germ is the criminal, an element which has no importance until the day where it finds the broth which makes it ferment'.[20] While his overall theory of criminality shared with the Lombrosian school a rejection of classical criminology's emphasis on rational individualism, and indeed a substantial biological-cum-psychological element, Lacassagne's focus on the role of social circumstances in criminal causation is something of a criminological landmark. Criminal behaviour is seen as the result of neither rational decision-making nor atavistic degeneration, but of the interaction between the individual and his or her environment. Basing his theories on extensive interviews and criminal autobiographies, Lacassagne noted that, for example, many criminals shared backgrounds involving violence, poverty, illness, and a lack of education.[21]

French criminologists played an important role in the development of a scientific approach not just to explaining crime but also to solving it. Alphonse Bertillon is a well-known figure here. As an assistant clerk in the identification bureau of the Paris police from 1879, Bertillon's primary responsibility was to record the details of felons (to assist in future identification). The system as he encountered it was inadequate, and, by yoking statistics, anthropology, and 'techniques of bodily measurement' he developed 'an intricate identification system based on the measurement of certain parts of the body believed to be unique to each person and unchanging in adults over time'.[22] Bertillon's system—known as Bertillonage—was, after some initial resistance, widely adopted by police forces around the world as a standard way of identifying suspects, and became something of a public phenomenon. Arthur Conan Doyle's Sherlock Holmes, for instance, is described by a prospective client in *The Hound of the Baskervilles* (1901–1902) as 'the second highest expert [in detection] in Europe' after 'Monsieur Bertillon'—much to his chagrin, of course.[23] Ironically, this reference to Bertillon's criminological preeminence was published at precisely the moment that fingerprinting, a much more reliable form of identification, was being introduced to Europe by the assistant commissioner at Scotland Yard Edward Henry, who along with two mathematically gifted Bengali police officers, Hem Chandra Bose and Qazi Azizul Haque, had developed techniques for classifying finger-print patterns.[24]

Lacassagne and his collaborators were also instrumental in the profes-sionalization and rationalization of investigative procedures. Lacassagne's approach was in some ways a mirror of Bertillon's. While the latter 'worked to *deconstruct* a living person's identity by breaking it down into small measurable parts', the former, 'worked in the opposite direc-tion, *reconstructing* a corpse's identity by compiling small parts to make a whole'.[25] What Lacassagne was developing (alongside his students and collaborators) was a rational, scientifically based approach to crime scene investigation, in which physical evidence—bloodstain patterns, the ana-lysis of entry wounds, rifling marks on bullets, and so on—could replace (or supplement) eye-witness testimony and potentially dubious confessions. Interestingly, these developments were occurring at the same time as Conan Doyle's stories were popularizing the procedures of rational, scientific investigation. Despite reservations about the certainty and speed displayed by Holmes, Lacassagne was fascinated by the character, and published two reviews of Doyle's tales in *Archives de l'anthropologie criminelle*, as well as supervising a thesis by Jean-Henri Bercher comparing the fictional detective's methodology with real-world practices. The main gap Bercher discovered in Doyle's work was the complete absence of autopsies.[26]

Modern Criminology

As the twentieth century began, many of the key ideas and practices in both criminology and policing were either established or under develop-ment. This is not to say, of course, that criminology was a full-fledged discipline by this point. Much remained to be done, but one way of seeing this work is to align it with, broadly speaking, the three strands of thinking about crime that had developed over the previous century, one empha-sizing the role of heredity and/or biology, one emphasizing social factors, and one emphasizing individual choice.

The first of these strands descends from Lombroso's positivist crimin-ology, and has, like his work, been highly controversial, frequently seen as tainted by racist and misogynist ideas, and widely and energetically debunked. While a number of criminologists attempted over the course of the twentieth century to offer more scientifically valid methods of phys-ically distinguishing criminals from non-criminals than, for example, Lombroso's phrenology, critics often attacked this work for faulty stat-istical analysis, or for relying on minor physiological differences between criminal and non-criminal individuals while ignoring social and envir-onmental explanations that could account for them.[27] Yet despite these setbacks, the urge to attribute criminality to particular biological or genetic traits has persisted, as demonstrated, for example, by James Q. Wilson and Richard Herrnstein's 1985 book *Crime and Human Nature*, a work ambitiously if inaccurately subtitled 'The Definitive Study of the Causes of Crime'. Wilson and Herrnstein argue that crime is strongly (though not exclusively) linked to factors such as body type, biological inheritance, and genetic composition.[28]

The last of these has remained a relatively robust area of study into the twenty-first century. While work has been carried out across a variety of fields, epigenetics, or the study of the heritable changes to gene activity (rather than to genes themselves), is an important area of research, particularly insofar as it combines biological and sociological approaches. A good example is Richard Tremblay and Moshe Szyf's recent work on the links between epigenetic markers, environmental factors such as pre- and postnatal maternal behaviour, and chronic childhood aggression.[29] The basic argument here is not, as in the crude biological determinism of Lombroso, that biology determines destiny, but that behaviour and environment influence biology, which in turn influences individual behaviour. Genetic explanations for criminal behaviour are, as Helena Machado and Rafaela Granja point out, 'symptomatic of the genetization, molecularization and biologization of our contemporary society', and as such are likely to continue to garner attention.[30]

The second, sociological, strand of thought mentioned earlier can be linked to the work of Lacassagne and the French school. It has led to many of the main developments in criminological thinking in the twentieth century. This disciplinary development should be seen in relation to an emerging cultural understanding of crime as a product of particular sets of socio-economic difficulties, such as the urban poverty and rural immiseration explored in works like Upton Sinclair's *The Jungle* (1906) and John Steinbeck's *The Grapes of Wrath* (1939).[31] In general terms, during much of the twentieth century a widespread understanding prevailed that the cause of a given crime seldom lay with a particular individual, but was instead related to much broader social factors.

A number of criminologists developed an extensive theoretical apparatus in support of this view. In the first half of the twentieth century, Clifford R. Shaw and Henry D. McKay (building on the work of previous criminologists) developed what is known as social disorganization theory. Based on studies of urban juvenile delinquency, they correlated high levels of social disorganization in particular neighbourhoods (meaning ineffective schools, churches, and other institutions of social organization) with high crime rates linked to inter-generational transfer of criminal behaviour patterns.[32] Social disorganization, they noted, was connected with, though not identical to, 'poverty, population heterogeneity, and mobility' which led to the failure of the institutions of social control.[33] In other words, in disorganized neighbourhoods, the existence of a poor, diverse, and transient population undermines the ability of one type of (acceptable) social institution, say an afterschool club or a church choir, to inculcate values and behaviour patterns. This creates the social space for another (unacceptable) institution, say the Vice Lords (a street gang), to teach a very different set of norms—with predictable if lamentable consequences. A development of this theory (or a new application of some of its insights) has been extremely influential in late twentieth century policing in America and the United Kingdom. Generally referred to as 'broken windows' theory after the title of an article published by James Q. Wilson and George L. Kelling in 1983, this approach emphasizes the role of 'disorderly social and physical conditions' in creating, maintaining, and intensifying a criminogenic environment.[34] This approach has been actively applied to policing in the United States—most notably in New York City, where it has underpinned zero tolerance policing since the 1990s—and lies behind any number of crime prevention measures targeting anti-social behaviour.

At roughly the same time as Shaw and McKay were developing their model, Robert K. Merton was also doing work that emphasized the importance of social values. However, in his 1938 article 'Social Structure and Anomie', Merton stressed the role of normative rather than deviant values in perpetuating criminal behaviour. Some social structures 'generate the circumstances in which infringement of social codes constitutes a "normal" response'.[35] Specifically, in a highly competitive society (like America's) which valorizes economic success and social mobility, but is less concerned with how these goals are achieved and denies many of its members legitimate opportunities to achieve them, there is a strong tendency towards what he calls, borrowing a term from Émile Durkheim, *anomie*, or 'cultural chaos'. Under these conditions, transgression of social norms in order to achieve desired goals becomes not deviant but normal.[36] Merton's arguments have proven fertile, and remained influential in the form of strain theory, which, as developed by Robert Agnew (and others) from the 1990s onwards, identifies a broader variety of stresses that have the potential to contribute to criminal behaviour, including negative treatment, personal loss, and the failure to achieve important goals. As Agnew puts it, the idea here is really very simple: 'when people are treated badly, they may get upset and engage in crime'.[37]

A third major social theory that was—and remains—influential was developed by Travis Hirschi from the late 1960s onwards. Social bond or social control theory, as it is known, adopts the interesting approach of asking not why some people commit crimes, but why many, indeed most, do not. After all, children routinely break social norms in order to achieve goals, or simply for the delight in exercising power over others. According to Hirschi, what prevents most adults from continuing this sort of behaviour is the 'bonds' they 'form to prosocial values, prosocial people, and prosocial institutions' based on psychological attachment, social commitment, social involvement, and social belief.[38] We don't commit crimes because we don't want to disappoint our friends and families, or because we don't want to lose our jobs, or because we are simply too busy working, or because we truly believe crime is bad, or, most likely, because of a complicated combination of all of these factors. Like Merton's work, Hirschi's ideas have remained influential, feeding directly into the life course or criminal career model that 'recognizes that individuals start their criminal activity at some age, engage in crime at some individual crime rate, commit a mixture of crimes, and eventually stop'.[39] At the same time, Hirschi has developed (alongside Michael Gottfredson) a self-control theory that emphasizes the importance not of the external social controls outlined in his earlier theoretical work, but of individual self-control developed through external bonds of family, friends, and social institutions, or the ability to 'avoid acts whose long-term costs exceed short-term benefits'.[40]

Despite the continued success of these diverse social theories of criminology, the classical theories first developed by Beccaria and others in the eighteenth century have also persisted. These 'decision-based theories of crime', based on the idea that criminal behaviour is largely a product of rational actors making rational choices, were largely supplanted by the biological and sociological theories discussed earlier for much of the nineteenth and twentieth century, but from the 1960s onwards they were revived in both theoretical and practical terms.[41] Key figures here include Gary Becker, who in 1968 offered an economic model of criminal activity built around the principles of rational choice, and Richard Posner, who studied, as the title of one of his early books has it, *The Economics of Justice*. Underpinning much of this work is the notion that 'crimes are purposive and deliberate acts, committed with the intention of benefiting the offender'.[42]

This assumption places responsibility for criminal acts squarely on the shoulders of the criminal. While there are many modifications and qualifications that can and have been made here (e.g. in the routine activity approach, which focuses on the ability to commit a crime rather than the intention), this emphasis on personal accountability resonated with increasingly conservative societies in both the United Kingdom and the United States. In response to rising crime rates in both countries throughout the 1960s and 1970s, and even more to media-fuelled perceptions of rising crime rates, communities and politicians (and some criminologists) abandoned approaches to crime that emphasized collective responsibility for the circumstances that led to crime, and judicial responses that emphasized rehabilitation and retraining, in favour of an increase in the frequency and duration of penal sanctions. When your city is (you believe) overrun by criminals, you are unlikely to care why young men (mostly) are stealing your car or mugging you on the subway (or why you are afraid of them doing so): you just want them to stop (or to stop worrying about them doing it).

James Q. Wilson's 1975 *Thinking About Crime* was hugely influential in the development of the 'get-tough, pro-prison movement' that has defined American, and to a lesser extent British, responses to crime for almost 50 years.[43] In terms of real-world, real-life impact, Wilson's argument that the most effective way to reduce crime is by 'physically preventing offenders from recidivating'[44] has led not to the selective incapacitation of high-rate criminals proposed in his work but to collective incapacitation through increases in the number of prison-punishable offences, mandatory minimum sentencing laws, and other techniques that bring huge numbers of people into the prison system and keep them there for long periods of time. Twenty-nine American states, for example, now have some form of 'three-strike' law mandating long or life sentences without the possibility of parole for repeat offenders. While these laws have been very popular with the public, they have, as James A. Norris notes with some under-statement, 'created some seeming injustices or disparities', such as non-violent offenders being sentenced to life in prison for shoplifting.[45] The same sort of assumptions about choice and individual responsibility have underpinned the disastrously ineffective, costly, and destructive war on drugs. All of this becomes particularly acute in light of the fact that these sorts of policies have had a disproportionate effect on women and racial minorities. For example, in the decade between 1986 and 1996, the number of women imprisoned on drug charges in America increased by an astounding 888 percent, with 75 percent of these women being single parents of young children, and in 2004 the incarceration rate for adult Black males in America was 4,919 per 100,000, a figure that was, almost unbelievably, more than five times as high as the comparable incarcer-ation rate in South Africa under the apartheid regime.[46] While this rate had fallen to 1,446 by 2019, it still remains almost six times as high as the rate for white adult males.[47]

Recent Developments in Criminology

Obvious inequalities like these underlie some of the more recent tendencies in criminological theory. One early development in this respect is known as radical or critical criminology, a broad movement that began in both Britain and America as an attempt to 'wrestle' the discipline 'away from etiologically-centered epistemologies of control, association, and learning, and to situate it firmly within the political economy'.[48] Critical criminology thus seeks to situate criminal activity in relation to broader social, economic, and political factors like extreme inequalities in the distribution of wealth and disparities in access to power, or in systematic forms of racial and gender discrimination. This critique was grounded in the counter-culture sensibilities of late 1960s radicalism, and it struggled, alongside many other left-wing forms of thought, throughout the late twentieth century in the face of a seemingly triumphant neo-liberal agenda. However, the serial crises of the twenty-first century (e.g. the bursting of the internet stock market bubble in 2001–2002, the financial crisis of 2007–2008, the European migration crisis of 2015, the @MeToo and BLM movements, the Covid pandemic, renewed inflationary pressures) have made the attempts of critical criminologists to conceptualize crime as 'rooted in the core structures of society, whether its class nature, its patriarchal form or its inherent authoritarianism' seem ever more relevant.[49]

While the range of criminological approaches that can be gathered under this rubric is startling, three major tendencies have had a major impact on, and seem likely to continue to shape, the overall field of criminology. The first of these are a set of ideas concerning gender and crime. Feminist criminology has arisen as a response to the fact that 'much of criminology ignores women and girls in conflict with the law'.[50] It places the operations of patriarchy, both structural and ideological, at the centre of its exploration of crime and criminality. This can mean, for example, studying patterns of female criminality both historically and in the present, or examining often-neglected crimes against women, such as domestic violence and femicide. A number of complimentary theories have developed exploring the ways masculine identities can be articulated through crime, ranging from an emphasis on physical violence to the valorization of competitiveness and success.[51] Both of these perspectives in turn are often linked with overlapping questions of race, racism, and ethnic identity. Critical criminology is, in other words, inherently intersectional in its approach, involving 'a critical analysis of the experiences of individuals or groups based on their social positions [...] in relation to their experiences with crime, the social control of crime, and any crime-related issues'.[52] As discussed earlier, the criminal justice system has a hugely disproportionate impact on the lives of non-white Americans, and to a lesser extent non-white British; this means that race is central to many examples of critical criminology. This is particularly true in America, where the ostensibly colour-blind legal system explored by Michelle Alexander in her seminal *The New Jim Crow: Mass Incarceration in the Age of Colorblindness* (2010) leads directly to the disenfranchisement and impoverishment of wildly disproportionate numbers of Blacks and Latinos.

Before concluding this chapter, it is vital to note a relatively new, and as yet not widely accepted field of study: environmental criminology. As the Sixth Assessment Report of the United Nations Intergovernmental Panel on Climate Change warns, 'global surface temperature will continue to increase until at least the mid-century under all emissions scenarios considered'.[53] Vast swathes of North America burn every summer in enormous wildfires, and long-standing temperature records fall regularly around the world. We are living, in other words, in an era of environmental crisis, yet traditional criminology has little to say about the crimes (if they are even conceived of as such) that have led us to this point. By adopting notions of environmental justice, ecological justice, and species justice, environmental criminology attempts to address this problem.[54] It represents, then, a widening of the sphere of criminological thought beyond its traditional focus on individuals and/ or their social context to include the natural environment within which they are situated.

Notes

1 Tim Newburn, *Criminology*, 3rd edition (London: Routledge, 2017), 4.
2 Ruth Ann Triplett, "Introduction," in *The Handbook of the History and Philosophy of Criminology*, edited by Ruth All Triplett (Hoboken, NJ: Wiley-Blackwell, 2018), 2.
3 Paul Rock, "Introduction: The Emergence of Criminological Theory," in *History of Criminology*, edited by Paul Rock (Aldershot: Dartmouth, 1994), xiii.
4 Ibid.
5 Vincenzo Ruggiero, *Crime in Literature: Sociology of Deviance and Fiction* (London: Verso, 2003), 39.
6 Pieter Spierenburg, "The Rise of Criminology in its Historical Context," in *The Oxford Handbook of the History of Crime and Criminal Justice*, edited by Paul Knepper and Anja Johansen (Oxford: Oxford University Press, 2016), 374.
7 Rock, "Introduction," xiv.
8 Cesare Beccaria, *On Crimes and Punishments and Other Writings*, edited by Aaron Thomas, translated by Aaron Thomas and Jeremy Parzen (Toronto: University of Toronto Press, 2008), 13.
9 Ibid., 79.
10 Ibid.
11 Travis C. Pratt, Jacinta M. Gau, and Travis W. Franklin, *Key Ideas in Criminology and Criminal Justice* (Thousand Oaks, CA: Sage Publications, 2011), 10–11.
12 Beccaria, *On Crimes and Punishments*, 86.
13 Cesare Lombroso, *Criminal Man*, translated by Mary Gibson and Nicole Hahn Rafter with assistance from Mark Seymour (Durham, NC: Duke University Press, 2006), 43.
14 Ibid.

15 Paul Knepper, "Laughing at Lombroso: Positivism and Criminal Anthropology in Historical Perspective," in *The Handbook of the History and Philosophy of Criminology*, edited by Ruth Ann Triplett (Chichester: Wiley-Blackwell, 2018), 62.

16 Lombroso, *Criminal Man*, 338.

17 Ibid., 341.

18 Douglas Starr, *The Killer of Little Shepherds: A True Crime Story and the Birth of Forensic Science* (New York: Knopf, 2010), 126.

19 Bruce DiCristina, "Criminology in 19th-Century France: Mainstays of the French 'Environmental' Tradition," in *The Handbook of the History and Philosophy of Criminology*, edited by Ruth Ann Triplett (Chichester: Wiley-Blackwell, 2018), 70–71.

20 Quoted in Jan Verplaetse, *Localizing the Moral Sense: Neuroscience and the Search for the Cerebral Seat of Morality, 1800–1930* (Dordrecht: Springer, 2009), 149.

21 Katherine Ramsland, *The Mind of a Murderer: Privileged Access to the Demons That Drive Extreme Violence* (Santa Barbara: Praeger, 2011), 12.

22 Haia Shpayer-Makov, "Detectives and Forensic Science: The Professionalization of Police Detection," in *The Oxford Handbook of the History of Crime and Criminal Justice*, edited by Paul Knepper and Anja Johansen (Oxford: Oxford University Press, 2016), 486.

23 Arthur Conan Doyle, *The Hounds of the Baskervilles* (London: Penguin, 2012), 7.

24 Shpayer-Makov, "Detectives and Forensic Science," 487.

25 Starr, *The Killer of Little Shepherds*, 67.

26 Ibid., 105–106.

27 Raymond Paternoster and Ronet Bachman, "The Positive School of Criminology: Introduction," in *Explaining Criminals and Crime: Essays in Contemporary Criminological Theory*, edited by Raymond Paternoster and Ronet Bachman (Los Angeles: Roxbury Publishing Company, 2001), 50.

28 John Monahan, "Slouching Toward Crime," *The Yale Law Journal* 95, no. 7 (1986), 1538.

29 Richard E. Tremblay and Moshe Szyf, "Developmental Origins of Chronic Physical Aggression and Epigenetics," *Epigenomics* 2, no. 4 (2010), 498.

30 Helena Machado and Rafaela Granja, *Forensic Genetics in the Governance of Crime* (Singapore: Palgrave Pivot, 2020), 40.

31 Pratt, et al., *Key Ideas in Criminology*, 42–43.

32 Ibid., 44.

33 Raymond Paternoster and Ronet Bachman, "Social Disorganisation and Crime: Introduction," in *Explaining Criminals and Crime: Essays in Contemporary Criminological Theory*, edited by Raymond Paternoster and Ronet Bachman (Los Angeles: Roxbury Publishing Company, 2001), 117.

34 Ralph B. Taylor, "The Ecology of Crime, Fear, and Delinquency: Social Disorganisation Versus Social Efficacy" in *Explaining Criminals and Crime: Essays in Contemporary Criminological Theory*, edited by Raymond Paternoster and Ronet Bachman (Los Angeles: Roxbury Publishing Company, 2001), 134.

35 Robert K. Merton, "Social Structure and Anomie," in *History of Criminology*, edited by Paul Rock (Aldershot: Dartmouth), 672.

36 Ibid., 399.

37 Robert Agnew, "On Overview of General Strain Theory," in *Explaining Criminals and Crime: Essays in Contemporary Criminological Theory*, edited by Raymond Paternoster and Ronet Bachman (Los Angeles: Roxbury Publishing Company, 2001), 161.

38 Pratt, et al., *Key Ideas in Criminology*, 58–59.

39 Alex R. Piquero, et al. "The Criminal Career Paradigm," *Crime and Justice* 30 (2003), 377, *JSTOR*. www.jstor.org/stable/1147702.

40 Travis Hirschi and Michael Gottfredson, "Self-control Theory," in *Explaining Criminals and Crime; Essays in Contemporary Criminological Theory*, edited by Raymond Paternoster and Ronet Bachman (Los Angeles: Roxbury Publishing Company, 2001), 83.

41 Ray Paternoster and Daren Fisher, "The Foundation and Re-emergence of Classical Thought in Criminological Theory: A Brief Philosophical History," in *The Handbook of the History and Philosophy of Criminology*, edited by Ruth Ann Triplett (Chichester: Wiley-Blackwell, 2018), 181, 174.

42 Ronald V. Clarke and Derek B. Cornish, "Rational Choice," in *Explaining Crime and Criminals: Essays in Contemporary Criminological Theory*, edited by Raymond Paternoster and Ronet Bachman (Los Angeles: Roxbury Publishing Company, 2001), 24.

43 Pratt, et al., *Key Ideas in Criminology*, 95.

44 Ibid., 91.

45 James A. Norris, "Three-Strikes Laws," in *American Prisons and Jails: An Encyclopedia of Controversies and Trends*, edited by Vidisha Barua Worley and Robert M. Worley, Vol. 2 (Santa Barbara, CA: ABC-CLIO, 2019), 649.

46 James Gray, *Why Our Drug Laws Have Failed and What We Can Do about It: A Judicial Indictment of the War on Drugs* (Philadelphia: Temple University Press, 2011), 44–45.
    Gray cites 6,919 rather than 4,919, but this seems to be a typo, as the source he refers to ("Prison and Jail Inmates at Midyear 2004" published by the Bureau of Justice Statistics) lists the latter number (see https://bjs.ojp.gov/cont ent/pub/pdf/pjim04.pdf).

47 Ann E. Carson, "Prisoners in 2019," in *Bulletin, U.S. Department of Justice, Office of Justice Programs, Bureau of Justice Statistics* (October 2020), 10, NCJ 255115, https://bjs.ojp.gov/content/pub/pdf/p19.pdf.

48 Travis Linnemann and Kyra A. Martinez, "Let Fury Have the Hour: The Radical Turn in British Criminology," in *The Handbook of the History and Philosophy of Criminology*, edited by Ruth Ann Triplett (Chichester: Wiley-Blackwell, 2018), 226.

49 J. Paul Walton and Jock Young, "Preface," in *The New Criminology Revisited*, edited by Paul Walton and Jock Young (London: St. Martin's Press, 1998), vii.

50 Walter S. DeKeseredy, *Contemporary Critical Criminology* (London: Routledge, 2011), 28.

51 Ibid., 34–36.

52 Hillary Potter, "Intersectional Criminology: Interrogating Identity and Power in Criminological Research and Theory," *Critical Criminology* 21, no. 3 (2013), 316.

53 "IPCC, 2021: Summary for Policymakers," in *Climate Change 2021: The Physical Science Basis. Contribution of Working Group I to the Sixth Assessment Report of the Intergovernmental Panel on Climate Change*, edited by Masson-Delmotte, et al. (Cambridge: Cambridge University Press, 2021), 17.

54 Rob White, *Crimes Against Nature: Environmental Criminology and Ecological Justice*. (Cullompton: Willan Publishing, 2012), 4.

3 A History of Crime Fiction

In most histories of crime fiction, the literary form is closely linked with modernity, and more specifically with Western modernity. Chris Baldick, for instance, has described the transformation of the detective story from a 'marginal curiosity of the Victorian imagination' to a 'national [and international] craze' as the 'most spectacular development in modern light fiction'.[1] Works like Edgar Allan Poe's C. Auguste Dupin stories (1841–1844), Andrew Forrester's 1864 collection *The Female Detective*, Émile Gaboriau's Monsieur Lecoq novels (1866–1869), Anna Katharine Green's 1878 novel *The Leavenworth Case*, and Arthur Conan Doyle's 1887 *A Study in Scarlet* may now seem like literary landmarks, but they were in their day rather peripheral works lying outside the boundaries of mainstream culture. The same cannot be said as we move into the early twentieth and twenty-first centuries, and narratives of crime and detection begin to occupy an ever more central place in both popular culture and in literary theory and history. It would be almost impossible to think, for example, about American fiction in the first half of the twentieth century without considering the impact of writers like Dashiell Hammett and Raymond Chandler. Yet this association between crime writing and modernity is at least to some extent tendentious.

The Origins of Crime Fiction

In fact, there has been a long-running and well-documented critical discussion, if not dispute, over the origins of the genre. In 1972, Julian Symons (who was himself a prolific and highly regarded crime writer) noted in his influential survey *Bloody Murder: From the Detective Story to the Crime Novel* that this issue divides literary historians into two opposing camps. One the one hand, there are those who argue that the detective story proper only becomes possible with the creation of the legal and administrative infrastructure of police and detective forces.[2] The 'modern crime novel'

DOI: 10.4324/9781003156581-5

as Jonathan Charley writes, 'can only come of age when the professional detective first stalks the city of Dickens and Dostoevsky'.[3] In this view, the history of the genre can be traced back to, say, the turn of the nineteenth century, as is indicated by the title of Stephen Knight's standard history of the genre *Crime Fiction Since 1800: Detection, Death, Diversity*.[4]

But this position has long been questioned. Crime has been a central feature of literature for as long as there has been something that can be referred to by that name. Some of our oldest stories contain, or are built around, behaviour that can be considered criminal. The *Epic of Gilgamesh* is frequently described as one of the first major literary works in history, and as we saw in Chapter 1, it is concerned with transgression and punishment, law and order. Critics have identified similar instances of crime and the application of rational processes of deduction to its investigation in sources ranging from the Bible to Voltaire, and have suggested that these represent early instances of what might be called detective fiction, or at least fictions of detection.[5] The great interwar mystery writer Dorothy L. Sayers was an early and effective proponent of this long-history approach. As she points out in her introduction to *Great Short Stories of Detection, Mystery, and Horror* (1928; re-published in America in 1929 as *The Omnibus of Crime*), the origins of detective stories (and horror tales) can be traced back to ancient times; some of the detective stories in her collection are in fact from texts such as Herodotus' *Histories* and Virgil's *Aeneid*.[6]

One way of thinking about the history of crime fiction, then, is to divide it into two large camps, a broader global pre-modern pre-history of writings concerning crime, investigation, detection, and punishment, and a history of crime fiction proper that starts roughly around the end of the eighteenth century and is primarily focused on developments in the West. This structure has the added advantage of paralleling the history of criminology, which, as we saw in Chapter 2, is also frequently divided into the work of a diverse set of pre-late eighteenth-century proto-criminologists and that of modern criminologists. Of course, not all of the features that we associate with the fully developed (or even rapidly developing) genre will be present in proto-crime fiction texts, but a history of the form and its development that ignores them completely would be only partial.

As Sayers indicated in her history of the genre (and as the example from the *Epic of Gilgamesh* referred to earlier indicates), it is not hard to find ancient literary texts that include the typical themes and tropes of crime fiction. In Judeo-Christian mythology, for instance, the first story about humans concerns a transgression of the law, with Adam and Eve's failure to follow God's prohibitions resulting in the punishment of exile. The central scene in the Biblical narrative of Cain and Abel has been described as the 'first ever recorded murder':[7] 'Cain said to his brother Abel, "Let us go out to the field." And when they were in the field, Cain rose up against his brother Abel, and killed him'.[8] Cain has a motive—jealousy over Abel's greater success in wooing the divinity with offerings—and a plan, basic but effective, to lure his victim to an isolated spot and kill him in secrecy. There is even an element of proto-detection when God appears as literature's first sleuth, learning of the crime by discovering clues: 'your brother's blood is crying out to me from the ground!'[9] However, it must be admitted that whatever its structural similarities, this is not what we generally think of when we discuss crime fiction. Nor, perhaps, is Sophocles' *Oedipus the King*, even though its protagonist, as Richard Bradford writes in his history of crime fiction, can be seen as 'a precursor to the modern detective' insofar as he 'conducts a meticulous investigation to unmask the murderer of his predecessor King Laius'.[10]

Another example of proto-crime fiction that is somewhat closer to contemporary generic expectations are the *Gong'an*, or court case fictions, that appeared in China between the tenth and fifteenth centuries CE in a variety of forms. As Wilt Idema describes the tales of Judge Bao (who along with Judge Dee is the best-known figure within this genre), each 'criminal case' typically involves 'a criminal act, a villain, a victim, and a judge'.[11] This is indisputably a type of crime fiction, or even detective fiction, and it forms an important part of China's literary heritage. But here, too, there are substantial differences from more familiar, modern (and Western) versions of the genre including a frequent reliance on supernatural intervention and the early introduction and identification of the criminal. The same can be said of early Arabic language tales of crime and detection, like those that appear in *Alf Layla wa-Layla* (*The Thousand and One Nights*), an anonymous medieval collection of stories from disparate sources assembled over several centuries. Here we find stories like 'The Tale of the Murdered Woman', which involves a familiar crime, uxoricide, and the dismemberment and disposal of the victim's body. However, there is no real investigation as the man ordered to solve the mystery, the Caliph's vizier Ja'far ibn Yahya, does nothing but stay at home in hopeless despair until the unexpected confession of the culprit reveals the story behind the murder.

Examples of this sort of proto-crime fiction could be multiplied, from Shakespeare's *Hamlet* (1599–1601), whose hero is directly or indirectly responsible for seven deaths, at least five of which are clearly criminal, to John Gay's 1728 runaway hit *The Beggar's Opera* (referred to in Chapter 2 as a form of pre-criminological discourse on crime) which drew enthusiastic audiences for 62 consecutive nights in its first season with its tale of larceny, corruption, and promiscuity,[12] to *The Newgate Calendar* (five-volume edition, 1774), which blended true-crime reportage with censorious moralizing and flights of grisly imagination. Another genre that plays an important role in the pre-history of crime fiction is the Gothic. Maurizio Ascari has argued in his 'counter-history' of the genre that various forms of supernatural fiction play an important, if sometimes suppressed or neglected, role in its development.[13]

While it is indisputably true that crime is an inherent part of much of the world's fiction,[14] considering all of this material under the rubric of crime or detective fiction would risk losing track of the very things that make the form recognizable, particular, and important. As Richard Bradford argues, to ignore these distinctions is to 'distort the definitive features' of 'the tradition that has thrived during the last two centuries'.[15] The case has been put even more robustly by John M. Reilly:

> Critics making these genealogical claims seem determined to establish an antique origin for crime and mystery writing that will distinguish it from the ephemeral and sensational work so commonly denigrated as merely popular, or even mass, literature. Still there is no escaping the fact that, while themes of evil and guilt in literature certainly are ancient and universal, the narrative form centering upon a criminal problem appears only in recent times.[16]

This returns us to the claim made by the first of the two literary-historical camps discussed at the start of this chapter: that a literature of crime and detection only really emerges under the conditions of modernity, and particularly alongside early developments in the modern criminal justice system, including a systematic criminology.

Crime Fiction and the Modern State

In part this is a question of institutions, in part of ideas. One of the fundamental preconditions for the emergence of crime fiction proper is the existence of a formal, regulated crime-fighting apparatus. You cannot have detective fiction without the detective. It is thus no coincidence that the development of a recognizable detective genre emerges at around the same time as the first modern police forces were being created in France and Britain, particularly in the rapidly expanding metropolises of Paris and London. In France, a '*Conseil de Police*' was established as early as 1666, with the '*lieutenant général de la ville, prévôté et vicomté de Paris*' leading 48 *commissaires* in the general task of maintaining urban order; from 1740 these were supplemented by a smaller body of *inspecteurs*, with responsibility for 'investigation and surveillance'.[17] In Britain, Henry Fielding (the famous novelist) was appointed magistrate in 1748, and in conjunction with his half-brother John Fielding organized 'a group of reliable constables to investigate and pursue offenders' who became known as the Bow Street Runners.[18] Both of these forces changed and expanded dramatically during and after the French revolution, culminating in the creation of the *Préfecture de police* in 1800 and the Metropolitan Police in 1829.

Some notable early examples of crime fiction emerged directly out of this institutional context. As mentioned in the introduction to this book, Eugène-François Vidocq was a petty criminal turned first informant and then policeman, finally serving as head of the plainclothes branch of the Prefectural Police, the *Brigade de la Sûreté*. His *Mémoires* (1828) were an international success and, given the imaginative licence displayed by his ghost writers, can be as accurately described as crime fiction as autobiography. A similar work deriving from the English context is the anonymous *Richmond; or, Scenes in the Life of a Bow Street Runner, Drawn Up from His Private Memoranda* published a year before Vidocq's memoirs. This, too, is clearly a work of fiction although it presents itself as a form of documentary record. Some of the most notable and enduring police characters in mid-nineteenth century fiction are found in the work of Charles Dickens, who also published a series of articles about the London police force in his periodicals *Household Words* and *All the Year Round*. A typical example is 'On Duty with Inspector Field', dealing with a night on the beat with his friend Charles Frederick Field (1805–1874) of the Scotland Yard. Field is generally considered to be the model for Inspector Bucket, who plays an important role in *Bleak House* (1852–1853) as perhaps the most fully developed of Dickens' detective figures.

Classic Crime Fiction

Stephen Knight argues that detection, while important in *Bleak House* and elsewhere in Dickens' work, remains secondary within his 'politicised, even spiritualized, version of the [...] city mystery'.[19] This is perhaps why authors like Dickens remain on the periphery of the crime fiction genre, despite their undoubted interest in criminality as a theme and a plot device. Other roughly contemporaneous writers produced work in which crime and its detection were much more central. Mary Elizabeth Braddon, for example, is usually described as a sensation novelist, but *The Trail of the Serpent* (1861; first published in 1860 as *Three Times Dead; or, The Secret of the Heath*) is very much a work of detective fiction. Its central investigative figure, the mute Joseph Peters, has been described as 'one of the most intriguing, challenging, and unique detectives of the genre'.[20] Wilkie Collins' 1868 *The Moonstone* has been described by no less a figure than T. S. Eliot as 'the first and greatest of English detective novels'.[21]

Eliot claimed that 'in detective fiction England probably excels other countries',[22] but America also played a central role in the development of the genre. This is particularly true of the example of Edgar Allan Poe. Poe was a writer of startling diversity, but his three stories featuring the detective C. August Dupin, 'The Murders in the Rue Morgue' (1841), 'The Mystery of the Marie Rogêt' (1842), and 'The Purloined Letter' (1845), have had a tremendous impact on the genre (and on academic responses to it). As Heather Worthington points out, in these tales Poe pioneers both methods and aspects of characterization that later became regular features of much better known and more popular detective stories.[23] Another American, Anna Katharine Green, has received increasing attention in recent years as an early and important author of full-length detective novels, including *The Leavenworth Case: A Lawyer's Story* (1878). Perhaps Green's most lasting contribution to the genre was the gradual development of the detective Ebenezer Gryce's character over ten further novels, and the introduction of a reappearing cast of supporting characters.[24] This technique of serial character development has become one the signature effects of the modern crime novel.

The most famous narratives of crime and detection in the world are without question the 4 novels and 56 short stories written by Arthur Conan Doyle between 1887 and 1927 featuring the 'consulting detective' Sherlock Holmes.[25] Their own success, and even more their tremendous legacy of imitation and adaptation, mean that for many readers they have come to represent, or even define, the genre. Doyle's work was very much in the tradition pioneered by Poe, who, according to Doyle, 'breathed the breath of life' into the form.[26] He also made a less complimentary and more competitive reference to Poe in Holmes' first appearance in *A Study in Scarlet* (1887). When Holmes' friend Watson compliments him on his deductive abilities by comparing him with Dupin (an early example of the sort of metafictional gesture so typical of detective fiction), Holmes responds acerbically:

> 'No doubt you think that you are complimenting me in comparing me to Dupin', he observed. 'Now, in my opinion, Dupin was a very inferior fellow. That trick of his of breaking in on his friends' thoughts with an apropos remark after a quarter of an hour's silence is really very showy and superficial. He had some analytical genius, no doubt; but he was by no means such a phenomenon as Poe appeared to imagine'.[27]

The key point here is not Holmes' condemnation of Dupin's meretricious detecting abilities, but his emphasis on analysis as a fundamental feature of the detective story. This sort of rational, deductive reasoning based on a detailed analysis of the external world is very much a characteristic of Doyle's detective stories, if one that is carried at times to improbable degrees. Importantly, it also aligns his work with one of the era's major intellectual currents, the rational, scientific, technocratic viewpoint known as positivism, which 'adopts the naturalistic method of the physical sciences and mathematics and looks to faith in science as the means whereby it is possible to achieve certain, concrete, objective, useful, positive, and precise knowledge [...]'.[28]

Before taking up a career as a writer, Doyle trained and practiced as a physician, and Holmes is based, at least in part, on Joseph Bell, a consulting surgeon at the Edinburgh Infirmary who was a famed diagnostician. Readers first encounter Holmes at St Bartholomew's Hospital, where he is conducting rather grisly experiments on cadavers, an activity that is, to the tastes of some, 'a little too scientific'.[29] Holmes is here, and throughout his career, an 'empirical detective'.[30] As Knight points out, science, or more broadly speaking a positivist reliance on rationality, organization, experimentation, evidence, and logic, is central to Doyle's 'claim to innovation and credibility'; these stories offer, he writes, 'the romance of science' alongside other 'disciplinary modes' of knowledge.[31] Thus Holmes (and his many epigones) can be seen as a fictional embodiment of his era's faith in the possibility of obtaining reliable knowledge and of using that knowledge for the overall good of society.

While the link between detective fiction, rationality, and scientific modes of thought is probably Doyle's most important legacy, Holmes was vital to the development of the genre in other ways. His tremendous commercial success both in periodical and book form created a vast reading public hungry for a steady supply of stories of crime and detection. Doyle also pioneered (or solidified) a number of other features that became, and to some extent remain, generic standards, including an emphasis on the extraordinary abilities of an exceptional and at the same time eccentric individual; the presence of a much less unusual companion; the reappearance of a relatively stable cast of characters in a protracted series of narratives; and a clear and repeatable plot structure involving a client, a problem, an investigation, and a solution, with the solution often being explained by the detective to the detective's companion (and the readers).

The Golden Age of Crime Fiction

The features of Doyle's work are also typical of what is often called the Golden Age of detective fiction, although this is a somewhat controversial label. Who, after all, is to say what constitutes a golden age? A less evaluative label for this era is interwar detective fiction, although this characterization presents its own problems. Writing in 1941, Howard Haycraft identified E. C. Bentley's pre-war *Trent's Last Case* (1913) as the inaugural text of the period, and many other literary historians have followed his lead.[32] Terminal dates are no simpler, as many of the main writers of the period continued to work well past the Second World War. Agatha Christie's last novel, *Postern of Fate*, for example, was published in 1973. But whichever term one uses, this was an extraordinary fertile period in the history of the genre, which extended and expanded on the legacy of classic detective fiction.

Perhaps the key characteristic of the era was the sheer popularity of the genre, which in Britain and elsewhere became central to the 'consumption of standardized "light" reading matter' that played an important role in a developing culture of private leisure activity.[33] Detective novels (and the novel replaced the short story as the dominant medium for crime narratives during this period) were one of many forms of reading material 'borrowed from one of the various commercial libraries and soon replaced by another book of a predictably similar kind'.[34] While this sounds, and indeed is, dismissive of the potential of the genre to offer meaningful aesthetic, intellectual, or emotional experiences to readers, it does capture something about the way many of the detective novels of the era were read. The famous poet W. H. Auden, for instance, was a self-pronounced addict of the form, writing that 'I forget the story as soon as I have finished it, and have no wish to read it again'.[35] Instead, he wants to read another detective novel, one which is, crucially, similar if not identical to the previous one.

What was it then about the Golden Age or interwar detective novel which made it so appealing—indeed irresistible—to a huge audience of eager readers? Building on the progress made by the classic detective story as developed by Arthur Conan Doyle and others, the Golden Age novel relied heavily on processes of deduction and rational analysis. However, it also added a number of new features to the genre. Perhaps most importantly, these novels generally adopted a clue-puzzle format which, as the name suggests, offered readers a comprehensive set of clues (and red herrings) which resulted in an intricate yet solvable puzzle comparable to other popular pastimes of the era like the crossword (which was introduced in its modern form in 1913). This puzzle-like structure is accompanied by a philosophy of fair play. Authors are expected to provide readers with all of the information they require in order to compete with the detective in solving the mystery. To facilitate this competition, Golden Age novels (unlike their classic nineteenth-century predecessors) often limit their settings to closed environments such as the generically typical country house or, most radically, the locked room. These formal features are frequently accompanied by an interest in psychology, particularly in relation to criminal motivation, that resonates with the interwar era's increased interest in the mind and its fragility. Finally, in terms of literary history this era is particularly interesting because it is now remembered almost exclusively for its female authors, the so-called queens of crime, Margery Allingham, Agatha Christie, Ngaio Marsh, and Dorothy L. Sayers.[36] While many male authors wrote very successful detective novels during this era, they have been largely neglected by posterity—a fascinating inversion of typical gendered patterns of literary reception.

Hardboiled Crime Fiction

The same certainly cannot be said for the second major literary tradition to emerge out of the interwar era, the hardboiled. This is a genre that explicitly situated itself in opposition to the Golden Age detective novel, and has frequently been read in exactly those terms. In his famous essay 'The Simple Art of Murder' the hardboiled writer Raymond Chandler directly critiqued the British tradition of detective novels '[...] they do not really come off intellectually as problems, and they do not come off artistically as fiction. They are too contrived, and too little aware of what goes on in the world'.[37] The hardboiled writer, in contrast (specifically Dashiell Hammett, but the argument implicitly applies to Chandler's own work and that of 'the realist in murder' more generally),[38] 'took murder out of the Venetian vases and dropped it into the alley' where it belongs.[39] This is a type of detective narrative that relies more on suspense than on mystery for its effects, and, importantly, prides itself on its realism. Critics have rebutted this latter claim, pointing out that the hardboiled novel is often every bit as mannered and contrived, as structured by convention and formal considerations, as any novel of the Golden Age, but the emphasis on realism remains nonetheless an important development in the history of crime fiction.

The hardboiled is in its origins a quintessentially American form. It developed in response to the substantial increase in violent crime—and the public perception of this increase—associated with the post-First World War era, and more specifically Prohibition (1920–1933), which saw a marked increase in homicide rates.[40] In literary terms, it had its origin in older genres such as the Western, and more recent ones such as the gangster story. The hardboiled took the iconic hyper-individualist hero of the Western, and placed him (and at this point it was always him) in the dangerous streets of America's hyper-capitalist cities.

These works tend to be much more openly violent than their British Golden Age equivalents, and rely more on the forward thrust of a fast-paced plot than on the pleasures of investigation, deduction, and the solution of problems. As Tzvetan Todorov points out in his seminal study 'The Typology of Detective Fiction', in the hardboiled narrative:

[...] we are no longer told about a crime anterior to the moment of the narrative; the narrative coincides with the action. No thriller is presented in the form of memoirs: there is no point reached where the narrator comprehends all past events, we do not even know if he will reach the end of the story alive.[41]

Instead of looking backwards to a crime that occurred at an earlier point, often one preceding the narration, we are now looking forward at a prospect of future crimes that will occur within the narrative itself. This form of fiction thus both responds to a different set of social circumstances, and offers readers a very different set of pleasures.

Early versions of the hardboiled found their home in serial publications such as *Black Mask, Dime Detective, Detective Fiction Weekly, Clues,* and *Detective Story.*[42] These magazines were known pejoratively as 'pulps' after the low-quality paper on which they were printed, but a very high-quality body of longer form fiction quickly developed. Works like Hammett's *Red Harvest* (1929) focus on endemic and institutionalized corruption and the lamentable overlap between organized crime and the government, while novels like Chandler's *The Big Sleep* (1939), featuring his iconic private eye Philip Marlowe, are similarly concerned with ethical degradation amongst the American ruling classes. They offer readers a vision of a world in which, in the words of Fredric Jameson, 'the rule of naked force and money is complete and undisguised'.[43]

As John Scaggs notes, the hardboiled has experienced a perhaps unexpected literary longevity.[44] While the interwar mystery has remained perennially popular among readers, and of continued interest to academic critics, the genre has not really flourished since the end of the Second World War (with the exception of screen adaptations, which have offered a welcoming home to many Golden Age luminaries). The hardboiled, on the other hand, has undergone something of a rebirth in the late twentieth and early twenty-first centuries, at least in part because it lends itself very effectively to 'gender, ethnic, and cultural appropriation'.[45]

Ironically, because the hardboiled in its classic form is so strongly gendered, and so strongly associated with white America, it has proven to be particularly susceptible to revisionist re-imaginings. Notable examples of this include Sue Grafton's Kinsey Millhone series, which, alongside works by writers like Marcia Muller, Sara Paretsky, and Amanda Cross, has repurposed and re-invigorated the hardboiled tradition by placing a woman in the role of private eye.[46] These works remain 'faithful to the tradition of tough-guy detective fiction while disrupting its gender codes'.[47] Similar points can be made about the work of Walter Mosley and Chester Himes, whose work disrupts the racial coding of the genre, or about some of the earlier novels by Haruki Murakami, who transplanted the isolated, individualist protagonist of the genre to the much more collective Japanese context.

The Police Procedural

If an unexpected flexibility has proven to be the strength of the hardboiled genre, its weakness has unexpectedly proven to be what Chandler originally claimed as its key strength: its relationship to reality. While Chandler attempted to argue that the American hardboiled was superior to its British clue-puzzle competitors due to its verisimilitude, it soon became clear that this claim was spurious. James Ellroy, who began his career writing in the hardboiled tradition, later noted that 'the last time a private eye investigated a homicide was never'.[48] The very structure of the hardboiled form, the investigation of a murder by a private detective, is in other words utterly implausible, a genre-specific convention rather than a reflection of reality.

Significantly, Ellroy attributed this critique of the hardboiled to Evan Hunter, author (under the pen-name Ed McBain) of over fifty 87th Precinct novels. Published between 1956 (*Cop Hater*) and 2005 (*Fiddlers*), these are some of the best-known examples of what is generally known as the police procedural. In this form of crime fiction, investigations into criminal activity are carried out not by eccentric amateur sleuths or by misanthropic, isolated private eyes, but by official groups of police and judicial investigators (depending on the context). The emphasis here shifts from individual abilities and individual actions to the collective corporate endeavours of state-sanctioned legal authorities. Alongside this emphasis on the group or team comes an increased focus on the routines, techniques, and technologies of modern crime fighting, including (depending on the era in which the novels are set) such things as the distribution of investigative responsibility between different levels of a police hierarchy, different aspects of forensic science, computerized record searches, and the remote surveillance of suspects. While it is not always the case, the crimes investigated in procedurals can also be less dramatic, and arguably more realistic, than the elaborate plots and cunningly contrived mysteries of other genres of crime fiction. Joseph Wambaugh's Hollywood Station series (2006–2012), for example, deals largely with the type of relatively minor crimes—shoplifting, drug offences, assaults—that shape the daily working life of beat cops (as reported to the author during 'dinner meetings at good restaurants where they [the police] could dine and drink and ventilate').[49] This level of technical and procedural detail and the promise of a true-to-life fidelity are perhaps the main attractions of the form. It has also lent itself very well to screen adaption, with television series like *Hill Street Blues* (1981–1987) and *The Wire* (2002–2008) demonstrating the effectiveness and popularity of the form's naturalistic, ensemble approach.

While many of the best-known police procedural writers are American (like McBain, Wambaugh, and Karin Slaughter), the form has deep international roots. Georges Simenon published 75 novels featuring Inspector Maigret of the Paris *Brigade Criminelle*, which have been hugely successful in France and abroad. J. J. Marric's Gideon novels (1955–1976) introduced the procedural in Britain, while Maj Sjöwall and Per Wahlöö's ten-volume *Story of a Crime* (1965–1975) adopted the form to the Swedish context, and were influential in the development of contemporary Scandinavian crime fiction. Recent examples of the procedural can be found globally, from Hideo Yokoyama, who exploits the resonances between its collective orientation and Japanese cultural norms in novels like *Six Four* (2012, English translation, 2017), to Deon Meyer, who uses its polyvocal narrative structures to examine the complexities of post-Apartheid South Africa in *Dead Before Dying* (1996, English translation, 1999).

Globalized Crime Fiction

The global reach of the police procedural points towards one of the key developments in contemporary crime fiction: its intense internationalization. In some ways, this sort of international reach has always been a feature of the genre. As Barbara Pezzotti argues, transnationalism, or mobility across national and cultural borders, is one of its intrinsic characteristics,[50] and crime fiction is, and always has been, an important constituent part of world literature. Edgar Allan Poe may be a key figure in American literary history, but his detective Dupin solves mysteries in Paris, and his influence has been recognized by one of the fathers of Japanese detective fiction, Tarō Hirai (1894–1965), better known under his pen name Edogawa Ranpo—say that name quickly as three words (Edogaw Aran Po) and the act of transnational homage will become clear. Sherlock Holmes is a quintessentially British figure, but he also belongs to the global imagination, as works like *The Mandala of Sherlock Holmes* (1999), by Tibetan author Jamyang Norbu (1999), or the Japanese television series *Miss Sherlock* (2018) indicate.

More recent examples of crime fiction as a transnational form include the astonishing international success of Scandinavian crime fiction (Nordic Noir or Scandinoir), a diverse set of works (for page and screen) that have been described as 'a widely transnational, translingual, and transmedial [...] phenomenon'.[51] Notable works in this subgenre include very successful series by Camilla Läckberg, Henning Mankel, Jo Nesbø, and, perhaps most famously, Stieg Larsson (*The Girl with the Dragon Tattoo* was without doubt the most successful crime novel of recent years). These novels (and television series and films) are written and set in Scandinavian countries, but circulate globally in translation. In fact, they are written as much for international as domestic markets, and have triggered a host of other local, national imitations (or adaptations) of their characteristic blend of a socially critical employment of the conventions of the police procedural—this is where the roots of the genre lie[52]—and the excitement and narrative propulsion of the crime thriller, with its focus on 'the crime and the criminal committing it'.[53]

This combination of genres goes some way to explain phenomenal success of Scandinavian crime fiction: it has tapped into the energies lying behind two of the most successful forms of crime writing of the twentieth century, and brought them into the globalized world of the twenty-first. The crime thriller has been to this point an obvious gap in this chapter's discussion of the history of crime fiction. After all, every great detective needs a great criminal (Doyle's Holmes–Moriarty dyad is paradigmatic here, as is so much else in his work), and even the more plausibly quotidian detectives of the hardboiled and the police procedural depend on their criminal antagonists for their very existence: no crime, no crime fiction. In many contemporary crime thrillers (of, for example, the Nordic Noir variety), almost as much attention is paid to the criminals (who may or may not remain anonymous while the narrative progresses) as to the attempts of the police to catch them. This, like all of the currently active sub-genres of crime fiction, is an approach with a long history. Patricia Highsmith, for example, wrote a number of hugely important studies of the criminal, especially the five novels of the so-called Ripliad (1955–1991), while Jim Thompson's novels (notably the 1952 *The Killer Inside Me*) 'plunge unwary readers into a harrowing world of psychopathic hustlers whose outward normalcy masks a seething rage against the mainstream society that spawned them'.[54]

Our fascination as readers with this sort of criminal abnormality shows no signs of waning, as is evident, for example, from the burgeoning of true crime narratives in the twenty-first century. Not does our desire to follow in the investigative footsteps of those tasked, either formally of informally, with protecting us from the very criminal transgression we find so fascinating. The history of crime fiction, as this chapter has indicated, is long, rich, and varied; it's future is certain to be just as exciting.

Notes

1 Chris Baldick, *The Modern Movement*, The Oxford English Literary History, Vol. 10, 1910–1940 (Oxford: Oxford University Press, 2005), 273.
2 Julian Symons, *Bloody Murder: From the Detective Story to the Crime Novel*, 3rd edition (New York: Mysterious Press, 1992), 19.
3 Jonathan Charley, "Drugs, Crime and Other Worlds," in *Writing the Modern City: Literature, Architecture, Modernity*, edited by Sarah Edwards and Jonanthan Charley (London: Routledge, 2012), 99.

4 In its first edition, this is *Crime Fiction 1800–2000: Detection, Death, Diversity*. The inaugural date remains unchanged in the updated version.

5 Symons, *Bloody Murder*, 19.

6 Dorothy L. Sayers, "Introduction," in *The Omnibus of Crime*, edited by Dorothy L. Sayers (New York: Garden City Publishing Company, 1929), 9.

7 John Byron, *Cain and Abel in Text and Tradition: Jewish and Christian Interpretations of the First Sibling Rivalry* (Leiden: Brill, 2011), 1.

8 *The New Oxford Annotated Bible with Apocrypha: New Revised Standard Version*, edited by Michael D. Coogan, et al. (Oxford: Oxford University Press, 2010), Gen. 4.8.

9 Ibid., Gen. 4.10.

10 Richard Bradford, *Crime Fiction: A Very Short Introduction* (Oxford: Oxford University Press, 2015), 1.

11 Wilt Lukas Idema, "Introduction," in *Judge Bao and the Rule of Law: Eight Ballad-Stories From the Period 1250–1450* (Singapore: World Scientific Publishing Company, 2009), xxviii.

12 Uwe Böker, Ines Detmers, and Anna-Christina Giovanopoulos, "From Gay to Brecht and Beyond: Imitation and Re-Writing of *The Beggar's Opera*— 1728 to 2004," in *John Gay's the Beggar's Opera 1728–2004: Adaptations and Re-Writings*, edited by Uwe Böker, Ines Detmers, and Anna-Christina Giovanopoulos (Leiden: Brill, 2006), 9.

13 Maurizio Ascari, *A Counter-History of Crime Fiction: Supernatural, Gothic, Sensational* (Houndmills: Palgrave Macmillan, 2007), xii.

14 Martin Priestman, *Crime Fiction from Poe to the Present* (Devon: Northcote House, 1998), 1.

15 Bradford, *Crime Fiction*, 2.

16 John M. Reilly, "History of Crime and Mystery Writing," in *The Oxford Companion to Crime & Mystery Writing*, edited by Rosemary Herbert (Oxford: Oxford University Press, 1999), 211.

17 Clive Emsley, *A Short History of Police and Policing* (Oxford: Oxford University Press, 2021), 55–56.

18 Ibid., 64.

19 Stephen Knight, *Crime Fiction Since 1800: Detection, Death, Diversity*, 2nd edition (Houndmills: Palgrave Macmillan, 2010), 47.

20 Janine Hatter, "Joseph Peters: Mary Elizabeth Braddon (1835–1915)," in *100 Greatest Literary Detectives*, edited by Eric Sandberg (Lanham, MD: Rowman & Littlefield Publishers, 2018), 145.

21 T. S. Eliot, "Wilkie Collins and Dickens," in *Selected Essays*, edited by Thomas Stearns (New York: Harcourt, Brace, & World, 1964), 413.

22 Ibid. 137.

23 Heather Worthington, *Key Concepts in Crime Fiction* (Houndmills: Palgrave Macmillan, 2011), xiv.

24 Patricia D. Maida, *Mother of Detective Fiction: The Life and Works of Anna Katharine Green* (Bowling Green, OH: Bowling Green State University Popular Press, 1989), 57.

25 Arthur Conan Doyle, *A Study in Scarlet* (London: Penguin, 2011), 22.

26 Dawn B. Sova, *Critical Companion to Edgar Allan Poe: A Literary Reference to His Life and Work* (New York: Facts on File, 2007), 323.
27 Doyle, *A Study in Scarlet*, 23.
28 Andrea Borghini, "Positivism," in *The Wiley-Blackwell Encyclopedia of Social Theory*, edited by B. S. Turner (Chichester: Wiley-Blackwell, 2017), *Wiley Online Library*.
29 Doyle, *A Study in Scarlet*, 7.
30 Reilly, "History of Crime and Mystery Writing," 213.
31 Knight, *Crime Fiction Since 1800*, 56.
32 Howard Haycraft, *Murder for Pleasure: The Life and Times of the Detective Story* (Mineola, NY: Dover, 2019), 113.
33 Baldick, *The Modern Movement*, 272.
34 Ibid., 273.
35 W. H. Auden, "The Guilty Vicarage: Notes on the Detective Story, by an Addict," *Harpers* (May 1948), 406.
36 Cora Kaplan, " 'Queens of Crime': The 'Golden Age' of Crime Fiction," in *The History of British Women's Writing, 1920–1945*, edited by Maroula Joannou (Houndmills: Palgrave Macmillan, 2013), 144.
37 Raymond Chandler, "The Simple Art of Murder," in *The Simple Art of Murder* (New York: Vintage, 1988), 11. This essay has a complex textual history, and exists in several different versions. See Miranda B. Hickman's "Introduction: The Complex History of a 'Simple Art'," 292–298.
38 Ibid., 17.
39 Ibid., 14.
40 Jeffrey A. Miron, "Violence and the U.S. Prohibitions of Drugs and Alcohol," *American Law and Economics Review* 1, no. 1-2 (1999), 91, https://doi.org/10.1093/aler/1.1.78.
41 Tzvetan Todorov, "The Typology of Detective Fiction," in *The Poetics of Prose*, translated by Richard Howard (Oxford: Basil Blackwell, 1977), 47.
42 Erin Smith, *Hard-Boiled: Working-Class Readers and Pulp Magazines* (Philadelphia: Temple University Press, 2000), 20.
43 Fredric Jameson, *Raymond Chandler: The Detections of Totality* (London: Verso, 2016), 10.
44 John Scaggs, *Crime Fiction* (London: Routledge, 2005), 30.
45 Ibid., 30.
46 Adrienne E. Gavin, "Feminist Crime Fiction and Female Sleuths," in *A Companion to Crime Fiction*, edited by Charles J. Rzepka and Lee Horsley (Chichester: Wiley-Blackwell, 2010), 264.
47 Ann Wilson, "The Female Dick and the Crisis of Heterosexuality," in *Feminism in Women's Detective Fiction*, edited by Glenwood Irons (Toronto: University of Toronto Press, 1995), 148.
48 Lee Horsley, *Twentieth-Century Crime Fiction* (Oxford: Oxford University Press, 2005), 100.
49 Joseph Wambaugh, "Feeding the Force," *Joseph Wambaguh: Grandmaster of Police Stories*, www.josephwambaugh.net/Police_Novels.html.

50 Barbara Pezzotti, "Transnationality," in *The Routledge Companion to Crime Fiction*, edited by Janice Allan, Jesper Gulddal, Stewart King, and Andrew Pepper (London: Routledge, 2020), 96.

51 Linda Badley, Andrew Nestingen, and Jaakko Seppälä, "Introduction: Nordic Noir as Adaptation," in *Nordic Noir, Adaptation, Appropriation*, edited by Linda Badley, Andrew Nestingen, and Jaakko Seppälä (Cham: Palgrave Macmillan, 2020), 7.

52 Paul Arvas and Andrew Nestingten, "Introduction: Contemporary Scandinavian Crime Fiction," in *Scandinavian Crime Fiction*, edited by Paula Arvas and Andrew Nestingen (Cardiff: University of Wales Press, 2011), 2.

53 Scaggs, *Crime Fiction*, 105.

54 Robert Lance Snyder, "Entropic Disintegration: Jim Thompson's *The Killer Inside Me, Savage Night,* and *A Hell of a Woman*," *Journal of American Culture* 44, no. 3 (2021), 177.

4   A History of Crime Fiction Studies

The history of crime fiction studies—or the critical and/or academic study of crime fiction as an independent body of work within the larger literary system—is almost as old as the genre itself. The birth of crime fiction as a separate literary genre can best be located somewhere in the second half of the nineteenth century (with all of the provisos that were discussed in the previous chapter), and by the late nineteenth and early twentieth centuries a handful of critics had begun to pay attention to the new genre. Howard Haycraft, an early historian and critic of crime fiction, claims that the first critical reference to mystery fiction appeared in the *Saturday Review* in 1883, and early criticism by G. K. Chesterton (author of the Father Brown mysteries) and F. W. Chandler appeared in the first decade of the twentieth century.[1] However, it is not until the 1920s that we begin to see what can be described as a systematic response to the genre.[2] This analysis did not come from outside the field—from, for example, universities or scholarly journals—but from within the genre itself. As John M. Reilly notes, 'practitioners of the form gave crime and mystery writing its first body of literary criticism'.[3]

It is also significant that early attempts by writers of detective and mystery fiction to analyse their own genre tended towards *apologia*. As summarized by George N. Dove, early twentieth-century self-reflexive criticism was generally defensive in tone and purpose. First of all, it was argued, detective fiction had moved out of the penny-dreadful or pulp class of fiction by attracting, at least in part, a respectable audience of 'statesmen, serious writers and college dons'. Second, it was pointed out that the form as a whole had a dignified, serious, well-documented, and important literary heritage that could be traced back to various literatures of the ancient world (as was discussed in Chapter 3). And finally, early critics plead for assessments of the genre to be based not on its worst exemplars, but on its best.[4] This of course begs the question: how are these works to be identified?

DOI: 10.4324/9781003156581-6

The Golden Age of Criticism

It was not until the advent of the Golden Age that a group of writers began to systematically answer this question by establishing clear guidelines for the effective production of mystery narratives. As Dove notes, between 1913 and 1928 writers of detective stories felt the need to explicitly state the rules they should follow, and to provide instructions on how they should be written.[5] Dove identifies six major contributions to this process of self-definition: Carolyn Wells' *The Technique of the Mystery Story* (1913), E. M. Wrong's introduction to the *Anthology of Crime and Detection* (1921), R. Austin Freeman's 'The Art of the Detective Story' (1924), Ronald Knox's 'Ten Commandments of Detection' (1928), Dorothy L. Sayers' introduction to *Great Stories of Detection, Mystery, and Horror* (1928), and S. S. Van Dine's 'Twenty Rules for Writing Detective Stories' (1928).[6] There are other examples of this sort of self-reflexive practitioner criticism. A. A. Milne, for example (most famous as the creator of Winnie the Pooh), published *The Red House Mystery* in 1922; four years later, when the book was republished, he added an introduction that, while ostensibly outlining only his own 'curious preferences',[7] is in fact a concise but thorough analysis of the key features of the genre in terms of style, structure, and presentation.

One major preoccupation of many of the genre's early auto-critics was the idea that it was, in fact, worthy of critical attention. For example, Sayers' playful but insightful essay 'Aristotle on Detective Fiction' re-applies the *Poetics*' (c. 335 BCE) analysis of tragedy to mysteries, the point being that if one form—tragedy—can be taken seriously by scholars and critics, the other—detective fiction—can be too. Aristotle, according to Sayers, 'in his heart of hearts [...] desired [...] a Good Detective Story'; tragedy was simply 'the literary form which the detective story took in his day'.[8]

Another key preoccupation of this era of criticism was fair play, or the idea that the alert and intelligent reader should have every opportunity to unravel the mystery before the investigator's concluding revelations. All of the relevant clues must be made available to the reader in a timely fashion. As Jesper Gulddal has argued, 'the clue is by general consent a constituent feature of crime fiction; it is the means by which the detective solves the mystery, the device that keeps the plot together, the interface that draws in the reader'.[9] At its most extreme, this emphasis on clues and fair play can lead to direct challenges from the author to the reader. Sayers, for instance, in her purest example of the clue-puzzle mystery, *Five Red Herrings* (1931), interrupts the narrative of Lord Peter Wimsey's investigation with the following parenthetical statement: '(Here Lord Peter told the Sergeant what he was to look for and why, but as the intelligent reader will readily supply these details for himself, they are omitted from this page)'.[10] It is not until some 200 pages later that the novel explains to the reader what the missing item was, and why it was an essential clue. This approach is not limited to the Golden Age, as is indicated by the success of the Japanese schools of *Honkaku* and *Shin-Honkaku* (Orthodox and New Orthodox) mystery writing, which, as Soji Shimada notes, are 'not only literature but also, to a greater or lesser extent, a game'.[11] Towards the conclusion of his own debut novel, the 1981 *The Tokyo Zodiac Killings*, Shimada interrupts the narrative to inform readers that they now have enough information to solve the puzzle on their own, and challenges them to do so.

While the concept of fair play is central to Golden Age criticism, there were other guidelines in relatively wide circulation as part of the critical superstructure for the developing genre. One idea that had a great deal of traction was that there was no place in the detective novel for romance or a love-interest. As Milne put it, 'a reader, all agog to know whether the white substance on the muffins was arsenic or face powder, cannot be held up while Roland clasps Angela's hand'.[12] Other ideas concern the import- ance of plotting, which is generally taken to be central to the genre: 'A detective story [...] is impossible without action, but there may be one without character'.[13] The overall thrust of all of these prescriptions, how- ever, was, as Dove writes of Van Dine's 20 rules, that 'the detective story was an intellectual game, and that game must be played according to rules as strict as those used in the working of a crossword puzzle'.[14]

The Question of Realism

One of the first major critical interventions in the analysis of detective fiction arose in response to exactly this view. For Raymond Chandler— who, like many of those mentioned earlier was primarily a writer rather than critic of crime fiction—the key point about the 'murder novel' (as he calls them in his landmark 1944 essay 'The Simple Art of Murder') is that it is precisely not a game.[15] 'Fiction in any form', he argues, 'has always intended to be realist', and it is this test that the writer he dismis- sively calls the 'ladies and gentlemen [...] of the Golden Age of detective fiction' fail, even on their own terms.[16] The clue-puzzle mystery, Chandler argues, must be a 'problem of logic and deduction' or 'it is nothing at all'.[17] Yet time after time (he claims) it fails to offer a realistic, plausible problem that is amenable to logical analysis and deductive reasoning, or to provide realistic solutions to the mysteries it proposes. It beggars belief, for instance, that because nobody 'could have done the murder alone' in Agatha Christie's famous *Murder on the Orient Express*, 'everybody did it together'.[18] The solution to this failing is realism (of motive for and method of murder), but this solution in turn causes another problem: '[…] if the writers of this fiction wrote about the kind of murders that happen, they would also have to write about the authentic flavor of life as it is lived'.[19] One sort of formal realism—the realism of the plot—demands another sort of realism—the realism of society, of psychology, of contemporary life.

Chandler locates this realism not in the British tradition of the clue-puzzle mystery (which was also widely written and read in America), but in the American tradition of the hardboiled to which he (who was a naturalized British subject) is such a notable contributor. He takes as his model Dashiell Hammett, whose Continental Op short stories (published in the pulp magazine *Black Mask* between 1923 and 1930) and five novels (published by Alfred E. Knopf between 1929 and 1934) were early and hugely important contributions to the genre. Hammett was the 'ace performer' of a larger group of realistic crime fiction writers.[20] His work was 'made up out of real things' and thus had the sense of lived reality, of a tangible likeness to the everyday world, that was so signally lacking in his Golden Age competitors.[21] Hammett, Chandler famously argued,

> […] gave murder back to the kind of people that commit it for reasons, not just to provide a corpse; and with the means at hand, not with hand-wrought duelling pistols, curare, and tropical fish. He put these people down on paper as they are, and he made them talk and think in the language they customarily used for these purposes.[22]

So here we have a realistic motivation (and thus realistic characters) and realistic murders (and thus by implication realistic investigations into these murders), with both conveyed to the reader in realistic language, the language of the street and of the day. Chandler adds one more important qualification here:

> The realist in murder writes of a world in which gangsters can rule nations and almost rule cities, in which hotels and apartment houses and celebrated restaurants are owned by men who made their money out of brothels, in which a screen star can be the finger man for a mob, and the nice man down the hall is a boss of the numbers racket; a world where a judge with a cellar full of bootleg liquor can send a man to jail for having a pint in his pocket, where the mayor of your town may have condoned murder as an instrument of moneymaking, where no man can walk down a dark street in safety because law and order are things we talk about but refrain from practicing; a world where you may witness a hold-up in broad daylight and see who did it, but you will fade quickly back into the crowd rather than tell anyone, because

the hold-up men may have friends with long guns, or the police may not like your testimony, and in any case the shyster for the defense will be allowed to abuse and vilify you in open court, before a jury of selected morons, without any but the most perfunctory interference from a political judge.[23]

This is an appeal for crime fiction to function as a sort of social realism, a type of writing that offers a believable and critical picture of modern society not as we might wish it to be (fair, equitable, just, etc.) but as we know it, when we are being honest, to be. Or, to put it differently, a call for the critical community to recognize that this is already what crime fiction is, at least some of the time: a genre capable of presenting a realistic, and trenchant, social analysis.

While Chandler is a very important, and early, proponent of this view of crime fiction as a genre yoked to realism, there are two qualifications that should be made here. First, the type of writing he proposes as a higher form of detective fiction, the hardboiled, is arguably every bit as mannered, conventional, and unrealistic as the most contrived Golden Age clue-puzzle mystery. As Miranda B. Hickman notes, the arguments put forward in 'The Simple Art of Murder' are so familiar, and are quoted so regularly, that they are more often taken for granted than subject to stringent analysis.[24] Second, Chandler was not alone (as he acknowledges in his essay) in criticizing the flaws of the Golden Age detective novel. Sayers, for example, (as a leading practitioner and theorist of the form) gradually became frustrated with its limitations, particularly its inability to integrate realistic, fully developed characters into its schematic, rule-bound format. She articulated this in her critical writings, but also, and most memorably, in her fiction. In her late novel *Gaudy Night* (1935), for example, her detective Lord Peter Wimsey and his romantic interest, the detective writer, Harriet Vane discuss the problems of her current novel: one character's 'behaviour isn't sufficiently accounted for'.[25] The obvious solution, to develop him as a character by giving him 'lifelike feelings' would, however, 'throw the whole book out of balance'.[26] This is the limitation of the 'jig-saw kind of story'—and perhaps one reason why Sayers herself soon gave up writing detective fiction.[27]

Before tracing the development of crime fiction studies further, it is worth noting that the sort of positive criticism of the genre discussed here was the exception rather than the rule. For many critics, the genre remained either beneath contempt, and thus critically invisible, or the object of an active and vociferous dislike. Edmund Wilson, for instance, one of America's leading critics in the first half of the twentieth century, was no fan of the genre. He described Agatha Christie's writing in one essay as 'of a mawkishness and banality which seem to me literally impossible to read',[28] and Sayers' in another as lacking 'any distinction at all'.[29] In Britain, an equivalent critique came from Queenie Leavis, a leading academic literary scholar of the era, who targeted detective fiction in general (and Sayers in particular) in an essay published in *Scrutiny* in 1937.[30] While this is not the place to go further into the details of these attacks on crime fiction, it is worth remembering that they formed the context for attempts to analyse the detective genre from its earliest days up to, roughly, the middle of the twentieth century.

Modern Criticism and Literary Theory

From the late 1950s onward critical work on detective fiction began to shift away from the practitioners of the genre itself, as academic criticism and literary scholarship more broadly began to consider its significance. The old debates over definition, value, form, and realism were displaced by the application of a range of different theoretical paradigms to detective fiction, both to illuminate particular aspects of the genre, and to cast light on particular issues arising within these theoretical approaches.

This is true, for example, of the sustained engagement of structuralist critics with detective fiction. As the label suggests, structuralist critics tend to be less interested in individual examples of narrative—say, an individual detective novel like Milne's *The Red House Mystery* or Chandler's *The Big Sleep*—and more interested in what these types of text can tell us about narrative more generally. One example of this approach is Umberto Eco's influential morphological study of Ian Fleming's James Bond stories which, in the style of Vladimir Propp's work on the morphology of Russian Folktales, breaks Fleming's narratives down into more or less generic functions to reveal the fact that

> in every detective story and in every hard-boiled novel, there is no basic variation, but rather the repetition of a habitual scheme in which the reader can recognize something he has already seen and of which he has grown fond.[31]

The relative simplicity of the crime novel here allows Eco to identify patterns which he (or his readers) can then apply to a broader range of literary texts.

Another key idea is that detective fiction, with its assemblage of clues and its delayed revelation of the true story, provides a working model for the understanding of other narratives, which less obviously, though just as importantly, rely on the giving and withholding of information for their impact. While early work was done in this area by the Russian Formalists (e.g. Victor Shklovsky's chapter on Sherlock Holmes in *Theory of Prose*),[32] a key text here is Tzvetan Todorov's 1966 'The Typology of Detective Fiction'. In this widely cited and much-discussed essay, Todorov focuses on the representation of time as a way of separating the sub-genres of crime fiction (and thus of thinking about genre as a literary category more generally). The classic detective novel, he points out, 'contains not one but two stories: the story of the crime and the story of the investigation',[33] with the story of the investigation completely effacing the story of the crime, which occurs, in fact, before the narrative proper even begins. Other versions of the crime narrative, Todorov argues, handle the relationship between these two separate stories differently. For Todorov, this argument is important not just for what it reveals about crime fiction, but for the emphasis it places on the distinction between the *fabula* (or the basic story material) and the *syuzhet* (or the way that material is arranged and narrated) in all forms of fiction. As Hetta Pyrönen notes, it is certainly possible to question the ability of models like this to fully reflect the dynamics of genre (the way they develop and change over time), or to allow for the way different subgenres interpenetrate each other.[34] Yet the structuralist approach of Todorov (and many others) was critical in moving the study of crime fiction towards the centre of the broader literary-critical context.

Other approaches have been adopted as part of what might be called the normalization of crime fiction studies, or its move into, or at least towards, the mainstream of literary studies. Post-structuralist and postmodernist critics, for example, have long been fascinated by the inherent self-reflexivity of the detective genre. This is a literary form that has since its inception acknowledged and celebrated its own fictionality. Consider, for example, Sherlock Holmes' famous condemnation in *A Study in Scarlet* of Edgar Allan Poe's detective C. Auguste Dupin, who is, in Holmes opinion, a 'very inferior fellow' and by no means 'such a phenomenon as Poe appeared to imagine'.[35] Holmes, a fictional detective, here asserts his own textual reality by inserting himself into the pre-existing textual reality of Poe's fictional detective. By treating Poe's fictional character as real, Doyle claims a sort of reality for his own character while simultaneously acknowledging that what is presenting itself as real (the world of Holmes and Watson in London) is in fact imaginary. This sort of 'self-aware mirroring of intertextuality' is a fundamental focus of post-structuralist and post-modern criticism, and is another example of the way the study of crime fiction has gradually become a more mainstream academic activity.[36] One of the clearest examples of this tendency is Patricia Merivale and Susan Elizabeth Sweeney's landmark 1998 collection *Detecting Texts: The Metaphysical Detective Story from Poe to Postmodernism*, which defined and studied a form of experimental crime story linked to both detective and modernist and postmodernist fiction.[37] Here, the study of crime fiction overlaps almost completely with some of the central preoccupations of literary study more generally.

Social Criticism

To this point, I have considered the development of crime fiction studies from a strongly textual perspective; that is to say I have been discussing criticism that focuses on narrative techniques, genre analysis, and so on. This is of course a perfectly sensible approach, as crime fiction is, like all fiction, before anything else text. But detective stories, again like all forms of fiction, have as much invested in the real, external world of people, places and things as they do in their own textual status. Indeed, some would argue that crime fiction is even more closely linked to the real, social world than many other forms of literature. As crime novelist Val McDermid has argued, 'the crime novel seems [...] to have become, at its best, the fictional form that represents the broadest picture of the way we live now'.[38] And this connection between the imagined world of crime fiction and the real world of crime has been another major focus for the study of the genre.

The basic point here is that crime fiction can be viewed as a form of cultural product (alongside a whole range of other cultural products, like ballet or beer) that can shed light on social attitudes that might otherwise remain invisible. This sort of cultural critique often reads crime fiction as an expression of an ideology that 'reproduces the values and subject positions' of those who are most deeply invested in 'the socio-cultural status quo'.[39] Stephen Knight, for example, in his 1980 study *Form and Ideology in Crime Fiction* contends that the success of Sherlock Holmes as a character arose from his unrivalled capacity for alleviating the 'anxieties of a respectable, London-based middle-class audience'.[40] In a rapidly growing metropolis like nineteenth-century London in which the rich and poor lived in uncomfortable proximity, and anonymity was a condition of existence, there was a need for precisely this sort of comfort. Similar arguments have been made about Agatha Christie's 'conservative social vision'[41] which presents 'a world embodying the virtues of the vanishing gentry' and which regularly evokes 'order out of disorder' while embodying 'a respect for the rule of law in defense of life and property'.[42] Time after time in this sort of fiction, readers are presented with a stable, hierarchical social milieu (the isolated village, the country house) which is disrupted by a crime; the arrival of the detective and the ensuing investigation are a sort of reparative social work, identifying and excising the damaged or sick organs of the social body—the criminal—to restore the tranquil continuity of the world. Examples are legion, but Dorothy L. Sayers' 1934 *The Nine Tailors* might well be exemplary, with its evocation of a rural community threated by the impact of the First World War and the transformations of modernity, but protected by the detective work of the aristocratic Lord Peter Wimsey.

The critical tradition has generally identified a rupture here between the Golden Age and the hardboiled. If Golden Age fiction extolls social continuity and tradition, and implicitly or explicitly serves the notion of an organic community, in the hardboiled the 'notion of the social system as a healthy organism' became 'nothing but a bad joke'.[43] The work of writers like Dashiell Hammett made this joke obvious. In *Red Harvest*, for example, we find a city in which the ruling class has let its 'hired thugs run wild' to defeat labour unrest, only to find that once 'the fight was over' they 'couldn't get rid of them'. 'Personville', Hammett writes, 'looked good to them and they took it over'.[44] The same sort of argument can be made regarding Raymond Chandler's novels or, to take a slightly later example, Ross McDonald's Lew Archer novels (1949–1976), which in the words of one commentator 'investigate the sources of rot in the American grain'.[45] This sort of reading emphasizes crime fiction's potential to function not as an expression of middle-class anxiety and values, but as a site of resistance to such ideological formations.

It should be noted however, that there are gaps in these claims for the social and political radicalism of the hardboiled. Philip Howell, for example, sees 'bourgeois ideological effects' as integral to crime fiction's 'claim to know the city' through the perspective of 'an individual detective around whom the production of meaning and therefore order revolves'.[46] When we read Chandler, we experience the world through the consciousness of his private eye Philip Marlowe, and thus experience it as a unified whole—perhaps an unpleasant and dangerous one, but one that is nonetheless coherent. As Fredric Jameson writes, Marlowe is able to 'tie its separate and isolated parts together'[47] in a way that a reader like Howell sees as fundamentally untrue to the lived experience of the polysemous and multifaceted city (which is better represented for Howell by the polyvocal police procedural, 'a more genuinely critical form of crime fiction').[48] Another widespread critique of the ostensibly radical politics of the hardboiled involves the identity of the single viewer: Marlowe (and Hammett's Continental Op, and many, many other hardboiled detectives) are socially isolated, white, heterosexual men. This is not, obviously, a universal or neutral subject position, particularly given the genre's troubling history of misogyny and racism.

Gender and race have in fact become central to some readings of hardboiled, and it is something of a critical commonplace to see the genre as promoting 'a masculinized view of the autonomous individual [...] in a tough and competitive world'[49] in which 'latent racial subtexts' persistently and repeatedly belittle and marginalize the non-white other.[50] One critical response to this has been to focus on writers like Sue Grafton and

Sara Paretsky, who challenge the male bias of the genre through the intro-duction of women to the central position of the private eye, or on writers like Chester Himes and Walter Mosely who do the same with African-American characters. Another response reads backwards into the canon, to focus on the aspects of older crime fiction that respond to interpret-ative strategies attuned to questions of sex or race. A critic might re-read Mickey Spillane's 1947 *I, The Jury* (a hugely successful hardboiled novel whose hero, Mike Hammer, sets out to avenge the murder of his friend) as a 'sadomasochistic project' that 'involves hurting women in self-defense'.[51] This sort of criticism has, once more, aligned crime fiction studies with broader currents in literary scholarship, where questions of race, gender, sexuality, identity, and representation have become ever more central in the twenty-first century.

This discussion should have indicated that assessments of the politics of crime fiction, and of its social impact, should not be yoked too closely to any particular subgenre or set of texts. The hardboiled can be read as a politically radical alternative to the staid conservatism of the Golden Age, but the same texts can be seen as offering 'a disillusioned populism' that is only a step away from a fascist worship of violence.[52] In the same way, many critics are now recuperating the Golden Age and rejecting easy conclusions about its ostensibly inherent conservatism. As Mary Evans, Sarah Moore, and Hazel Johnstone note in the context of Agatha Christie and Gladys Mitchell (another important if less well-remembered Golden Age author), 'detective fiction, in the hands of these women, was not about maintaining the political and intellectual orthodoxies of the first decades of the twentieth century'.[53] Thus while some Golden Age crime fiction may well be conservative and some hardboiled crime fiction may well be radical, a more valuable perspective might be to see crime fiction as an inherently ambivalent genre that operates in an uncomfortable space between full-throated support for state power, law enforcement, and social order and a persistent probing critique of these claims.

Notes

1 Heta Pyrhönen, *Murder from an Academic Angle* (Columbia, SC: Camden House, 1994), 4.

2 Howard Haycraft, *Murder for Pleasure: The Life and Times of the Detective Story* (Mineola, NY: Dover, 2019), 272.

3 John M. Reilly, "Criticism, Literary," in *The Oxford Companion to Crime & Mystery Writing*, edited by Rosemary Herbert (Oxford: Oxford University Press, 1999), 109.

4 George N. Dove, "The Rules of the Game," *Studies in Popular Culture* 4 (1981), 68.

5 Ibid., 67.

6   Ibid.
7   A. A. Milne, "Introduction," in *The Red House Mystery* by A. A. Milne (London: Vintage, 2009), xi.
8   Dorothy L. Sayers, "Aristotle on Detective Fiction," *English* 1, no. 1 (1936), 24–25.
9   Jesper Gulddal, "Clues," in *The Routledge Companion to Crime Fiction*, edited by Janice Allan, Jesper Gulddal, Stewart King, and Andrew Pepper (London: Routledge, 2020), 194.
10 Dorothy L. Sayers, *Five Red Herrings* (Toronto: Signet, 1967), 22.
11 Tara Cheesman, "A Brief Introduction to *Honkaku* and *Shin Honkaku* Mysteries," *Crime Reads*, September 25, 2020, https://crimereads.com/the-honkaku-and-shin-honkaku-mysteries-of-seishi-yokomizo/.
12 Milne, "Introduction," x.
13 Dorothy L. Sayers, "Aristotle on Detective Fiction," *English* 1, no. 1 (1936), 26.
14 George N. Dove, "The Rules of the Game," 70.
15 Raymond Chandler, "The Simple Art of Murder," in *The Simple Art of Murder* (New York: Vintage, 1988), 2. This essay has a complex textual history. See Miranda B. Hickman's "Introduction: The Complex History of a 'Simple Art'," 292–298, for a full discussion.
16 Ibid., 1, 5.
17 Ibid., 6–7.
18 Ibid., 7.
19 Ibid., 11.
20 Ibid., 13–14.
21 Ibid., 14.
22 Ibid., 14–15.
23 Ibid., 17.
24 Miranda B. Hickman, "Introduction: The Complex History of a 'Simple Art'," *Studies in the Novel* 35, no. 3 (2003), 292.
25 Dorothy L. Sayers, *Gaudy Night* (New York: Avon, 1968), 255.
26 Ibid., 256.
27 Ibid.
28 Edmund Wilson, "Why Do People Read Detective Stories?," *New Yorker*, October 14, 1944, www.newyorker.com/magazine/1944/10/14/why-do-people-read-detective-stories.
29 Edmund Wilson, "Who Cares Who Killed Roger Ackroyd: A Second Report on Detective Fiction," *New Yorker*, June 20 (1945), 60.
30 Q. D. Leavis, "The Case of Miss Dorothy Sayers," *Scrutiny* (December 1937), 334–340.
31 Umberto Eco, "Narrative Structures in Fleming," translated by R. A. Downie, in *The Poetics of Murder: Detective Fiction and Literary Theory*, edited by Glenn W. Most and William W. Stowe (San Diego, CA: Harcourt Brace Jovanovich, 1983), 113.
32 Viktor Shklovksy, *Theory of Prose*, translated by Benjamin Sher (Normal, IL: Dalkey Archive Press, 1991), 101–116.

33 Tzvetan Todorov, "The Typology of Detective Fiction," in *The Poetics of Prose*, translated by Richard Howard (Oxford: Basil Blackwell, 1977), 45.

34 Pyrhönen, *Murder from an Academic Angle*, 30–31.

35 Arthur Conan Doyle, *A Study in Scarlet* (London: Penguin, 2011), 23.

36 Pyrhönen, *Murder from an Academic Angle*, 35.

37 Patricia Merivale and Susan Elizabeth Sweeney, "The Game's Afoot: On the Trail of the Metaphysical Detective Story," in *Detecting Texts: The Metaphysical Detective Story from Poe to Postmodernism*, edited by Patricia Merivale and Susan Elizabeth Sweeney (Philadelphia: University of Pennsylvania Press, 1998), 1.

38 Val McDermid, "Preface," *Crime Fiction Studies* 1, no. 1 (2020), v.

39 Pyrhönen, *Murder from an Academic Angle*, 81.

40 Stephen Knight, *Form and Ideology in Crime Fiction* (London: MacMillan, 1980), 67.

41 John Scaggs, *Crime Fiction* (London: Routledge, 2005), 48.

42 Charles Rzepka, *Detective Fiction* (Cambridge: Polity Press, 2005), 153.

43 Peter Messent, *The Crime Fiction Handbook* (Chichester: Wiley-Blackwell, 2013), 17.

44 Dashiell Hammett, *Red Harvest* (New York: Vintage, 1972), 9–10.

45 Nicholas Dawidoff, "Ross Macdonald, True Detective," *The New Republic*, September 15, 2017, https://newrepublic.com/article/144537/ross-macdonald-true-detective-noir-novelist-investigated-sources-rot-american-grain.

46 Philip Howell, "Crime and the City Solution: Crime Fiction, Urban Knowledge, and Radical Geography." *Antipode* 30, no. 4 (1998), 360, 365.

47 Jameson, *Raymond Chandler*, 7.

48 Howell, "Crime and the City Solution," 365.

49 Jopi Nyman, *Hard-boiled Fiction and Dark Romanticism* (Frankfurt: Peter Lang, 1998), 9–10.

50 Elisabeth V. Ford, "Miscounts, Loopholes, and Flashbacks: Strategic Evasion in Walter Mosley's Detective Fiction," *Callaloo* 28, no. 4 (2005), 1075. *JSTOR*, www.jstor.org/stable/3805589.

51 David Willbern, *The American Popular Novel after World War II: A Study of 25 Best Sellers, 1947–2000* (Jefferson, NC: McFarland, 2013), 14.

52 John M. Reilly, "The Politics of Tough Guy Mysteries," *University of Dayton Review* 10 (1973), 29–30.

53 Mary Evans and Sarah Moore, with Hazel Johnstone, *Detecting the Social: Order and Disorder in Post-1970s Detective Fiction* (Cham: Palgrave MacMillian, 2019), 4.

5   The Criminology of Crime Fiction

The connections between the material covered in the four preceding chapters may not be immediately obvious. Crime is a social phenomenon and an aspect of human experience; criminology is a field of study with aspirations towards a scientific methodology which aims to understand this phenomenon. Both are thus closely related to the real world of facts. Crime fiction on the other hand is a form of narrative that is at least in part, as its name suggests, defined by its fictionality. It is, whatever the pretensions of particular sub-genres, authors, or texts made-up, unreal, fantastic. And crime fiction studies is thus the study of works of imagination, of make-believe. The relationship between these two discourses or fields of study, criminology on the one hand and crime fiction on the other, may therefore seem remote or even tendentious.

However, it is possible to argue that the relationship between criminology and crime fiction is much closer than this focus on facticity versus fictionality suggests. First of all, we need to be attentive to the fact that both criminology and crime fiction originate towards the end of the eighteenth and the beginning of the nineteenth century. This was a time (as we have seen in previous chapters) when a range of social, political, and legal factors intertwined in places like Britain and France, leading to a radical transformation in both the conceptualization of crime and the social and judicial responses to it. One factor was the way in which religious authority was over time replaced by the rule of secular law in these societies, with crime coming to be seen as less an affront to the divine order and more a challenge to the prevailing socio-economic elite.[1] Another important consideration was the tremendous transformation in legal responses to crime. To take Britain as an example, radical changes took place around the end of the nineteenth century. During the era of what has come to be known as the Bloody Code (c. 1723–1832), there were over 200 offences punishable by the death. By 1861, this number had been reduced to five: murder, arson in the Royal Dockyards, espionage, piracy with violence, and

DOI: 10.4324/9781003156581-7

treason. While each country and region has its own historical particular-ities, in the broadest terms we can claim that similar changes happened in many other parts of the world at around the same time. Perhaps the best way of thinking about these transformations is as part of the whole package of modernity, with criminology and crime fiction emerging more or less simultaneously as part of a broader cultural response to these new, modern conditions, and to look at them as admittedly different, but none-theless related, forms of discourse.

Cultural Criminology

A key context here has been the emergence of a field of study known as cultural criminology which, according to Karin Scholfield, 'advocates the blending of ideas and approaches from a range of theoretical orientations, most notably media and cultural studies, through which the social con-struction of crime and criminal behaviour(s) can be interrogated and theorised'.[2] As Scholfield points out, traditional criminologists draw on relatively few sets of information about crime, deviance, victimhood, and so on in their work, including statistical, legislative, and psychological sources, often combined or filtered through pre-existing criminological theorization. Cultural criminologists, on the other hand, insist on the value of a vastly expanded range of sources and theories in an approach that, importantly, 'reflects the multi-mediated nature of much criminality in late modernity'.[3] We live in a world in which crime always appears in the context of representations of crime, and is at times inseparable from these representations.

To take a single example, we might ask if it is possible, or if possible useful, to consider the still unsolved 1997 murder of rapper Christopher Wallace, better known as the Notorious B.I.G, separately from the fact that roughly a third of the most popular commercial rap hits released between 1989 and 2000 contained at least one reference to homicide (a proportion that would be much higher in Wallace's own genre of gangsta rap),[4] or the extensive media coverage—or media construction—of the East Coast vs. West Coast hip-hop feud that was a backdrop to his death, or a film like Brad Furman's 2021 *City of Lies* (based on Randall Sullivan's book, *LAbyrinth*) which reconsiders the murder decades later? Or, to adopt an even broader perspective, would it be meaningful to think about Wallace's murder without considering the ubiquity of late twentieth-century media- and racism-fuelled stereotypes of young Black men as 'incarnations of vio-lence'?[5] This is not the traditional stuff of criminology, but for a cultural criminologist it would represent important, and neglected, information.

As this example illustrates, proponents of cultural criminology believe that it has the potential to 'loosen the methodological, theoretical and substantive constraints' of the conventions of traditional criminology with its emphasis on large-scale statistical data analysis and abstract theorization, and thus free the study of crime and criminality from a 'stranglehold on meaning, style and interpretation'.[6] Crime, cultural criminologists believe, is so central to society—its self-image, its success or failure, its ability to provide equality and justice for all its members—that it is vital to adopt as broad and as flexible a perspective as possible to understanding it. As Jeff Ferrell, Keith Hayward, Wayne Morrison, and Mike Presdee write:

> Theories of crime and crime control are too important to leave to statisticians or theoreticians floating adrift from the immediacy of transgression. The criminological production of numeric summaries, cross-correlations, statistical residues and second-hand data sets may serve the needs of the crime control industry, the campaigns of politicians, or the careers of academic criminologists—but let's no longer fool ourselves that they serve to make sense of crime and crime control, or move us toward social arrangements less poisoned by fear, violence and exploitation.[7]

The point here is straightforward: few bodies of information and theory, few discourses in other words, have a more direct and immediate impact on the members of a society than criminology—particularly on its most vulnerable members.

As an example of this fact, consider the history of the so-called 'superpredator'. In the mid-1990s Princeton-based criminologist John J. Dilulio Jr., alongside other conservative criminologists, developed the idea that 'superpredators', or a small number (six percent, to be precise) of young men, generally Black city-dwellers, were responsible for the vast majority of serious crimes. This idea was immediately taken up by the popular press, with articles about America's looming superpredator-driven crime wave appearing in publications from *Newsweek* to *Reader's Digest*.[8] Now thoroughly debunked, the theory was at the time accepted not just by the public, but by the judicial system, as in the case of Keith Belcher who was sentenced in 1997 to an extraordinary 60 years imprisonment for a crime he committed at the age of 14 (sexual assault and robbery of an elderly woman) on the explicit grounds that he was, in the words of Judge Michael Hartmere, 'a charter member' of the 'superpredator[s]', or 'radically impulsive, brutally remorseless youngsters who assault, rape, rob and burglarize'.[9] This sentence has now been thrown out by the Connecticut Supreme Court specifically on the grounds that 'the superpredator myth is precisely the type of materially false information that courts should not rely on in making sentencing decisions'.[10] Dilulio himself has long since expressed regret at his association with the discredited idea.[11] The point

I want to make here is not to diminish the seriousness of Belcher's crime, or others like it, but to reinforce the idea that criminological theories have direct and real impacts on real people. Belcher's 60-year sentence was, by all usual legal standards and judicial precedents, excessive, even for a reprehensible, violent assault. Yet a single criminological theory, supported by a dubious selection of misrepresented statistical data[12]—and a catchy name—was sufficient to overturn these norms. This clearly indicates that criminology should be, as cultural criminologists argue, a site of contestation, experimentation, and innovation.

A less elaborate way of putting this would be to say that the stories we tell about crime are every bit as important as the crimes themselves, which from the perspective of a cultural criminologist, are inseparable from the cultural narratives within which they are embedded. In the words of Jeff Ferrell, Keith Hayward, and Jock Young, this is one of 'cultural criminology's founding concepts: *cultural dynamics carry within them the meaning of the crime* [emphasis in original]'.[13] Culture, from this perspective, 'interweave[s] with the practice of crime and crime control and contemporary society' with each crime becoming a contested site of 'meaning, representation, and power'.[14] Indeed, under the conditions of late modernity (or post-modernity) cultural criminologists would contend that 'as a result of the pervasiveness of digital media, images of crime and its control are becoming almost as "real" as crime and criminal justice itself'.[15] In order to study this dynamic palimpsest of fluid meanings in which the representation of crime is superimposed on real crime, and crime occurs in media-saturated environment, cultural criminologists examine a wider range of texts that 'promulgate the social "story" of crime and crime control' including (according to Ferrell, Hayward, and Young) television shows and films, comic books and graphic novels, photography and other visual artworks, and the imagery of the news media.[16]

Cultural Criminology and Crime Fiction

This is of course a partial list, intended to represent rather than encompass the range and diversity of the materials from which cultural criminology draws inspiration. But the omission of crime fiction from Ferrell, Hayward, and Young's list is interesting. Nor is it unique. In her discussion of cultural criminology, Karin Scholfield very usefully identifies five modes of inquiry, only one of which has space for fiction, the 'Communicational Mode' which includes the study of 'broadcast, print media, fiction, film, theatre, art, photography and public debate' as 'barometers of social process and change' and as indications of 'behavioural and societal attitudes'.[17] Here at least fiction gets a look in, however briefly. Scholfield also discusses Mike Presdee's *Cultural Criminology and the Carnival of*

Crime as describing the 'interrelationship of crime and culture through cultural texts' as 'illustrated by the popularity of the genres of crime and deviance within film, television and literary texts'.[18] But Presdee's book makes almost no reference to literary texts, instead drawing on 'life histories, images, music and dance'.[19]

Presdee is most interested in the everyday cultural acts (from bare-knuckle fighting to genital piercing to raving) through which people challenge the stultifying status quo of neo-liberal capitalism. When he does deal with more formal texts, he is almost exclusively interested in television (his index refers to more than ten television programmes, but no works of fiction). For Presdee, detective stories, crime novels, and police procedurals are not, apparently, part of everyday life. Similarly, Ferrell, Hayward, and Young include a very interesting criminological filmography in *Cultural Criminology: An Invitation* listing movies, documentaries, and television series from Nicholas Ray's *Rebel Without a Cause* (1955) to David Simon's *The Wire* (2005–2008). They include no equivalent list of works of crime fiction. There is nothing wrong with this approach, of course—film and television and now various forms of streaming media and video games are central aspects of twenty-first century culture—but it does indicate the existence of a gap in the overall field of cultural criminology.

Addressing this blind spot in the field of study is important for a number of reasons. Crime fiction offers a body of texts stretching from the very earliest epochs of our literary history to the present day. Even restrictive definitions of the genre locating its origins in the early nineteenth century give us close to two centuries of cultural material to work with, offering an incredibly deep and broad reflection on crime and criminal justice. This is our most sustained and enduring form of cultural engagement with crime. While YouTube videos and Instagram posts may provide a rich source of information on the contemporary attitudes to, say, drug use, if we want to put that information into a historical context, by comparing it for instance with prohibition-era attitudes towards alcohol, crime fiction will provide a valuable source of information.

Crime fiction is also an extremely popular form of discourse. While information about book sales is carefully controlled for commercial reasons,[20] the statistics that are available indicate that crime fiction is likely the most popular genre of adult fiction in Britain, where eight out of the ten most-borrowed authors in the national public library system in 2020–2021 were writers of crime fiction.[21] The same is true in America, where just over 50 percent of the works of fiction that spent two weeks or more on the *New York Times* best-seller list in 2022 were crime novels.[22] Agatha Christie is reputed to have sold more than a billion copies, making her the best-selling novelist of all time.[23] The extraordinary reach of crime fiction is extended by the legion of adaptations for small and large screens. In

2012, Guinness World Records announced that Sherlock Holmes holds
the record for screen appearances by a human literary character, with 48
more than Shakespeare's Hamlet.[24]

This cultural reach is complemented by depth. Crime fiction has paid
sustained, protracted attention to the problem of crime, devoting tremendous energy, attention, and imagination to particular crimes, criminals,
eras, investigations, judicial processes, and more. Crime fiction is also a
diverse, global phenomenon, with novels from every country and culture
contributing to what might be described as a 'mega-text' (to borrow Daniel
Broderick's characterization of the collective text of science fiction novels)[25]
of crime. Finally—and this is a key point for my purposes—it is a discourse
that is closely linked both historically and thematically to other discourses
on crime, offering us what might be seen as a sort of popular criminology.

It is thus clear that crime fiction represents an important part of cultural criminology, or, to situate it within a different field, of what has
been described as the criminal humanities, a 'kaleidoscope of scholarly
traditions, disciplines, theories, and methods' that overlays 'literature
and narrative on to the study of criminals and their victims, the evolution of the criminal justice system, and the epistemology of punishment
and deterrence [...]'.[26] This is an approach that, as Michael Arntfeild and
Marcel Daneshi have argued, may offer 'the most cogent inroad to the
critical study of criminal offending, criminal investigation, deviance, and
penology, as well as how humans have defined justice over our history'.[27]
It also offers inroads into the study of crime fiction, as the relationship
between the two fields is not unidirectional.

At this point, I would like to address the specific areas where crime
fiction and criminology overlap or intersect as alternate forms of discourse.
Both are, as their names indicate, interested in and focused on the problem
of crime. In their different ways they both explore 'what counts as crime'
in different times, places, and situations.[28] They are deeply interested in
the criminal, and the way the criminal operates as an individual or as part
of a larger criminal enterprise. They are interested in the ways crimes are
committed, but also concerned with the ways crime can be fought—either
avoided, prevented, or investigated—and ameliorated. And, as Matthew
Levay argues (and as we have seen in the preceding chapters) they are
both diffuse, widespread fields of activity that resist the imposition of any
single overarching framework of understanding. These are 'messy' fields
that reflect the messiness of crime.[29]

Literary Criminology

One of the most direct ways of thinking about the relationship between
crime fiction and criminology is to identify points at which they have

developed similar or related concepts about the definition of crime, about explanations for it, about adequate responses to it, and so on. This has happened, as Levay notes, quite regularly: 'crime fiction is filled with examples of criminal logical thought, in which characters voice sometimes prevailing, sometimes emerging notions of criminality that map onto the very same concerns that occupied criminologists of the period'.[30] We can thus use (as Jon Frauley has done with film in his study *Criminology, Deviance, and the Silver Screen: The Fictional Reality and the Criminological Imagination*) the fictions presented on the page to illustrate the ideas and theories that are found in more traditional or mainstream version of criminology.[31] Sherlock Holmes, for example, can diagnose (or detect) criminality in the lineaments of a suspect's body and face, as when he meets his arch-nemesis Moriarty in 'The Final Problem' (first published in *The Strand Magazine* in 1893). It is immediately obvious to Holmes that Moriarty 'had hereditary tendencies of the most diabolical kind. A criminal strain ran in his blood', a taint visible, to the trained detective, through physiognomy and behaviour: 'his face protrudes forward, and is forever slowly oscillating from side to side in a curiously reptilian fashion'.[32] This sort of anthropological, biological discourse concerning the heredity (and racialized) nature of criminal behaviour can be traced back to Lombroso, and in this case more directly to Havelock Ellis' 1890 *The Criminal*, which offered a physiological system for identifying criminal types inspired by Lombroso's criminal anthropology.[33] This is a clear instance of what Rafe McGregor describes as the way fictional texts (be they films or novels) 'are able to represent criminological concepts and theories in a particularly dramatic or captivating way that cannot be reproduced in the classroom or in an academic monograph'.[34]

A second approach that McGregor has identified is to use fictional texts to provide case studies 'against which criminological concepts and theories can be tested for their relevance for and application to social reality'.[35] 'Fictional worlds', as Frauley writes, 'offer contained social realities that can be used to exemplify abstract concepts and can also operate as empirical referents to which our concepts and theories can be applied'.[36] In other words, fiction can make abstract criminological concepts and theories appear more real—or help determine if they are in fact real in any meaningful sense.[37] As an example of this, we might return to Dilulio's criminological theory of the superpredator. A traditional criminological approach would perhaps critique the statistical information on which this theory is based (e.g. the claim that 'about six percent of young males are responsible for half the serious crimes committed by their age group')[38] or its interpretation, as William Chamblis does, pointing out that the serious crimes these six percent are involved in include almost no life-threatening incidents, thus rendering the term superpredator inaccurate and otiose.[39] A literary criminologist might instead (or in addition) look to a text like Richard Price's 1992 novel *Clockers*, which explores the life of the low-level drug-dealer Ronald 'Strike' Dunham, presenting him not as a superpredator but as a young man responding as best he can to grossly limited opportunities, intolerable social pressure, and, in the words of one reviewer, personal humiliation 'at the hands of nearly everyone: his boss, his girlfriend, the police and the vast majority of whites with whom he comes into contact'.[40] Strike, though a fictional character, can be read as a refutation of the simplistic, reductive, and dehumanizing presentation of the young Black men in Dilulio's theory.

What is being illustrated by these examples is one of the central contentions of cultural criminology, and more specifically of the way the study of literary texts—crime fictions—can function within this larger enterprise. Considering crime through the lens of cultural production allows us to see, as Keith Haward writes, that 'the true meaning of crime and crime control' is not found only 'in the essential (and essentially false) factuality of crime rates' but instead 'in the contested processes of symbolic display, cultural interpretation, and representational negotiation'.[41] Statistics and other factual forms of information are important, but they do not speak for themselves; fictional narratives are an important part of 'a circuit of culture where collective meaning is made and remade' as part of the 'dynamic relationship between crime and its representation'.[42]

The next two sections of this book will explore this dynamic relationship in more detail, looking closely at the ways criminological concepts are present in, and tested by, the facts of crime fiction. We will be thinking about how crime fiction can help us understand crime as 'an expressive human activity' which occurs in a wide variety of complex contexts and therefore demands interpretation, not simply enumeration and condemnation, and about how it can serve to both represent and 'critique the perceived wisdom surrounding the [...] politics of crime and criminal justice'.[43]

Notes

1 Heather Worthington, *Key Concepts in Crime Fiction* (Houndmills: Palgrave Macmillan, 2011), 10–11.
2 Karin Scholfield, "Collisions of Culture and Commodification of Crime: Media Sexual Abuse," in *Cultural Criminology Unleashed*, edited by Jeff Ferrell, Keith Hayward, Wayne Morrison, and Mike Presdee (London: Glasshouse Press, 2004), 121.
3 Ibid., 129.
4 Gwen Hunnicutt and Kristy Humble Andrews, "Tragic Narratives in Popular Culture: Depictions of Homicide in Rap Music," *Sociological Forum* 24, no. 3 (2009), 618.

5 Michael Collins, "Biggie Envy and the Gangsta Sublime," *Callaloo* 29 (2006), 912.
6 Jeff Ferrell, Keith Hayward, Wayne Morrison, and Mike Presdee, "Fragments of a Manifesto: Introducing *Cultural Criminology Unleashed,*" in *Cultural Criminology Unleashed*, edited by Jeff Ferrell, Keith Hayward, Wayne Morrison, and Mike Presdee (London: Glasshouse Press, 2004), 1.
7 Ibid., 1–2.
8 William J. Chambliss, *Power, Politics and Crime* (New York: Routledge, 2018), 52–53.
9 James Forman Jr. and Kayla Vinson, "The Superpredator Myth Did a Lot of Damage. Courts Are Beginning to See the Light," *The New York Times*, April 20, 2022, www.nytimes.com/2022/04/20/opinion/sunday/prison-sentencing-parole-justice.html.
10 Kelan Lyons, "CT Supreme Court tosses 60-year term of man judge called 'superpredator' Keith Belcher to be resentenced," *The CT Mirror*, January 24, 2022, https://ctmirror.org/2022/01/24/ct-supreme-court-tosses-60-year-term-of-man-judge-called-superpredator/.
11 Elizabeth Becker, "As Ex-Theorist on Young 'Superpredators,' Bush Aide Has Regrets," *The New York Times*, February 9, 2001, www.nytimes.com/2001/02/09/us/as-ex-theorist-on-young-superpredators-bush-aide-has-regrets.html.
12 Chambliss, *Power, Politics and Crime*, 52–53.
13 Jeff Ferrell, Keith Hayward, and Jock Young, *Cultural Criminology: An Invitation*, 2nd edition (London: Sage, 2008), 2.
14 Ibid.
15 Jeff Ferrell and Keith Hayward, "Cultural Criminology Continued," in *Alternative Criminologies*, edited by Pat Carlen and Leando Ayres França (London: Routledge, 2018), 27.
16 Ibid., 81.
17 Scholfield, "Collisions of Culture," 129.
18 Scholfield, "Collisions of Culture," 122.
19 Mike Presdee, *Cultural Criminology and the Carnival of Crime* (London: Routledge, 2000), 15.
20 Melanie Walsh, "Where is All the Book Data," *Public Books*, October 4, 2022, www.publicbooks.org/where-is-all-the-book-data/.
21 "PLR Most Borrowed," *British Library*. n.d. www.bl.uk/plr/popular-loans.
22 "The New York Times Fiction Bestseller List 2022," *Booklistqueen*, 2023, www.booklistqueen.com/the-new-york-times-fiction-bestseller-list-2022/.
23 Olivia Rutigliano, "Agatha Christie is the best-selling novelist in history," *Lithub*, April 3, 2020, https://lithub.com/agatha-christie-is-the-best-selling-novelist-in-history/.
24 Ashley D. Polasek, "Surveying the Post-Millennial Sherlock Holmes: A Case for the Great Detective as a Man of Our Times," *Adaptation* 6, no. 3 (2013), 385.
25 Damien Broderick, *Reading by Starlight: Postmodern Science Fiction* (London: Routledge, 1995), 157.
26 Michael Arntfeild and Marcel Daneshi, "Introduction: Rise of the Criminal Humanist," in *The Criminal Humanities: An Introduction*, edited by Michael Arntfeild and Marcel Daneshi (New York: Peter Lang, 2016), 3–4.

27 Ibid., 4–5.

28 Matthew Levay, "Crime Fiction and Criminology," in *The Routledge Companion to Crime Fiction*, edited by Janice Allan, Jesper Gulddal, Stewart King, and Andrew Pepper (London: Routledge, 2020), 273.

29 Ibid.

30 Ibid.

31 Rafe McGregor, *Critical Criminology and Literary Criticism* (Bristol: Bristol University Press, 2021), 4.

32 Arthur Conan Doyle, "The Final Problem," in *The Memoirs of Sherlock Holmes*, by Arthur Conan Doyle (London: Penguin, 2011), 286, 289.

33 Ronald R. Thomas, "The Fingerprint of the Foreigner: Colonizing the Criminal Body in 1890s Detective Fiction and Criminal Anthropology," *ELH* 61, no. 3 (1994), 660–661.

34 McGregor, *Critical Criminology*, 4.

35 Ibid.

36 Jon Frauley, *Criminology, Deviance, and the Silver Screen: The Fictional Reality and the Criminological Imagination* (New York: Palgrave Macmillan, 2010), 2.

37 Ibid., 13.

38 Quoted in William J. Chambliss, "The Politics of Crime Statistics," in *The Blackwell Companion to Criminology*, edited by Colin Sumner (Malden, MA: Blackwell Publishing, 2004), 464.

39 Chamblis, *Power, Politics and Crime*, 53.

40 Jim Shepard, "Clockers," *The New York Times*, June 21, 1992, www.nytimes.com/1992/06/21/books/clockers.html.

41 Keith Hayward, "Opening the Lens: Cultural Criminology and the Image," in *Framing Crime: Cultural Criminology and the Image*, edited by Keith Hayward and Mike Presdee (Milton Park: Routledge, 2010), 1.

42 Alexandra Campbell, "Imagining the 'War on Terror': Fiction, Film, and Framing," in *Framing Crime: Cultural Criminology and the Image*, edited by Keith Hayward and Mike Presdee (Milton Park: Routledge, 2010), 98.

43 Ferrell, Hayward, and Young, *Cultural Criminology: An Invitation*, 4.

Section 2

Equip You

6   Defining Crime

Politicians tend to speak of crime as if it were a simple, obvious concept. When Donald Trump opened his presidential election campaign in 2015 with the claim that Mexican immigrants were 'bringing crime' across the border, American voters may have agreed or disagreed with him, and supported or deplored his attitude. But they would not, generally speaking, have been confused about what Trump meant by crime. His explanation that Mexicans 'are bringing drugs' and that 'they are rapists'[1] may well be a gross and grossly racist stereotype, but as examples of crimes, drug smuggling and sexual assault are relatively uncontroversial. However, different political perspectives can easily reveal that the apparent obviousness of crime is illusory. In the years following the mass protests of 2012, Vladimir Putin and the Russian government broadened (some might say transformed) the definition of espionage to include reporting and other journalistic activities. As Masha Gessen writes, this means that 'contrary to popular perception and common sense, in Russia, "espionage" does not need to mean working for a foreign intelligence service or even a foreign government', but includes 'gathering information for any foreign organization the Russian government sees as threatening the security of the country'.[2] In other words, the basic functions of the press have been redefined as crimes.

Adding a historical dimension to the discussion, as we did in the first chapter of this book, adds to the complexity of the issue. As Louise A. Knafla points out:

A further problem is the ever-changing definition of what constitutes crime or criminal activity. For example, in modern times we have lost much of petty theft as authorities—on whom the burden of prosecution now rests—become increasingly loathe to prosecute low-valued monetary crimes because of the increasing cost of the public prosecutorial system. But we have also seen a tremendous increase in sexual

DOI: 10.4324/9781003156581-9

crimes as society's sensitivity has changed from toleration to degrees of nonacceptance in the area of customary gender relations.[3]

So on the one hand petty theft—once punishable in Britain by hanging or deportation—is now classified as a misdemeanour below a certain monetary threshold, and becomes fodder for social media videos and outraged commentary (as in online videos and reports of Covid and post-Covid era shoplifting across America) rather than for police action. On the other hand, marital rape was not a crime in all American states until 1993. And expanding the time scale simply magnifies these disparities. Witchcraft, for example, became a crime punishable by death in Britain in 1542, with some 500 people executed for the offense before the laws were repealed in 1736 (though fines and imprisonment for people who claimed to be able to use magic, such as mediums, were in force until 2008);[4] today witchcraft, or Wicca, is practiced publicly, and proudly, by hundreds of thousands of people in Britain and around the world,[5] and in 2022 Nicola Sturgeon, First Minister of Scotland, publicly apologized to 'all those accused, convicted, vilified or executed under the Witchcraft Act of 1563'.[6]

Crime and Power

What all of this amounts to is that crime, as Robert Reiner notes, 'is far from simple'.[7] A crime in one jurisdiction is not a crime in another; what was accepted behaviour (at least from a legal standpoint) at one time becomes a crime a few years later; what was a capital crime in one era becomes a social problem in another. At first this may seem to imply a wild relativism that would leave crime essentially indefinable. As Brendan O'Flaherty and Rajiv Sethi write, in this case 'the only consistently applicable definition of crime' would be 'the set of activities that governments have decided to punish severely'.[8] While this may seem like a radical approach to crime, it is important to note that it is one with a very long history. The first two books of Plato's *Republic* (c. 375 BCE) are concerned with the definition of justice. One of Socrates' interlocutors, the Sophist Thrasymachus, argues that it 'is nothing else than the interest of the stronger'.[9] Sophocles of course sets out to refute this view—and being Sophocles soon has Thrasymachus tied into knots—but its presence in this foundational text of Western philosophy indicates the durability of the stance.

There is certainly a tradition within crime fiction that has taken this reductive definition of crime onboard, generally for the purposes of critique. Perhaps the clearest examples of this deal with periods in which governments have acted in ways that are themselves criminal. For instance, Didier Daeninckx's 1984 *Meurtres pour mémoire* (*Murder in Memoriam*) opens on 17 October 1961 with a massive, and massively violent, police action against a peaceful pro-Algerian protest in Paris:

> Rifle butts came down on bare heads shielded only by arms and hands. A policeman threw a woman to the ground giving her hard heavy kicks; he struck out at her over and over again before moving on. Another one was using a club on the stomach of a young boy with such force that the wood broke. He kept on, using the sharpest fragment. His victim held up his hands to shield himself, trying to catch at the wooden handle. He soon lost all control of his broken fingers.[10]

The crime of this crime fiction—and it is important to note that the events Daeninckx narrates are closely based on the historical Paris Massacre of 1961—is state-sanctioned and orchestrated; only by re-defining peaceful protest as a criminal activity can the state justify its actions. Nor is this, as Daeninckx's novel indicates, an aberration. While investigating a murder that takes place some 20 years following the massacre, the novel's detective-figure Inspector Cadin uncovers a chain of connections to another state-sanctioned crime, the deportation to Nazi extermination camps of French Jews by the Vichy government during the Second World War. The novel's murderer turns out to be a Director of Criminal Affairs who is attempting to cover up his own involvement as a 'zealous bureaucrat' who 'scrupulously administered the transportation of Jewish families to the transit center at Drancy'.[11] He committed this crime not out of anti-Semitism or ideological conviction; he was simply 'obeying the rules and carrying out the orders of the hierarchy'.[12] The crimes in question in this novel are the government's routine bureaucratic functions of administration and security.

A similar set of critiques appears, though in less extreme circumstances, in the ten volumes of Maj Sjöwall and Per Wahlöö's novel cycle *Roman om ett brott* (*The Story of a Crime*) published between 1965 and 1975. The series is superficially a standard police procedural offering readers a series of team-based investigations (led by the main character Martin Beck) into a range of serious crimes set in realistically depicted urban settings. As Philip Howell has argued, the procedural tends to have an identifiable and clearly marked social role: to propagate and reinforce bourgeoise social order through narratives that present the police state, or the state of ubiquitous policing, as natural, inevitable, and desirable.[13] This could be taken as a fairly accurate description of the first novel in the series, *Roseanna*, in which a large team of police officers sifts through the evidence produced by almost a hundred suspects spread out over four continents in order to locate the killer of the titular murder victim. This 'Herculean' task of policing ensures public safety, but also polices private personal behaviour by identifying and punishing (on the level of plot) sexual deviance.[14] As Michael Tapper points out the murder victim, who is sexually active in ways that challenge patriarchal norms, is discussed by many of the (male) investigators as if her 'unsound sexual appetite' were responsible for her death.[15] However, as Tapper argues the novel as a whole is 'ideologically open-ended', amenable to readings emphasizing either the role of male violence or the consequences of a sexually permissive society.[16] Roseanna's killer, Folke Bengtsson, is presented by Sjöwall and Wahlöö as quintessentially normal: his first name associates him directly with the people as a whole, and he is repeatedly described as 'rather ordinary' or 'nothing special'.[17] This could well indicate the presence of a deeper level of social critique.

This sort of criticism becomes much clearer in later novels in the series. In the sequel to *Roseanna*, *The Man Who Went Up in Smoke* (1966), the investigation leads to the arrest of a man who has killed a vile misogynist, but who seems in other respects a perfectly decent human being. The fact that justice must be done, at least on the level that standard juridical norms permit, leaves Martin Beck feeling, as he puts it with typically Scandinavian understatement, 'not well'.[18] In the remaining eight novels of the series the policing of Swedish society is presented as bifurcated between an increasingly bureaucratized and militarized system with right-wing, or even fascist, tendencies and Beck and his colleagues who work almost in opposition to the police force at large. At times the awareness of the social situation that lies behind criminal behaviour becomes an outright transposition of the roles of victim and criminal. In *Murder at the Savoy* (1970), for example, a corporate executive and arms merchant is shot by a laid-off employee, but the text makes it clear that the real criminal is the man who sold weapons to the racist regime in Rhodesia, not the working class shooter who will have to 'rot away the best years of his life in a prison cell'—to say nothing of the broader political and social system that enables the situation.[19] By the time the final novel in the series is published in 1975, *The Terrorists*, 'violence has rushed like an avalanche throughout the whole of the Western world', and to be a police officer is to have 'the wrong job' at 'the wrong time' in 'the wrong system'.[20]

These sorts of story represent extremes, either of situation (as in the 'state terror' exposed in *Murder in Memoriam*)[21] or of perspective (as Sjöwall and Wahlöö's unusually dystopian vision of twentieth-century Sweden). Both exemplify crime fiction's potential to engage with, and challenge, reductive definitions of crime. But the genre is also interested in more nuanced examples of this sort of questionable definition of crime. Consider, for example, the ethical complexities of William Defoe's 1722 *Moll Flanders*, a pseudo auto-biographical novel that employs the narrative structure of the then popular short non-fictional criminal biography, expanding the tale of youthful crime followed by reformation, and bringing it to a happy conclusion (rather than the more typical gallows). Moll Flanders is, first of all, born in effect already condemned for a crime committed by her mother, a 'petty theft scarce worth naming, viz. having an opportunity of borrowing three pieces of fine holland of a certain draper in Cheapside', for which she is lucky to be transported instead of hung, thus leaving her daughter 'a poor desolate girl without friends, without clothes, without help or helper in the world'.[22] Later in life Flanders becomes a criminal in her own right, describing herself as a 'complete thief, hardened to the pitch above all the reflections of conscience or modesty'.[23] But she qualifies this by arguing that she was brought to the state by 'irresistible poverty', (and the devil—this is an eighteenth-century novel, after all) and that if 'a prospect of getting my bread by working presented itself then, I had never fallen into this wicked trade'.[24] As Joshua Gass points out, the novel offers an implicit critique of the social structures that have driven her to actions that are necessary to her survival, but are defined by that society as crimes.[25] While the novel's heroine certainly commits deeds that would be widely considered criminal, and even relishes her place in the underworld, her life of crime is at the same time clearly marked as a product of social injustice. Is it, Defoe in effect asks, really a crime to steal the food you need to survive, or to feed and clothe your children?

Ambivalent Crimes

Questions of this type become particularly interesting when crime fiction deals with transgressions that fall outside of what Brendan O'Flaherty and Rajiv Sethi describe as the 'set of activities that are considered intrinsically bad, or *mala in se* in legal doctrine, and are outlawed almost everywhere' such as 'murder, rape, robbery, assault, burglary, larceny, motor vehicle theft, and arson',[26] or which complicate in some other way the presentation and interpretation of such crimes. A very good example of the way this works can be seen in one of the earliest, and most famous, Sherlock Holmes narratives, 'A Scandal in Bohemia', first published in *The Strand Magazine* in 1891, and collected in *The Adventures of Sherlock Holmes* in 1892. It is worth prefacing a discussion of this story with a reminder that Conan Doyle's work has frequently been seen as epitomizing a range of generally conservative social attitudes linked to a fear of social contamination either from foreign organized crime or from blowback from the British imperial project.[27] He is, in Stephen Knight's words, a figure of 'disciplinary authority' and a 'shield against criminal disruption'.[28] Yet 'A Scandal in Bohemia' sees Holmes playing a very different role.

First of all, as the narrator Dr Watson notes, while the case is 'surrounded by none of the grim and strange features' which generally make Holmes' detective work so interesting, it is nonetheless of interest because of 'the exalted station of' Holmes's client, 'Wilhelm Gottsreich Sigismond von Ormstein, Grand Duke of Cassel-Felstein, and hereditary king of Bohemia'.[29] But this client is, in point of fact, the criminal in the case. Having unwisely left the 'well-known adventuress' Irene Adler in possession of a photograph of the two together, he now fears she will send it (as she has apparently threatened) to his fiancé, a member of the Swedish royal family which is noted for its 'strict principles'.[30] There is nothing in the story to indicate that Adler is in fact an adventuress; nor would it be a crime in any jurisdiction to simply send a picture to someone (there is no threat of blackmail here). But the king's fears are enough to justify an extraordinary series of genuine crimes. Even before Holmes becomes involved, attempts have been made to retrieve—or more accurately steal—the picture: 'Twice burglars in my pay ransacked her house. Once we diverted her luggage when she travelled. Twice she has been waylaid. There has been no result'.[31] The king is thus by his own admission implicated in burglary, robbery, and theft. Holmes and Watson are willing to add to this list of crimes, 'breaking the law' and 'running a chance of arrest' because the 'cause is excellent',[32] though exactly what constitutes its excellence is never made clear. Perhaps it is the thousand pounds in gold and currency that the king pays for Holmes's services.

In any case, Adler quickly sees through Holmes' plot, and flees Britain with her new husband. Watson is 'heartily ashamed' of his role in the conspiracy,[33] while Holmes is merely full of admiration for Adler's quick wit and resolute behaviour. But neither of the two characters seems capable of registering the fact that they have committed (or attempted to commit) a crime at the behest of a serial offender whose only redeeming feature is his social position. Adler's crime—and structurally she occupies the place of the criminal in this narrative—is to resist and threaten the combined might of class and patriarchy. Holmes is revealed here (very near the outset of his career) as a servant of power, who will accept power's definition of anything which threatens it as a crime. Neil McCaw has pointed out that Holmes exhibits a 'fluid relationship with the established legal system in which the detective is just as likely to apply his own sense of natural justice as he is to rely on the official standards of the law'.[34] Yet in this case at least there is little of this sense of 'natural justice' on display. Instead, 'A Scandal in Bohemia' illustrates crime as 'a political process, whereby people in positions of power are able to impose their will on everyone else'.[35]

All of the texts discussed here can be read, then, in relation to a constructivist view of crime (or to use an alternative nomenclature, a nominalist view). This is to say that they see crime not as a product of 'any intrinsic characteristic of the behavior so labeled', or the actions described as criminal, but as a 'product of perception and political process'.[36] To phrase it more carefully, these texts can be *read* as seeing crime as a social construction. This is one of the caveats that needs to be attached to any literary criminological enterprise. While not all texts validate all readings, all texts are capable of sustaining a range of interpretations. Some will be more limited, offering less room for successful or plausible readerly inter-pretation, while others will be more open to the creative, meaning-making intervention of the reader. This is the fundamental distinction that Roland Barthes proposed in his seminal 1970 work *S/Z* between the *lisible*, or readerly, text and the *scriptable*, or writerly, text: the former is, rela-tively speaking, straightforward, direct, undemanding, and offers a fairly constrained set of possibilities of meaning; the latter is self-consciously dif-ficult, and demands in effect an act of co-creation on the part of the reader which means that it is a much more malleable text, open to a wider range of interpretations.[37]

Of course, no one would be likely to describe Doyle's Sherlock Holmes stories as self-consciously difficult, but that does not mean that they are unavailable to the operation of interpretation as Barthes defines it: 'To interpret a text is not to give it a (more or less justified, more or less free) meaning, but on the contrary to appreciate what plural constitutes it'.[38] Here, the plurality of the text that is of interest is its relationship to the definition of crime. In some cases, as in *Moll Flanders*, this plurality is very much in evidence, constituting a major theme in the novel itself, with crime presented as a sin, as a delight, and as a rational response to social injustice, at times all within a single page or even paragraph. Other texts will be less amenable to readings attempting to identify multiple or conflicting definitions of crime. Sjöwall and Wahlöö's *Cop Killer* (1974), for example, leaves little room for interpretation when it contrasts the small-time criminal and erroneously suspected titular cop killer as a 'lad [...] who has never shot anyone or employed any kind of violence at all' with one of his ostensible police victims, a man who has been 'shouting and swearing, pushing, kicking, hitting people with his truncheon, or slapping them [...]' for 20 years, who 'had always been the stronger, had always had the advantage of arms and might and justice against people who were weaponless and powerless and had no rights'.[39] Sjöwall and Wahlöö were not, generally speaking, restrained in their socio-political criticism.

A key distinction can be made here between defining and evaluating laws. This is an element of legal positivism, which, in what is described as the separability thesis, sees the law as a legal reality distinguish-able and separable from the moral or ethical evaluation of that law. The most extreme examples of the divergence between these tend to be found in totalitarian states—the distinction would be highly relevant, for example, to a discussion of Daeninckx's *Murder in Memoriam*, in which the bureaucrats running the Vichy 'human disposal machine' of mass deportation are clearly following a valid law, but one which is just as clearly utterly immoral.[40] Or consider the Nazi-era 'Law for the Defence of German Blood and Honour' which banned sexual relations (marital or otherwise) between Jews and other Germans.[41] This law was, as the expression of the will of the state presented through the appropriate channels and in the appropriate forms, valid; it was not, however, ethical, moral, or acceptable. Philip Kerr's hardboiled novels, set during and after the Nazi era, are very much about this gap between the legal validity of the law and the imperative to evaluate the law from an ethical standpoint—as are many of the other 150 crime novels that Katharina Hall has identified as confronting 'the National Socialist past and its legacy in the postwar era'.[42] Even in less extreme circumstances it is not difficult to find places where the law (or a particular law) and widely held beliefs about ethical value come into conflict. One example is America's mandatory minimum sentencing laws (discussed in Chapter 2) which frequently result in legal decisions that seem to many inherently wrong.

Natural Law

There is, however, a place or set of circumstances where the law and the good seem to be aligned more strongly or regularly than our discussion to this point would indicate. As legal philosopher H. L. A. Hart writes, some laws 'overlap with basic moral principles vetoing murder, violence, and theft'.[43] He goes on to argue that all legal systems inevitably intersect with morality at these crucial points.[44] The concept of natural justice may not resonate with the readings I have proposed of, for example, the works of Sjöwall and Wahlöö or Daniel Defoe—natural injustice would seem closer to the mark—but it is a useful one for thinking about other powerful versions of the 'essentially contested concept' of crime.[45]

As Robert Reiner argues, there is a widespread agreement about the basic concept of crime: some things are wrong, and generate 'revulsion, fear, pain or disapproval', however different our views of what these things are in specific circumstances.[46] This disapprobation and disgust is an important pointer towards a second major conceptualization of crime, the realist position (as opposed to the constructivist position) which holds that 'crime represents real problems, which exist whether or not they are labeled as crime'.[47] In other words, in a complete inversion of the constructivist paradigm, some forms of behaviour are seen as fundamentally, essentially, and naturally wrong, whether a particular legal system identifies them as crimes or not. This is perhaps the most widely accepted approach to defining crime, covering a range of common sense, normative, and generally understandable definitions that allows criminologists and others involved in judicial processes to get on with the business of developing effective criminal countermeasures, be they based on enforcement, sentencing, or rehabilitation. After all, if you are a fully paid-up member of a capitalist system, it is arguably not very useful to have it pointed out, as the French anarchist Pierre-Joseph Proudhon did in 1840, that property is theft.[48] Instead, you are much more likely to be concerned with how you can stop your apartment from being burgled, or at least find out who committed the crime, and discourage them from repeating the offence.

This realist view of crime is one that appears, in a variety of forms, throughout crime fiction. One way of writing about crime—and one with a very long history—connects it directly with social and religious views on moral and immoral behaviour. Classic and Golden Age detective fiction, for example, frequently offers strongly moralistic attitudes towards criminal behaviour. This position was clearly articulated in the early theorization of the genre. G. K. Chesterton, for example, author of the Father Brown mystery stories (published between 1911 and 1935), argues that 'by dealing with the unsleeping sentinels who guard the outposts of society', the genre 'tends to remind us that we live in an armed camp, making war with a chaotic world, and that the criminals, the children of chaos, are nothing but the traitors within our gates'.[49] Similarly, in his introduction to the 1926 anthology *Crime and Detection*, E. M. Wrong argues that while it may be true that 'art in general should have no moral purpose, [...] the art of the detective story has one and must have; it seeks to justify the law and to bring retribution on the guilty. The criminal must be unmasked, the detective represents good and must triumph'.[50]

These sorts of views reappear regularly in the critical and theoretical literature, and are also a prominent feature in many examples of Golden Age detective fiction. Agatha Christie's Miss Marple, for example, takes a dubious view of the ethical condition of humanity in general—she notes in her quiet way that 'the depravity of human nature is unbelievable'—but she reserves her strongest disapprobation for those who have failed to struggle against their inherently fallen natures.[51] As she states in *Nemesis*, 'I do not like evil beings who do evil things'.[52] A similarly clear-cut attitude towards the identification and condemnation of crime appears in *The Body in the Library*, in which Miss Marple observes that she is 'quite pleased to think' that the murderer will hang.[53] This is not an expression of bloodthirstiness, but of a view of criminal behaviour rooted in the ethical and theological underpinnings of a realist conceptualization of crime.[54] While this sort of attitude towards crime may seem reductively simple, we should not underestimate the importance of its regular, persistent appearance in various forms of popular crime narrative. Agatha Christie is, after all, the best-selling author in history, and her novels have been read by billions (and seen by many more in adaptations). It is no stretch to think, then, that her view of crime as a manifestation of evil (rather than as a product of social forces and legal processes) may have had a powerful impact on popular attitudes towards crime.

Nor have more modern theories of crime completely rejected the relationship between morality and the definition of crime. Michael Moore, for example, has argued that crime is fundamentally defined by its immoral nature: a crime is a 'morally wrongful action' and a criminal is 'morally culpable' for doing this action.[55] Modern crime fiction has also continued to embrace this sort of association between morality and criminality. Walter Mosely's Easy Rawlins, the detective hero of a series of revisionist, African American hardboiled novels published between 1990 and 2021 has been described as driven by 'his experience of duality and by a resultant ambiguity of attitude toward the cases he investigates [...]'.[56] Yet Rawlins' attitude towards crime is not always as nuanced as this sort of reading would suggest. In the first novel in the series, *Devil in a Blue Dress*, for example, we read that 'back in Texas, in Fifth Ward, Houston, men would kill over a dime wager or a rash word. And it was always the evil ones that would kill the good or the stupid'.[57] Although complications abound in this novel and elsewhere in the series—they are in fact what make Mosely's work so successful—they exist alongside an implied definition of crime as ethical transgression, as an immoral act, or, not to put too fine a point on it, as evil.

The Problem of Evil

Evil is of course not a concept that is widely used in criminological discourse—it is theological rather than sociological in origin. But it certainly plays a role in many different varieties of crime writing. We have seen how it appears and reappears in the work of Golden Age novelists like Christie, widely seen as bastions of conservatism, but also in the work of a writer like Mosely who is more closely associated with a critical approach to questions of justice (and injustice in a racist nation). Further examples from across the crime genre, from the police procedural to Scandinavian noir, would be easy to identify, to say nothing of crime novels (like, for example, Jim Thompson's 1952 *The Killer Inside Me*) that place the murderous criminal at the centre of the narrative. Even a writer like David Simon, the creator of the seminal HBO police drama *The Wire*, who is keenly aware of the sociological, economic, and structural issues that underlie crime and criminal behaviour, needs to describe certain criminals in terms that are more familiar from demonology than criminology. A suspected child rapist and murderer is described in his novelistic true crime study of Baltimore murder police *Homicide: A Year of the Killing Streets* (1991) as 'the devil himself [...] evil incarnate'.[58] Yet this suspect is at the same time utterly normal:

> The suspect stepped slowly from the room, a thirty-one-year-old black man, thinly built, with receding, close-cropped hair and deep brown eyes. His face is rounded, his wide mouth marked by gap teeth and a long overbite. His sweatsuit is a size too big, his high-top tennis shoes well worn. Nothing in his appearance gives truth to his abominable deed: There is nothing in the face to inspire fear, nothing in the eyes to call extraordinary. He is altogether ordinary [...].[59]

This ordinariness (what Hannah Arendt would describe in the context of the Holocaust as banality) pushes us as readers away from the concepts of good and evil, inherent vice, original sin; away from our powerful, visceral reactions against wrong-doing, and towards the broader, cultural, political, economic, and social context within which crime occurs. This is a fundamental tension in the definition of crime: it is at once a contingent socio-political artefact, shaped and created by different societies and different times and in different places for different purposes, and a felt and lived reality of a wrongness that needs to be fought. The best of crime writing is able to negotiate both of these positions, perhaps not reconciling them—they may not be reconcilable—but holding them insistently up for our attention even when we may prefer to avert our eyes.

Notes

1 Katie Reilly, "Here Are All the Times Donald Trump Insulted Mexico," *Time*, August 31, 2016, https://time.com/4473972/donald-trump-mexico-meeting-insult/.

2 Masha Gessen, "How Putin Criminalized Journalism in Russia", *The New Yorker*, April 7, 2023, www.newyorker.com/news/our-columnists/how-putin-criminalized-journalism-in-russia.

3 Louis A. Knafla, "Structure, Conjuncture, and Event in the Historiography of Modern Criminal Justice History," in *Crime History and Histories of Crime: Studies in the Historiography of Crime and Criminal Justice in Modern History*, edited by Clive Emsley and Louis A. Knafla (Westport, CT: Greenwood Press, 1996), 35.

4 "Witchcraft," *UK Parliament*, 2022, www.parliament.uk/about/living-heritage/transformingsociety/private-lives/religion/overview/witchcraft/.

5 Ethan Doyle White, *Wicca: History, Belief, and Community in Modern Pagan Witchcraft* (Eastbourne: Sussex Academic Press, 2022), 2.

6 Maria Cramer, "Scotland Apologizes for History of Witchcraft Persecution," *The New York Times*, March 9, 2022, www.nytimes.com/2022/03/09/world/europe/scotland-nicola-sturgeon-apologizes-witches.html#:~:text=Nicola%20Sturgeon%2C%20the%20first%20minister,the%2016th%20and%2018th%20centuries.

7 Robert Reiner, *Crime: The Mystery of the Common-Sense Concept* (Cambridge: Polity, 2016), 1.

8 Brendan O'Flaherty and Rajiv Sethi, *Shadows of Doubt: Stereotypes, Crime, and the Pursuit of Justice* (Cambridge, MA: Harvard University Press, 2019), 40.

9 Plato, *The Republic*, translated by Benjamin Jowett (Oxford: Clarenden Press, 1888), 338c, retrieved from www.gutenberg.org/files/55201/55201-h/55201-h.htm#pref.

10 Didier Daeninckx, *Murder in Memoriam*, translated by Liz Heron (London: Serpent's Tail, 1991), 24.

11 Ibid., 171.

12 Ibid.

13 Philip Howell, "Crime and the City Solution: Crime Fiction, Urban Knowledge, and Radical Geography," *Antipode* 30, no. 4 (1998), 358–359.

14 Maj Sjöwall and Per Wahlöö, *Roseanna*, translated by Lois Roth (London: 4th Estate, 2016), 71.

15 Michael Tapper, *Swedish Cops: From Sjöwall and Wahlöö to Stieg Larsson* (Bristol: Intellect Books, 2014), 87.

16 Ibid., 87.

17 Sjöwall and Wahlöö, *Roseanna*, 174.

18 Maj Sjöwall and Per Wahlöö, *The Man Who Went Up in Smoke*, translated by Joan Tate (New York: Harper Perennial, 2006), 198.

19 Maj Sjöwall and Per Wahlöö, *The Murder at the Savoy*, translated by Joan Tate (London: 4th Estate, 2016), 238.

20 Maj Sjöwall and Per Wahlöö, *The Terrorists*, translated by Joan Tate (London: 4th Estate, 2016), 323–324.

21 James House and Neal MacMaster, *Paris 1961: Algerians, State Terror, and Memory* (Oxford: Oxford University Press, 2006), 15.

22 Daniel Defoe, *The Fortunes & Misfortunes of the Famous Moll Flanders* (Westminster: Folio Society, 1954), 2.

23 Ibid., 191.

24 Ibid.

25 Joshua Gass, "*Moll Flanders* and the Bastard Birth of Realist Character," *New Literary History* 45, no. 1 (2014), 113, www.jstor.org/stable/24542584.

26 Brendan O'Flaherty and Rajiv Sethi, *Shadows of Doubt: Stereotypes, Crime, and the Pursuit of Justice* (Cambridge, MA: Harvard University Press, 2019), 41.

27 Martin Priestman, *Crime Fiction from Poe to the Present* (Plymouth: Northcote House, 1998), 17.

28 Stephen Knight, *Crime fiction Since 1800: Detection, Death, Diversity*, 2nd edition (Houndmills: Palgrave Macmillan, 2010), 57, 63.

29 Arthur Conan Doyle, "A Scandal in Bohemia," in *The Adventures of Sherlock Holmes* (London: Penguin, 2011), 14, 10.
30 Ibid., 10–12.
31 Ibid., 11–12.
32 Ibid., 19.
33 Ibid., 24.
34 Neil McCaw, "Sherlock Holmes: Sir Arthur Conan Doyle (1859–1930)," in *100 Greatest Literary Detectives*, edited by Eric Sandberg (Lanham, MD: Rowman & Littlefield Publishers, 2018), 91.
35 Stephen Jones, *Criminology*, 7th edition (Oxford: Oxford University Press, 2021), 21.
36 Reiner, *Crime*, 6.
37 Roland Barthes, *S/Z*, translated by Richard Miller (Oxford: Blackwell, 2002), 3–5.
38 Ibid., 5.
39 Maj Sjöwall and Per Wahlöö, *Cop Killer*, translated by Thomas Teal (London: 4th Estate, 2016), 220, 182.
40 Daeninckx, *Murder in Memoriam*, 153.
41 Saul Friedländer, *The Years of Persecution: Nazi Germany and the Jews 1933–1939* (London: Phoenix, 2007), 142.
42 Katharina Hall, "The 'Nazi Detective' as Provider of Justice in Post-1990 British and German Crime Fiction: Philip Kerr's *The Pale Criminal*, Robert Harris's *Fatherland*, and Richard Birkefeld and Göran Hachmeister's *Wer übrig bleibt, hat recht*," *Comparative Literature Studies* 50, no. 2 (2013), 288.
43 H. L. A. Hart, "Positivism and the Separation of Law and Morals," *Harvard Law Review* 71, no. 4 (1958), 623. https://doi.org/10.2307/1338225.623.
44 H. L. A. Hart, "Positivism and the Separation of Law and Morals," *Harvard Law Review* 71, no. 4 (1958), 623. https://doi.org/10.2307/1338225.623.
45 Reiner, Crime, 3.
46 Ibid., 5.
47 Ibid., 7.
48 Pierre-Joseph Proudhon, *What Is Property?: An Inquiry into the Principle of Right and of Government*, translated by Benj. R. Tucker (New York: Dover, 1970), 10. Technically, the phrase should be translated as property is 'robbery' but I use here the more familiar English version of 'c'est le vol!.'
49 G. K. Chesterton, "A Defence of Detective Stories," *The Detective*, The Society of Gilbert Keith Chesterton, 2002, www.chesterton.org/a-defence-of-detective-stories.
50 E. M. Wrong, "Introduction to Crime and Detection (1926) by E. M. Wrong," *Golden Age of Detection Wiki*, edited by Juergen Lull, November 28, 2008. http://gadetection.pbworks.com/w/page/7930836/Introduction%20to%20Crime%20and%20Detection.
51 Agatha Christie, "Strange Jest," in *Miss Marple: The Complete Short Stories* (London: HarperCollins, 1997), 244.
52 Agatha Christie, *Nemesis* (London: HarperCollins, 2016), 140.
53 Agatha Christie, *The Body in the Library* (London: HarperCollins, 2016), 211.
54 Reiner, *Crime*, 38.

55 Michael Moore, *Placing Blame: A General Theory of the Criminal Law* (Oxford: Clarendon Press, 1997), 35.
56 Helen Lock, "Invisible Detection: The Case of Walter Mosley." *Melus* 26, no. 1 (2001), 79. https://doi.org/10.2307/3185497.
57 Walter Mosely, *Devil in a Blue Dress* (New York: Washington Square Press, 2020), 34.
58 David Simon, *Homicide: A Year on the Killing Streets* (New York: Owl Books, 2006), 521.
59 Ibid.

7 Explaining Crime

This chapter explores the overlapping ways that criminology and crime writing attempt to explain crime, in other words to account for its ubiquitous presence and its extraordinary persistence. There is a certain amount of conceptual overlap between this enterprise and the attempt, discussed in the previous chapter, to define crime. After all, to some extent to define a phenomenon is to explain it. However, the range of specific explanations that have been proposed for crime and criminal behaviour are much broader than the opposition between constructivist and realist perspectives on the definition of crime.

Consider the example (discussed in Chapter 6) of Agatha Christie's *Nemesis* and Miss Marple's condemnation of crime and criminals: 'I do not like evil beings who do evil things'.[1] This is straightforward enough in isolation, but the claim becomes more interesting when it is placed in a fuller narrative context. Marple's remark occurs while she is discussing a young man, Michael Rafiel, with the criminal psychiatrist Professor Wanstead: 'From his earliest youth', Michael has been, as Wanstead puts it, 'completely unsatisfactory'.[2] This is both a widely held view—he is described by another character as 'a wicked devil' and 'a bad lot from the day he was born'[3]—and something of an understatement, as Wanstead acknowledges. Michael is 'a young delinquent, a young thug, a bad lot, a person of diminished responsibility [...] a criminal type' who has 'joined gangs [...] beaten people up [...] stolen, [...] embezzled' and so on. He went on from these relatively minor repeat offenses to committing 'assault and rape against a young girl'; after a period of imprisonment he was convicted of strangling another young woman and attempting to prevent identification of the corpse by smashing her face with 'heavy stones or rocks'.[4] This is unquestionably a bad record capped by a horrific crime, and it may well deserve the label that Miss Marple attaches to it, as well as justify her refusal to 'urge an unhappy childhood' or 'blame bad environment' for his crimes.[5] Professor Wanstead, for one, concurs, and adds to

DOI: 10.4324/9781003156581-10

the list of possible—but rejected—alternative explanations for a persistent pattern of criminal behaviour: criminals have no control over the 'genes with which they are born'.[6]

As *Nemesis*' intricate plot unfolds, it eventually becomes clear that despite his many failings and admitted criminal propensities, Michael is not in fact guilty of murder, though this is rather beside the point for the purposes of this discussion. What we are seeing here is the way crime fiction can and does articulate a range of possible explanations for criminal behaviour, favouring some over others depending on a range of factors from historical period to authorial preference. Christie, for example, reliably settles on a theologically rooted vision of crime as a manifestation of evil.[7] But at the same time she brings a range of other, competing explanations for crime into play; Miss Marple and Professor Wanstead, for instance, refer to childhood trauma, environmental factors, and genetic predisposition as possible drivers of criminal behaviour. And as we learn later in the novel, the actual murderer, Clotilde Bradbury-Scott, commits her crimes (multiple murders) for none of these reasons. Her motivation is a very traditional—even prosaic—one: jealousy. So jealous is she of Verity Hunt's choice of 'marriage and the normality of happiness' with Michael Rafiel over her own less socially acceptable love that she kills her, and then commits other crimes to both frame him and protect herself.[8] Thus we can add intense emotional agitation (the proverbial crime of passion) to the growing list of criminal explanations found in a single crime novel.

All of these motivations or explanations have featured, and indeed continue to feature, in criminological discourse, as have a startling variety of other explanatory paradigms. For the sake of simplicity, it is probably useful to think of these competing or co-existing theories as situated along a continuum, with the individual at one end and society writ large at the other. Some theoretical approaches tend to explain crime and criminal behaviour by focusing on the individual, though from a number of different perspectives; others tend to situate criminal behaviour in relation to larger groups and social phenomena.

Crime as a Rational Phenomenon

To begin at one end of this imaginary spectrum—with explanations for crime focusing on the individual—we can consider classical criminology as represented by figures like Cesare Beccaria and Jeremy Bentham. As a rule, the classical school is less interested in accounting for the origins of crime than in developing the most appropriate judicial and administrative responses to it. However, in so far as they do consider motivations for criminal behaviour, Beccaria and Bentham focus on the individual responsibility of individual actors making individual choices. For Beccaria, for example, the law is intended to fight 'the private usurpations of each particular individual, since everyone always tries to withdraw not only his own share but also to usurp that belonging to others'.[9] This is, in essence, rational behaviour, unless the penalties for doing so (and for Beccaria critically the likelihood of experiencing these penalties) outweigh the good to be obtained by transgression. Bentham, too, identifies individual free will governed by rationality as central to the issue, arguing that 'all men pursued their ends deliberately, after rational consideration of the divergent elements involved'.[10] The point is to establish systems that made it irrational to break the law.

This has, quite rightly, been described as a 'remarkably simplistic assessment of human nature',[11] but it does nonetheless have an important role to play in the analysis of criminal behaviour as it appears in crime fiction. In *Nemesis*, Clotilde Bradbury-Scott's first crime is irrational—'Because you love her, you killed her' as Miss Marple puts it—but her subsequent crimes are highly rational.[12] She kills a second woman to frame Michael for the murder and thus punish him for stealing Verity, and then kills a third to avoid detection. These crimes are perfectly rational by Benthamite utilitarian standards: you cannot be hung three times, so there is no logical reason for Clotilde not to commit further murders to achieve her ends and attempt to escape justice. As Miss Marple notes, 'you know one doesn't stop at one murder. I have noticed that in the course of my life and in what I have observed of crime'.[13] This emphasis on the almost inevitable seriality of murder is in fact a typical feature of the Golden Age mystery, and is no doubt related at least in part to the form's overall emphasis on rationality.

Another, much earlier, instance of the link between rationality and crime can be seen in Fyodor Dostoevsky's *Crime and Punishment*. First published in 1866, this is not a work that is traditionally viewed as a crime novel—although this has as much to do with the dubious cultural status of the genre as it does with the taxonomically relevant features of the text. However, it is, as its title indicates, deeply concerned with criminality (and of course its consequences), and it integrates a clear element of rational choice into its analysis of crime—although importantly this is only one element.

As the novel opens, the main character Raskolnikov, an impoverished ex-student in St Petersburg, has decided to murder and rob an elderly and unpleasant pawnbroker. He has thought this crime through in some detail. The first stage of his planning has involved the question of detection: 'why', he wonders, are 'almost all crimes [...] so easily detected and solved', and how can he avoid the 'morbid revolutions' of the mind that he believes lead to the capture of most criminals.[14] He then determines that what he is contemplating is in fact 'not a crime'.[15] His planned murder is, he believes (or convinces himself), an ideological act of self-overcoming; he wants 'to become a Napoleon' unafraid to take bold and conventionally immoral steps to advance his career, and thus enable himself to contribute to society. This will also allow him to help his mother and his sister, saving them both from poverty. So, on one side of the scales there is a 'stupid, meaningless, worthless, wicked, sick old Crone', and on the other 'fresh, young forces that are wasted for lack of support, [...]! A hundred, a thousand good deeds and undertakings that could be arranged and set going by the money that old woman has [...]'.[16] These words are not Raskolnikov's—he overhears the argument being made by a stranger—but '*exactly the same thoughts* [emphasis in original] had just been conceived in his own head'.[17] By killing the pawnbroker, Raskolnikov will be able to make a contribution to the well-being of his family and society. This is of course purely utilitarian thinking, a dramatic and bloody acting out of Bentham's 'fundamental axiom' that 'it is the greatest happiness of the greatest number that is the measure of right and wrong'.[18]

Obviously, this is not the whole story of Raskolnikov's crime. Dostoevsky offers readers a much wider range of explanations for the murder than this suggests. Raskolnikov is suffering from desperate poverty and weeks of near starvation, and 'concentrated anguish' has left him in a condition of dubious mental health.[19] Nor is his condition unique: the novel can be read as an indictment of a deeply unjust, hierarchical society that allows the rich to prey on the poor, and does little if anything to alleviate the sufferings of the vulnerable. Ideological and religious considerations are also central to Dostoevsky's analysis of this crime. But it is an example of the way crime narratives can and do integrate rational decision-making into their explorations of crime.

Before moving on, I would like to look at one more example of the way a much more contemporary writer explores the rationality of crime, if only to indicate that this is by no means a merely historical phenomenon. Richard Price is an important figure in contemporary American crime writing. His novels have garnered critical acclaim, and he has contributed to some of the most critically (and commercially) successful TV crime dramas of the twenty-first century, notably David Simon's *The Wire* (2002–2008). He is particularly noted for his ability to evoke the widespread social and economic malaise of contemporary, ex-working-class America, a condition linked in the words of one reviewer to 'poverty [...] silence, institutionalized racism, indifference, and ignorance'.[20] Yet even within his highly contextualized examinations of America's criminogenic environment, Price presents rational decision-making as an important part of criminal behaviour.

In his 1992 novel *Clockers* (adapted for the big screen by Spike Lee in 1995) (also discussed in Chapter 5), for example, the main character Strike

Dunham is a low-level drug dealer (or clocker) managing the retail distribution of cocaine out of a housing estate in the fictional city of Dempsey, New Jersey. There is little about Strike's life as a dealer—a 'street-corner-prince'[21]—that is attractive. He suffers from the stupidity and insubordination of his underlings, the almost constant abuse and harassment of the police, and the contempt and intimidation of his superiors in the drug trade. All of this has left him with chronic, near-debilitating anxiety (and ulcers).

Strike knows perfectly well that the life he is leading is all too likely to end in the morgue or prison. Nonetheless, his decision—and it is a decision—to work as a drug dealer is presented as rationally motivated, not just the result of 'racism, the pigs, or society in general'.[22] First of all, he has a plan: 'dealing' is 'short term [...] he'd end it quick, coming back [...] rich and on the level'.[23] This is of course harder to achieve than to say, but it is not as if Strike has many other options. His older brother Victor, for example, has avoided crime by working 80 hours a week at two jobs; he has a stable home life and children, and makes 'six hundred and twenty-five dollars a week'.[24] To get out of the projects, he needs an 8,000 dollar down payment for an apartment which will then cost 850 dollars a month. The arithmetic makes Victor's likely destiny painfully obvious, and by contrast justifies, or at least explains, Strike's choices. After all, he has more than 20,000 dollars saved after a short career on the streets, a sum his brother will likely never be able to save. One of the policemen who routinely harasses Strike complains that he is 'nice-looking, clean, bright, you know, all things considered, so what's he do with himself? He sits out there running a crew like clocking's all the world has to offer him [...]'.[25] This is precisely the point: this is all the world has to offer him, and his decision to risk imprisonment or death is thus rational.

These examples indicate that classical criminology's emphasis on the individual and individual choice has some continued relevance to an analysis of the causes of crime. As a monocausal explanation it may be an abject failure, but it nonetheless draws our attention to rational choice as a contributing factor in criminal activity.

Crime as a Biological Phenomenon

There are of course other criminological approaches that can also be situated on or towards the individual end of the causal continuum described earlier. The biological positivism associated with Cesare Lombroso, for example, also accounts for criminal activity by studying the individual. As discussed in Chapter 2, Lombroso and his followers explained high rates of recidivism through biological determinism. Criminals are in fact biologically different from non-criminals—they have 'weak or diseased minds' and thus (in a complete reversal of the classical position) 'lack free will'.[26] This view of the criminal as biologically different—and not just different, but degenerate and identifiable through what has been described as a 'taxonomy of criminal stigmata'[27]—appears regularly in earlier examples of crime fiction, indicating the extent to which Lombroso's theories penetrated the popular consciousness.

Arthur Conan Doyle's Sherlock Holmes tales regularly present criminals as physically recognizable types, or as atavistic throwbacks to bygone eras of savagery, as in the following description of the escaped convict who haunts the moors in *The Hound of the Baskervilles* (1902):

> Over the rocks, and the crevice of which the candle burned, there was thrust out an evil yellow face, a terrible animal face, all seamed and scored with vile passions. Foul with mire, with a bristling beard, and hung with matted hair, it might well have belonged to one of those old savages who dwelt in the burrows on the hillsides. The light beneath him was reflected in his small, cunning eyes, which peered fiercely to right and left through the darkness, like a crafty and savage animal who has heard the steps of the hunters.[28]

This sort of direct reference to degeneracy and animalism has largely disappeared from crime writing. It has had a persistent half-life, however, in ways that are less obviously linked to Lombroso's theories, but nonetheless associate non-normative or deviant physical appearance to criminal behaviour. We can see this in older texts like Wilkie Collin's *The Woman in White* (published serially in 1859 and 1860), in which the villainous Count Fosco appears as what has been called a 'corpulent criminal mastermind'.[29] But it is also a feature of much more recent works: the *femme fatal* of interwar and postwar American fiction can be seen as exhibiting just this type of degeneracy, perhaps most famously in Raymond Chandler's descriptions of Carmen Sternwood in *The Big Sleep* (1939), a murderer whose sexual and ethical degeneracy is marked by her expressionless 'slate-grey' eyes, her 'little sharp predatory teeth', her 'thin, too taut lips', and her 'curiously shaped thumb, thin and narrow like an extra finger, with no curve in the first joint'.[30] These markers of a predisposition towards crime appear very early in the novel, and it comes as no great surprise to the alert reader when Carmen is eventually revealed as one of the novel's killers.

While Lombroso's theories of inherent degeneracy have long been discarded by criminologists, there is a relatively new field of study that associates criminal behaviour with a range of biological factors. In *Why Crime?* (2009), Matthew B. Robinson and Kevin M. Beaver discuss three different levels on which biology can influence criminal behaviour: the cellular level (genetic inheritance predisposes individuals to criminal behaviour), the organ level (brain function and misfunction related to neurotransmitters, hormones, and trauma predispose individuals to criminal behaviour), and the organism level (factors such as personality type, intelligence, nutrition, drug use, and mental illness predispose individuals to criminal behaviour).[31] It is important to note that few if any reputable scientists would directly link these sorts of biological factors (particularly in terms of genetics and brain function) to crime. As Siri Hustvedt warns us, 'the road from genes to an organism's structure is torturous and depends on many factors'—to say nothing of the winding road from genes to the type of social behaviour associated with criminality.[32]

This justifiable caution over reductive or reductively presented scientific claims is perhaps one reason that these sorts of explanatory paradigms have not figured largely in crime fiction. One exception to this would be the type of cautionary tale represented by Philip K. Dick's 1956 novella 'The Minority Report' (adapted for the big screen by Steven Spielberg in 2002), in which technological advances have allowed the 'the post-crime punitive system of jails and fines' to be supplanted by a predictive system that identifies and arrests future criminals before they commit the offense for which they are imprisoned; 'In our society', one expert explains, 'we have no major crimes [...] but we do have a detention camp full of would-be criminals'.[33] While the science-fiction structure of this story makes no reference to genetic predisposition, the ethical implications of linking biological traits to criminal behaviour are not dissimilar to those raised by Dick.

Crime as a Group Phenomenon

At this point we can begin to move towards theories that emphasize not the role of the individual (be the focus on their choices or their biology) in explaining crime, but the role of the social group immediately or proximately surrounding that individual. Two main strands of thought co-exist (or compete) at this level: social learning theories and social control theories. The first of these sees criminal (or deviant) activity as a form of learned behaviour. This is the type of theoretical paradigm exemplified by, for example, Edwin Sutherland's *Principles of Criminology* (1939, revised 1947), which argued that criminal behaviour is learned 'through a process of interaction among small, intimate groups'.[34] Thus an individual will learn law-breaking behaviour from, for example, their family or their peer-group, who will teach them (directly or indirectly) how to commit crimes (we are not born knowing how to hotwire a car) and, even more importantly, a set of mental frames or orientations that are favourable towards criminal behaviour (we are not born thinking it is acceptable or even admirable to hotwire a car). Ronald Akers, who developed

Sutherland's social learning theory, offers a four-part model in which an individual learns a set of criminal behaviours and attitudes towards them from a sub-group within their immediate social circle, often in contrast with other competing values and norms of behaviour.[35] The teenage peer group may think hotwiring cars is acceptable; the high school teachers whose cars are hotwired are not likely to agree.

The second strand referred to earlier (social control theories) approaches the problem of criminality from the opposite direction. If 'social learning theories suggest that peers and family members are important for explaining why people *do* commit crimes'—they teach, in a very broad sense, criminal behaviour—'social control theories suggest that peers and family members are important for explaining why people do *not* commit crimes'.[36] Most closely associated with the work of Travis Hirschi, this approach focuses on a range of restraining factors that impede criminal behaviour including effective and durable group relationships, institutional presence and participation, and the presence of conventional moral codes and values, all of which help regulate individual behaviour. When these factors are 'weak or rendered ineffective, people are freer to deviate from legal and moral norms' and under these conditions 'crime and delinquency become possible, if not likely, outcomes'.[37] Taken together, these group-level theories offer a robust set of explanations for individual participation in criminal behaviour that takes a much wider range of circumstances into account than more individually focused theories can accommodate.

The novel, in its classical form, is highly invested in the representation and exploration of the relationship between the individual and society. This is true of, for example, the *bildungsroman*, which can be seen as dealing with 'the integration of the individual into society', asking to what extent 'the individual is a product and creature of society'.[38] But it is also true of many other variants of the novel. It is thus unsurprising that the crime novel frequently articulates a perspective that is very close to both social learning and social control theory. This is certainly true of Price's *Clockers*, which, as we saw earlier, presents the criminal behaviour of its protagonist Strike as at least partially rational, or rationally explicable, the result of an independent decision based on a set of available options and considering both rewards and punishments. However, the novel also explores—more prominently and urgently—the social situation that both teaches Strike to be a criminal and fails to control this impulse.

Clockers lays a great deal of emphasis on the inter-generational transmission of criminal behaviour. Strike has of course not entered into his life as a dealer in a vacuum. He has instead been groomed or prepared for the position, first by life-long exposure to the ongoing drug trade, which functions as a normalized and routine part of the life of Roosevelt Houses, if one that is surreptitiously loathed by the neighbourhood's law-abiding residents, and then through contact with Rodney Little, a local drug baron. Strike worked in Rodney's store for a year—'making five dollars an hour under the table, straight, no-nonsense mule-team shopkeeping'—before 'Rodney sat him down one day and offered him a different kind of job'.[39] Rodney has the personal charisma to attract and sway the young men he surrounds himself with—it is likened to an 'underwater surge'—and he also actively assumes the role of mentor within the drug trade.[40] In one scene, he takes a group of young dealers to an upscale restaurant, and lectures them 'about having the proper mentality on the street', arguing that their activities 'ain't even criminal, man, it's just survival' through good business practices.[41] Strike himself then passes on this learned criminal behaviour to a young boy from his neighbourhood in whom he sees potential as a 'spy boy, ounce mule, brightful and young, too young to be noticed',[42] and more generally as a perverse sort of surrogate child (or 'little brother')[43] with whom he can share the lessons he has himself learned about crime.

As the novel develops its rich picture of life in Dempsey, we also become aware of the near total absence (or utter ineffectiveness) of the sort of social controls Hirschi and others identify as working against criminal behaviour patterns. Neither Strike nor Tyrone nor any of the young men in the novel have intact families, with fathers as well as mothers being dead or absent; school is little more than 'time away from making money'; religion has little impact on people who are, in the words of a minister, 'unchurched'.[44] The only thing left, it seems, to hold society together here are the police—and they are all too often racist, aggressive, and ineffective, an 'army of occupation' rather than a police force.[45]

While a novel like *Clockers* integrates a criminological emphasis on individual choice, it can also be read in relation to criminological traditions that emphasize the role of the group, for good or for ill, in enabling or preventing criminal behaviour. A fuller consideration of the overall plot and patterning of the novel would be required to determine which of these aspects plays a larger role, but the key point here is that *Clockers* is able to both articulate, exemplify, and even critique, a range of criminological theories within its fictional matrix. It can also help us see how different forms of crime writing align (or align more easily) with different theoretical perspectives. *Clockers* is perhaps best described as a combination of a crime novel (focusing on the experience and perspective of the criminal) and a police procedural (focusing on the physical and administrative routines of police investigation). These forms seem to address themselves quite naturally to a group-level focus. A classic whodunnit or clue-puzzle mystery, on the other hand, would generally be less heavily invested in social explanations of criminal behaviour. Criminals in these sorts of texts tend to operate individually (or at most in pairs) and their (mis)behaviour is, as we have seen, generally linked to individual traits (be these rational, emotional, biological, or moral).

Crime as a Social Phenomenon

By moving one step further along the continuum of explanations for criminal behaviour we may be able to bring these two strands of analysis back together, although this will require a certain interpretative stretch. We will need to move our attention from the smaller groupings of friends, family, and other social units to society in general. Here we find a set of criminological theories that emphasize the role of, for example, breakdowns or deteriorations in social norms arising from changes or tensions in a given society (e.g. Merton's strain theory, discussed in Chapter 2), or, more radically, forms of critical criminology that, whatever their differences, 'locate one of the prime "causes" or origins of criminal behavior in the economic structure of society and the inequalities of the class system that this structure generates'.[46] Crime, from this perspective, is not so much a product of individual decision or group dynamic, but an inherent feature of social structures, inequalities, and injustices.

As we saw in Chapter 6, this sort of position has been articulated in a substantial number of crime novels, such as Sjöwall and Wahlöö's socially critical police procedurals. The hardboiled also frequently explores a broad, high-level malaise or corruption in a way that distributes the responsibility for crime across an entire society, rather than focusing it on an individual or group. Perhaps the classic example here would be Dashiell Hammett's 1929 *Red Harvest* in which the 'damned town' of Personville—called 'Poisonville' in the novel—acts synecdochally for society more generally.[47] It is certainly no stretch to read Price's *Clockers* through this sort of lens. The large-scale social failures that have led to the existence of deprived communities like Roosevelt Houses are not highlighted in the novel, but they are nonetheless present in references, more or less obvious, to income disparities, drug addiction, the AIDS crisis, police corruption, endemic street violence that reaches well beyond deprived neighbourhoods, an entrenched class system, and misogyny. Rodney Little articulates this position quite clearly when he argues (while training his drug dealers) that 'this whole country run by criminals—Wall Street, the govament [sic], the po-lice. How you think the dope gets in town to begin with?'[48]

Whether the book as a whole endorses this position is another question. Price's novel articulates a broad range of positions regarding the aetiology of crime. In this, we might be tempted to say, it is fundamentally different from classic mystery writing, which, as we saw at the start of this chapter, tends to focus on the individual. To take one paradigmatic example, Agatha Christie's 1926 *The Murder of Roger Ackroyd* (probably her most famous work),[49] places responsibility for the titular crime squarely on the shoulders of the criminal, who is first of all financially greedy (he has been blackmailing Ackroyd's wife) and second, immoral or disturbed in some (unspecified) way. As his sister says, he has always had a 'strain of weakness'.[50] There is no suggestion here that there is anything wrong with society except the presence of a murderer, and the investigative and deductive expertise of Hercule Poirot is quickly able to cauterize this wound on the social body.

Yet a consideration of the overall generic pattern of the Golden Age novel may help reconcile these seemingly irreconcilably different explanations for crime, and show how crime fiction can articulate criminological perspectives that may at first seem very foreign to a particular sub-genre or text. The key point is that *The Murder of Roger Ackroyd* does not appear alone. It is, like so many crime narratives, part of a larger series. Each Sherlock Holmes story can be read in isolation, but it also exists as part of a narrative sequence in which stasis (the repetition of a pattern) and change (the differing details of each narrative) collaborate to generate and maintain readerly interest. As Ruth Mayer points out, detective fiction 'operates by reeling off ever new beginnings or, rather, loops of action' within individual narratives, across multiple narratives, and indeed across the genre itself.[51] Poirot supresses the danger to society in *The Murder of Roger Ackroyd*, but then he must do so again and again, in novel after novel, all the way up to *Curtain: Poirot's Last Case* almost 50 years later. Add to this sense of criminal inevitability the fact that the killers in Christie's world almost always come from within its own middle-class, domestic confines—this is a world in which every friendly neighbour and every apparently loving family member is a potential murderer—and you could make the case that crime in her fiction is every bit as much a structural or social phenomenon as in any radical police procedural or critical crime novel. What I have presented in this chapter as a spectrum of criminological causality running from individual to collective becomes, when considered through the lens of crime fiction, a fluid continuum, with every member of every society at least potentially a criminal.

Notes

1 Agatha Christie, *Nemesis* (London: HarperCollins, 2016), 140.
2 Ibid., 138.
3 Ibid., 108.
4 Ibid., 140.
5 Ibid.
6 Ibid., 141.

7 Nick Baldock, "The Christian World of Agatha Christie," *First Things*, April 8, 2009, www.firstthings.com/web-exclusives/2009/08/the-christian-world-of-agatha-christie.

8 Christie, *Nemesis*, 265.

9 Cesare Beccaria, *On Crimes and Punishments and Other Writings*, edited by Aaron Thomas, translated by Aaron Thomas and Jeremy Parzen (Toronto: University of Toronto Press, 2008), 10.

10 Gilbert Geis, "Pioneers in Criminology VII–Jeremy Bentham (1748–1832)." *Journal of Criminal Law and Criminology* 46, no. 2 (1955), 163.

11 Stephen Jones, *Criminology*, 7th edition (Oxford: Oxford University Press, 2017), 79.

12 Christie, *Nemesis*, 265.

13 Ibid., 266.

14 Fyodor Dostoevsky, *Crime and Punishment*, translated by Richard Pevear and Larissa Volokhonsky (London: Vintage, 2007), 70–71.

15 Ibid., 71.

16 Ibid., 65.

17 Ibid., 65–66.

18 Jeremey Bentham, *A Comment on the Commentaries and A Fragment on Government*, edited by J. H. Burns and H. L. A. Hart, in *The Collected Works of Jeremy Bentham*, general editors J. H. Burns, J. R. Dinwiddy, F. Rosen, and T. P. Schofield (London: Athlone Press, 1977), 393.

19 Dostoevsky, *Crime and Punishment*, 11.

20 Rich, Nathaniel, "American Dreams: 'Clockers' by Richard Price," *The Daily Beast*, July 14, 2017, www.thedailybeast.com/american-dreams-clockers-by-richard-price.

21 Richard Price, *Clockers* (London: Bloomsbury, 2009), 299.

22 Ibid., 157.

23 Ibid., 105.

24 Ibid., 289.

25 Ibid., 350.

26 Cesare Lombroso, *Criminal Man*, translated by Mary Gibson and Nicole Hahn Rafter with assistance from Mark Seymour (Durham, NC: Duke University Press, 2006), 43.

27 Anna Neill, "The Savage Genius of Sherlock Holmes," *Victorian Literature and Culture* 37, no. 2 (2009), 613. doi:10.1017/S1060150309090378.613.

28 Arthur Conan Doyle, *The Hounds of the Baskervilles* (London: Penguin, 2012), 100.

29 Joanne Ella Parsons, "Fosco's Fat: Transgressive Consumption and Bodily Control in Wilkie Collins' *The Woman in White*," in *The Victorian Male Body*, edited by Joanne Ella Parsons and Ruth Heholt (Edinburgh: Edinburgh University Press, 2018), 216.

30 Raymond Chandler, *The Big Sleep* (New York: Vintage Crime/Black Lizard, 1992), 5–6.

31 Matthew B. Robinson and Kevin M. Beaver, *Why Crime?: An Interdisciplinary Approach to Explaining Criminal Behavior*, 2nd edition (Durham, NC: Carolina Academic Press, 2009), 84, 135, 171–172.

32 Siri Hustvedt, *A Woman Looking at Men Looking at Women: Essays on Art, Sex and the Mind* (New York: Simon & Schuster, 2016), 168.

33 Philip K. Dick, "The Minority Report," in *The Minority Report and Other Classic Stories* by Philip K. Dick (New York: Citadel Press, 1987), 72.

34 Ruth Triplett, "Crime, Social Learning Theory of," in *The Blackwell Encyclopedia of Sociology*, edited by George Ritzer, *Wiley Online Library*, 2015, https://doi.org/10.1002/9781405165518.wbeosc157.pub2.

35 Ibid.

36 Matthew B. Robinson and Kevin M. Beaver, *Why Crime?*, 181.

37 James D. Orcutt, "Crime, Social Control Theory of," in *The Blackwell Encyclopedia of Sociology*, edited by George Ritzer, *Wiley Online Library*, 2016, https://doi.org/10.1002/9781405165518.wbeosc156.pub2.

38 John R. Maynard, "The Bildungsroman," in *A Companion to the Victorian Novel*, edited by Patrick Brantlinger and William Thesing (Malden, MA: Blackwell Publishing, 2002), 287.

39 Richard Price, *Clockers*, 24.

40 Ibid., 28.

41 Ibid., 299.

42 Ibid., 194.

43 Ibid., 413.

44 Ibid., 27, 469.

45 Ibid., 328.

46 Martin D. Schwartz and Henry H. Brownstein, "Critical Criminology", in *The Handbook of Criminological Theory*, edited by Alex R. Piquero (Chichester: Wiley Blackwell, 2016), 301.

47 Dashiell Hammett, *Red Harvest* (New York: Vintage, 1972), 145.

48 Richard Price, *Clockers*, 301.

49 Richard Bradford, *Crime Fiction: A Very Short Introduction* (Oxford: Oxford University Press, 2015), 21.

50 Agatha Christie, *The Murder of Roger Ackroyd* (New York: Pocket Books, 1986), 255.

51 Ruth Mayer, "In the Nick of Time?: Detective Film Serials, Temporality, and Contingency Management, 1919–1926," *Velvet Light Trap* 79 (2017): 21. doi:10.7560/VLT7903.

8   Investigating Crime

The first thing that needs to be said about the focus of this chapter, criminal investigation, is that it is not strictly speaking an aspect of criminology. Instead, it is generally viewed as part of the separate though related field of criminal justice. Criminology is broadly adjacent to, and frequently intertwined with, disciplines like sociology and psychology. It aims to develop a theoretical understanding of crime and criminal behaviour that may feed into policy making. Criminal justice, on the other hand, can be seen as an applied form of criminology. If criminology develops theories regarding criminal motivation and behaviour, criminal justice puts these theories into effect within the framework of the many different systems involved in the enforcement of the law, such as police forces, courts, and prisons. In practice, despite these substantive differences, there is a great deal of overlap between the two fields:[1] people who study criminology, for example, may well go into careers in the criminal justice system. The distinction nonetheless remains important, and it places the practical aspects of investigating crime firmly in the criminal justice camp.

Crime fiction, as anyone who has been even superficially exposed to the genre can attest, is deeply interested in precisely this aspect of criminal justice. It is in fact frequently referred to as detective fiction, thus emphasizing the processes of investigating crime rather than crime itself. Mary Evans, Sarah Moore, and Hazel Johnstone argue in *Detecting the Social Order and Disorder in Post-1970s Detective Fiction* that while the two terms are frequently used interchangeably, the label detective fiction is useful or indeed preferable for two key reasons. First, crime does not always involve the death of individual people, and detective fiction has generally been concerned primarily, though not exclusively, with a death or series of deaths caused by another person's actions. Second, it highlights the processes of detecting which are so central to the genre.[2] Evans, Moore, and Johnstone quote Anthony Horowitz's metafictional mystery *The Word is Murder* (2017), which offers a useful reminder of the potential relevance

DOI: 10.4324/9781003156581-11

of nomenclature: 'They're not called murder victim stories. They're not called criminal stories. They're called detective stories'.[3]

A further point is that in its broadest sense detection is an activity that is not just of relevance to students of crime fiction (or detective fiction) or criminology (or criminal justice). The concept has much wider implications, as Evans, Moore, and Johnstone argue:

> How to detect, what to look for, what to regard as reliable or unreliable evidence are all part not just of detection in fiction but of every form of research, be it in the social sciences, the humanities or the natural sciences. We cannot find out anything that we need to know unless we have some certainty about how we will proceed. And what detective fiction has done, from its very earliest years is to offer some diverse possibilities about how to find out what is going on in the world.[4]

Investigation, or detection, is thus of direct relevance not just to almost all of the narratives that we gather under the somewhat unstable labels of detective or crime fiction but also to all of our systematic attempts to learn about the world through organized, coherent forms of study. Consider, for example, the close relationship between the early detective fiction of Arthur Conan Doyle and medicine. Holmes was famously (though only partially) based on Doyle's medical school lecturer, Dr Joseph Bell, who offered a model of keen observation and diagnostic virtuosity that could be applied well beyond the limited confines of his field. A recent article in the *British Medical Journal* applies this process in reverse, arguing that 'analogies between diagnostic reasoning and the investigative strategies found in detective literature may provide us with some clues on how to confront the problems posed by the burgeoning number of available technologies' in medical practice.[5] Even more broadly, the idea of detection, or the systematic use of investigation to answer questions, plays an important role in our general sense of our place in the world. Detection is a fundamental aspect of our epistemology, of how we know what we know, and as such demands a central place in any study of the overlapping fields of criminology and crime fiction.

Amateur Detection

At this point, I would like to narrow my focus back down from the universal—detection as a basic model for human understanding, for knowing what we know and how we know it—to the particular—detection as a central component of crime fiction. David Geherin notes in his study of the detective figure that while the history of literature is rich in characters who are driven by 'a desire to figure out something that demands an explanation' (another example of the universal resonance of the concept of detection), crime fiction as a genre has tended to place narrative responsibility for this task with one of three main character types: the amateur detective, the private eye, and the police officer.[6] Geherin uses this familiar distinction to discuss the evolution of crime fiction, but it also indicates one of the key differences between detection in the real world of criminal justice and detection in the imagined world of crime fiction—realism.

Early detectives in the classical and Golden Age traditions tended to be amateur detectives of one kind or another. Edgar Allan Poe's C. Auguste Dupin is an early, well-known, and important example. He is a 'young gentleman [...] of an excellent, indeed of an illustrious family [...] reduced to such poverty that the energy of his character succumbed beneath it, and he ceased to bestir himself in the world, or to care for the retrieval of his fortunes'.[7] In his unambitious lassitude (he is what might have been called a few decades ago a dropout; in more contemporary parlance, he is lying flat) he wanders through Paris, exercising his undoubted observational and analytical abilities on the varied sights and experiences the city offers the night-time *flaneur*, until he is drawn into an investigation out of curiosity. Another widely discussed example of this type is Doyle's Sherlock Holmes (although describing Holmes, a 'consulting detective', as an amateur is something of a stretch).[8]

Both of these detectives rely largely, though not exclusively, on rational deduction and analysis in order to solve the mysteries (they are not always crimes) they encounter. Dupin's first appearance in 'The Murders on the Rue Morgue' (1841) is prefaced with a discussion of the nature of the 'mental features discoursed of as the analytical' which can be 'described, although not defined, as the capacity for resolving thought into its elements',[9] and Holmes' first appearance in *A Study in Scarlet* includes a similarly abstract discussion of 'the Science of Deduction and Analysis' in the form of an article written by Holmes called 'The Book of Life' in which he argues that life is a 'great chain, the nature of which is known whenever we are shown a single link of it'.[10] Both detectives are thus able to combine observation and logic in order to reach conclusions unavailable to the 'simple diligence and activity' of the police (as Dupin describes it).[11] Dupin's trick of breaking in on his companion's silent train of thought is a famous example of this approach, as is Holmes' repeatedly demonstrated ability to determine profession, class, family background, and so on from minor external details. In 'The Yellow Face' (1893), to take a single instance, he determines that the owner of a particular pipe is 'obviously a muscular man, left-handed, with an excellent set of teeth, careless in his habits, and with no need to practise economy'.[12]

In terms of realism, there are two problems here. Amateur detectives played little or no role in the nineteenth-century criminal justice system.

Despite local differences, this was largely built around patrolmen, whose job was crime prevention and the maintenance of social order, and plainclothes detectives who actively investigated serious crimes.[13] In addition, the police detectives who actually investigated crimes were far more likely to rely on informants and their extensive knowledge of the community (criminal and otherwise) than on the elaborate application of deductive or analytical ability.[14] Indeed, as one Metropolitan Police Commissioner put it in 1878, 'the real practical fact is that in ninety-nine cases out of a hundred cases of crime, the detection is most humdrum work, and it only requires just ordinary care and intelligence. You do not want a high class mind to do it at all'.[15] There is in reality no need for the powerful intellect of a Dupin or a Holmes.

The lack of realism involved in the investigative paradigms of classic detective fiction becomes even more acute if we focus on the interwar realm of the clue-puzzle or Golden Age mystery. Here we find implausible investigators like Agatha Christie's elderly spinster Miss Marple or John Dickson Carr's obese Gideon Fell, who is only able to walk with the assistance of two canes. These characters' physical limitations highlight the mental nature of their investigations. Miss Marple's decades of 'observing village life, sometimes with binoculars, have [...] given her an understanding of human nature and behavior on which to base deductions'.[16] The local, domestic, and familiar can be applied, the Marple novels indicate, to the understanding of the deeply unfamiliar world of criminal behaviour. This is a charming and popular conceit, as indicated by the persistent success of the character, but it is not what one would call realistic. Carr's investigator Fell is an exuberantly odd character who specializes in solving seemingly impossible 'locked room' crimes that are, as he notes in *The Hollow Man* (1935), openly—and again exuberantly—fictional: 'I will now lecture', said Dr Fell, inexorably, 'on the general mechanics and development of the situation which is known in detective fiction as the "hermetically sealed chamber". Harrumph. All those opposing can skip this chapter. Harrumph'.[17] This sort of metafictional acknowledgement of the fictionality of the detective text is by no means unheard of in clue-puzzle mysteries, but it, along with the bizarre nature of the crimes Fell investigates, can be seen as representing an extreme form of Golden Age investigative implausibility. In these novels unrealistic crimes are investigated in unrealistic ways—much to the delight of generations of readers.

Private Detection

As we saw in Chapter 3, hardboiled detective fiction was at least in part a direct response to the implausibility of the Golden Age model. Instead of presenting unrealistic amateur detectives using unrealistically sophisticated analytical procedures to solve unrealistically outré crimes, the hardboiled offers (at least in theory) the more realistic figure of the professional private detective solving realistic crimes in realistic ways for realistic reasons. Dashiell Hammett's work is exemplary in this regard (as in many others). Hammett had himself worked for a number of years for the Pinkerton Detective Agency before becoming a writer, and was thus able to develop the realism of the detective figure in terms of their social position (private eyes are paid employees rather than enthusiastic amateurs); motivation (private eyes have financial, professional, and potentially ethical reasons to solve crimes); and most importantly method, for 'the private eye's success comes not from logical deduction but from methodical trial and error'.[18]

The private eye in hardboiled fiction is no longer able to rely on the masterful analysis of the clue—the seemingly insignificant scrap of material evidence upon which Golden Age detectives build their elaborate logical castles. In the hardboiled private eye novel the whole function of the clue is, as Jesper Gulddal puts it, 'subjected to extensive self-reflexive critique as the crime genre reinvents itself on the basis of new epistemologies better aligned with the modern world'.[19] In practice, what this means is that the clue becomes unreliable. What looks like a clue may not be one, while other genuine clues may be ignored or misinterpreted by the private eye. These 'empty, unnoticed or misunderstood clues' indicate, Gulddal argues, that the hardboiled private eye's strength 'lies in his ability to navigate the unmeaning chaos of modern urban life rather than in his intellectual prowess'.[20] This navigation can be taken quite literally; if the prototypical figure of the Golden Age novel is the immobile, rational, armchair detective who analyses clues within a strictly delimited physical space, the hardboiled private eye is a much more physical and physically mobile figure who follows leads—the new name indicating a new role—across the varied spaces of the modern metropolis. We can think of figures like Raymond Chandler's Philip Marlowe or Hammett's Sam Spade not just as more realistic versions of the detective but also as social explorers, whose active, mobile investigations involving travel, interviews, surveillance, and physical confrontation offer readers a synthetic overview of a new, and rapidly developing, social and physical urban reality.

Yet despite its tremendous success, this fictional paradigm was, as we have seen, eventually subject to criticism in turn for its own lack of realism—recall James Ellroy's claim that 'the last time a private eye investigated a homicide was never'.[21] The private eye is, in other words, as unrealistic as the amateur sleuth. This critique tends to focus on the social and institutional position of the private eye. In the real world, private eyes are far, far more likely to be involved with investigations of marital infidelity or suspect insurance claims than with murder.

Sue Grafton is one of the few authors of private eye novels to have acknowledged this fact and integrated it into her fiction. The investigator of her Alphabet series, Kinsey Millhone, appeared in 25 novels between 1982 (*A is for Alibi*) and 2017 (*Y is for Yesterday*). Alongside characters like Marcia Muller's Sharon McCone and Sara Paretsky's V. I. Warshawski, Millhone represents a clear challenge to the masculine norms of the hardboiled. Part of this comes from the emphasis Grafton places on the dailiness of her work as a private investigator.[22] Millhone operates 'on a modest scale, supporting [her]self by doing missing-person searches, background checks, witness location, and the occasional service of process'.[23] Readers are treated to full accounts not just of the marginally dramatic events that regularly fall to the lot of the working private eye, such as serving a restraining order, but also to detailed descriptions of the paperwork that accompanies the process:

> In the car again, I logged the time I'd spent and the mileage on my car. I drove back into downtown Santa Teresa and parked in a lot near a notary's office. I took a few minutes to fill out the affidavit of service, then went into the office, where I signed the return and had it notarized. I borrowed the notary's fax machine and made two copies, then walked over to the courthouse. I had the documents file-stamped and left the original with the clerk.[24]

This sort of material tends to give way in the Millhone novels to more dramatic plotlines involving murder, but we are still well on our way here to the police procedural, a form that places a great deal of emphasis on the realistic evocation of accurately rendered and extremely detailed aspects of the criminal justice system, including but not limited to investigation.

Police Detection

The police procedural as a whole has found it difficult to shake off completely the hardboiled's emphasis on the individual and frequently isolated investigator. For instance, despite the fact that Sjöwall and Wahlöö's *Story of a Crime* (1965–1975) focuses on a very broad cast of characters, the series is often marketed and discussed as the Martin Beck novels. But even so there is a clear sense within the procedural that the hardboiled is an inadequate form for representing the modern world and, more specifically, the way criminal investigations occur within it. Harry Bosch, for instance, the hero of Michael Connelly's successful police series (referred to, predictably enough, as the Harry Bosch novels) may 'seem like the loner type. A Private Eye, not a man who has to take orders from men he doesn't respect', but this is, as Bosch himself knows, something of an illusion. 'There are no more private operators', he explains, 'everybody takes orders'.[25]

The representation of criminal investigation in the police procedural thus tends to be a much more collaborative affair than in other iterations of the detective novel, with clearly defined roles for different participants working within a clearly articulated and elaborately depicted institutional framework. An important point here is that as a genre or sub-genre the procedural is not based on a purely literary tradition (with each new fictional form building on or challenging the legacy of its predecessors). Instead, it is based, as Heather Worthington writes, 'on the actualities of police work carried out by ordinary men [sic] dealing with crimes that their employment *requires* them to investigate'. The crimes these men and women investigate are not 'solved by genius or intuition' as in the classic and Golden Age detective story, 'but by practical methods' (a trait shared with the hardboiled) and most significantly 'by teamwork'.[26]

In his textbook on the topic, Steven G. Brandl has identified three interlinked components of criminal investigation: (1) the investigative process, which is intended to collect (2) crime-related information or evidence to achieve (3) particular goals such as, most importantly, solving the crime.[27] The investigative process is conducted by a range of actors, from patrolmen to detectives, and involves a wide range of activities, such as interviewing victims and witnesses, gathering physical objects from the crime scene, and identifying potential witnesses. The results of this process are then recorded in reports. While the classic or Golden Age detective is interested in *clues*, and the private eye follows *leads*, the investigators in the police procedural need *evidence* if they are to achieve their desired goal of arrest and, hopefully, criminal conviction.

This evidence can take a range of forms, from verbal and/or written statements such as witness identifications or outright perpetrator confessions, to the types of physical evidence that rely on expert scientific analysis for validity, such as DNA profiling and gunshot analysis. All of this evidence must be gathered and secured in accordance with relevant local laws, and must be strong enough in aggregate to lead to an arrest. This is of course quite different from the circumstances that condition fictional investigations in, for example, a Golden Age mystery, where the detective's ratiocination (based on the presence of clues) is generally enough to lead to a narrative dénouement, if not an arrest and conviction. This is one of the reasons the genre so often allows the criminal to escape justice via suicide: the 'small piece of half charred paper' with the cryptic message 'll and' found in Agatha Christie's *The Mysterious Affair at Styles* (1920) may be more than enough to confirm Hercule Poirot's suspicions (he 'expected it'), but it certainly would not stand up in court as evidence.[28]

The police protagonist of the first novel in the Harry Bosch Series, *The Black Echo* (1992), exhibits many of the typical characteristics of the private eye. He is like Chandler's Marlowe a 'Private "I" ' who 'hides his true motivation and identity behind a tough-talking mask',[29] and he also matches LeRoy Panek's description of the hardboiled detective as 'a man in a perverse relationship with authority and circumstances'.[30] Bosch lives alone, has no family or close friends, and is strongly attracted to Edward Hopper's famous painting of urban loneliness, *Nighthawks* (he 'once [...] stood in front of it studying it for nearly an hour').[31] Finally, as an 'outsider in an insider's job' he is in perpetual conflict with his superior officers, internal affairs, and the Los Angeles Police Department in general.[32] Yet *The Black Echo* nonetheless hews much more closely to the real-world model of criminal investigation than would be typical, or even imaginable, in other forms of detective fiction.

Bosch may talk and live (and drink) like a private eye, but he investigates like a trained police officer. As the novel opens, he is called out to investigate what looks like the 'no-count case' of Vietnam veteran Billy Meadows' heroin overdose; not on the face of it a promising or interesting mystery, and certainly not one he has chosen to investigate. The scene of the death is examined not by Bosch alone, but by a team of specialists, including patrolmen, his partner, and a number of crime scene technicians.[33] The process is facilitated by access to mobile computer terminals (high technology in the novel's late twentieth-century setting), and documented by photographs and video recordings. Important evidence is provided by a detailed autopsy examination conducted by a medical examiner, who notes in fluent bureaucratese that 'the totality of the medical evidence indicates death at the hands of others'.[34] Further information is provided by accessing police databases, such as the 'Gang-Related Information Tracking' system run by 'Community Resources Against Street Hoodlums',[35] a real-world unit of the LAPD shut down in the wake of the 2000 Rampart Scandal. Interviews with witnesses are also important, with some of the novel's key scenes set in an 'eight-by-eight' interview room, where statements are recorded for future consultation.[36] As the case develops (this is of course not a mere overdose), interagency cooperation becomes important, with the FBI and the LAPD working together on the investigation.

The Black Echo offers, in other words, a narrative that maps very closely onto the real-world processes of criminal investigation. Perhaps most strikingly, several of Bosch's biggest breaks in the case come not from clues or leads or dazzling chains of thought or even intuitive hunches, but from reading reports. First a 'thick sheaf of papers' containing the complete military records of the victim leads to an unexpected development in the case (connecting the victim to an FBI supervisor in a deeply suspicious fashion); later, while reviewing 'the murder book and other files on the

Meadows case [...]. looking for anything, a new name, a discrepancy in somebody's statement, something that has been discarded earlier as unimportant but would look different to him now', Bosch discovers more vital information (revealing yet another layer of FBI malfeasance—the bureau does not come out well in this novel).[37] The particular details of Bosch's investigation and its rather far-fetched results are less important than the way the narrative offers readers a view of a criminal justice system operating in a highly bureaucratized world.

As I have argued, Connelly's Bosch is in effect a hardboiled character ported into a police novel, and this combination of genres has been hugely successful. Examples could be multiplied almost endlessly from across the globe, from Ian Rankin's Inspector Rebus series (Scotland, 24 novels published from 1987 to 2022), to Henning Mankell's Kurt Wallander series (Sweden, 13 novels published from 1991 to 2009), to Qiu Xiaolong's Inspector Chen Cao series (China, 12 novels published from 2000 to 2021), to Deon Meyer's Benny Griessel series (South Africa, 8 novels published from 2004 to 2020). All of these situate the individualistic character of the hardboiled private eye tradition within the realities of modern policing—and this sort of detailed, realistic examination of criminal justice as a modern bureaucratic system is even more typical of the pure police procedural form represented by, for example, Sjöwall and Wahlöö's *Story of a Crime*, J. J. Marric's twenty-one Gideon novels (1955–1976), or Ed McBain's fifty-three 87th Precinct novels (1956–2005).

Investigative Realism: Forensics

Yet it would be a mistake to accept too easily or completely the outline I have proposed here. Yes, one can trace the development of fictional criminal investigation from the classic and clue-puzzle forms, through the hardboiled and into the police procedural, and link each step to a greater emphasis on the realistic depiction of criminal investigation. But it is important to realize that earlier forms of crime writing were also at times heavily invested in the details of real-world criminal investigation. Charles Dickens, for example, although not strictly speaking a crime writer, was an important early innovator in the use of mystery and detection in his plotting. He was also, as Haia Shpayer-Makov writes, 'more than any of his counterparts, the writer who heightened interest in police agents'.[38] Dickens was, as we saw in Chapter 3, in close contact with the Metropolitan Police, and wrote extensively about the routines and investigative practices of police officers like his friend Charles Frederick Field. This real-world knowledge was transformed into a fictional register in *Bleak House* (1852–1853), where Inspector Bucket repeatedly demonstrates his ability to navigate, silently and discretely, the complex social and physical realities of London. This 'sharp-eyed man in black' is a keen observer who has an uncanny ability to 'lurk and lounge', silently observing and yet mysteriously influencing the life of the streets.[39] The generically named Mr Inspector of *Our Mutual Friend* (1864–1865) is another Dickensian police officer, described by one critic as a character who 'maintains [Bucket's] tradition of being imperturbable, omnicompetent, firm but genial, and an accomplished actor'.[40] While speaking of realism in the context of Dickens is problematic, both of these characters embody the normal institutional working practices of the police of their time and place.

Another example of the early integration of investigative realism into crime fiction can be seen in Arthur Conan Doyle's Sherlock Holmes stories. The great detective may be a patent figure of fantasy—Marshall McLuhan scathingly calls him the 'superman of our dreams'[41]—and his investigative practices may frequently border on the tendentious (can you really determine so very much about a man by the condition of his hat?), but he is nonetheless an imaginative participant in the emergence of forensic science and rationalized criminal investigation. As James F. O'Brien writes in his definitive study of the scientific background to the Holmes' stories, 'Conan Doyle set out to write about a detective who actively employed science in his work', and referred to some aspect of science in each of the 60 stories that make up the Holmes canon.[42] Holmes calls himself a 'scientific detective' in his second appearance in *The Sign of the Four* (1890) and explains to Watson (and the reader) the value of a range of technical investigative techniques, from the 'Distinction between the Ashes of the Various Tobaccos' (he has written a monograph on the subject) to 'the uses of plaster of Paris as a preserver of impresses'.[43] Seven Holmes tales refer to fingerprints,[44] including the 1903 story 'The Norwood Builder'. Here, fingerprint evidence plays an important role, and this only two years after Scotland Yard had begun using the new technique. However, this is not yet pure forensic investigation, for the fact that 'no two thumb-marks are alike' is less important in this story than the fact that one particular thumb mark 'had been put on during the night' in an attempt to frame a particular suspect.[45]

Holmes also operates a private version of the extensive databases that are such a key feature of modern investigation. In 'A Scandal in Bohemia', for instance, he consults his index to learn more about Irene Adler:

> For many years he had adopted a system of docketing all paragraphs concerning men and things, so that it was difficult to name a subject or a person on which he could not at once furnish information. In this case I found her biography sandwiched in between that of a Hebrew Rabbi and that of a staff-commander who had written a monograph upon the deep-sea fishes.[46]

This index is the forerunner of the many electronic databases available to investigators today offering information needed during criminal investigations (of the sort Harry Bosch consults in *The Black Echo*), ranging from the FBI's National Crime Information Center (NCIC) to the Interpol Case Tracking System (NLETS).[47] Perhaps less comfortably, it is also the forerunner of the indexing system developed by Reinhard Heydrich of the SS security service and (later) the Reich Security Main Office before and during the Second World War to record information about political opponents and foreign nationals slated for execution.[48] Investigative technologies can, unfortunately, be applied for both good and ill.

The role of the science and technology of crime in the Golden Age mystery is also interesting. This is the last place one would expect to find a realistic deployment of forensic (or administrative) technology to crime solving. After all, the Golden Age mystery is a form of game, an intellectual puzzle in which 'detection is rational rather than active or intuitional'.[49] In Agatha Christie's first novel, *The Mysterious Affair at Styles* (1920), for instance, Hercule Poirot claims that 'one should not ask for outside proof—no, reason should be enough'.[50] Any appeal to technical veracity in this context would seem to be deeply out of place. As A. A. Milne puts it in his introduction to his 1922 detective novel *The Red House Mystery*:

> Away with the scientific detective, the man with the microscope! What satisfaction is it to you or me when the famous Professor examines the small particle of dust which the murderer has left behind him, and infers that he lives between a brewery and a flour-mill? What thrill do we get when the blood-spot on the missing man's handkerchief proves that he was recently bitten by a camel? Speaking for myself, none. The thing is so much too easy for the author, so much too difficult for his readers.[51]

This is a stinging (if comic) repudiation of the sort of forensic detection pioneered by Doyle, but the fact remains that other Golden Age writers made extensive use, at least at times, of technical aspects of investigation.

Consider Dorothy L. Sayers' Lord Peter Wimsey, whose undoubted logical strength is supported by an equally impressive ability to read the text of the physical world, as in *Whose Body?* (1923), when the examination of a corpse—an improvised post-mortem of sorts—reveals 'one or two little contradictions' (e.g. manicured nails but dirty ears) that are central to the mystery.[52] This 'mastery of the material world' is in part reliant on Wimsey's use of technical means, including, for example, a magnifying monocle, the latest photographic equipment, and sophisticated chemical tests.[53] Sayers' 1930 novel, *The Documents in the Case* (written with Robert Eustace), takes this technical, forensic interest to something of an extreme. While it is obvious enough who has committed the crime (a poisoning), obtaining proof of that fact is much more difficult; the investigation ultimately relies on a very sophisticated chemical analysis intended to determine the difference between synthesized muscarine (the poison in the poisonous fly agaric) and the natural product. The organic substance, we learn, displays 'a kind of bias—a lop-sidedness'.[54] In other words, it is molecularly asymmetrical rather than symmetrical like a synthesized substance. This difference is detectable in a laboratory using specialized optical equipment and polarized light, and the scene in which this test is carried out is the most dramatic in the novel.

Taking a very broad view we can agree, then, with Andy Williams when he notes that 'over the last 150 years, the excitement and interest in crime and the criminal have' been matched by 'ideas and developments around *forensics* [emphasis in original]'.[55] Williams goes on to point out that the blend of 'crime, criminals and forensics is so potent that it has spawned vast educational, economic, and technological industries that have increasingly influenced our social, cultural and political worlds'.[56] One manifestation of this broad cultural fascination is the forensic crime novel, a hugely successful sub-genre represented by the work of authors such as Patricia Cornwell, Jeffery Deaver, and Kathy Reichs. This is a genre in which, as Nicole Kenley points out, the main formal characteristic is the presence of scenes of forensic investigation and interpretation.[57] Kenley argues that the effect of this forensic focus is to reassert the 'detective fiction's traditional function of reassurance and containment in the face of destabilizing elements'—in other words to make crime fiction comforting again—by 'delimiting the field of potential solutions through ever-more-minute investigative techniques' and 'the wonders of forensic science'.[58] The promise of forensic fiction is certainty in an uncertain world.

Patricia Cornwell's *Post-Mortem* (1990) is an early example of the type. It introduces Kay Scarpetta, 'first among forensic detectives',[59] and while the character has developed over the course of her long literary career, one factor has remained constant in Cornwell's novels: a textual commitment to the processes and procedures of forensic investigation as a solution—*the* solution—to the dangers of modern urban and suburban American life. The world of *Post-Mortem* is one in which a serial killer can operate with near impunity. Someone is raping and killing women in Richmond, Virginia, where Scarpetta works as Chief Medical Examiner, but despite an extensive police investigation he 'could be anybody and he was nobody'.[60] Only the exhaustive, and exhaustively narrated, technical work of the forensic scientist is able to narrow down the vast field of suspects provided by a highly mobile and anonymous population. Analysis indicates, for example, that the attacker must be a nonsecreter (meaning 'his blood-type antigens could not be found in his other body fluids, such as saliva or semen or sweat'), but that only limits the suspect pool to 'twenty per-cent of the population', or 'approximately forty-four thousand people in a city the size of Richmond. Twenty-two thousand if half of that number is male'.[61] Further investigation is obviously required to restore order—and the reader's sense of security.

The bodies of the victims are the focus of Scarpetta's investigation, with lengthy autopsies functioning as a both primary points of textual interest, and as plot devices for moving the investigation forward. Scarpetta's tech-nical mastery is key here. Her 'diplomas and certificates' from 'Cornell, John Hopkins, Georgetown, et al.'[62] are markers of an officially accredited expertise which is repeatedly demonstrated in scenes set in the Forensic Science Bureau, a 'beehive, a honeycomb of cubicles filled with labora-tory equipment and people wearing white lab coats with plastic safety glasses'.[63] Here, a wide range of technological processes are applied to the victims' bodies, their clothing, and other pieces of evidence, including detailed wound analysis, studies of fibre residue, and laser-assisted obser-vation based on the fact that 'if an atom is excited by heat, and if light of a certain wavelength is impinged upon it, an atom can be stimulated to emit light in phase'.[64] This sort of scientific description is offered for a number of different forensic processes, including an early use of DNA profiling (the first real-world arrest based on this technology—of Colin Pitchfork, a British double murderer—took place in 1987, only three years before the publication of *Post-Mortem*). 'For Cornwell', as Kenley notes, 'the body remains ever legible, and technology renders it ever more so'.[65] It is also worth noting that this forensic work is supported by an elaborate administrative apparatus, and by advanced (for 1990) infor-mation and communication systems like modem-enabled computers and police databases.

This modern (if now dated—this is one of the inherent dangers of this type of fiction) investigative approach is contrasted throughout the novel with older forms of detective work, represented here by Sergeant Marino. Scarpetta dismissively describes one of his theories as 'a wonderful plot for Agatha Christie'.[66] Forensic detection is thus presented as not only a technological panacea for the dangers of modern society—its anonymity, its amorality, its violence—but also as yet another stage in crime fiction's ongoing internal struggle for the mantle of realism. As Scarpetta says, 'in real life murder is usually depressingly simple. I think these murders are simple. They are exactly what they appear to be, impersonal random murders committed by someone who stalks his victims long enough to figure out when to strike'.[67] Given this realistic element of randomness, Cornwell's novel (and indeed the forensic genre as a whole) implies that the sophisticated deployment of cutting-edge technology is the only way to fight crime.

As Ronald R. Thomas notes in his early and important study of forensics in detective fiction, the fictional detective makes a claim to a certain type of authority by applying 'strategies of interpretation and authentication' to 'the body of the criminal and the victim alike'.[68] These literary strategies—these fictional employments of technologies—also 'relate to broader questions of subjectivity and cultural authority' so that 'the history of detective fiction is deeply implicated with the history of forensic technology'.[69] While Thomas' work focuses on nineteenth and early twentieth century crime fiction, this claim can be made regarding later forms of the genre, perhaps most particularly the forensic crime novel. While there is much to be said about the vision of the self proposed in this type of fiction—the individual seen, for example, as a monitored, measured, and analysed subject of biomedical/judicial processes—a fascinating point is the way this form of crime writing has had an impact on real-world criminal investigations. I am referring to what is known as the CSI-effect, defined recently as 'the perception commonly held by lawyers, judges, police officers, and even the general public that, due to the apparent availability of forensic evidence on crime television shows such as CSI, jurors may be either unwilling to convict in the absence of such evidence or overly reliant on it when it is presented'.[70] As the name suggests, this phenomenon is much more likely to be associated with popular television dramas than with crime novels, but it remains a fascinating example of the way crime fiction and real-world criminology are intertwined.

By way of conclusion, I would like to discuss the way the very fictionality of crime fiction—its freedom from the constraints of reality—allows it to re-think the contemporary emphasis on forensics in criminal investigation. The text I would like to consider is Tom Hillenbrand's *Drohnenland*, or *Drone State* (2014), which in 2015 won both the Glauer Award for best German crime novel and the Lasswitz Award for the best German science fiction novel. Set at in indeterminate moment in a future European Union damaged, though not destroyed, by nuclear war in the Middle East, the ensuing energy crisis, and the impact of ongoing climate change, Hillenbrand's police officers deploy extraordinarily sophisticated technologies to fight crime. Fleets of drones and powerful computers allow them to practice 'virtual forensics'[71] through the 'forensic replication'[72] of crime scenes, which are recorded in precise detail for future access in a fully immersive virtual reality space—there is also an even more sophisticated version of this known as 'mirror space', a 'continuous real-time replication' based on 'all the data we can compile—from security videos, humming-drone pictures, recordings from survey drones, signatures from all cars and people [...]'.[73] The results of this meta-surveillance are then fed into a super computer capable of using its enormous database to predict criminal behaviour: 'based on the suspect's data corona' the computer can generate a 'predictive criminal record' (166). This all makes for very effective policing—it is almost impossible for a fugitive to escape the authorities, for example, in a society that is so thoroughly monitored—but the dystopian potential of such sophisticated investigative technologies is also clear, constituting, in fact, the main plot of the novel.

What Hillenbrand is offering here is an extrapolation of our developing surveillance society, a fictional exploration of the fact that, as Florian Zappe and Andrew S. Grosse argue, 'surveillance practices and technologies have infiltrated all aspects of our lives and caused fundamental shifts in established notions of privacy and subjectivity, thus altering the status of the individual within the social realm'.[74] This is true both of our participation in cyberspace, which can be thought of as 'a separate socio-spatial dimension [...] a distinct jurisdiction requiring its own constitution and legal system, its own law enforcement agents and practices', and of our lives in the real, embodied world.[75] This is particularly acute in urban China, where a report published in 2020 estimates that there are 372.8 surveillance cameras in operation per thousand people, but it is also a fact of life in other major cities around the world.[76] We are increasingly watched, recorded, and monitored by agents public and private wherever we are and whatever we do. As Heike Hendersen argues in her discussion of *Drone State*, 'surveillance is [...] never neutral; it always participates in social ordering and cultural developments'.[77] The same argument can be made for forensics, and indeed criminal investigation, more generally: the technologies that enable effective policing are never neutral. One of crime fiction's jobs, then, is to participate in the ongoing social evaluation demanded by the existence of these powerful tools.

Notes

1 David E. Duffee, Alissa Pollitz Worden, and Edward R. Maguire, "Directions for Theory and Theorizing in Criminal Justice," in *Criminal Justice Theory*, 2nd edition, edited by Edward R. Maguire and David E. Duffee (London: Routledge, 2015), 453–454.

2 Mary Evans and Sarah Moore, with Hazel Johnstone, *Detecting the Social: Order and Disorder in Post-1970s Detective Fiction* (Cham: Palgrave MacMillan, 2019), 1–2.

3 Anthony Horowitz, *The Word Is Murder* (London, Century, 2017), 61.

4 Mary Evans et al., *Detecting the Social*, 2.

5 Claudio Rapezzi, Roberto Ferrari, and Angelo Branzi, "White Coats and Fingerprints: Diagnostic Reasoning in Medicine and Investigative Methods of Fictional Detectives," *British Medical Journal* 331, no. 7531 (2005), 1491.

6 David Geherin, "Detectives," in *The Routledge Companion to Crime* Fiction, edited by Janice Allan, Jesper Gulddal, Stewart King, and Andrew Pepper (London: Routledge, 2020), 159.

7 Edgar A. Poe, "The Murder in the Rue Morgue," *Graham's Lady's and Gentleman's Magazine* 18 (1841), 167, *Hathi Trust*, https://babel.hathitrust. org/cgi/pt?id=osu.32435051465326&view=1up&seq=16.

8 Arthur Conan Doyle, *A Study in Scarlet* (London: Penguin, 2011), 22.

9 Edgar A. Poe, "The Murder in the Rue Morgue," 166.

10 Arthur Conan Doyle, *A Study in Scarlet*, 20.

11 Edgar A. Poe, "The Murder in the Rue Morgue," 171.

12 Arthur Conan Doyle, "The Yellow Face," in *The Memoirs of Sherlock Holmes* (London: Penguin 2011), 38–39.

13 Clive Emsley, *A Short History of Police and Policing* (Oxford: Oxford University Press, 2021), 113–114.

14 Ibid. 116.

15 Bob Morris, "History of Criminal Investigation," in *Handbook of Criminal Investigation*, edited by Tim Newburn, Tom Williamson, and Alan Wright (London: Routledge, 2007), 20.

16 Christine R. Simpson, "Marple, Miss Jane," in *The Oxford Companion to Crime & Mystery Writing*, edited by Rosemary Herbert (Oxford: Oxford University Press, 1999), 278.

17 John Dickson Carr, *The Hollow Man* (London: Orion, 2013), 152.

18 David Geherin, "Detectives," 161.

19 Jesper Gulddal, "Clues," in *The Routledge Companion to Crime Fiction*, edited by Janice Allan, Jesper Gulddal, Stewart King, and Andrew Pepper (London: Routledge, 2020), 199.

20 Ibid., 200.

21 Lee Horsley, *Twentieth-Century Crime Fiction* (Oxford: Oxford University Press, 2005), 100.

22 Eric Sandberg, "Peanut-Butter-and-Pickle-Sandwiches: Sue Grafton's Alphabet Series and Everyday Life," *Mean Streets: A Journal of American Crime and Detective Fiction* 1, no. 1 (2020), 75–76.

23 Sue Grafton, *W is for Wasted* (New York: Berkley Books, 2014), 3.

24 Sue Grafton, *Q is for Quarry* (New York: Berkley Books, 2003), 30.

25 Michael Connelly, *The Black Echo* (London: Orion, 2017), 216.

26 Heather Worthington, *Key Concepts in Crime Fiction* (Houndmills: Palgrave Macmillan, 2011), 69.

27 Steven G. Brandl, *Criminal Investigation*, 3rd edition (Thousand Oaks: SAGE Publications, 2014), 3–4.

28 Agatha Christie, *The Mysterious Affair at Styles* (London: HarperCollins, 1989), 45.

29 John Scaggs, "Double Identity: Hard-Boiled Detective Fiction and the Divided 'I,'" in *Investigating Identities: Questions of Identity in Contemporary International Crime Fiction*, edited by Marieke Krajenbrink and Kate M. Quinn (Amsterdam: Rodopi, 2009), 133.

30 LeRoy L. Panek, *The Special Branch: The British Spy Novel, 1890–1980* (Bowling Green: Bowling Green University Popular Press, 1981), 226.

31 Michael Connelly, *The Black Echo*, 222.

32 Ibid., 105. As the series progresses, Bosch eventually retires, and subsequently works as a private investigator.

33 Ibid., 12.

34 Ibid., 65.

35 Ibid., 123, 121.

36 Ibid., 170.

37 Ibid., 364, 424.

38 Haia Shpayer-Makov, *The Ascent of the Detective: Police Sleuths in Victorian and Edwardian England* (Oxford: Oxford University Press, 2011), 230.

39 Charles Dickens, *Bleak House* (London: Penguin, 2012), 371, 373.

40 Philip Collins, *Dickens and Crime* (Bloomington, IN: Indiana University Press, 1968), 213.

41 Marshall McLuhan, *The Mechanical Bride: The Folklore of Industrial Man* (London: Routledge & Kegan Paul, 1951), 108.

42 James F. O'Brien, *The Scientific Sherlock Holmes: Cracking the Case with Science and Forensics* (Oxford: Oxford University Press, 2013), xx.

43 Arthur Conan Doyle, *The Sign of Four* (London: Penguin, 2014), 4–5.

44 James F. O'Brien, *The Scientific Sherlock Holmes*, 50.

45 Arthur Conan Doyle, "The Norwood Builder," in *The Return of Sherlock Holmes* by Arthur Conan Doyle (London: Penguin, 2008), 52, 59.

46 Arthur Conan Doyle, "A Scandal in Bohemia," in *The Adventures of Sherlock Holmes* by Arthur Conan Doyle (London: Penguin, 2011), 10.

47 Steven G. Brandl, *Criminal Investigation*, 272.

48 Robert Gerwarth, *Hitler's Hangman: The Life of Heydrich* (New Haven, CT: Yale University Press, 2011), 55, 135.

49 Stephen Knight, *Crime Fiction Since 1800: Detection, Death, Diversity*, 2nd edition (Houndmills: Palgrave Macmillan, 2010), 78.

50 Agatha Christie, *The Mysterious Affair at Styles*, 149.

51 A. A. Milne, "Introduction," in *The Red House Mystery* by A. A. Milne (London: Vintage, 2009), x, xi.

52 Dorothy L. Sayers, *Whose Body?* (London: New English Library, 1977), 32.

53 Eric Sandberg, *Dorothy L. Sayers: A Companion to the Mystery Fiction* (Jefferson, NC: McFarland, 2022), 70.

54 Dorothy L. Sayers and Robert Eustace, *The Documents in the Case* (London: New English Library, 1978), 208.

55 Andy Williams, *Forensic Criminology* (London: Routledge, 2015), 1.

56 Ibid.

57 Nicole Kenley, "Global Crime, Forensic Detective Fiction, and the Continuum of Containment," *Canadian Review of Comparative Literature* 46, no. 1 (2019), 96, https://doi.org/10.1353/crc.2019.0006.

58 Nicole Kenley, "Global Crime, Forensic Detective Fiction, and the Continuum of Containment," *Canadian Review of Comparative Literature* 46, no. 1 (2019), 96, https://doi.org/10.1353/crc.2019.0006.

59 Ruth Heholt, "Kay Scarpetta: Patricia Cornwell (1956–)," in *100 Greatest Literary Detectives* edited by Eric Sandberg (Lanham, MD: Rowman & Littlefield, 2018), 165.

60 Patricia Cornwell, *Post-Mortem* (London: Warner Books, 1992), 5.

61 Ibid., 92.

62 Ibid., 43.

63 Ibid., 113.

64 Ibid., 27.

65 Nicole Kenley, "Global Crime, Forensic Detective Fiction, and the Continuum of Containment," 100.

66 Patricia Cornwell, *Post-Mortem*, 82.

67 Ibid., 82–83.

68 Ronald R. Thomas, *Detective Fiction and the Rise of Forensic Science* (Cambridge: Cambridge University Press, 1999), 3.

69 Ibid.

70 Evelyn M. Maeder and Richard Corbett, "Beyond Frequency: Perceived Realism and the CSI Effect," *Canadian Journal of Criminology and Criminal Justice 57*, no. 1 (2015), 84.

71 Tom Hillenbrand, *Drone State*, translated by Laura Caton (n.p.: Prinn & Junzt, 2014), 32.

72 Ibid., 96.

73 Ibid.

74 Florian Zappe and Andrew Gross, "Introduction," in *Surveillance I Society I Culture*, edited by Florian Zappe and Andrew Grosee (Berlin: Peter Lang, 2019), 10.

75 Fraser Sampson, "Cyberspace: The new frontier for policing?," in *Cyber Crime and Cyber Terrorism Investigator's Handbook*, edited by Babak Akhgar, Andrew Staniforth, and Francesca Bosco (Amsterdam: Elsevier, 2014), 6.

76 Paul Bischoff, "Surveillance Camera Statistics: Which Cities have the Most CCTV Cameras?," *Comparitech.com*, July 11, 2022, www.comparitech.com/vpn-privacy/the-worlds-most-surveilled-cities/.

77 Heike Henderson, "Mapping the Future? Contemporary German-Language Techno Thrillers," *Crime Fiction Studies* 1, no. 1 (2020), 101.

9   Experiencing Crime

Crime takes the form of a grammatically complete sentence: when a crime occurs, someone does something to someone. There are exceptions to this rule, but they are so unusual that they receive a special label; these are so-called victimless crimes, and, as an early work on the subject notes, the term 'is subject to much controversy'.[1] There is in the first instance no clear consensus on which crimes are in fact victimless. Some people would consider morality offenses as prototypical victimless crimes; drug use and prostitution, for example, are behaviours which while undoubtedly risky, arguably have no substantial impact on anyone other than the person doing drugs or selling sex. Many other people—and many or indeed most judicial systems—nonetheless view these activities as criminal. Some might point to the fact that self-victimization is nonetheless victimization, and is seldom entirely based on free choice, or to the generally ignored victimization suffered by non-participant residents of areas where victimless crimes like drug use or sex work are carried out.[2] Similarly, while some financial crimes, like credit card or insurance fraud, are sometimes seen as victimless (losses are absorbed by the financial system in general rather than by any particular individual), a recent study argues that it can have serious consequences for those involved ranging from depression to health problems.[3] All of which is to point out that even victimless crimes have, or can be construed as having, victims. Again, crime takes the form of a sentence, with a subject, a verb, and, even when it is not immediately apparent, an object.

Despite this fact, however, the discourses of both criminology and crime fiction have tended to be directed towards the subject and verb of the criminal sentence, focusing their attention on the people who commit crimes and the nature of the crimes they commit. This is perfectly understandable. If criminological theory is intended first to understand and then to reduce crime, it makes sense to attend to the motivations and circumstances of the people committing the crimes and on the crimes they commit. We thus

DOI: 10.4324/9781003156581-12

find throughout the history of criminology any number of approaches that focus on the perpetrator. Classical criminological theory was built around the self-interest and free will of the criminal, but had little interest in the victims of this behaviour; Cesar Lombroso and his school of criminologists postulated a different explanation for criminal behaviour, and had a great deal to say about the criminal as a biological and psychological type, but had equally little to say about the victim. Similar observations can be made about other, more recent approaches. Many, indeed almost all, of the major theoretical criminological paradigms developed in the twentieth and twenty-first centuries, from Travis Hirschi's social bond/social control theory (non-criminal behaviour arises out of 'prosocial values, prosocial people, and prosocial institutions')[4] to Terrie Moffit's life course theory (distinguishing between 'life-course persistent offenders' and 'adolescent-limited offenders') are dedicated to understanding the transgressive activities of the criminal.[5] It is only relatively recently that criminologists and other scholars have begun to study 'crime victims and the circumstances surrounding their victimization'.[6]

Missing Victims

If crime fiction is seen as a form of discourse aimed at the cultural processing of criminal behaviour, its focus on the figure of the criminal and his or her actions makes good sense—and good stories. It is thus unsurprising that for much of its history the crime genre has paid relatively little attention to victims, or to the impact of criminal behaviour on individuals, families, communities, and society. As Rebecca Mills argues, while in many crime fiction narratives, the victims' personalities, bodies, and lives are examined for their evidentiary values as clues, and perhaps also to evoke readerly sympathy for their suffering, the results of this process at times cast blame on the victims (whose personality or lifestyle may be presented as contributing to their fate), or simply 'dehumanize and de-individualize the victim, as the corpse becomes evidence [...] and the personality is reduced to a type'.[7] Instead, as Mills goes on to point out, narrative attention is lavished on the criminal, both in terms of their psychological profile and their criminal methodology, or on the behaviour of figures like the investigators, witnesses, and suspects.[8] This leaves little or no room within the text for the victims of crime.

Consider for example the narrative model of the Golden Age mystery, with its focus on clues and logical deduction. Here, the victim of a given crime frequently appears as little more than an excuse for the beginning of the detective plot, a 'cipher' or 'signal for a battle of wits to begin' between the criminal and the detective on the one hand, the author and the reader on the other.[9] In part this is a structural feature of narrative form. As Tzvetan Todorov points out, this type of novel (he calls it the 'whodunnit') is built around a fundamental split or 'duality'. It 'contains not one but two stories: the story of the crime and the story of the investigation. In their purest form, these stories have no points in common'. The story of the crime comes first in chronological terms, and in fact ends before the second story starts.[10] We read, however, the second story (that of the investigation), not the first (that of the crime), and only through the second story learn about or gain the information we need to reconstruct the first. Critically, the victim belongs to this hidden or concealed first story, what Ernst Bloch calls 'the darkness before the beginning', appearing in the second only as a corpse.[11] And the corpses of Golden Age fiction are frequently, as Gill Plain argues, 'intensely underwritten', 'empty signifiers' whose 'corporeal complexity' is 'secondary to their function as instigators of narrative causality'.[12] In Agatha Christie's *The Murder of Roger Ackroyd*, for example, the most salient fact about Roger Ackroyd is that he has been murdered. Nothing else about his life or personality or experience is of particular relevance to the novel. The same could be said of the victims in many other Golden Age crime novels.

Even in more recent crime fiction, the focus of narrative attention seldom rests on the victim except insofar as their life (such as their family or professional situation, or their personality) might yield clues to fuel the investigation. Val McDermid's 1995 *The Mermaids Singing*, for instance, devotes lavish attention to the psychology of the serial killer 'Handy Andy'. Along with the profiler Tony Hill (and his police partner Carol Jordan), readers spend much of the novel trying to 'find [their] way into Handy Andy's head and map a path through the tortured labyrinth of his unique logic'.[13] The novel's multiple victims appear as the object of their killer's obsessive desire and savage violence, but are otherwise of interest only insofar as their lifestyle similarities contribute to Hill's profile. Hill notes in *The Last Temptation* (2002) that 'before he could contemplate a profile of the killer, he first had to profile the victims'.[14] This sounds promising, seeming to give the traditionally neglected victim an unexpected level of attention, but it nonetheless renders them (however inadvertently) secondary or subordinate to their killer. They become a means to an end: the victims of crime here are 'usually as much a physical signature as the actions the offender took to make the crime uniquely his'.[15] They are, this implies, a sort of product of the killer.

Victim-Centred Criminology

As I noted before, in recent years the object of the criminal sentence, the victim, has gradually come to assume greater importance both within criminological theory and the criminal justice system. In the first instance, a number of approaches have been developed that emphasize the fact that it is not possible to understand crime—how and why it occurs—without understanding victimization, or the processes by which people become victims of crime.[16] According to Bonnie S. Fisher, Bradford W. Reyns, and John Sloan III's useful analysis of the development and typology of victimology theories, this victim-centred approach has been conceptualized in a number of different ways. Early work in the field focused on the concept of victim precipitation, an approach which indicates that victims in some way make a contribution to the criminal event that affects them, and developed elaborate typologies of victims based on, for example, psychological attributes or degrees of responsibility for their victimization.[17] This developed into (or was supplemented and/or replaced by) approaches that emphasized the role of opportunity in victimization: lifestyle exposure theory points out that victimization is not random, but disproportionately affects some groups (based on, for example, age, gender, or marital status), while routine activity theory emphasizes changes in everyday life patterns (such as greater participation of women in the labour force) that create criminal opportunities.[18] This has, broadly speaking, remained the dominant paradigm in victimization studies, with questions of opportunity and lifestyle central to discussions of who becomes the victims of crime and why they do so.

It is worth noting that the victim-centred approach has had a major and important impact on the criminal justice system in many parts of the world, largely through the victim support movement. This can be seen as the place where 'the professional interests of the police, the care agencies, the academic world and the policy field come together' in practices such victim compensation schemes and mediation programmes.[19] While this sounds very positive, it is not entirely unproblematic. As Lucy Welsh, Layla Skinns, and Andrew Sanders write, in the British context the victim movement has grown in influence in terms of both 'substance and rhetoric', not because it is necessarily 'synonymous with increased rights for victims' but because 'crime control policies are often (spuriously) justified in this way'.[20] In other words, the natural and laudable concern for the victims of crime which is addressed by victim-oriented programmes can be used as window-dressing for an otherwise 'repressive criminal justice policy'[21] and used to justify, for example, inequitable and biased stop-and-search policies that disproportionately affects minorities.

Victim-Centred Crime Fiction

This transformation within criminology and criminal justice has also appeared in more recent works of crime fiction, where at times the focus has shifted away from the traditional criminal-investigator binary towards a greater awareness of victims. Historian of the form Martin Edwards has traced this shift back to the 1940s and novels like Vera Caspary's *Laura*,[22] but it has only become a regular feature of the genre more recently than this, probably from the late twentieth century onwards. I would like to take as a first example a fairly standard work of crime fiction by Ruth Rendell in order to illustrate the way this re-focussing of attention can work.

Rendell, who died in 2015, was for many decades one of Britain's most successful and critically acclaimed crime novelists. A recent appreciation describes her as a 'mistress of dark adaptation, shifting her perspective to explore and interrogate the lives and minds of the disturbed, the abnormal, the transgressive'.[23] This is a fair assessment of much of Rendell's work, and indeed a fair description of a great deal of contemporary crime fiction, but its focus on the figure of the criminal does not apply well to *Road Rage* (1997), one of Rendell's long-running (1964–2013) Inspector Wexford series.

This police novel pays an unexpected level of attention to what it is like not to commit a crime, or investigate it, but to experience it as a victim. This attention appears first in an almost comic, and certainly a dismissive, register. Tanya Payne works as a receptionist at a car hire firm in the (fictional) town of Kingsmarkham. Early in the novel, she is the victim of a seemingly senseless workplace robbery. Her first response when questioned by the police about the crime is to demand attention precisely as a victim: 'I'm confused now. They tied me up and gagged me and it was *horrible* and I want counselling. I'm a victim'.[24] When a police office visits her again to continue the investigation, she at first imagines that he is a 'concerned social worker checking up on whether she had been given the counselling she had asked for'.[25] Payne is a 'total solipsist', and the implication here is that an over-emphasis on victimhood is a sign of this personal failing.[26] As Ross McGarry and Sandra Walklate note in their study of victimhood, 'to acquire victim status, an individual's victimisation must be acknowledged by others'.[27] Here, Payne's victimhood is formally acknowledged by the police, but rejected by the novel as a whole.

However, as the plot develops, Rendell substantially modifies this perspective. Payne's experience was only one step in a larger kidnapping plot, in which an (apparent) environmental terrorist group attempts to stop the construction of a bypass road through an ecologically sensitive area by taking hostages. Inspector Wexford's wife Dora is through sheer bad luck one of the hostages, and Wexford is thus in the improbable and uncomfortable position of investigating his own wife's disappearance. The impact of this event transforms his self-perception: 'He walked about, looking at things, not seeing, aware that eyes were on him in a new and curious way. He had become a victim'.[28] When Dora is released by the kidnappers, she is also presented as a victim (though like her husband, and unlike Payne, as a reticent and stoic one who refuses to self-dramatize her experiences). She delays medical attention to provide evidence for the investigation, but is so obviously traumatized, looking 'pale' and 'tired' after her ordeal,[29] that a senior officer asks if it might help 'her to have counselling'.[30]

This is all relatively mild, of course, and *Road Rage* remains generally focused on the more traditional material of crime fiction. But it does offer evidence for a shift in narrative focus towards the realities of experiencing crime, and towards the fact that victims of crime may want 'compensation and support' instead of or in addition to the 'retribution and revenge' that are traditionally offered by both the real-world judicial system and by crime fiction.[31] The information provided in the novel about the experiences (and sufferings) of the other hostages is also an indication of this shift in focus: one suffers from debilitating claustrophobia, while another develops a version of Stockholm syndrome. Equally important is the experience of the extended circle of victims, those (like Wexford) whose loved ones have been kidnapped (and in one case died):

> To suggest counselling to this woman, some kind of bereavement support, would be insulting. All he could do was look at her and say, feeling how wretchedly inadequate it was, 'I am very, very sorry. You have my deepest sympathy'.[32]

This new emphasis also appears at the level of the novel's mystery plotting. As the investigation progresses, Wexford repeatedly tells his team that 'the backgrounds of the hostages should be of no particular interest to them or their operation'.[33] These are apparently random hostages, after all, and the individual life histories and experiences of the victims are irrelevant to the investigation, just as they are to the typical crime narrative. Yet in this case, the opposite proves to be true; the solution to the mystery lies precisely in the backgrounds of the hostages (some of whom are not actually victims, but the criminals). Rendell's plotting thus indicates that attention to the experience of victimization is not only a moral good and a social obligation but also a key aspect of the investigative process. If the criminal event is, to go back to the metaphor with which I started this chapter, a grammatically complete sentence, it is illegible without its object.

New Victims

While *Road Rage* represents only a tentative fictional embrace of this stance, other, more recent works of crime fiction have made the victim and the experience of victimization much more central to their narrative texture. One key feature of this development has been a new awareness that victimization is not a uniform phenomenon. While it is true that the statistical information consistently indicates that men experience (or at least report) higher rates of personal victimization, the victims of many key types of criminal activity are disproportionately children, women, and the elderly.[34] A great deal of the attention of the victims' right movement has been directed towards the first two of these groups; indeed, one of the main motivating factors in the development of victims' rights was a feminist response to 'victim-blaming arguments' that were until quite recently a lamentably common feature of the judicial response to crimes targeting women such as sexual assault and domestic violence.[35] Many recent crime narratives (in both crime fiction and the adjacent field of true crime) have, like the victims' rights movement, responded to this fact by focusing on women and children and their experience of victimization, thus displacing to a certain extent the traditional interest in the (frequently male) perpetrator and investigator.

The first example of this phenomenon I would like to consider is Kate Atkinson's 2004 *Case Histories*, the first novel in what is often referred to as the Jackson Brodie series. This sounds conventional enough—an ex-police officer turned private eye is not exactly a ground-breaking concept—but *Case Histories* places an unusual amount of narrative attention on the victims of a series of interlinked crimes. In part, this may be because Atkinson is more interested in character than plot. As Brien Diemert points out in his monograph on the author, she builds her work not around crime itself, but around the characters it affects.[36] The fact that Atkinson has distanced herself from the crime fiction label is also significant: she has described *Case Histories*, for instance, as 'just my novel with crime in it'.[37]

This relative freedom from generic convention may well have contributed to Atkinson's refocusing of the narrative on the experience of the victims. This includes both the primary victims of crime—in this case women and children—and the secondary victims, generally family, created by the experience of bereavement. One of the multiple mysteries Brodie investigates, for example, concerns the unsolved, and seemingly inexplicable, murder of Laura Wyre. Not only do we learn about Laura herself (her life, her personality, and so on) in greater detail than is generically typical, but we also learn about the continuing impact of her death on her father, who keeps the equivalent of a 'police incident room' in his house complete with 'ghastly pictures of his daughter's body'.[38] Wyre is, as Brodie notes, 'stuck somewhere near the beginning of the bereavement process' ten years after his daughter's murder, refusing or simply unable to 'get on with his life'.[39] Similarly, when two women hire Brodie to investigate their baby sister's disappearance 34 years ago, it is gradually revealed that this disappearance, stemming from their recently deceased father's crimes (he was a child abuser and rapist) has profoundly impacted the shape of their lives, and that of their older sister, the main target of their father's abuse and the accidental killer of the missing girl. Overall, the narrative suggests very powerfully that victimization is not a one-off event, but an ongoing process; that it is not limited to the individual who is in legal terms the victim of a given crime, but ramifies widely within families and society more generally; and that this experience, this reality, is every bit as important as the crime itself or the process of solving it. Indeed, Brodie's primary strength as an investigator is not his intellect, or intuition, or intrepidity, but as Diemert observes the fact that he 'easily identifies with victims and with their family members'.[40]

This sort of focus on the victim's experience, and particularly on the experience of women (and children) as victims is having an undeniable impact on contemporary crime fiction. Consider the success, for example, of works like Alice Sebold's *The Lovely Bones* (2002), Emma Donoghue's *Room* (2010), and Abigail Dean's *Girl A* (2021), all of which focus not, in the words of one reviewer, on the question of 'who committed a crime' but instead on 'how to carry on with life in its aftermath'.[41] It is possible—although only possible—that we are near the beginning of fundamental re-orientation of crime fiction away from perpetrators and towards victims.

Although it would be rash to speculate as to the long-term success of this new form of victim-oriented fiction (the traditional criminal–crime–investigator–investigation pattern is still dominant), those who applaud this development (such as author Amanda Kabak, who notes that while 'crime is everywhere and in seemingly every form' the perspective of the victim 'is largely underrepresented')[42] can take some comfort from the success of true crime victim-centred narratives on both screen and page. Consider, for example, the 2019 Netflix mini-series *Unbelievable* dealing with the aftermath of a series of rapes in the northwest United States, and the reluctance of the police to accept victim testimony, or Ed Perkins' 2019 documentary about the long-term impact of child abuse on survivors, *Tell Me Who I Am*. Another example is Ken Burns' 2012 *The Central Park Five*, which focuses on the victims not of crime as it is traditionally depicted, but on the victims of a miscarriage of justice, and in doing so complicates or challenges notions of what exactly constitutes victimhood. Even much more traditional true crime narratives, like Netflix's 2022 series *Monster: The Jeffrey Dahmer Story*, have to grapple with this shifting focus, if only due to the public and critical backlash they can face for what has been described as the 'apparent glamorisation of a serial killer and perceived insensitivity towards the families of Dahmer's victims'.[43]

While victim-oriented perspectives can lead to critical and conceptual challenges to more traditional perpetrator-oriented crime narratives, the reverse is equally true. Consider the example of British-American historian

Hallie Rubenhold's 2019 *The Five: The Untold Lives of the Women Killed by Jack the Ripper*. This is a work that is directly and openly opposed to the longstanding focus of 'Ripperology' on the identity of the infamous nineteenth-century serial killer and his possible motives. Rubenhold focuses instead on 'the story of the canonical five victims of the Ripper' through what has been described as 'a feminist victimological perspective'.[44] Her conclusion that the victims were not, as has generally been claimed, sex workers, has aroused heated controversy (particularly in online Ripper fandom communities), in part because she challenges long-held beliefs in a dense and crowded field that is almost uniquely situated at the intersection of academic and public interest, but also because of the very choice of her narrative and historical focus. By not identifying a potential suspect, by ignoring the countless possible identities that have clustered around the Ripper label, Rubenhold undercuts one of the central focuses of criminological activity. Placing victims and their life experiences at the centre of a crime narrative, whether it in true crime or crime fiction, can thus represent a real challenge to widely held perceptions of crime and the ways in which it should be understood.

Notes

1   Wendy Serbin Smith, *Victimless Crime: A Selected Bibliography* (n.p.: National Institute of Law Enforcement and Criminal Justice, 1977), v.
2   Richard A. Aborisade, Adeleke A. Oladele, and Oshileye A. Temitope, "Victims of the 'Victimless Crimes': The Narratives of Residents of Red-Light Districts in Ibadan, Nigeria," *Gender & Behaviour* 16, no. 1 (2018), 10874.
3   Mark Button, Chris Lewis, and Jacki Tapley, "Not a Victimless Crime: The Impact of Fraud on Individual Victims and their Families," *Security Journal* 27, no. 1 (2014), 52, 43.
4   Travis C. Pratt, Jacinta M. Gau, and Travis W. Franklin, *Key Ideas in Criminology and Criminal Justice* (Thousand Oaks, CA: Sage Publications, 2011), 58.
5   Ibid., 157.
6   Bonnie S. Fisher, Bradford W. Reyns, and John Sloan III, *Introduction to Victimology: Contemporary Theory, Research, and Practice* (New York: Oxford University Press, 2016), 7.
7   Rebecca Mills, "Victims," in *The Routledge Companion to Crime Fiction*, edited by Janice Allan, Jesper Gulddal, Stewart King, and Andrew Pepper (London: Routledge, 2020), 149.
8   Ibid.
9   Martin Edwards, "Victim", in *The Oxford Companion to Crime and Mystery Writing*, edited by Catherine Aird and John M. Reilly (Oxford: Oxford University Press, 1999), 478.
10 Tzvetan Todorov, "The Typology of Detective Fiction," in *The Poetics of Prose*, translated by Richard Howard (Oxford: Basil Blackwell, 1977), 44.

11 Ernest Bloch, "A Philosophical View of the Detective Novel," in *Literary Essays,* translated by Andrew Joron et al. (Stanford: Stanford University Press, 1998), 219.

12 Gill Plain, *Twentieth-Century Crime Fiction: Gender, Sexuality, and the Body* (Edinburgh, Edinburgh University Press, 2001), 31.

13 Val McDermid, *The Mermaids Singing* (London: HarperCollins, 2006), 212.

14 Val McDermid, *The Last Temptation* (New York: St Martin's Paperbacks, 2003), 220.

15 Ibid., 224.

16 Fisher et al., *Introduction to Victimology,* 8.

17 Ibid., 11–13.

18 Ibid., 36–43.

19 Hans Boutellier, *Crime and Morality: The Significance of Criminal Justice in Post-Modern Culture* (Dordrecht, NL: Kluwer Academic Publishers, 2000), 61.

20 Lucy Welsh, Layla Skinns, and Andrew Sanders, *Sanders and Young's Criminal Justice,* 5th edition (Oxford: Oxford University Press, 2021), 606.

21 Boutellier, *Crime and Morality,* 61.

22 Edwards, "Victim", 479.

23 Andrew Wilson, "Ruth Rendell: An Appreciation," *Contemporary Women's Writing* 11, no. 1 (2017), 123.

24 Ruth Rendell, *Road Rage* (London: Arrow Books, 1998), 40.

25 Ibid., 119.

26 Ibid.

27 Ross McGarry and Sandra Walklate, *Victims: Trauma, Testimony and Justice* (London: Routledge, 2015), 16.

28 Ibid., 96–97.

29 Rendell, *Road Rage,* 166.

30 Ibid., 193.

31 Antony Pemberton and Inge Vanfraechem, "Victims' Victimization Experiences and their Need for Justice," in *Victims and Restorative Justice* (London: Routledge, 2015), 37.

32 Ibid., 355.

33 Ibid., 142.

34 Fisher et al., *Introduction to Victimology,* 176–177.

35 William G. Doerner and Steven P. Lab, *Victimology,* 6th edition (Amsterdam: Elsevier, 2012), 14.

36 Brian Diemert, *Understanding Kate Atkinson* (Columbia, SC: University of South Carolina Press, 2020), 51.

37 Amy Scribner, "Kate Atkinson: Scandal in Scotland," *BookPage,* October 2006, https://bookpage.com/interviews/8372-kate-atkinson#.YYi_h-mQyUk.

38 Kate Atkinson, *Case Histories* (New York: Back Bay Books, 2005), 105.

39 Ibid., 106.

40 Diemert, *Understanding Kate Atkinson,* 54.

41 Flynn Berry, "What Happens to Siblings Who Survive a House of Horrors?" *The New York Times,* February 2, 2021, www.nytimes.com/2021/02/02/books/review/girl-a-abigail-dean.html.

42 Amanda Kabak, "We Need More Victim-Focused Narratives," *Crime Reads*, July 19, 2021, https://crimereads.com/we-need-more-victim-focused-nar ratives/.

43 Michele Ruyters, Greg Stratton, and Jarryd Bartle, "'They're Making Money off Tragedy'—Netflix's Dahmer Series Shows the Dangers of Fictionalising Real Horrors," *The Conversation*, October 10, 2022, https://theconversation. com/theyre-making-money-off-tragedy-netflixs-dahmer-series-shows-the-dang ers-of-fictionalising-real-horrors-192006.

44 Paul Bleakley, "A New Front in the History Wars? Responding to Rubenhold's Feminist Revision of the Ripper," *Criminology & Criminal Justice* 22, no. 5 (2021), 660.

10 Punishing Crime

Every example of the criminal event considered as a complete process begins with an individual or a group of individuals transgressing a social boundary that has been codified in law as a criminal offence. It continues through a process of investigation more or less rigorous depending on circumstance, and ends either with an escape from the strictures of justice, in which the criminal eludes judicial processes and legal responsibility for their actions, or with some sort of a response on the part of society to the criminal activity in question, ranging from a fine to imprisonment to execution. However, crime fiction has been somewhat reluctant to deal with what might be described as the conclusion of the cycle of crime, and for early examples of fictional engagement with retribution we have to look to the margins of the crime fiction genre, and works like Feodor Dostoyevsky's 1866 *Crime and Punishment* and Émile Zola's 1867 *Thérèse Raquin.*

Punishment and Genre

The first observation it is important to make about Dostoyevsky and Zola's novels is that their interest in punishment, in the broadest sense, is one of several factors that places them outside the boundaries of the crime fiction genre. While there is an investigator present in *Crime and Punishment*— the police detective Porfiry Petrovich—there is no mystery. Readers have full access to the young Raskolnikov's planning and (extremely clumsy) implementation of a double murder and robbery. His behaviour following the crime seems intended to draw suspicion to himself, and Petrovich has little doubt as to his guilt (even when someone else confesses). In addition, the novel is intensely interested in Raskolnikov's punishment, both in terms of his personal and persistent sense of guilt (and his struggle against it—'I only killed a louse' he claims at one point, 'a useless, nasty, pernicious louse'),[1] and in legal terms. In the novel's epilogue, we learn that 'the court proceedings in his case went without great difficulties', and that a

DOI: 10.4324/9781003156581-13

range of extenuating circumstances 'contributed in the end to mitigating the accused man's sentence'.[2] The final result is 'penal servitude of the second class for a term of only eight years', and the novel even follows him a year into his sentence, at which point the narrator indicates that this is the start of a new story, one of 'gradual regeneration'.[3]

Similarly, there is no mystery surrounding the titular protagonist of *Thérèse Raquin* and her lover Laurent's murder of her husband Camille. Readers have full access to its background, motivation, planning, and execution. There is a police presence here, as well, but rather than investigating and solving Camille's murder, these are 'imbeciles' who are inadvertently 'protecting' Thérèse and Laurent 'from all suspicion'.[4] And like Dostoyevsky, Zola is fascinated by the punishment that follows crime, in this case an informal but highly effective punishment for the very success of the murder. Thérèse and Laurent are haunted by persistent hallucinations of their victim, and 'their marriage' and 'the anguish generated by their union' is 'the inevitable punishment for the murder'.[5] Their only escape from the psychological torment they suffer as a result of their crime is joint suicide.

All of this—the lack of mystery, the lack of sustained interest in a police investigation, and the emphasis on both formal and informal punishment—is exceptional in terms of crime fiction's traditional interests and patterns. This is a genre that is generally interested in criminals and their motivations; the actual crimes they commit; the investigators who are responsible for exploring these crimes and uncovering the concealed truth about them; and, to a lesser extent, the impact of these crimes on individuals and society. There are of course some exceptions to this tendency: the hugely popular legal thrillers of a writer like John Grisham (e.g. *The Firm*, 1991) are obviously concerned with legal processes, trials, and the ensuing punishments. But as the name of the genre suggests, these books are somewhat peripheral to crime fiction in general. In many or even most forms of crime fiction, what happens to the criminals after the detective's investigation is of little interest.

Criminology, Criminal Justice, and Punishment

Punishment is, however, of prime interest to theoreticians and practitioners of both criminology and criminal justice. Criminology adopts a range of critical approach to the law and how it is applied in society, while criminal justice studies the implementation of the law as it operates within the overall criminal justice system. But both fields are deeply interested in punishment. The origins of criminology as a coherent field of study, for example, lie in eighteenth-century efforts to reform the criminal justice system, with punishment being a specific target of critique.[6] As was discussed in Chapter 1, Cesare Beccaria is frequently seen as the father of the classical school of criminology, and his *On Crimes and Punishments* (1764) was, as its title suggests, specifically interested in how society should respond to the criminal's abrogation of the implied social contract with punishment 'in a manner that ultimately benefited society' through a process of deterrence based on 'certainty, severity, and promptness'.[7] Similarly, as Julian V. Roberts notes, the question of why to punish offenders, and how to punish them are 'the oldest and most fundamental [...] in criminal justice'.[8] After all, while criminologists may theorize about the nature of appropriate and effective punishments, members of the criminal justice system have to actually put these theories into practice through a range of punitive practices that must consider both 'the seriousness of the harm caused' and the 'risk the offender may pose to society'.[9]

Crime fiction is in many ways linked to this eighteenth-century transformation in attitudes towards crime and its punishment. As we have seen in Chapter 3, while crime fiction as a genre has an extensive and fascinating pre-history with many very early forms of literature including scenes of criminal activity, it was only with the rise of modern judicial systems from the eighteenth century onwards that crime fiction began to develop as a powerful and popular genre in its own right. In part this is related to transformations in punishments. In the pre-modern era, crime was largely attributed to and explained by supernatural forces—'spiritualism and demonology'—and legal systems were structured around this point of view. There was thus little room for the sort of investigative pattern that forms the backbone of crime fiction.

While torture as an investigative tool was not widely used in all jurisdictions (in England for example, only 89 warrants for torture were issued by the Crown between 1540 and 1640),[10] punishments were, and long remained, extraordinarily ferocious. In his *Discipline and Punish: The Birth of the Prison* (1975), Michel Foucault details the horrific penalty exacted upon the attempted regicide Robert-François Damiens in 1757:

[...] he was to be 'taken and conveyed in a cart [...] to the Placede Grève, where, on a scaffold that will be erected there, the flesh will be torn from his breasts, arms, thighs and calves with red-hot pincers, his right hand, holding the knife with which he committed the said parricide, burnt with sulphur, and, on those places where the flesh will be torn away, poured molten lead, boiling oil, burning resin, wax and sulphur melted together and then his body drawn and quartered by four horses and his limbs and body consumed by fire, reduced to ashes and his ashes thrown to the wind.[11]

This execution was witnessed by Giacomo Casanova (better-known for his amorous adventures), who recorded in his memoirs that he 'had to turn aside from the sight of the martyrdom of this victim of the Jesuits, and to stop [his] ears to keep out his piercing shrieks of agony'.[12] Casanova's sympathy, however, was not shared by his companions, who seem to have been unmoved by the spectacle of Damiens' suffering—two of them in fact spent the hours of the torture 'teasing and cajoling and caressing' each other, a perhaps extreme example of the fact that public executions offered spectators opportunities for pleasure.[13]

Early forms of crime writing tend to downplay this potential pleasure in the suffering of others in favour of what is presented as moral edification. The *Newgate Calendar*, for example, offered eighteenth- and nineteenth-century readers records of a selection of crimes, testimonies, and executions. There certainly was an element of pleasure to be had in the just punishment of villainy—this is a form of literary *schadenfreude*—but there is generally an element of moral redemption integrated into the narrative. James Sparr, William Sparry, and William Biddle, for example, may have forged the last will and testament of Jeffery Henville to defraud his housekeeper and intended beneficiary Anne Ferte, and once convicted were 'launched into eternity' at the end of a rope, but they all behaved 'penitently and with resolution' on their day at Tyburn.[14] The reader is presumably intended to learn from their punishment—crime doesn't pay—but also from their display of penitence and fortitude in face of death.

This form of public, spectacular, and exemplary punishment was replaced, as Foucault points out, by a regimented system of penal discipline, exemplified in *Discipline and Punish* by a set of rules drawn up in the mid-nineteenth century for a juvenile detention centre. This code involved the minute regimentation of the routines of the incarcerated, from the start of the day 'at six in the morning in winter and at five in summer' to its end at 'half-past seven in summer, half-past eight in winter' when 'the prisoners must be back in their cells [...] undress, and [...] get into bed' with 'supervisors' tasked with maintaining 'order and silence'.[15] For Foucault, the key point is that the modern prison does not exist in isolation; rather it is part of a much larger system of social control involving not just prisons, but also schools, asylums, and factories.[16] Of course, this wide-ranging carceral system was accompanied for many years (and still is in some jurisdictions) by continued recourse to the death penalty or other forms of corporal punishment, though as public execution rapidly comes to be seen as an 'intolerable' and 'shameful' exhibition of 'tyranny, excess, the thirst for revenge' it is generally carried out away from public attention.[17] For my purposes, what is important in this transformation is that this modern rationalization of punishment was part of the general reassessment of crime in the modern world that led to (or coincided with) the proliferation of crime writing in a variety of forms.

Crime Fiction and the Problem of Punishment

Despite this historical synchronicity—or perhaps because of it—crime fiction was, and to some extent remains, generally uninterested in the details of the punishment that awaits its criminals. This is certainly true of classic, nineteenth-century detective fiction, where the detection of the criminal is the primary, indeed at times almost the exclusive focus of attention. Consider the typical narrative pattern of a Sherlock Holmes story, for example. In his *Theory of Prose* (1925), Russian literary theorist Viktor Shklovsky offers a 'general schema' of Conan Doyle's detective stories broken down into nine stages, starting with 'anticipation, conversation concerning previous cases, analysis' and 'the appearance of the client' and concluding with an 'analysis of the facts made by Sherlock Holmes' (which corrects the 'false resolution' offered by the official authorities).[18] What is notably absent from this analysis of Doyle's narrative scaffolding is any reference to punishment. Once the criminal is unmasked, the story ends; neither Holmes nor the reader is much concerned with what comes next, at least not in terms of the official administration of justice.

In the 1891 story 'The Red-Headed League' for example, the criminal John Clay is unmasked by Holmes, but his arrest is little more than a narrative footnote. The 'murderer, thief, smasher, and forger' is captured and taken by cab to Scotland Yard; this is the last we hear of him.[19] The implication is that he will stand trial and no doubt be found guilty, but neither Doyle nor his readers are particularly interested in the details of this process. At other times in Doyle's work less formal resolutions are offered, as in for example the 1892 story 'The Blue Carbuncle'. Here, James Ryder, 'Head Attendant at the Hotel Cosmopolitan' has stolen the titular priceless jewel from a guest.[20] Holmes tracks him down and extracts a confession, but then allows the hapless neophyte criminal to flee, pointing out to Watson that he 'is not retained by the police to supply their deficiencies' and that a penal sentence for Ryder would be counterproductive: 'send him to gaol now, and you make him a gaolbird for life'.[21] Holmes is thus doing the work of the courts for them by distinguishing between the punishments appropriate to a hardened repeat offender (like Clay) and those appropriate to a misguided and sorely tempted but otherwise harmless individual (like Ryder). But in both cases, punishment is an afterthought to the discovery of the criminal and the solution of the mystery.

Another possible extra-judicial resolution available to the classic mystery writer is a convenient death which provides both clear narrative closure and, at times, avoids any discussion of potential ethical ambiguities. In *A Study in Scarlet* (1887), for instance, the murder of two American visitors to London, Enoch Drebber and his secretary Joseph Stangerson, is quickly solved by Sherlock Holmes. The killer is another American, Jefferson Hope, and in the extended narrative analepsis that makes up the second part of the novel, readers learn of his motivation. Many years ago in Utah, Drebber and Stangerson (both Mormons) were involved in the abduction and forced marriage of Hope's fiancé (also a Mormon), and the murder of her father. Hope, despairing of any viable legal route to punish the men for their crime, has 'determined' that he shall act as their 'judge, jury and executioner all rolled into one'.[22] He has even arranged matters so that 'the high God' (or chance) can 'judge between' them: he offers each man a choice of pill, one poisoned, the other harmless, and himself takes the one that remains.[23]

The narrative cards are stacked very clearly against Drebber and Stangerson, the ostensible victims who are in fact the criminals, but nonetheless the 'forms of the law must be complied with' and Hope must appear before the magistrates, charged with murder.[24] This is not, apparently, a satisfying narrative conclusion. In the first place, the 'testimony' of Holmes and Watson at the trial would be entirely redundant—we have already heard it, and repetition would be otiose. In the second place, a formal trial would be, at least potentially, offensive to readers' sense of justice. Sharon Hayes notes that justifications for punishment have traditionally focused on a limited number of concepts: 'retribution, just deserts, deterrence, societal protection, and/or rehabilitation'.[25] Retribution is not a compelling motive in for punishing Hope, as he is in fact already exacting retribution on his victims, and the same can be said for the concept of just deserts. If Hope gets what he deserves, the narrative implies, he will not be going to jail, much less face hanging as a murderer. In fact, Drebber and Stangerson have already gotten what they deserved. Neither deterrence nor societal protection offer a more compelling reason to prosecute Hope, who is unlikely to ever encounter again a set of circumstances as outlandish and provocative as these. Nor is Hope in need of rehabilitation, as he is, barring these two murders, a productive and peaceful member of society. There is thus little to justify his inevitable punishment but the outraged majesty of the law, and the need to protect the state's monopoly on violence. This is of course not the sort of satisfaction a typical reader of crime fiction is looking for. Any punishment Doyle metes out to Hope to satisfy the demands of the law (and to maintain a level of social realism) would thus interfere with the reader's pleasure in seeing villains like Drebber and Stangerson punished. The solution Doyle offers is a *deus ex machina* that dispatches Hope to 'a tribunal where strict justice would be meted out to him': a burst aneurism kills him in his sleep, and saves everyone concerned from facing an ethically uncomfortable situation.[26]

This narrative escape hatch remained popular throughout the Golden Age of interwar detective fiction, which was in general no more interested in the question of punishment than nineteenth-century crime fiction. If, or more accurately when, the criminal is revealed towards the end of a Golden Age novel, and the detective has explained his or her view of the case, that novel tends to stop. What comes next—the entire legal process from arraignment to trial to in all likelihood execution—is quite simply left out. To take a single example, in Agatha Christie's 1942 Miss Marple novel, *The Body in the Library*, the penultimate chapter ends with the capture of one of the novel's two criminals in the very act of attempting yet another murder: the 'iron grasp' and 'voice of the law' are brought to bear in a 'dramatic *finale*' arranged by the ingenious detective.[27] This is followed in the final chapter by Miss Marple's explanation of how she came to suspect the criminals, but Christie provides no information about their ultimate fate. Instead, we learn that two of the other characters in the novel are going to marry, as the criminal plot of the novel transitions smoothly into a romantic plot, and gestures towards that most satisfying and traditional of narrative conclusions, a marriage.

This move is revealing; readers are, it seems uninterested or uncomfortable with the punishment that awaits the victim (to invert, with intentional provocation, the common use of the term) of the detective's activities. After all, until 1965 in Britain, the potential penalty for a conviction for murder was death, and it remains so to this day in many places around the world—in 2021, 18 countries carried out at least 579 executions (a number that does not include the estimated thousands carried out in China).[28] This means that the stakes are high (if only in imaginative terms) for readers. Carol Westron has argued that 'the death penalty was the most potent and exciting cliff-hanger' for Golden Age writers, as 'death was the ultimate gamble'.[29] This is certainly true, but readers do not seem to want to enter into the details of the results of the criminal's failed toss of the dice. After all, as readers we have spent a great deal of time with the criminal character, who almost by default must be a reasonably attractive or at least normal character, one not obviously and malignantly criminal in nature (if they were, we would know whodunnit too quickly). While we may in theory approve of justice being done, we may not want to share the spectacle of, for example, an attractive young woman choking her life out in a hempen noose. This is why, as Miss Marple notes about her plan to catch the murderers in the act in *The Body in the Library*, 'it's so nice to be *sure*, isn't it?'—something of an understatement.[30]

However, even when detectives and readers are sure of who killed whom and how and why, they often remain uncomfortable with the repercussions of this fact. Ignoring the issue through narrative elision is one response; a timely accidental death, as in *A Study in Scarlet*, is another.

A final technique, and one that was very popular during the Golden Age, is having the killer commit suicide. In Agatha Christie's *The Murder of Roger Ackroyd* (1926), for example—'the best known and most widely discussed' novel in Christie's vast body of work—the narrator, Dr James Sheppard, fills the generically typical role of Watson (to Hercule Poirot's Holmes).[31] In a controversial rupture of generic norms, however, Sheppard is ultimately revealed as the murderer. This presents Christie with exactly the difficulty discussed above. Readers have by the end of the novel spent considerable time listening to Sheppard's voice, and become accustomed to his own positive self-presentation. He is, after all, the character who mediates between the average reader and the apparent genius of the detective, and to discover that he is a murderer and thus subject to execution is certainly a shock. There is, however, as Poirot points out to Sheppard, 'one way out'—Sheppard will kill himself with veronal (as the victim of his blackmail, Mrs Ferrars, did), thus offering a 'kind of poetic justice' while at the same time allowing him, and the readers, to avoid the real thing in all its protracted unpleasantness.[32]

The suicide solution also appears in the Lord Peter Wimsey novels of Dorothy L. Sayers, Christie's collaborator and competitor. Like Christie, she at times allows her more personable killers the narrative luxury of a convenient escape from the wheels of justice. In *The Unpleasantness at the Bellona Club* (1928), for instance, the murderer Dr Penberthy is given the opportunity 'to make a clean job of it all' rather than face formal justice, and at the same time to avoid implicating other innocent parties in the inevitable scandal.[33] It is implied that this is because the doctor's wartime service has left him callous, indifferent to human life, and ruthless in pursuit of his goals. In effect, his war service is presented as an extenuating factor. Similarly, the killer in *Murder Must Advertise* (Mr Tallboy) is advised by Lord Peter Wimsey to allow a drug gang to kill him, thus sparing his family the trauma of his arrest and execution, while at the same time demonstrating the sort of personal bravery he associates (the poor fish) with the upper classes: by allowing himself to be killed he will finally 'achieve the Eton touch' that he has vainly aspired to throughout his sad lower-middle-class life.[34] However, even less sympathetic characters are at times offered the same escape. The murderer Mary Whittaker of *Unnatural Death* (1927) is described as an 'evil woman, if ever there was one',[35] but she, too is allowed to evade formal justice through suicide, though it is worth noting that Whittaker is not offered this out by Wimsey, but hangs herself with a bedsheet in her cell after her arrest. We may well need to distinguish here between two types of permission, one homodiegetic, offered by the detective figure as a sort of reward or form of recognition, the other heterodiegetic, offered by the author for narrative convenience.

Crime Fiction and the Rewards of Punishment

Sayers makes a particularly interesting case here. While she certainly makes use of suicide as a form of narrative closure, this does not seem to have been due to a lack of interest in the moral implications of punishment. In fact, Sayers' work demonstrates how a sense of the problematics of justice can inform and deepen detective fiction. In *Strong Poison* (1930), for example, she introduces the character Harriet Vane, who becomes a central investigative (and romantic) partner for Lord Peter Wimsey. When she first appears, however, she is on trial for a murder she did not commit. The novel opens with a lengthy, and generically unusual, court scene and invests a great deal of energy in making the death penalty—so often a mere abstraction—feel real. Some years later, in *Gaudy Night* (1935), a group of Oxford dons debate the efficacy and morality of capital punishment: one argues that while 'murder must be prevented and murderers kept from doing further harm [...] they ought not to be punished and they certainly ought not to be killed'.[36] Others argue that while execution is certainly a deplorable and uncivilized practice, some form of punishment is certainly needed.

It is worth pausing to note that this tension between the need to protect society and the degrading distastefulness of some forms of, or indeed all, punishment is still very much alive. As Hyman Gross writes in *Crime and Punishment: A Concise Moral Critique* (published close to a century after Sayers' novel), 'criminal punishment appears to be indispensable, but it is not a social practice that can fill us with pride'.[37] He goes on to link the punishment of criminals with other 'deeply objectionable' activities that have at different times and places 'enjoyed considerable respectability' including slavery, war, torture, and execution.[38] Sayers' detective Lord Peter Wimsey is himself subject to considerable emotional stress over the implications of his work. In *Whose Body?* (1923) he experiences a recurrence of his post-First World War shellshock when he faces up to the 'very grave responsibility' of having a criminal hanged,[39] and in the last of Sayer's novels (*Busman's Honeymoon* [1937]) Wimsey arranges for the defence of a criminal he has himself caught, and visits him in jail while he awaits execution to request forgiveness. These novels could thus be seen as representing a shift of sorts, a place at which interest in a series of questions about the criminal justice system in general, and in the punishment of criminals in particular, became more acute, and began to play a larger role in crime fiction.

This is an issue that becomes much more important in later twentieth-century and twenty-first-century crime fiction. As Stuart Sim has argued, crime narratives are always to some extent 'morality tales, but of late what those tales are saying is becoming more and more disturbing'.[40] The basic issue here is that while the detective has traditionally operated as a locus of moral value, opposed obviously to the immorality of the criminal, this binary has blurred or even vanished in novels dealing with 'a society apparently sliding into a condition of moral crisis' in which 'neither the justice system nor the legal system are commanding much respect'.[41] This is exacerbated by a widespread mistrust in other social institutions, including both political and business organizations. Some modern crime fiction indicates that in a world where the machinery of justice is broken or functions in favour of elites, detectives may well 'find themselves compelled to commit criminal acts in order to punish criminals'.[42]

This sense of a systematic failure of both the criminal justice system in particular, and of systems of governance more generally, is perceptible as far back as the emergence of hardboiled in America during the interwar years. Dashiell Hammett is well-known for his 'deeply critical and sceptical attitude towards American society'.[43] *Red Harvest* (1929), for instance, tells a story of deeply rooted, intractable governmental corruption: the town of Personville has been taken over more or less completely by organized crime. Fredric Jameson's description of Raymond Chandler's Los Angeles applies just as well to Hammett's novel: it 'takes place inside the microcosm, in the darkness of a local world without the benefit of the federal constitution, as in a world without God'.[44] This is an America re-imagined as a place where 'the rule of naked force and money is complete and undisguised'.[45] Hammett's detective, the nameless Continental Op, is only able to solve the town's problems—and punish those guilty of crime—by first orchestrating a gang fight in which various factions kill each other off, and then by arranging the intervention of the state governor and the National Guard. This level of central authority is, at this point at least, imagined as safe from the taint of corruption, and justice is done—if one is willing to forget that Elihu Willson, the businessman who set in motion the chain of events that led to the town's downfall, faces no consequences for his actions, and as the novel ends has Personville 'back, all nice and clean and ready to go to the dogs again'.[46]

Contemporary Crime Fiction and the Failure of Justice

In more recent crime fiction, even this dubious level of external or formal justice is often unavailable. This is very evident, for example, in the work of James Ellroy. In the 'LA Quartet', which consists of *The Black Dahlia* (1987), *The Big Nowhere* (1988), *LA Confidential* (1990), and *White Jazz* (1992), the Los Angeles Police Department are depicted as both thoroughly corrupt, and, despite its regular recourse to extraordinary levels of brutality, utterly unable to contain the violence that regularly rips through the city. As Sim points out, the main police characters in this novel sequence are driven by a need for 'absolute justice', which is essentially a form of revenge achieved through vigilante activity.[47] In *The Black Dahlia*, for instance, the policeman Dwight 'Bucky' Bleichert tracks down the killer of Elizabeth Short (a real woman whose 1947 murder remains unsolved), one George Tillden, and kills him in an act of vigilante justice. He learns later in the novel that, first, his partner had solved the case long ago, but used the knowledge to blackmail the wealthy Emmett Sprague (Tillden's employer), and second, that the actual killer was Sprague's wife, who goes unpunished. Once the 'legal machinery took over' the rich and powerful are effectively insulated from the repercussions of their actions.[48] This conclusion leaves readers at an impasse: the expected consequence of the standard narrative sequence of crime, investigation, and detection is punishment. But here both formal and informal approaches (the judicial system and vigilante vengeance) fail to achieve the desired and expected goal.

Ellroy's work offers a fine example of the way in which a great deal of contemporary crime writing is built around a sense of the failure of the criminal justice system, or at least a sense of its inability to cope adequately with contemporary criminality. This is particularly true when it deals with what Vincenzo Ruggiero describes as the 'crimes of the powerful' who are often able to elude punishment.[49] These are people who are able, or feel able, to break the law with relative impunity.[50] Crime fiction that deals with questions of gender and/or race in relation to justice, or more accurately injustice, frequently adopts this perspective. For a woman, or a member of a vulnerable minority community, all crimes can be seen as crimes of the powerful, and all offenders as capable of evading formal justice. *A is for Alibi* (1982), for instance, the first novel in Sue Grafton's Alphabet series, famed for its feminist revision of hardboiled norms, ends with an act of violent self-defence on the part of PI Kinsey Millhone. Millhone, the first-person narrator of the novel, has investigated and faced threats from the murderer Charlie Scorsoni; in the novel's final sentence, she proudly proclaims 'I blew him away'.[51] In Stieg Larsson's global phenomenon, *The Girl with the Dragon Tattoo* (2008, first published as *Män som hatar kvinnor*, or *Men Who Hate Women*), the heroine Lisbeth Salander exacts private revenge on her rapist by tattooing a 'message [...] written in caps over five lines that covered his belly, from his nipples to just above his genitals: I AM A SADISTIC PIG, A PERVERT, AND A RAPIST'.[52] This textual fantasy of retribution and permanent labelling of the offender clearly resonated with readers, offering a sign of the way crime fiction can act as an imaginative or fantastic surrogate for actual justice.

This radical mistrust of the efficacy of the justice system has appeared even in the police procedural, a genre which might be expected to exhibit both a greater interest in the workings of the criminal justice system and a greater respect for its capacities. But here, too, we find uncertainty over the efficacy of formal, legal approaches to crime. To take a single example, consider Don Winslow's 2017 novel *The Force*. It deals with the officers of the Manhattan North Special Task Force, a fictional elite crime-fighting squad based on units like the Los Angeles Police Department's CRASH unit, the Baltimore Gun Trace Task Force, and Memphis' SCORPION team that have regularly made the news in the twenty-first century for brutality and corruption. Winslow's fictional unit is, no surprise, brutal and corrupt, and as one reviewer points out, more or less equivalent to the gangs that rule the city, 'all of them lords and barons of their territory, ruling with violence'.[53] The novel's protagonist, Denny Malone, eventually wrestles with his own criminality, and faces up to its consequences, but along the way he carries out a number of vigilante killings of criminals who think they will evade justice. His indictment of the ruling and administrative class of the city is stinging—'I call *you* corrupt. You're the corruption, you're the rot in the soul of this city, this country'—but more performative than effective: 'they got friends in DC' and unlike Malone or the criminals he kills are unlikely to suffer for their crimes.[54] What we are left with here, as in so much recent crime fiction, is a regression to 'the primitive system of revenge' that preceded, and perhaps at least imaginatively still underlies, our own responses to criminal behaviour.[55]

Notes

1 Fyodor Dostoevsky, *Crime and Punishment*, translated by Richard Pevear and Larissa Volokhonsky (London: Vintage, 2007), 416.
2 Ibid., 535–537.
3 Ibid., 537, 551.
4 Émile Zola, *Thérèse Raquin*, translated by Andrew Rothwell (Oxford: Oxford University Press, 2008), 140.
5 Ibid., 169.
6 Travis C. Pratt, Jacinta M. Gau, and Travis W. Franklin, *Key Ideas in Criminology and Criminal Justice* (Thousand Oaks, CA: Sage Publications, 2011), 7.
7 Ibid., 9–10.
8 Julian V. Roberts, *Criminal Justice: A Very Short Introduction* (Oxford: Oxford University Press, 2015), 57.
9 Ibid., 58.
10 Roger Hopkins Burke, *Criminal Justice Theory: An Introduction* (London: Routledge, 2012), 3.
11 Michel Foucault, *Discipline and Punish: The Birth of the Prison*, translated by Alan Sheridan (New York: Vintage, 1995), 3.
12 Giacomo Casanova, *The Memoirs of Jacques Casanova* (New York: Modern Library, 1929), 185.

13 Ibid.
14 *The Complete Newgate Calendar*, volume 4, edited by G. T. Crook (London: Navarre Society, 1926), 4.
15 Foucault, *Discipline and Punish*, 7.
16 Burke, *Criminal Justice Theory*, 19.
17 Foucault, *Discipline and Punish*, 73.
18 Viktor Shklovksy, *Theory of Prose*, translated by Benjamin Sher (Normal, IL: Dalkey Archive Press, 1991), 115.
19 Arthur Conan Doyle, "The Red-Headed League," in *The Adventures of Sherlock Holmes* (London: Penguin, 2011), 78.
20 Arthur Conan Doyle, "The Blue Carbuncle," in *The Adventures of Sherlock Holmes* (London: Penguin, 2011), 199.
21 Ibid., 205.
22 Arthur Conan Doyle, *A Study in Scarlet* (London: Penguin, 2011), 143.
23 Ibid., 151.
24 Ibid., 154.
25 Sharon Hayes, *Criminal Justice Ethics: Cultivating the Moral Imagination* (London: Routledge, 2015), 179.
26 Doyle, *A Study in Scarlet*, 155.
27 Agatha Christie, *The Body in the Library* (London: HarperCollins, 2016), 204, 212.
28 "Executions Around the World." *Death Penalty Information Center*, 2023, https://deathpenaltyinfo.org/policy-issues/international/executions-aro und-the-world.
29 Carol Westron, "The Golden Age: Authors and the Death Penalty Dilemma." *Promoting Crime Fiction by Lizzie Hayes*, December 16, 2018, https://promoti ngcrime.blogspot.com/2018/12/authors-and-death-penalty-dilemma.html.
30 Christie, *The Body in the Library*, 212.
31 Howard Haycraft, *Murder of Pleasure: The Life and Times of the Detective Story* (Mineola, NY: Dover Publications, 2019), 130.
32 Agatha Christie, *The Murder of Roger Ackroyd* (New York: Pocket Books, 1986), 255.
33 Dorothy L. Sayers, *Unpleasantness at the Bellona Club* (New York: HarperPaperbacks, 1995), 236.
34 Dorothy L. Sayers, *Murder Must Advertise* (New York: Harper Paperbacks, 1995), 348.
35 Dorothy L. Sayers, *Unnatural Death* (London: New English Library, 1974), 244.
36 Dorothy L. Sayers, *Gaudy Night* (New York: Avon, 1968), 283.
37 Hyman Gross, *Crime and Punishment: A Concise Moral Critique* (Oxford: Oxford University Press, 2012), 161.
38 Ibid., 161–162.
39 Dorothy L. Sayers, *Whose Body?* (London: New English Library, 1977), 167.
40 Stuart Sim, *Justice and Revenge in Contemporary American Crime Fiction* (Basingstoke: Palgrave Pivot, 2015), 3.
41 Ibid., 2.
42 Ibid., 3.

43 Naremore, James. "Dashiell Hammett and the Poetics of Hard-Boiled Detection," in *Essays on Detective Fiction*, edited by Bernard Benstock (London: Macmillan Press, 1983), 62.
44 Fredric Jameson, *Raymond Chandler: The Detections of Totality* (London: Verso, 2016), 10.
45 Ibid.
46 Dashiell Hammett, *Red Harvest* (New York: Vintage, 1972), 187.
47 Sim, *Justice and Revenge in Contemporary American Crime Fiction*, 16.
48 James Ellroy, *The Black Dahlia* (London: Arrow Books, 2005), 376.
49 Vincenzo Ruggiero, *Power and Crime* (London: Routledge, 2015), 18.
50 Ibid., 47.
51 Sue Grafton, *A is for Alibi* (New York: Holt, Rinehart and Winston, 1982), 208.
52 Stieg Larsson, *The Girl with the Dragon Tattoo*, translated by Reg Keeland (New York: Alfred E. Knopf, 2010), 209.
53 Jason Sheehan, " 'The Force' is Basically 'Game Of Thrones' With Cops—And That's Pretty Great," June 24, 2017, *NPR*, www.npr.org/2017/06/24/532976297/the-force-is-basically-game-of-thrones-with-cops-and-thats-pretty-great.
54 Don Winslow, *The Force* (London: HarperCollins, 2018), 466–467.
55 Mark Jones and Peter Johnstone, *History of Criminal Justice*, 5th edition (Amsterdam: Elsevier, 2012), 23.

Section 3

Enable You

Case Study 1 Arthur Conan Doyle's *The Sign of Four*

Imperial Crimes

Arthur Conan Doyle's *A Study in Scarlet*, in which Sherlock Holmes appeared before the public for the first time, was first published in the 1887 issue of *Beeton's Christmas Annual*. The novel was generally well-received, but Doyle did not immediately follow up this success with another work of detective fiction. Instead, he devoted himself to researching and writing the ambitious historical novel *Micah Clarke*; this was a genre he felt would allow him to combine 'a certain amount of literary dignity with [...] scenes of action and adventure'—the implication being, of course, that detective fiction lacked this particular quality.[1]

It was thus not until 1890 that Holmes reappeared, this time in the pages of *Lippincott's Monthly Magazine* in the novel *The Sign of Four* (under its original title *The Sign of the Four; or The Problem of the Sholtos*). Here, Holmes and Watson investigate the mysterious death of Bartholomew Sholto—killed with a poisoned dart from a blowgun—and the disappearance of the Agra treasure, an extremely valuable collection of Indian jewels, that belongs in part to their client Miss Morstan through inheritance. The ensuing investigation reveals ethically troubling connections between Britain and its imperial possessions. These have been a prime focus for many post-colonial critics, who read the novel as displaying a deep anxiety over the stability and fate of the British Empire, and as revealing (through, for example, Holmes' famous cocaine use), 'uncomfortable points of comparison between the detective and England's imperial subjects'.[2] Another approach to the novel focuses less on its politics, and more on what one critic describes as 'the epistemological stances espoused by Holmes', whose sense of control (both of himself and others) renders him (in Ernest Mandel's words) 'the epitome of bourgeois rationality in literature'.[3] Both of these critical traditions are of interest, but *The Sign of Four* also responds to a range of more criminologically inspired approaches.

The most obviously relevant criminological lens through which to examine the novel is the magnifying glass so often associated with

DOI: 10.4324/9781003156581-15

Holmes as a character (or caricature). As James F. O'Brien suggests, 'a strong component' of the Holmes' 'ongoing appeal and success is his knowledge of science and frequent use of the scientific method', particularly in relation to the employment of 'scientific forensic techniques in his investigations'.[4] Throughout his career Holmes remains on or near the cutting edge of the developing science of forensic criminology. Techniques that are referred to in the Holmes canon include methods of criminal identification including both the Bertillon system developed by the eponymous French anthropologist and the system of fingerprinting that supplanted it; a wide range of analytical chemical tests; the analysis of handwriting; and the typological classification of physical substances from tobacco ash to stationery. This forensic reading is, it should be noted, very much in line with the view of the detective as an embodiment of middle-class epistemology and positivist rationalism: the forensic techniques Holmes deploys so successfully are the physical manifestations of a cultural tendency to valorize rationality at the expense of, for example, emotion or intuition.

Holmes' forensic apparatus is on full display in *The Sign of Four*. When Holmes and Watson first inspect Pondicherry Lodge, the Sholto home, and the scene of the murder, the detective repeatedly uses his magnifying lens to examine 'marks which appeared [...] to be mere shapeless smudges of dust' to the untrained and unaided eye, but are to the well-equipped forensic detective considerably more significant.[5] Muddy prints on the windowsill of the murdered man's room are examined and revealed to be 'the impression of a wooden stump' and the mark of a 'heavy boot with a broad metal heel',[6] while the attic above the room reveals 'the prints of a naked foot [...] scarce half the size of those of an ordinary man' (with, as we later learn, unusually widely spaced toes).[7] Watson, and perhaps the reader, 'cannot conceive anything which will cover the facts', but Holmes faces no such difficulty; with the assistance of his various forensic tools he is able to reconstruct the events of the evening, and even provide a detailed physical description of the two people involved in the murder.[8] In fact, this initial forensic investigation has more or less solved the mystery. What remains of the narrative is something much closer to an adventure story, culminating in a high-speed river boat chase that, *mutatis mutandis*, could have appeared in an episode of *Miami Vice*.

Essentially, Doyle's novel can be read as a paean to the emerging science of forensic criminal investigation which, combined with the intellectual tools of the science of deduction ('The Science of Deduction' is in fact the title of the first chapter of the novel), promises readers an unprecedented level of security from crime and other forms of social disruption. It is worth noting, however, that Holmes' forensic expertise and superhuman reasoning abilities are potentially problematic. As Watson notes at the beginning of *The Sign of Four*, Holmes' attitudes make him appear at times to be 'an automaton—a calculating machine' who is 'positively inhuman'.[9] This is not the most comforting of images.

A second criminological approach to reading *The Sign of Four* focuses not on the figure of the superhuman (and not-quite-human) detective, but on the identities of the criminals he so efficiently pursues and captures. Here, as is so frequently the case in early detective fiction, the theories of Cesare Lombroso cast a long shadow. The key figure is not Jonathan Small, the mastermind of the robbery of the Sholtos' jewels, but his companion-cum-servant Tongo, a 'little Andaman Islander' who, while 'staunch and true' to Small, is nonetheless unable to govern his murderous impulses.[10] Watson's description of Tongo clearly maps on to Lombroso's linkage of criminality and the people he calls 'savages', among whom 'crime is not the exception but almost a general rule'.[11] Tongo is (for Watson) a 'savage, distorted creature' with 'a great, misshapen head and a shock of tangled, dishevelled hair', along with 'features [...] deeply marked with all bestiality and cruelty' in which his 'small eyes glowed and burned with a sombre light, and his thick lips were writhed back from his teeth, which grinned and chattered at us with half-animal fury'.[12] Even Small, who relies heavily on Tongo's abilities to carry out his criminal enterprise, dismisses him as a 'little hell-hound' and a 'little devil' whose inability to control his bloodlust has led to Sholto's murder (for which Small disclaims all responsibility).[13] A reading like this, that emphasizes Doyle's employment of Lombroso's association of non-whiteness with savagery and criminal behaviour, clearly resonates with post-colonial readings of the text that, for example, explore 'the concepts of the racial type and the criminal type as they inform both ethnographic taxonomies of India and the structures of Doyle's detective tale'.[14]

A third criminological approach sheds a different light on *The Sign of Four*. We can think about the crime around which Holmes and Watson's investigation circulates—the theft of the Agra jewels and the murder of Bartholomew Sholto—in relation to what Vincenzo Ruggiero describes as 'crimes of the powerful'.[15] This is a broad category, ranging from the white-collar crime of corporations to the actions of states as they obtain and consolidate power. In *The Sign of Four*, we would need to (again) consider the colonial context, in which the history of the Sholto's treasure is intertwined at every stage with unequal power relations that, at least in Small's opinion, undercut any easy notion of justice ('Justice! [...] A pretty justice! Whose loot is this if not ours?').[16] Small was sent as a young man to soldier in India to escape 'a mess over a girl'—in itself an injustice.[17] There he worked as an overseer on an indigo plantation, thus participating in a deeply unjust colonial economy. He is caught up in the Indian mutiny (more properly rebellion) of 1857, which Small and the other colonizers view as an interruption of their legitimate rule, but which is from another perspective an attempt to achieve the overthrow of an unjust system of governance. During the Mutiny, Small and his three associates (Sikhs, to whom Small displays a high level of colour-blind loyalty) obtain the jewels by murdering the servant of a rajah. Small justifies their crime by pointing to the rajah's betrayal of the British colonial government: 'his property becomes the due of those who have been true to their salt'.[18] This says nothing of the rajah's servant, of course, who is murdered precisely for staying true to *his* salt. Small and his associates are arrested for their crime and sent to a prison colony on the Andaman Islands; here they are betrayed by Bartholomew Sholto and Miss Mortstan's fathers, prison guards who agreed to free them for a share of the treasure.

Thus, when Watson claims that 'the treasure [...] or part of it, belonged rightfully to Miss Morstan' it is by no means clear that this is true.[19] So deeply involved are the jewels in a history of unequal power relations and systematic criminality that it would be difficult to determine who their legitimate owner is. Small's solution to this dilemma is to dump the treasure into the Thames when his capture becomes inevitable. While Small's motivation is selfish—he cannot bear the thought of 'another man at his ease in a palace with the money that should be mine'—he has perhaps stumbled upon the only possible solution to an otherwise insoluble problem.[20] Even Sherlock Holmes' vaunted rationality might not be able to untangle the knot of justice and injustice surrounding the Agra jewels.

For Further Study

The association between Sherlock Holmes and the forensic sciences is in some ways straightforward and is certainly well-recognized in the critical literature. It would be interesting to consider, however, the relationship between the relatively poorly developed, or even rudimentary, technical infrastructure which Holmes deploys (the lens and tape measure, for example) and the extraordinary results he regularly achieves. To what extent, in other words, do Doyle's Sherlock Holmes stories represent a form of rationalist propaganda, offering the Victorian readership a fantasy of a world in which technological progress is able to combat not so much crime itself as the fear of it? It might also be interesting to consider this question in relation to much more recent developments, such as the tremendous popularity of forensic crime fiction and (even more) forensic crime television serials. More than a century on from Sherlock Holmes, we might ask, are we still living in a world of technological fantasy?

Notes

1 Russell Miller, "Enter Sherlock Holmes," in *The Sign of the Four* by Arthur Conan Doyle (N.P.: Penguin, 2014), 137.

2 Benjamin D. O'Dell, "Performing the Imperial Abject: The Ethics of Cocaine in Arthur Conan Doyle's *The Sign of Four*," *Journal of Popular Culture* 45, no. 5 (2012), 980.

3 Nathanael T. Booth, "*The Sign of the Four* and the Detective as a Disrupter of Order," *Clues* 37, no. 1 (2019), 9.

4 James F. O'Brien, *The Scientific Sherlock Holmes: Cracking the Case with Science and Forensics* (Oxford: Oxford University Press, 2013), xiv.

5 Arthur Conan Doyle, *The Sign of Four* (London: Penguin, 2014), 37.

6 Ibid., 41.

7 Ibid., 43.

8 Ibid., 44.

9 Ibid., 14.

10 Ibid., 122.

11 Cesare Lombroso, *Criminal Man*, translated by Mary Gibson and Nicole Hahn Rafter with assistance from Mark Seymour (Durham, NC: Duke University Press, 2006), 175.

12 Doyle, *The Sign of Four*, 92.

13 Ibid., 95.

14 McBratney, John. "Racial and Criminal Types: Indian Ethnography and Sir Arthur Conan Doyle's *The Sign of Four*." *Victorian Literature and Culture* 33, no. 1 (2005), 150.

15 Vincenzo Ruggiero, *Power and Crime* (London: Routledge, 2015), 10.

16 Doyle, *The Sign of Four*, 102.

17 Ibid., 103.

18 Ibid., 110.

19 Ibid., 68.

20 Ibid., 103.

Case Study 2 Agatha Christie's *Crooked House*

Family Crimes

Agatha Christie is best known for her detective characters Hercule Poirot and Miss Marple, but some of her most interesting fiction falls outside of these two popular series. Similarly, while Christie is strongly associated with the interwar peak of the Golden Age of detective fiction, much of what today looks like her strongest work postdates the Second World War. In part this may be attributable to the fact that Christie's novels rely more on 'wonderfully engineered plots' than on effective characterization, so that the absence of her most famous creations does her novels no harm.[1] In part it may be because in her later work she demonstrated a perhaps unexpected ability to register and respond to the social changes that radically reshaped post-war Britain, acknowledging, as Barry Forshaw notes, that 'real life is lived outside the privileged circle in which the majority of her characters move, and that people can reside in inner cities as well as in quaint English villages'.[2]

The novel I want to consider here, *Crooked House*, is a fine example of Christie's post-war, non-serial fiction. Published in 1949, it is one of Christie's own 'special favourites', a novel that was 'pure pleasure' to write.[3] It features neither Poirot nor Miss Marple, instead relying on the narrator Charles Hayward, his father Sir Arthur Hayward, and Chief Inspector Taverner to investigate the murder of the elderly millionaire Aristide Leonides, who has been killed by the simple expedient of replacing his insulin with his own eserine-based eye medicine. This very intimate method of murder casts suspicion directly on his own large family. Realistically, the medicines in question are only accessible to family members, and—as is generically typical—despite their initial protestations many of Leonides' relatives have motives for murder.

Unsurprisingly, then, the novel has frequently been read in relation to its focus on family. J. C. Bernthal, for example, places it within a group of novels Christie published in the decade following 1945 that 'participated in contemporary debates about the nature and even the relevance of the

DOI: 10.4324/9781003156581-16

traditional, "normal" or "ideal" family'.[4] Bernthal points out that the family as Christie depicts it in these texts is 'anything but knowable, secure and nostalgically traditional'; instead, it is as 'confused and inconsistent' as the larger society within which it is situated.[5] Similarly, the fact that the murderer ultimately turns out to be Josephine Leonides, Aristide's 12-year-old granddaughter, challenges traditional notions concerning children (their innocence, their vulnerability, and so on).

This sociological approach is persuasive, but *Crooked House* also responds to a variety of more criminologically focused readings. The way that the narrator Charles Hayward becomes involved in investigating Aristide's murder, for example, enables an interpretation building on the relatively recent school of criminology focused on victims of criminal activity, victimology. Hayward is not a detective, but he is in love with Aristide's granddaughter Sophia Leonides (Josephine's older sister). They plan to marry, but if the murder is not solved, it will leave a miasma of suspicion surrounding the entire family. While Charles is more than willing to overlook this, Sophia is not: 'I'm devilishly proud. I want our marriage to be a good thing for everyone [...]'.[6] Other members of the family experience similar personal disruptions and dislocations from the crime that has occurred in their midst. Thus, while the primary victim of Josephine's crime is Aristide himself, the impact of his murder extends well beyond him. If the family serves here as a metaphor for society more generally—and the fact that the Leonides are such a large and diverse group, including representatives of multiple generations, professions, and personal backgrounds lends credence to this view—the novel as a whole can be read in relation to theories that link criminal behaviour, especially violent criminal behaviour, with social atomization and diminished levels of inter-personal trust.[7] Ultimately, by both disrupting the Leonides household (and leading towards its dissolution) and threatening the marriage of Sophia and Charles, Josephine's crime can be read as representing a radical threat to society as a whole, which becomes the ultimate victim of her crime.

Another approach arising out of the relationship between victim and murderer in *Crooked House* would be to focus on its exploration of the role of heredity in criminal behaviour. Josephine murders her grandfather because he refuses to allow her to take '*bally* [ballet] *dancing*' lessons— the misspelling is an indication of the murder's childishness—but this motive is grossly inadequate to the crime (not to mention the further crimes Josephine commits to conceal it).[8] The narrator Charles (and the novel as a whole) is thus left to seek alternative explanations. Josephine, as Charles notes, has 'an authoritarian ruthlessness of her grandmother's family, and the ruthless egoism of Magda [her mother], seeing only her own point of view' along with 'the essential crooked strain of old

Leonides'—these are 'the various factors of heredity' that meet and mingle with disastrous results in the young criminal's makeup, her 'precocious mental development' and 'retarded moral sense'.[9] The fact that this crime is so unmotivated (or under-motivated) leaves the field of causal explanation open for a purely hereditary explanation. Josephine has committed her crime because of who she is, and she is who she is because of her genetic heritage.

This sort of explanation for criminal behaviour has, of course, a long and controversial history. In the nineteenth century, Cesare Lombroso attempted to map correlations between heredity and patterns of criminal activity. His findings led him to develop an 'atavistic theory of criminality' that argued that some criminals 'were actually throwbacks to an earlier stage in man's development as evidenced' by a range of physical markers including 'slanting foreheads and large, protruding jaws'.[10] Compare this with Charles's description of the 'fantastically ugly' Josephine: 'the face [...] was round with a bulging brow, combed back hair and small, rather beady, black eyes [...] attached to a body—a small skinny body'.[11] Josephine's potential criminality, which is a result of her biological makeup, is clearly marked by her physiognomy.

While Lombroso's work had been quite thoroughly debunked (or at least savagely criticized) in academic and criminological circles by the time Christie wrote *Crooked House*, its general influence—the way it had diffused into the broader culture—was still very much in evidence. And while Lombroso's own work was out of fashion, new generations of criminologists were offering alternative explanations of the apparent linkages between heredity and criminality. In 1942, for instance, William Sheldon published *The Varieties of Temperament: A Psychology of Constitutional Differences*, which sought to link body types with personalities and temperaments, including criminal tendencies (which he associated with mesomorphic builds).[12] Thus Christie's association of heredity and criminality in *Crooked House* (and indeed elsewhere in her body of work) can be seen in relation to, and as contributing to, an ongoing social and scientific discourse.

More recently, biosocial approaches have tended to look to a combination of 'biological, environmental, and social factors' to explain individual tendencies towards criminal behaviour.[13] This synthetic approach would allow us to consider not just Josephine's potential genetic pre-disposition towards crime—her heredity—but also the range of social and environmental factors that *Crooked House* brings into play. This is a child, after all, who has 'suffered [...] from the stigma of being unattractive', particularly as the only ugly member of an otherwise very attractive family.[14] We might also want to consider the fact that she has grown up in a household that is defined by the 'different kinds of ruthlessness' of its inhabitants;

everyone in the family is, in their own way, 'queer', and tends to place their own interests before those of others.[15] And at the centre of this microcosm of society is the figure of Aristide. He is the victim in this case, but he is also 'crooked', the sort of man who thrives in the economic margins of legality: 'nothing he ever did was illegal', as Inspector Taverner notes, 'but as soon as he got on to it, you have to have a law about it'.[16]

A biosocial reading of Josephine's crime would thus situate her own propensity for crime (presented in Christie's novel as a question of heredity) within the criminogenic context of her family home, and by implication, her society more generally. Bernthal argues that *Crooked House* ends with a 'lingering, but compromised, sense of optimistic futurism in its conclusion as Sophia [...] is taken out of her house and out of her country'.[17] But this is, readers might feel, a substantial compromise. The crooked house of post-war England cannot be saved: it can only be abandoned for the potentially delusive hope of the blank page that follows the ending of the novel.

For Further Study

This case study has focused on two potential criminological approaches that can enhance a reading of Agatha Christie's *Crooked House*: victimology and a biosocially influenced criminology. It might be worth considering to what extent other texts in the Christie corpus respond to these approaches. One major novel that might be of interest here is *Murder on the Orient Express*, which manipulates in a very overt fashion the standard victim-criminal relationship, while linking the victim's own behaviour to his victimization, and exploring the way a single crime can resonate outwards to destabilize society. On a larger scale, we might ask whether the interest a writer like Christie displays here (and elsewhere) with biosocial explanations for criminal behaviour might be used to challenge conventional characterizations of the Golden Age detective novel as a sort of empty social vessel, a content-free game designed for entertainment rather than edification.

Notes

1 Barry Forshaw, *Crime Fiction: A Reader's Guide* (Harpenden: Oldcastle Books, 2019), 25.

2 Ibid., 26.

3 Agatha Christie, "Foreword," in *Crooked House*, by Agatha Christie (London: HarperCollins Publishers, 2017), vii.

4 J. C. Bernthal, *Queering Agatha Christie: Revisiting the Golden Age of Detective Fiction* (n.p.: Palgrave Macmillan, 2016), 162.

5 Ibid.
6 Agatha Christie, *Crooked House* (London: HarperCollins Publishers, 2017), 11.
7 Marie R. Garcia, Ralph B. Taylor, and Brian A. Lawton, "Impacts of Violent Crime and Neighborhood Structure on Trusting Your Neighbors," *Justice Quarterly* 2, no. 4, (2007), 680.
8 Christie, *Crooked House*, 239.
9 Ibid., 237–238.
10 Glenn D. Walters and Thomas W. White, "Heredity and Crime: Bad Genes or Bad Research," *Criminology* 27, no. 3 (1989), 456.
11 Christie, *Crooked House*, 83.
12 Walter and White, "Heredity and Crime: Bad Genes or Bad Research," 456.
13 J. C. Barnes, Brian B. Boutwell, and Kevin M. Beaver, "Contemporary Biosocial Criminology" A Systematic Review of the Literature: 2000–2012," in *The Handbook of Criminological Theory*, edited by Alex R. Piquero (Malden, MA: Wiley Blackwell, 2016), 76.
14 Christie, *Crooked House*, 238.
15 Ibid., 29.
16 Ibid., 16.
17 Bernthal, *Queering Agatha Christie*, 190.

Case Study 3 Walter Mosley's *Devil in a Blue Dress*

Racial Crimes

A great deal of attention has been paid in recent years to the alarmingly high rates of incarceration in the United States,[1] where imprisonment rates and the size of the overall prison population are well above historical norms.[2] This over-incarceration is, as penal theorist Loïc Wacquant points out, unequally distributed: the 'gargantuan penal state' is 'finely targeted' by class, race, and place in ways that lead to the '*hyper*incarceration of (sub) proletarian African American men'.[3] This phenomenon can, and should, be situated within America's long history of institutionalized racism and segregation. As Michelle Alexander writes, 'like Jim Crow (and slavery), mass incarceration operates as a tightly networked system of laws, policies, customs, and institutions that operate collectively to ensure the subordinate status of a group defined largely by race'.[4]

This reality has not, however, registered very strongly in crime fiction. The genre has, after all, been repeatedly and insistently described as an 'inherently, uniquely, conservative' one, with a clear ideological bias.[5] Crime fiction, in this reading, works to naturalize systemic inequalities and injustices through the power of narrative. It is thus not surprising that the genre in general has not always been attentive to the discriminatory elements of the criminal justice system in America (and elsewhere). This is perhaps particularly true of that quintessentially American subgenre, the hardboiled, in which 'the dominant consciousness' as Maureen T. Reddy writes, is 'indisputably a white consciousness'.[6]

A major exception to this omission is found in the revisionist hardboiled of Walter Mosely, who, though he has a number of important predecessors (like Chester Himes and Anthony Gar Haywood), has been given credit for the appearance of fully developed African-American characters in crime fiction.[7] In the 13 Easy Rawlins novels he has published to date (and in one collection of short stories), Mosley, in the words of Daylanne K. English, 'uses crime fiction as the ideal form in which to expose and narrate the still-lived experience of what his detective [...] terms being

DOI: 10.4324/9781003156581-17

"criminal by color" '.[8] Like all serial fiction, the Easy Rawlins novels develop over time, and are probably best considered as a whole, but even in the first novel in the series, *Devil in a Blue Dress* (1990), Mosley's critical attitude towards American racism, particularly as it intersects with questions of crime and justice, is abundantly clear. This is a novel than demands to be read, in other words, from the perspective of critical criminology with its insistence on the inherently political and politicized nature of crime and punishment.[9]

The issue of race dominates *Devil in a Blue Dress* from its opening scene, in which a white man walks into Joppy's bar and Easy Rawlins feels 'a thrill of fear' at the sight.[10] This reaction is a vestigial reflex from Rawlins' Southern past, and his experiences of its racist violence. His role as a combat soldier in World War Two has more or less cured him of his fear of white men, who he has discovered are 'just as afraid to die' as he is.[11] The novel suggests, however, that Rawlins might have been better off listening to his gut instinct in this case. Mr Albright is no ordinary white man; instead, he is a sort of emblematic distillation of whiteness. He wears 'an off-white linen suit and shirt with a Panama straw hat and bone shoes over flashing white silk socks'; his skin is 'smooth and pale with just a few freckles'; his eyes are 'pale' to the point of abnormality; and he carries an enormous gun in 'a white leather shoulder holster'.[12] This gun is a clear marker of his potential for violence; Albright is a ruthless and extremely dangerous man, who 'can kill with no more trouble than drinking a glass of bourbon'.[13] And the offer he makes Rawlins in Joppy's bar—he will pay him one hundred dollars to help locate a young woman—leads Rawlins into direct confrontation with the institutionalized racial violence of American policing.

A key point here is the way Albright and Easy Rawlins, considered in relation to each other, challenge the basic social preconceptions of the entanglement of crime and race in America. Albright, the epitome of whiteness, is utterly ruthless; even worse, he positively enjoys inflicting pain. This is revealed in a scene in which he rescues Rawlins from an altercation with a group of drunk, racist teenagers. Rawlins is more than capable of defending himself, but he hesitates because he doesn't 'kill children' (even racist ones), a fact Albright finds amusing.[14] He has no such reservations, and clearly enjoys humiliating and terrifying the teenaged ringleader. Nor, Rawlins knows, would he have hesitated to 'kill that boy' if he had shown any resistance.[15] But Albright, despite his almost limitless capacity for violence, is an establishment figure. He has worked as a defence lawyer in the South, and now provides services to some of Los Angeles' wealthiest and most influential businesspeople—he 'does favors for friends, and friends of friends'.[16] Nonetheless, he is a criminal, more than ready to kill or betray when the opportunity to make a profit arises.

His whiteness allows him to operate on both sides of the law without difficulty.

Rawlins, on the other hand, appears at the start of the novel as a regular citizen: a working man, a property owner, and a taxpayer. He has an important job on the shop floor of an aircraft manufacturer, and is a sort of embodiment of the American dream, working hard, saving money, and bettering himself through participation in the expanding post-war economy—except for the key fact that he is the wrong colour to fill this role. As the novel opens, he has refused to accept the racist assumptions of his workplace, an industrialized version of the Southern plantation where 'the bosses see all the [black] workers like they're children, and everyone knows how lazy children are', and has thus lost his job.[17] This expulsion from the legitimate economy is what exposes him to the danger embodied by Albright: he needs to earn money to pay his mortgage. By the end of the novel, he has become a private investigator who helps, in a mirror image of Albright's business model, 'people I know and people they know'.[18]

We thus have on the one hand a highly amoral, highly dangerous criminal, Albright, and on the other a hard-working citizen who is simply trying to make ends meet by unravelling criminal conspiracies and solving crime. But Albright and Rawlins are not seen this way by other characters. As bodies start piling up around the novel's titular femme fatale, Daphne Monet, Rawlins is almost instantly perceived as a suspect by the police, represented here by Officers Miller and Mason, who make a mockery of Rawlins' assertion of his basic rights: ' "You got a right to fall down and break your face, nigger. You got a right to die," [Mason] said. Then he hit me in the diaphragm'.[19] This is only the first in a series of beatings Rawlins endures at the hands of the police, who assume without any evidence that he is behind the murders they are investigating.

The novel's open representation of this highly racialized and racist version of justice is central to its social critique, and to its challenge to the generic norms of crime fiction. As J. Madison Davis writes,

> the traditional crime novel is inconceivable in many black communities. Bad cops are not simply corrupt bullies, as they are in, say, Raymond Chandler's or Dashiell Hammett's novels. They are bullies because of what they perceive as their racial superiority.[20]

We might extend this by pointing out that they are not simply racist bullies, either; instead, they are the representatives of an entire legal and social system built on and around racist assumptions.

Of course, it would be easy enough to say that this sort of systematic racism belongs in the past. However, the evidence of recent works of criminology like Alexander's *The New Jim Crow* suggests otherwise, as does

Devil in a Blue Dress and subsequent novels in the Easy Rawlins series. While the series is set in the past, it is narrated from a time much closer to the present, and as English argues, despite this 'historical settings, the past is not past for the detective, and the series shows that much remains the same for him in Los Angeles even across decades'.[21] The more things change, it seems, the more they stay the same.

For Further Study

Mosely's work is not simplistic or simple minded about what is required for a Black private eye to survive, much less thrive, in a racist system. Rawlins' success comes at a cost. In *Devil in a Blue Dress*, for example, this is revealed at the end of the novel, when he is forced to turn over a fellow African-American—and one who might even be described as a friend, although not an innocent man—to Mason and Miller in order to avoid the endless persecution they have threatened him with. It would be worth considering to what extent this sort of compromise with the racist legal and judicial system appears throughout the series, and asking whether it is a regular feature of revisionist crime fiction texts that challenge or subvert the white, masculine heteronormativity of the genre. Even in openly critical or radical fictional texts, in other words, is some sort of compromise with the status quo inevitable?

Notes

1 Kali N. Gross, "Black Women, Criminal Justice, and Violence," in *The Oxford Handbook of Crime and Criminal Justice*, edited by Michael Tonry (Oxford: Oxford University Press, 2019), 285.

2 David Brown, "Mass Incarceration," in *Alternative Criminologies*, edited by Pat Carlen and Leandro Ayres França (London: Routledge, 2018), 369–371.

3 Loïc Wacquant, "Class, Race & Hyperincarceration in Revanchist America." *Daedalus* 139, no. 3 (2010), 74.

4 Michelle Alexander, *The New Jim Crow: Mass Incarceration in the Age of Colorblindness*, revised edition (New York: The New York Press, 2012), 13.

5 Philip Howell, "Crime and the City Solution: Crime Fiction, Urban Knowledge, and Radical Geography." *Antipode* 30, no. 4 (1998), 358–359.

6 Maureen T. Reddy, *Traces, Codes, and Clues: Reading Race in Crime Fiction* (New Brunswick, NJ: Rutgers University Press, 2003), 9.

7 J. Madison Davis, "Expanding the World of the Private Eye: Walter Mosley Becomes a Grand Master." *World Literature Today* 90, no. 3–4 (2016), 33.

8 Daylanne K. English, "The Modern in the Postmodern: Walter Mosley, Barbara Neely, and the Politics of Contemporary African-American Detective Fiction." *American Literary History* 18, no. 4 (2006), 773–774.

 9 Paul Roberts, "Thinking through Critical Criminology," in *Social Censure and Critical Criminology: After Sumner*, edited by Anthony Amatrudo (London: Palgrave Macmillan, 2017), 24–25.
10 Walter Mosley, *Devil in a Blue Dress* (New York: Washington Square Press, 2020), 1.
11 Ibid.
12 Ibid., 1, 18.
13 Ibid., 23.
14 Ibid., 62.
15 Ibid., 59.
16 Ibid., 5.
17 Ibid., 64.
18 Ibid., 218.
19 Ibid., 70.
20 J. Madison Davis, "Expanding the World of the Private Eye," 34.
21 Daylanne K. English, "The Modern in the Postmodern," 774.

Case Study 4   Maj Sjöwall and Per Wahlöö's *The Man on the Balcony*

Social Crimes

The ten novels of Maj Sjöwall and Per Wahlöö's *The Story of a Crime* were published in Sweden between 1965 and 1975. Inspired by Ed McBain's 87th Precinct series, they are clear examples of the police procedural, and are generally considered to be the inaugural texts or predecessors of the internationally popular genre of Scandinavian crime fiction known as Nordic noir. Their influence on crime fiction remains undiminished. To take a single example of the reach of Sjöwall and Wahlöö's work, in director Park Chan-wook's 2022 Korean thriller *Decision to Leave*, the police detective Jang Hae-joon keeps a stack of the novels on his desk, with the subject of this case study, the third novel in the cycle, *The Man on the Balcony* (1967), on top.[1]

The Story of a Crime as a whole represents something of an exception to the generally reactionary politics of the police procedural. Peter Messent has pointed out that the police novel (as represented by McBain and Joseph Wambaugh, another prominent American police novelist) generally 'works to conservative ends',[2] and even argues that this is a built-in feature of the genre which is 'necessarily structured around the protection [...] of the existing social order'.[3] This is not, however, the case with Sjöwall and Wahlöö's work, which instead offers a critique of policing, the judicial system, and bourgeoise capitalism more generally. These are novels that ask the question that Andrew Pepper has identified as typical of radical crime fiction more broadly: 'what has caused this problem called "crime" in the first place?'[4]

Critics have frequently attributed the success of Nordic Noir in general, and Sjöwall and Wahlöö's work in particular, to its articulation of an 'ideological agenda', its critique of both the state's relationship to crime (and to the way this is articulated in relation to questions of gender).[5] This is certainly true, but *The Man on the Balcony* also resonates strongly with a number of different criminological perspectives. In part, this is because the novel deals with two very different crimes committed by two very

DOI: 10.4324/9781003156581-18

different criminals, and embeds their crimes in a social context that could be described as criminogenic. In other words, the crimes investigated are tied up on multiple levels with the novel's overall social critique.

The first criminal the reader encounters is a mugger who has for the 'eighth time in two weeks' savagely assaulted and robbed a person in a city park.[6] This is a robber 'who knows his business'—he only targets 'defenceless old men and women'.[7] This pattern of criminal activity could be read through the lens of victimology. As Afreen A. Hussain notes, one of the primary focal areas of this field is the study of various factors that render an 'individual or a group of individuals susceptible to becoming a victim of a crime or a violent attack'.[8] In this case, the mugger's victims are susceptible because they are elderly and, at the time of the assaults, isolated. One could also argue that in some of the assaults, there is an element of victim precipitation. This is a theory that postulates that in some cases of homicide the actions or choices of the victim may have played a significant role in leading to their own death.[9] Consider, for example, the case of the woman in *The Man on the Balcony* who not only walks through Vanadis Park alone late in the evening, and thus presents a tempting target of opportunity, but also wrestles with the mugger for her handbag, thus leading to a much more severe assault than would otherwise have occurred. Add to this the fact that 'she had just shut up her fruit and confectionary kiosk and was on her way home' with 'the entire day's takings in her handbag', and you have another way in which the victim could be described as having facilitated her own victimization. At least one of the police officers investigating the case seems to endorse this view when he notes that 'people are crazy' for taking risks like this.[10]

This would, however, be an inaccurate reading of the way Sjöwall and Wahlöö present the perpetrator of these crimes, a young man named Rolf Evert Lundgren. First, we have a chapter narrated from his perspective, in which he is revealed as a thoroughly amoral, calculating perpetrator. When he is working—and this is his work—he spends literally hours selecting the targets least likely to struggle and most likely to offer suitable financial rewards for the risks he takes, 'weigh[ing] the pros and cons' of each potential victim before striking.[11] He is a sort of embodiment of the classical criminology that can be traced back to the work of Cesare Beccaria, which sees 'human beings as rational, self-interested, possessing of [sic] free will, and capable of making decisions based on a cost-benefit analysis', and thus views crime as 'a free choice'.[12] Just as importantly, he is in the words of his former girlfriend, 'very dangerous': he owns submachine guns, and has claimed (inaccurately) that 'he'll never let himself be taken alive'.[13] The novel thus offers us a picture of a young man of violent tendencies who makes rational, if highly selfish, decisions.

Lundgren's patterns of life (and crimes) are contrasted throughout the novel with the life (and crimes) of the titular man on the balcony, and the focus of the novel's investigation, Ingemund Fransson. Fransson is a child rapist and a murderer (his crimes are loosely based on the real-life 1963 rape and murder of two young girls in Stockholm).[14] There is no question in the novel that these are horrific acts of violence, and that their perpetrator must be stopped. But while Fransson is presented not as an object of sympathy—that would be difficult if not impossible given the nature of his attacks—he is presented as a manifestation or symptom of a broader problem. One way of looking at his crimes is in relation to Travis Hirschi's social bond theory (as developed in his 1969 *Causes of Delinquency*), which argues that 'delinquent acts result when an individual's bond to society is weak or broken'.[15] Hirschi argues that attachment and commitment to, alongside involvement and belief in, prosocial individuals and institutions prevent individuals from giving in to their innate anti-social or delinquent desires.[16] And Fransson is presented throughout *The Man on the Balcony* as a man without bonds of any sort.

This profound isolation from society can be seen in the unnerving opening chapter of the novel, in which Fransson sits and smokes on his apartment balcony in a state of affectless isolation, with 'no particular feeling about anything'.[17] His background, revealed towards the end of the novel, is equally indicative of social isolation. He lost his parents relatively young, and moved from one part of the country to another doing menial labour. He was pensioned off as 'unfit to work' about a decade before the events in the novel, and is described in the records by the state doctors as 'very unsociable' with 'no need of human contact'.[18] A convenient diagnosis, for at this point the state and society in general have given up on him: 'Since then none of the authorities had had reason to concern themselves with Fransson [...]'.[19] It is only when he gives in to what are described as his 'inclinations' and begins killing that this neglect ends, and he becomes an object of social concern.[20]

Of course, none of this excuses Fransson's crimes, or even fully explains them (there are indications in the novel of the power of his overwhelming compulsions, and it is implied that his actions are based on a profound psychological disturbance), but it does contextualize them. This is especially true when Fransson is compared with an earlier suspect in the investigation, Ericksson, 'a human wreck, an outcast from the dubious fellowship that surrounded him, and utterly alone'.[21] Ericksson's crimes are much less serious than Fransson's, but Sjöwall and Wahlöö imply that they too are at least partially explicable by the failure of society to attend to and care for its weak, its damaged, and its sick.

In a final twist away from the value system generally at work in the police procedural (and in crime fiction more generally), it gradually becomes clear that the real object of the novel's disgust is not so much the individual crimes that are the object of Beck and his colleagues' investigation, but what is described as the 'swift gangsterization of [...] society', as revealed through both a high level of background violence and criminality, and through the willingness of the public to use violence to protect itself through vigilantism.[22] This phenomenon is, as one of the police inspectors reflects, 'a product' of society, and all of the 'people who lived in it and had a share in its creation'.[23] Crime in this view (and it is one that is developed at length over the course of the series) is 'caused by a catastrophic philosophy which had been provoked by the prevailing system. Consequently society should be duty bound to produce an effective counterargument. One that was not based on smugness and more police officers'.[24] Fransson's crimes—and indeed Lundgren's—are thus located within what the novel defines as a much larger and much more important crime that is attributable to society itself. To be a police officer in these circumstances, as is noted in *The Terrorists*, the final novel *The Story of a Crime*, is to have 'the wrong job' at the 'wrong time' in 'the wrong system'.[25]

For Further Study

The police procedural is a genre that tends to reify or naturalize the dominant assumptions, or ideology, of the society within which it is produced. However, as Theodore Martin has argued, crime fiction has played a 'concerted role' in 'alternately contesting and abetting the postwar transformation of the United States into a carceral state'.[26] *The Man on the Balcony* can clearly be seen as a novel that contests the development of the carceral or police state (albeit in Sweden rather than America). It remains an open question, however, whether a genre as deeply imbued with conservative politics as the police procedural can effectively be turned against itself. Is the sort of radical critique present throughout Sjöwall and Wahlöö's work effective, we might wish to ask, or has its longer-term legacy in the form of Scandinavian crime fiction tended to drift back towards a set of more conservative attitudes towards crime?

Notes

1 Chan-wook, Park, *Decision to Leave* (Moho Film, 2022).
2 Peter Messent, *The Crime Fiction Handbook* (Chichester: Wiley-Blackwell, 2013), 23.
3 Ibid., 26.
4 Andrew Pepper, *Unwilling Executioner: Crime Fiction and the State* (Oxford: Oxford University Press, 2016), 12.

5 Dawn Keetley, "Unruly Bodies: The Politics of Sex in Maj Sjöwall and Per Wahlöö's Martin Beck Series." *Clues* 30, no. 1 (2012), 54.

6 Maj Sjöwall and Per Wahlöö, *The Man on the Balcony*, translated by Alan Blair (New York: Harper Perennial, 2007), 7.

7 Ibid., 8.

8 Afreen A. Hussain, "Crimes Against Persons," in *Victimology: A Comprehensive Approach to Forensic, Psychosocial and Legal Perspectives*, edited by Rejani Thudalikunnil Gopalan (Cham: Springer, 2022), 273.

9 Martin E. Wolfgang, "Victim Precipitated Criminal Homicide." *Journal of Criminal Law, Criminology & Police Science* 48, no. 1 (1957), 1.

10 Sjöwall and Wahlöö, *The Man on the Balcony*, 37.

11 Ibid., 21.

12 Travis C. Pratt, Jacinta M. Gau, and Travis W. Franklin, *Key Ideas in Criminology and Criminal Justice* (Thousand Oaks, CA: Sage Publications, 2011), 11.

13 Ibid., 77.

14 Michael Tapper, *Swedish Cops: From Sjöwall and Wahlöö to Stieg Larsson* (Bristol: Intellect Books, 2014), 89.

15 Travis Hirschi, *Causes of Delinquency* (New Brunswick, NJ: Transaction Publishers, 2002), 16.

16 Travis C. Pratt, Jacinta M. Gau, and Travis W. Franklin, *Key Ideas in Criminology and Criminal Justice* (Thousand Oaks, CA: Sage Publications, 2011), 58–59.

17 Maj Sjöwall and Per Wahlöö, *The Man on the Balcony*, 3.

18 Ibid., 185.

19 Ibid.

20 Ibid., 118.

21 Ibid., 50.

22 Ibid., 35.

23 Ibid.

24 Ibid., 141.

25 Maj Sjöwall and Per Wahlöö, *The Terrorists*, translated by Joan Tate (London: 4th Estate, 2016), 323–324.

26 Theodore Martin, "War-on-Crime Fiction." *PMLA* 136, no. 2 (2021), 226.

Case Study 5   Neal Stephenson's *Zodiac*

Environmental Crimes

Neal Stephenson's novels have been described as gleefully defying 'any category, genre, precedent or label'.[1] But this doesn't stop people from trying, and labels ranging from satire to cyberpunk to sci-fi to historical fiction have been attached to his work.[2] The one descriptor that hasn't been applied is crime fiction. It might thus seem perverse to use his second novel, *Zodiac* (1988), as a case study in this book, but the inclusion is defensible for two reasons. First, Stephenson notes in *Zodiac*'s acknowledgments that 'the hard-boiled detective fiction of James Crumley' was the inspiration for the novel.[3] Second, and for my purposes more importantly, this is an early example of a novel that applies the tropes of crime fiction to questions of systematic ecological damage. It thus responds well to a reading based on 'green criminology' or 'eco-critical criminology', a set of approaches that examines 'environmental concerns within notions of power, harm and justice'.[4]

Zodiac has not attracted a great deal of critical attention, perhaps because it is an early work in Stephenson' substantial oeuvre, perhaps because it is something of a generic outlier. However, the few critics who have given the novel consideration have registered its environmental focus. Nicholas P. Spencer, for instance, offers a reading of the novel emphasizing its three main areas of concern, 'toxic pollution, animal exploitation, and nuclear energy',[5] in conjunction with its reassessment of the relationship between activism and politics. Yet very little attention has been paid to *Zodiac* as a crime novel, and specifically an ecological crime novel. This is surprising given the fact that Stephenson is very clear about the intertwining of ecological and criminal issues. *Zodiac* opens with a scene of environmental destruction, albeit a relatively minor one narrated in a comic register: 'Roscommon came and laid waste to the garden an hour after dawn, about the time I usually get out of bed and he usually passes out on the shoulder of some freeway'.[6] This minor act of ecological vandalism (carried out by the narrator's landlord) prefigures the much

DOI: 10.4324/9781003156581-19

greater acts of corporate eco-crime that are the object of the protagonist Sangamon Taylor's investigations.

Sangamon is in some ways a generically typical first-person hardboiled narrator: he lives an unconventional, relatively isolated life, has difficulty in maintaining relationships with women, and is, by his own account, a 'congenital pain in the ass', especially in relation to authority figures.[7] However, Sangamon has turned his obstreperousness, alongside his mechanical and chemical abilities, into a career as 'a professional asshole' for GEE, or the 'Group of Environmental Extremists'.[8] In fact, he is an eco-sleuth or environmental detective, investigating what Reece Walters describes as a primary focus of green criminology, 'environmental damage' and the 'human and non-human victimisation' that results from the 'abuse of state and corporate power'.[9]

He is sometimes referred to around Boston (his home and the centre of his investigative activities) as a 'Granola James Bond'—a sort of hippie super-agent.[10] This work takes him to 'the dirtiest, the most dangerous, the most crime-ridden neighborhood in Boston'.[11] So far, so familiar: these are, in Raymond Chandler's famous formulation, the 'mean streets' down which the investigator must go 'in search of a hidden truth'.[12] But Sangamon isn't 'talking about crack dealers, tenements, or minority groups'—white middle-class America's version of the mean streets—but 'the zone around the Mystic River where most of New England's heavy industry is located', and where 'the nation's poisoner's congregate' to pollute the local watershed with the impunity that comes from public ignorance, private greed, and official negligence.[13] This is a narrative version of the fundamental tenet of ecological or green criminology, which is dedicated to the study of 'transgressions committed against ecosystems, human beings, and non-human beings'.[14]

This investigative focus changes several fundamental things about the way a private eye figure like Sangamon operates. Like a standard hardboiled detective, he works adjacent to rather than alongside official law enforcement. In part this is because the criminals he pursues are corporations with their own squads of 'rent-a-cops and rent-a-dicks'[15] who have access to much of the paraphernalia of law enforcement, from Ford Broncos with 'too many antennas' to dossiers full of 'photographic representations' of Sangamon and other activists.[16] But more importantly, the actual legal bodies responsible for policing and enforcing the 'eco-laws'[17] are toothless. The Environmental Protection Agency ('the chemical Keystone Kops' with 'offices full of mediocre chemists, led by the lowest bottom-feeders of them all: political appointees') 'don't have the balls to take preventive measures' and 'punitive action doesn't even enter their minds. The laws are broken so universally that they don't know what to do. They don't even look for violators'.[18]

In this context, not only must Sangamon investigate outside the established legal framework, using very different tools and techniques from the typical private eye, but he must also pursue justice differently once he has gathered evidence. Investigations rely largely on Sangamon's titular zodiac, his test tubes for collecting samples, and his encyclopaedic knowledge of Boston Harbor's 'dark, carcinogenic side', its 'thousands of inlets' and 'every single goddamn pipe that empties into it'.[19] Once evidence has been gathered, however, there is little point in taking it to the police or other law enforcement officials, who would be reluctant or unable to take serious action against the interests of corporate America. Instead, Sangoman (and his associates in GEE) take direct action to stop pollution, and simultaneously stage public relation events intended to attract attention and generate outrage.

In one example of this 'system of laissez-faire justice',[20] GEE first sabotages a 'mile long toxic-waste diffuser' operated by a company Sangoman refers to as the 'Swiss Bastards', which will shut their chemical plant down at least temporarily, and then organizes a 'full-scale media circus'.[21] This results not in the arrest of the company executives that have been running the illegal waste disposal system, but of Sangoman and his team. This may be a 'totally awful, bogus bust' and the 'charges will probably be dropped anyway',[22] but it illustrates a fundamental difference in the activities of a traditional detective and Stephenson's eco-detective. The police may not like the private operator of hardboiled fiction, and to some extent they may work at cross purposes, but at least they generally agree on what defines criminal activity. Murder is murder, but as Mark Halsey and Rob White note, 'many of the most serious forms of environmental harm in fact constitute "normal social practice"' rather than criminal activity.[23] All companies everywhere (and all individuals) dispose of their waste (and carry out a wide range of other practices) in ways that are from one perspective perfectly routine, but from another are clear examples of what F. J. W. Herbig and S. J. Joubert define as 'conservation crime': 'any intentional or negligent human activity or manipulation that impacts negatively on the earth's biotic and/or abiotic natural resources, resulting in immediately noticeable or indiscernible (only noticeable over time) natural resource trauma of any magnitude'.[24]

The main plotline of the novel centres around exactly this sort of crime on a grand scale, as a company called Basco Industries attempts to conceal its history of polluting Boston Harbor with polychlorinated biphenyls (PCBs, extremely carcinogenic compounds that were widely used in industrial and consumer products throughout much of the twentieth century) by releasing an untested genetically modified bacteria that consumes the chemical, but also releases its own toxins. There are two particularly interesting things about this plot from an eco-criminological perspective.

The first is the way the offending company is presented as an inherently criminal enterprise. Not only do they have a decades-long history of ecological crime, but when they feel threatened by Sangamon's investigations they are more than willing to move beyond monitoring and intimidation, and resort to direct violence. Traditional crime and ecological crime are in this view intertwined. Second, this criminality is presented not as an aberration external to the dominant systems that rule America, but as fundamentally entangled with them. Not only was Basco ('the avant-garde of the toxic waste movement') a major producer of Agent Orange, the 'toxic waste' the American military used during the Vietnam war as a defoliant, but one of the Pleshys, the family that founded the company, is running for president of the United States.[25]

Sangamon's investigations, and the ensuing media storm, derail Pleshy's political ambitions, but the point Stephenson is making remains valid. The perpetrators of ecological crime are not outsiders who threaten the status quo or the orderly running of society; they are the most powerful people in society, and the status quo they represent is, from an ecological perspective, inevitably criminal. It is also critical that criminal charges are highly unlikely to occur: 'Of course, even when you have legally correct evidence, corporations rarely suffer in this country. Look at any big government contractor for the Pentagon or NASA. They can get away with murder'.[26] Even if Basco does eventually go bankrupt—or 'eat shit and die' as Sangamon puts it—this will change very little about the underlying system that not just allows, but facilitates, eco-crime.[27] And it is not, *Zodiac* reminds us as it ends, just the corporations that are at fault here. When Sangamon revs up his zodiac's engine and heads back out into the harbour on his crusade against pollution, he gives 'all the well-dressed people […] the finger'—and we are included in that gesture.[28]

For Further Study

In *The Great Derangement*, his 2016 study of the relationship between climate change, culture, and politics, Amitav Ghosh argues that the traditional realist novel, or what we culturally construe as 'serious fiction', has proved itself to be incapable of dealing with the realities of our unfolding global ecological catastrophe.[29] Instead, he argues, climate change tends to register in science fiction texts, which have provided a welcome home for 'cli-fi' stories of climate disaster and ensuing dystopias.[30] But as Ghosh argues, there is a problem here: 'cli-fi is made-up mostly of disastrous stories set in the future', but this is only 'one aspect of the Anthropocene' which also includes 'the recent past, and, most significantly, the present'.[31] For generic reasons, cli-fi thus tends to miss the immediacy or presentness of the climate emergency, as well as its roots in the past. Might crime fiction, with its generically typical intertwining of the past and present, represent a potential mode for effective consideration of the causes and current consequences of climate change? If so, how does this eco-criticism register in crime fiction texts?

Notes

1 Lev Grossman, "Isaac Newton, Action Hero." *Time*, September 8 (2003), 91.
2 "Stephenson, Neal 1959–." *Concise Major 21st Century Writers*, edited by Tracey L. Matthews, Vol. 5 (Detroit, MI: Gale, 2006), 3422–3425.
3 Neal Stephenson, "Acknowledgements," *Zodiac* (London: Arrow Books, 2001), n.p.
4 Reece Walters, "Green Criminology," in *Alternative Criminologies*, edited by Pat Carlen and Leandro Ayres França (London: Routledge, 2018), 166.
5 Nicholas P. Spencer, "Ecological Struggle in Neal Stephenson's *Zodiac*," in *Tomorrow Through the Past" Neal Stephenson and the Project of Global Modernization*, edited by Jonathan P. Lewis (Newcastle-upon-Tyne: Cambridge Scholars Press, 2006), 48.
6 Neal Stephenson, *Zodiac* (London: Arrow Books, 2001), 1.
7 Ibid., 6.
8 Ibid.
9 Walters, "Green Criminology," 169.
10 Stephenson, *Zodiac*, 2.
11 Ibid., 16.
12 Raymond Chandler, "The Simple Art of Murder," in *The Simple Art of Murder* (New York: Vintage Books, 1988), 18.
13 Stephenson, *Zodiac*, 16.
14 David Rodríguez Goyes, *Southern Green Criminology: A Science to End Ecological Discrimination* (Bingley: Emerald Publishing, 2019), 3.
15 Stephenson, *Zodiac*, 49.
16 Ibid., 17.
17 Ibid., 18.
18 Ibid., 55.
19 Ibid., 55.
20 Ibid., 55.
21 Ibid., 73–75.
22 Ibid., 81.
23 Mark Halsey and Rob White, "Crime, Ecophilosophy and Environmental Harm," in *Environmental Crime: A Reader*, edited by Rob White (Cullompten: Willan Publishing, 2009), 28.
24 F. J. W. Herbig and S. J. Joubert, "Criminological Semantics: Conservation Criminology–Vision or Vagary?," in *Environmental Crime: A Reader*, edited by Rob White (Cullompten: Willan Publishing, 2009), 57.
25 Stephenson, *Zodiac*, 44, 20.
26 Ibid., 290.
27 Ibid., 291.

28 Ibid.
29 Amitav Ghosh, *The Great Derangement: Climate Change and the Unthinkable* (Chicago: University of Chicago Press, 2017), 11.
30 Ibid., 72.
31 Ibid.

Case Study 6   Natsuo Kirino's *Out*

Gendered Crimes

In the introduction to their recent study of feminism in Japan, Julia C. Bullock, Ayako Kano, and James Welker note that while feminism has shaped modern Japanese society in both theoretical and practical terms, the country's government and powerful forces within its society have long sought to impose 'a conservative vision of normative femininity grounded in conventional domestic roles for women'.[1] They also point out that within this deeply patriarchal context, a persistent strand of feminist thought has been articulated not only through intellectual and political interventions, but also, and just as importantly, through cultural production.[2]

This sort of conflict between a powerful set of officially and socially sanctioned norms and an undercurrent of resistance offers a fertile zone for crime fiction, which, at least in its more radical forms, is well suited to probing the open wounds of the body politic. While many of the examples discussed in this book are rooted in Western contexts—American, British, and European—crime fiction's critical edge has been exploited just as effectively in other traditions. This may be particularly true of Japan, where crime fiction has flourished as a genre, in no small part due to its ability to offer sustained socio-political critique in a popular form. Japanese crime fiction has also been very successful internationally, offering strong evidence of crime fiction's status as a 'transnational phenomenon' possessed of an 'inherent transnational mobility'.[3]

The tension between patriarchy and feminism is one of the contexts within which I would like to situate Natsuo Kirino's novel *Out* (1997; English translation, 2004). Kirino is, after all, a writer who, in Kathryn Hemmann's words, puts 'anger at phallocentric discourse and the double standards imposed by a patriarchal society' to 'literary use in her bestselling crime and suspense stories'.[4] The second context is feminist criminology, which has moved over the past half century from the periphery of the criminological world towards its centre; indeed, the study of 'gender, women and deviance' has recently been characterized as one of the most

DOI: 10.4324/9781003156581-20

enduring and vital aspects of contemporary criminology.[5] While this is a diverse field with a long tradition of development, controversy, and internal critique (Kerry Carrington, for instance, has identified five major distinct approaches), it is focused on women's experience of crime and the justice system as both victims and perpetrators.[6] One of the most interesting things about Kirino's novel is the way it explores this criminal-victim binary, putting the notion (which Carrington describes as plaguing feminist criminology) that 'men are violent and women as passive' under extreme pressure.[7] While it has long been true that men are responsible for much higher levels of violence than women, and direct much of that violence against women, this is not always and everywhere the case, as recent statistics on women's imprisonment indicate.[8] Nor is it helpful to relegate women in the cultural imaginary to a perpetual state of victimhood.

Out deals with a group of women who work the gruelling night shift in a boxed meal factory; while each of the four main characters (Masako, Yoshie, Yayoi, and Kuniko) is a very different person, they have all been marginalized or exploited to a greater or lesser extent by Japan's patriarchal society. Yoshie, for instance, is a widow, and must care not only for her daughter but also for her mother-in-law, a situation that puts her under immense psychological and financial strain. Masako has lost her job in a credit union due to her refusal to accept workplace discrimination; after she requested a long over-due management position, and asked to be 'given the same work as the male employees' she was subject to 'blatant harassment' that culminated in a 'humiliating assault' and a forced resignation.[9] Kuniko is punished by Japan's male-dominated society for her failure to meet female beauty norms: being 'ugly and fat' means she is unable to participate effectively in the economy, and when she is abandoned by her partner she is left deep in debt.[10] These examples of structural male violence crystalize around the last member of the group, Yayoi, who has not only seen her husband spend the family savings on gambling and escorts, but has been beaten by him when she protests. As if all of this were not enough, the women working in the factory are being preyed on by a 'strange man' who has pulled several of the workers 'into the shadows and assaulted' them.[11] This overall situation can be read through the lens of a feminist criminology that sees gendered violence as part of a social system predicated on male dominance over women, and that works to 'erase and normalise women's victimization'.[12]

Yayoi acts as a catalyst in *Out*, precipitating first a recognition on the part of the women of their systematic victimization and their justifiable anger, and then a shift from victimization to transgression. When Yayoi's husband returns home drunk again, and complains that she should 'be nice once in a while', she loses control and strangles him with a belt.[13] Yayoi is shocked at her response to the crime: it 'feels so good' to be freeing the 'cruelty inside'.[14] Once her husband is dead, she calls Masako for help, who (with Yayoi and Kuniko) chops up and disposes of the body, and thus conceals the crime. Significantly, both the murder and the disposal of the body are described in ways that emphasize the agency and power of the women. *Out* thus neatly inverts the traditional association of women with passive victimhood by presenting this group (especially Masako) as actively participating in a serious criminal enterprise.

This inversion becomes even more pronounced when they put their grisly experience to work and set up a business disposing of corpses for profit. The novel here drifts loose from its social-realist moorings, introducing a heightened, even Gothic, level of violence along with what Barbara Creed describes in her discussion of feminist cinema as a form of monstrous or abject femininity, excessive, uncontrollable, and highly disruptive of patriarchal norms.[15] Kirino situates the monstrous (in Creed's sense) violence of its female protagonists in relation to an intensified version of the misogynist violence that has triggered their transgression. This occurs when the police, investigating Yayoi's husband's death, focus on a marginal underworld figure, the pimp and gambling club owner Mitsuyoshi Satake. While their investigations are fruitless—he has nothing to do with the murder—they nonetheless disrupt his carefully constructed life, leaving him eager for revenge. This is particularly dangerous as Satake has a history of psychopathic violence against women: as a young gangster, he raped, tortured, and murdered a woman who had crossed the gang in a fashion so brutal that even his criminal peers 'looked at him in disgust when they saw what he had done'.[16] While the text initially attributes Satake's violence to sadism, by the end of the novel it has been redefined as a pure distillation of misogyny. When he attacks Masako, ostensibly to get revenge, he tells her he hates her (and thus will rape, torture, and kill her) 'because you're a woman'.[17]

The final scenes of *Out* have attracted a great deal of the critical attention dedicated to this novel.[18] This is understandable, given their extreme violence, Kirino's double narration of Satake's attack on Masako (from both of their perspectives), and the distinctly odd dynamic of reciprocal understanding that develops between the two characters. At the very least, to hear Masako claim that she understands her rapist because 'I see that we're the same [...]' is deeply unsettling.[19] The novel as a whole remains open, however, to a reading emphasizing not Masako's masochism, but both the role of misogyny as a 'pervasive and historic form of hatred that transcends time, space and place' and the fact that 'many women who fear or have experienced male violence recognise that gender, both theirs and that of their assailant' is central to their experience.[20] The only solution to this systematic, institutionalized hatred of women, Kirino's *Out* suggests, is escape to the 'freedom' Masako is sure 'must be out there somewhere'.[21]

This is an optimistic gesture at the conclusion of a deeply pessimistic novel, but one that may well be no more than rhetorical. What part of the world, after all, is free from patriarchal misogyny?

For Further Study

Kirino's *Out* is clearly a novel that depends for much of its effect on the particularities and specificities of its Japanese setting. But it is worth asking if its central dynamic, the tension between women-as-victims and women-as-perpetrators, appears more generally in feminist crime fiction. Is this duality a feature, for example, of the great American tradition of revisionist hardboiled novels exemplified by the work of authors like Sue Grafton, Marcia Muller, and Sara Paretsky? How do novels by authors like these, or more recent works of female-oriented crime fiction like the Claire DeWitt trilogy by Sara Gran, present the relationship of their female characters to a patriarchal social and justice system that is geared towards their victimization?

Notes

1 Julia C. Bullock, Ayako Kano, and James Welker, "Introduction," in *Rethinking Japanese Feminisms*, edited by Julia C. Bullock, Ayako Kano, and James Welker (Honolulu: University of Hawai'i Press, 2018), 1, 5.

2 Ibid., 2.

3 Stewart King, "The Reader and World Crime Fiction: The (Private) Eye of the Beholder," in *Criminal Moves: Modes of Mobility in Crime Fiction*, edited by Jesper Gulddal, Stewart King, and Alistair Rolls (Liverpool: Liverpool University Press, 2019), 195, 207.

4 Kathryn Hemmann, "Dangerous Women and Dangerous Stories: Gendered Narration in Kirino Natsuo's *Grotesque* and *Real World*," in *Rethinking Japanese Feminisms*, edited by Julia C. Bullock, Ayako Kano, and James Welker (Honolulu: University of Hawai'i Press, 2018), 171.

5 Kerry Carrington, "Feminist Criminologies," *in Alternative Criminologies*, edited by Pat Carlena and Leandro Ayres França (London: Routledge, 2018), 110.

6 Ibid., 110–111.

7 Ibid., 120.

8 Ibid.

9 Natsuo Kirino, *Out*, translated by Stephen Snyder (London: Vintage, 2004), 202–203.

10 Ibid., 16.

11 Ibid., 2.

12 Dana M. Britton, "Feminism in Criminology: Engendering the Outlaw," in *Girls, Women, and Crime: Selected Readings*, 2nd edition, edited by Dana M. Britton (Thousand Oaks, CA: Sage Publications, 2013), 44.

13 Ibid., 61.

14 Ibid.

15 Barbara Creed, *Return of the Monstrous-Feminine: Feminist New Wave Cinema* (London: Routledge, 2022), 6.

16 Natsuo Kirino, *Out*, 48.

17 Ibid., 48, 504.

18 Mina Qiao, "Fifty Shades of Noir: Female Masochism and Evolving Male Characterization as Cultural Critique in Kirino Natsuo's Writing." *Japan Forum* 33, no. 4 (2021), 679.

19 Natsuo Kirino, *Out*, 517–518.

20 Marian Duggan and Hannah Mason-Bish, "A Feminist Theoretical Exploration of Misogyny and Hate Crime," in *Misogyny as Hate Crime*, edited by Irene Zempi, and Jo Smith (London: Routledge, 2022), 19.

21 Natsuo Kirino, *Out*, 520.

Bibliography

Aborisade, Richard A., Adeleke A. Oladele, and Oshileye A. Temitope, "Victims of the 'Victimless Crimes': The Narratives of Residents of Red-Light Districts in Ibadan, Nigeria." *Gender & Behaviour* 16, no. 1 (2018): 10874–10888.

Agnew, Robert. "On Overview of General Strain Theory." In *Explaining Criminals and Crime: Essays in Contemporary Criminological Theory*, edited by Raymond Paternoster and Ronet Bachman. 161–174. Los Angles: Roxbury Publishing Company, 2001.

Alexander, Michelle. *The New Jim Crow: Mass Incarceration in the Age of Colorblindness*. Revised edition. New York: The New York Press, 2012.

Armitt, Lucie. *Fantasy Fiction: An Introduction*. New York: Continuum, 2005.

Arntfeild, Michael and Marcel Daneshi. "Introduction: Rise of the Criminal Humanist." In *The Criminal Humanities: An Introduction*, edited by Michael Arntfeild and Marcel Daneshi. 1–8. New York: Peter Lang, 2016.

Arvas, Paul and Andrew Nestingten. "Introduction: Contemporary Scandinavian Crime Fiction." In *Scandinavian Crime Fiction*, edited by Paula Arvas and Andrew Nestingen, 1–17. Cardiff: University of Wales Press, 2011.

Ascari, Maurizio. *A Counter-History of Crime Fiction: Supernatural, Gothic, Sensational*. Houndmills: Palgrave Macmillan, 2007.

Atkinson, Kate. *Case Histories*. New York: Back Bay Books, 2005.

Auden, W. H. "The Guilty Vicarage: Notes on the Detective Story, by an Addict." *Harpers* (May 1948): 406–412.

Badley, Linda, Andrew Nestingen, and Jaakko Seppälä. "Introduction: Nordic Noir as Adaptation." In *Nordic Noir, Adaptation, Appropriation*, edited by Linda Badley, Andrew Nestingen, and Jaakko Seppälä. 1–14. Cham: Palgrave Macmillan, 2020.

Baldick, Chris. *The Modern Movement*. The Oxford English Literary History. Volume 10, 1910–1940. Oxford: Oxford University Press, 2005.

Baldock, Nick. "The Christian World of Agatha Christie," *First Things*, April 8, 2009. www.firstthings.com/web-exclusives/2009/08/the-christian-world-of-aga tha-christie

Barnes, J. C., Brian B. Boutwell, and Kevin M. Beaver, "Contemporary Biosocial Criminology: A Systematic Review of the Literature: 2000–2012." In *The*

Handbook of Criminological Theory, edited by Alex R. Piquero. 75–99. Malden, MA: Wiley Blackwell, 2016.

Barthes, Roland. *S/Z*, translated by Richard Miller. Oxford: Blackwell, 2002.

Beccaria, Cesare. *On Crimes and Punishments and Other Writings*, edited by Aaron Thomas. Translated by Aaron Thomas and Jeremy Parzen. Toronto: University of Toronto Press, 2008.

Becker, Elizabeth. "As Ex-Theorist on Young 'Superpredators,' Bush Aide Has Regrets." *The New York Times*. February 9, 2001. www.nytimes.com/2001/02/09/us/as-ex-theorist-on-young-superpredators-bush-aide-has-regrets.html

Bentham, Jeremey. "A Comment on the Commentaries and a Fragment on Government." In *The Collected Works of Jeremy Bentham*, edited by J. H. Burns and H. L. A. Hart. General Editors J. H. Burns, J. R. Dinwiddy, F. Rosen, and T. P. Schofield. London: Athlone Press, 1977.

Bernthal, J. C. *Queering Agatha Christie Revisiting the Golden Age of Detective Fiction*. N.P.: Palgrave Macmillan, 2016.

Berry, Flynn. "What Happens to Siblings Who Survive a House of Horrors?" *The New York Times*. February 2, 2021. www.nytimes.com/2021/02/02/books/review/girl-a-abigail-dean.html

Bischoff, Paul. "Surveillance Camera Statistics: Which Cities Have the Most CCTV Cameras?." *Comparitech.com*. July 11, 2022. www.comparitech.com/vpn-privacy/the-worlds-most-surveilled-cities/

Bleakley, Paul. "A New Front in the History wars? Responding to Rubenhold's Feminist Revision of the Ripper." *Criminology & Criminal Justice* 22, no. 5 (2021): 659–675.

Bloch, Ernst. "A Philosophical View of the Detective Novel." In *Literary Essays*, translated by Andrew Joron et al. 209–227. Stanford: Stanford University Press, 1998.

Blumstein, Alfred. "Some Trends in Homicide and Its Age-Crime Curves." In *Wiley Handbooks in Criminology and Criminal Justice: The Handbook of Homicide*, edited by Fiona Brookman, et al. Chichester: Wiley-Blackwell, 2017. *Credo Reference*. https://doi.org/10.1002/9781118924501.ch3

Boatright, John R. "London Interbank Offered Rate (LIBOR) Scandal." In *The Sage Encyclopedia of Business Ethics and Society*, Volume 1, edited by Robert W. Kolb. 2115–2117. Thousand Oaks, CA: Sage Publications, 2018.

Böker, Uwe, Ines Detmers, and Anna-Christina Giovanopoulos. "From Gay to Brecht and Beyond: Imitation and Re-Writing of The Beggar's Opera –1728 to 2004." In *John Gay's the Beggar's Opera 1728–2004: Adaptations and Re-Writings*, edited by Uwe Böker, Ines Detmers, and Anna-Christina Giovanopoulos. 9–31. Leiden: Brill, 2006.

Booth, Nathanael T. "The Sign of the Four and the Detective as a Disrupter of Order." *Clues* 37, no. 1 (2019): 9–18.

Borghini, Andrea. "Positivism." In *The Wiley-Blackwell Encyclopedia of Social Theory*, edited by B. S. Turner. Chichester: Wiley-Blackwell, 2017. *Wiley Online Library*. https://doi-org.ezproxy.cityu.edu.hk/10.1002/9781118430873.est0731

Boutellier, Hans. *Crime and Morality: The Significance of Criminal Justice in Post-Modern Culture*. Dordrecht, NL: Kluwer Academic Publishers, 2000.

Bowden, Charles. *Murder City: Ciudad Juárez and the Global Economy's New Killing Fields*. New York: Nation Books, 2010.

Bradford, Richard. *Crime Fiction: A Very Short Introduction*. Oxford: Oxford University Press, 2015.

Brandl, Steven G. *Criminal Investigation*. 3rd edition. Thousand Oaks, CA: Sage Publications, 2014.

Briggs, John, Christopher Harrison, Angus McInnes, and David Vincent. *Crime and Punishment in England: An Introductory History*. London: University College London Press, 1996.

Britton, Dana M. "Feminism in Criminology: Engendering the Outlaw." In *Girls, Women, and Crime: Selected Readings*. 2nd edition, edited by Dana M. Britton. 39–51. Thousand Oaks, CA: Sage Publications, 2013.

Broderick, Damien. *Reading by Starlight: Postmodern Science Fiction*. London: Routledge, 1995.

Brown, David. "Mass Incarceration." In *Alternative Criminologies*, edited by Pat Carlen and Leandro Ayres França. 364–385. London: Routledge, 2018.

Bullock, Julia C., Ayako Kano, and James Welker. "Introduction." In *Rethinking Japanese Feminisms*, edited by Julia C. Bullock, Ayako Kano, and James Welker. 1–11. Honolulu: University of Hawai'i Press, 2018.

Burke, Roger Hopkins. *Criminal Justice Theory: An Introduction*. London: Routledge, 2012.

Button, Mark, Chris Lewis, and Jacki Tapley. "Not a Victimless Crime: The Impact of Fraud on Individual Victims and their Families." *Security Journal* 27, no. 1 (2014): 36–54.

Byron, John. *Cain and Abel in Text and Tradition: Jewish and Christian Interpretations of the First Sibling Rivalry*. Leiden: Brill, 2011.

Campbell, Alexandra. "Imagining the 'War on Terror': Fiction, Film, and Framing." In *Framing Crime: Cultural Criminology and the Image*, edited by Keith Hayward and Mike Presdee. 98–114. Milton Park: Routledge, 2010.

Carr, John Dickson. *The Hollow Man*. London: Orion, 2013.

Carrington, Kerry. "Feminist Criminologies." In *Alternative Criminologies*, edited by Pat Carlena and Leandro Ayres França. 110–124. London: Routledge, 2018.

Carson, E. Ann. "Prisoners in 2019." *Bulletin, U.S. Department of Justice, Office of Justice Programs, Bureau of Justice Statistics*. October 2020. NCJ 255115. https://bjs.ojp.gov/content/pub/pdf/p19.pdf

Casanova, Giacomo. *The Memoirs of Jacques Casanova*. New York: Modern Library, 1929.

Chambliss, William J. "The Politics of Crime Statistics." In *The Blackwell Companion to Criminology*, edited by Colin Sumner. 452–470. Malden, MA: Blackwell Publishing, 2004.

Chambliss, William J. *Power, Politics and Crime*. New York: Routledge, 2018.

Chandler, Raymond. *The Big Sleep*. New York: Vintage Crime/Black Lizard, 1992.

Chandler, Raymond. "The Simple Art of Murder." In *The Simple Art of Murder*. 1–18. New York: Vintage Crime/Black Lizard, 1988.

Charley, Jonathan. "Drugs, Crime and Other Worlds." In *Writing the Modern City: Literature, Architecture, Modernity*, edited by Sarah Edwards and Jonanthan Charley, 97–107. London: Routledge, 2012.

Cheesman, Tara. "A Brief Introduction to Honkaku and Shin Honkaku Mysteries." *Crime Reads*, September 25, 2020, https://crimereads.com/the-honkaku-and-shin-honkaku-mysteries-of-seishi-yokomizo/

Chesterton, G. K. "A Defence of Detective Stories." *The Detective*. The Society of Gilbert Keith Chesterton, 2002. www.chesterton.org/a-defence-of-detective-stories

Christie, Agatha. *The Body in the Library*. London: HarperCollins, 2016.

Christie, Agatha. *Crooked House*. London: HarperCollins, 2017.

Christie, Agatha. "Foreword." In *Crooked House*, by Agatha Christie. vii. London: HarperCollins Publishers, 2017.Christie, Agatha. *The Murder of Roger Ackroyd*. New York: Pocket Books, 1986.

Christie, Agatha. *The Mysterious Affair at Styles*. London: HarperCollins, 1989.

Christie, Agatha. *Nemesis*. London: HarperCollins, 2016.

Christie, Agatha. "Strange Jest." In *Miss Marple: The Complete Short Stories*. 242–255. London: HarperCollins, 1997.

Clarke, Ronald V. and Derek B. Cornish. "Rational Choice." In *Explaining Crime and Criminals: Essays in Contemporary Criminological Theory*, edited by Raymond Paternoster and Ronet Bachman. 23–42. Los Angeles: Roxbury Publishing Company, 2001.

Collins, Michael. "Biggie Envy and the Gangsta Sublime." *Callaloo* 29 (2006): 911–938.

Collins, Philip. *Dickens and Crime*. Bloomington, IN: Indiana University Press, 1968.

The Complete Newgate Calendar. Volume 4, edited by G. T. Crook. London: Navarre Society, 1926.

Connolly, Michael. *The Black Echo*. London: Orion, 2017.

Cornwell, Patricia. *Post-Mortem*. London: Warner Books, 1992.

Cramer, Maria. "Scotland Apologizes for History of Witchcraft Persecution." *The New York Times*. March 9, 2022. www.nytimes.com/2022/03/09/world/europe/scotland-nicola-sturgeon-apologizes-witches.html#:~:text=Nicola%20Sturgeon%2C%20the%20first%20minister,the%2016th%20and%2018th%20centuries

Creed, Barbara. *Return of the Monstrous-Feminine: Feminist New Wave Cinema*. London: Routledge, 2022.

Daeninckx, Didier. *Murder in Memoriam*, translated by Liz Heron. London: Serpent's Tail, 1991.

Davis, J. Madison. "Expanding the World of the Private Eye: Walter Mosley Becomes a Grand Master." *World Literature Today* 90, no. 3-4 (2016): 32–34.

Dawidoff, Nicholas. "Ross Macdonald, True Detective." *The New Republic*. September 15, 2017. https://newrepublic.com/article/144537/ross-macdonald-true-detective-noir-novelist-investigated-sources-rot-american-grain

Defoe, Daniel. *The Fortunes & Misfortunes of the Famous Moll Flanders*. Westminster: Folio Society, 1954.

DeKeseredy, Walter S. *Contemporary Critical Criminology*. London: Routledge, 2011.

Dick, Philip K. "The Minority Report." In *The Minority Report and Other Classic Stories*, by Philip K. Dick. 71–102. New York: Citadel Press, 1987.

Dickens, Charles. *Bleak House*. London: Penguin, 2012.

DiCristina, Bruce. "Criminology in 19th-Century France: Mainstays of the French 'Environmental' Tradition." In *The Handbook of the History and Philosophy of Criminology*, edited by Ruth All Triplett. 67–83. Chichester: Wiley-Blackwell, 2018.

Diemert, Brian. *Understanding Kate Atkinson*. Columbia, SC: University of South Carolina Press, 2020.

Dingledy, Frederick W. "The *Corpus Juris Civilis*: A Guide to its History and Use." *Legal Reference Services Quarterly* 35, no. 4 (2016): 231–255.

Dostoevsky, Fyodor. *Crime and Punishment*. Translated by Richard Pevear and Larissa Volokhonsky. London: Vintage, 2007.

Doyle, Arthur Conan. "The Blue Carbuncle." In *The Adventures of Sherlock Holmes*, by Arthur Conan Doyle. 179–206. London: Penguin, 2011.

Doyle, Arthur Conan. "The Final Problem." In *The Memoirs of Sherlock Holmes*, by Arthur Conan Doyle. 283–307. London: Penguin, 2011.

Doyle, Arthur Conan. *The Hounds of the Baskervilles*. London: Penguin, 2012.

Doyle, Arthur Conan. "The Norwood Builder." In *The Return of Sherlock Holmes*, by Arthur Conan Doyle. 30–62. London: Penguin, 2008.

Doyle, Arthur Conan. "The Red-Headed League." In *The Adventures of Sherlock Holmes*, by Arthur Conan Doyle. 56–87. London: Penguin, 2011.

Doyle, Arthur Conan. "A Scandal in Bohemia." In *The Adventures of Sherlock Holmes*, by Arthur Conan Doyle. 1–31. London: Penguin, 2011.

Doyle, Arthur Conan. *The Sign of Four*. London: Penguin, 2014.

Doyle, Arthur Conan. *A Study in Scarlet*. London: Penguin, 2011.

Doyle, Arthur Conan. "The Yellow Face." In *The Memoirs of Sherlock Holmes*, by Arthur Conan Doyle. 36–60. London: Penguin, 2011.

Drapkin, Israel. *Crime and Punishment in the Ancient World*. Lexington, MA: Lexington Books, 1989.

Duffee, David E., Alissa Pollitz Worden, and Edward R. Maguire. "Directions for Theory and Theorizing in Criminal Justice." In *Criminal Justice Theory*. 2nd edition, edited by Edward R. Maguire and David E. Duffee. 425–457. London: Routledge, 2015.

Duggan, Marian and Hannah Mason-Bish. "A Feminist Theoretical Exploration of Misogyny and Hate Crime." In *Misogyny as Hate Crime*, edited by Irene Zempi, and Jo Smith. 19–39. London: Routledge, 2022.

Eco, Umberto. "Narrative Structures in Fleming." Translated by R. A. Downie. In *The Poetics of Murder: Detective Fiction and Literary Theory*, edited by Glenn W. Most and William W. Stowe. 93–117. San Diego, CA: Harcourt Brace Jovanovich, 1983.

Edwards, Martin. "Victim." In *The Oxford Companion to Crime and Mystery Writing*, edited by Catherine Aird and John M. Reilly. 478–479. Oxford: Oxford University Press, 1999.

Eisner, Manuel. "From Swords to Words: Does Macro-Level Change in Self-Control Predict Long-Term Variation in Levels of Homicide?" *Crime and Justice* 43, no. 1 (2014): 65–134.

Eliot, T. S. "Wilkie Collins and Dickens." In *Selected Essays*, edited by Thomas Stearns. 409–418. New York: Harcourt, Brace, & World, 1964.

Ellroy, James. *The Black Dahlia*. London: Arrow Books, 2005.

Emsley, Clive. *A Short History of Police and Policing*, Oxford: Oxford University Press, 2021.

English, Daylanne K. "The Modern in the Postmodern: Walter Mosley, Barbara Neely, and the Politics of Contemporary African-American Detective Fiction." *American Literary History* 18, no. 4 (2006): 772–796.

The Epic of Gilgamesh. Translated by Andrew George, New York: Penguin Books, 1999.

Evans, Mary and Sarah Moore, with Hazel Johnstone. *Detecting the Social: Order and Disorder in Post-1970s Detective Fiction*. Cham: Palgrave MacMillian, 2019.

"Executions Around the World." *Death Penalty Information Center*. 2023. https://deathpenaltyinfo.org/policy-issues/international/executions-around-the-world

Ferrell, Jeff and Keith Hayward. "Cultural Criminology Continued." In *Alternative Criminologies*, edited by Pat Carlen and Leando Ayres França. 17–33. London: Routledge, 2018.

Ferrell, Jeff, Keith Hayward, Wayne Morrison, and Mike Presdee. "Fragments of a Manifesto: Introducing *Cultural Criminology Unleashed*." In *Cultural Criminology Unleashed*, edited by Jeff Ferrell, Keith Hayward, Wayne Morrison, and Mike Presdee. 1–9. London: Glasshouse Press, 2004.

Ferrell, Jeff, Keith Hayward, and Jock Young. *Cultural Criminology: An Invitation*. 2nd edition. London: Sage, 2015.

Fisher, Bonnie S., Bradford W. Reyns, and John Sloan III. *Introduction to Victimology: Contemporary Theory, Research, and Practice*. New York: Oxford University Press, 2016.

Ford, Elisabeth V. "Miscounts, Loopholes, and Flashbacks: Strategic Evasion in Walter Mosley's Detective Fiction." *Callaloo* 28, no. 4 (2005): 1074–1090. *JSTOR*, www.jstor.org/stable/3805589.

Forman, James Jr. and Kayla Vinson. "The Superpredator Myth Did a Lot of Damage. Courts Are Beginning to See the Light." *The New York Times*. April 20, 2022. www.nytimes.com/2022/04/20/opinion/sunday/prison-sentencing-parole-justice.html

Forshaw, Barry. *Crime Fiction: A Reader's Guide*. Harpenden: Oldcastle Books, 2019.

Foucault, Michel. *Discipline and Punish: The Birth of The Prison*. Translated by Alan Sheridan. New York: Vintage, 1995.

Frauley, Jon. *Criminology, Deviance, and the Silver Screen: The Fictional Reality and the Criminological Imagination*. New York: Palgrave Macmillan, 2010.

Freud, Sigmund. *Totem and Taboo: Resemblances Between the Psychic Lives of Savages and Neurotics*. Translated by A. A. Brill. New York: Moffat, Yard and Company, 1919.

Friedländer, Saul. *The Years of Persecution: Nazi Germany and the Jews 1933–1939*. London: Phoenix, 2007.

Garcia, Marie R., Ralph B. Taylor, and Brian A. Lawton. "Impacts of Violent Crime and Neighborhood Structure on Trusting Your Neighbors." *Justice Quarterly* 2, no. 4, (2007): 679–704.

Gass, Joshua. "*Moll Flanders* and the Bastard Birth of Realist Character." *New Literary History* 45, no. 1 (2014): 111–130. JSTOR, www.jstor.org/stable/24542584.

Gavin, Adrienne E. "Feminist Crime Fiction and Female Sleuths." In *A Companion to Crime Fiction*, edited by Charles J. Rzepka and Lee Horsley. 258–269. Chichester: Wiley-Blackwell, 2010.

Geggel, Laura. "Cold Case Closed: Scientists Pin 33,000-Year-Old Murder on a Left-Handed Paleo Killer." *Live Science*, July 3, 2019. www.livescience.com/65849-paleolithic-man-murdered.html.

Geherin, David. "Detectives." In *The Routledge Companion to Crime Fiction*, edited by Janice Allan, Jesper Gulddal, Stewart King, and Andrew Pepper. 159–167. London: Routledge, 2020.

Geis, Gilbert. "Pioneers in Criminology VII—Jeremy Bentham (1748–1832)." *Journal of Criminal Law and Criminology* 46, no. 2 (1955): 159–171.

Gerwarth, Robert. *Hitler's Hangman: The Life of Heydrich*. New Haven, CT: Yale University Press, 2011.

Gessen, Masha. "How Putin Criminalized Journalism in Russia." *The New Yorker*, April 7, 2023. www.newyorker.com/news/our-columnists/how-putin-criminalized-journalism-in-russia

Ghosh, Amitav. *The Great Derangement: Climate Change and the Unthinkable*. Chicago: University of Chicago Press, 2017.

Golding, William. *The Inheritors*. London: Faber & Faber, 1961.

Goode, Erich and Nachman Ben-Yehuda. *Moral Panics: The Social Construction of Deviance*. 2nd edition. Chichester: Wiley-Blackwell, 2009.

Goyes, David Rodríguez. *Southern Green Criminology: A Science to End Ecological Discrimination*. Bingley: Emerald Publishing, 2019.

Grafton, Sue. *A is for Alibi*. New York: Holt, Rinehart and Winston, 1982.

Grafton, Sue. *Q is for Quarry*. New York: Berkley Books, 2003.

Grafton, Sue. *W is for Wasted*. New York: Berkley Books, 2014.

Gray, James. *Why Our Drug Laws Have Failed and What We Can Do about It: A Judicial Indictment of the War on Drugs*. Philadelphia: Temple University Press, 2011.

Gross, Hyman. *Crime and Punishment: A Concise Moral Critique*. Oxford: Oxford University Press, 2012.

Gross, Kali N. "Black Women, Criminal Justice, and Violence." In *The Oxford Handbook of Crime and Criminal Justice*, edited by Michael Tonry. 285–298. Oxford: Oxford University Press, 2019.

Grossman, Lev. "Isaac Newton, Action Hero." *Time*, September 8 (2003): 91.

Gulddal, Jesper. "Clues." In *The Routledge Companion to Crime Fiction*, edited by Janice Allan, Jesper Gulddal, Stewart King, and Andrew Pepper. 194–201. London: Routledge, 2020.

Hall, Katharina. "The 'Nazi Detective' as Provider of Justice in Post-1990 British and German Crime Fiction: Philip Kerr's *The Pale Criminal*, Robert Harris's *Fatherland*, and Richard Birkefeld and Göran Hachmeister's *Wer übrig bleibt, hat recht.*" *Comparative Literature Studies* 50, no. 2 (2013): 288–313.

Halsey, Mark and Rob White. "Crime, Ecophilosophy and Environmental Harm." In *Environmental Crime: A Reader*, edited by Rob White. 27–49. Cullompten: Willan Publishing, 2009.

Hammett, Dashiell. *Red Harvest*. New York: Vintage, 1972.

Hart, H. L. A. "Positivism and the Separation of Law and Morals." *Harvard Law Review* 71, no. 4 (1958): 593–629. https://doi.org/10.2307/1338225.623

Hatter, Janine. "Joseph Peters: Mary Elizabeth Braddon (1835–1915)." In *100 Greatest Literary Detectives*, edited by Eric Sandberg. 144–146. Lanham, MD: Rowman & Littlefield Publishers, 2018.

Haycraft, Howard. *Murder for Pleasure: The Life and Times of the Detective Story*. Mineola, NY: Dover, 2019.

Hayes, Sharon. *Criminal Justice Ethics: Cultivating the Moral Imagination*. London: Routledge, 2015.

Hayward, Keith. "Opening the Lens: Cultural Criminology and the Image." In *Framing Crime: Cultural Criminology and the Image*, edited by Keith Hayward and Mike Presdee. 1–17. Milton Park: Routledge, 2010.

Heholt, Ruth. "Kay Scarpetta: Patricia Cornwell (1956–)." In *100 Greatest Literary Detectives*, edited by Eric Sandberg. 165–166. Lanham, MD: Rowman & Littlefield, 2018.

Hemmann, Kathryn. "Dangerous Women and Dangerous Stories: Gendered Narration in Kirino Natsuo's *Grotesque* and *Real World*." In *Rethinking Japanese Feminisms*, edited by Julia C. Bullock, Ayako Kano, and James Welker. 170–184. Honolulu, University of Hawai'i Press, 2018.

Henderson, Heike. "Mapping the Future? Contemporary German-Language Techno Thrillers." *Crime Fiction Studies* 1, no. 1 (2020): 96–113.

Herbig, F. J. W and S. J. Joubert. "Criminological Semantics: Conservation Criminology — Vision or Vagary?." In *Environmental Crime: A Reader*, edited by Rob White. 50–62. Cullompten: Willan Publishing, 2009.

Hickman, Miranda B. "Introduction: The Complex History of a 'Simple Art'." *Studies in the Novel* 35, no. 3 (2003): 285–304.

Hirschi, Travis. *Causes of Delinquency*. New Brunswick, NJ: Transaction Publishers, 2002.

Hirschi, Travis and Michael Gottfredson. "Self-control Theory." In *Explaining Criminals and Crime: Essays in Contemporary Criminological Theory*, edited by Raymond Paternoster and Ronet Bachman. 81–96. Los Angeles: Roxbury Publishing Company, 2001.

Hoebel, E. Adamson. *The Law of Primitive Man: A Study in Comparative Legal Dynamics*. Cambridge, MA: Harvard University Press, 2006.Horowitz, Anthony. *The Word Is Murder*. London: Century, 2017.

Horsley, Lee. *Twentieth-Century Crime Fiction*. Oxford: Oxford University Press, 2005.

House, James and Neal MacMaster. *Paris 1961: Algerians, State Terror, and Memory*. Oxford: Oxford University Press, 2006.

Howell, Philip. "Crime and the City Solution: Crime Fiction, Urban Knowledge, and Radical Geography." *Antipode* 30, no. 4 (1998): 357–378.

Hunnicutt, Gwen, and Kristy Humble Andrews. "Tragic Narratives in Popular Culture: Depictions of Homicide in Rap Music." *Sociological Forum* 24, no. 3 (2009): 611–630.

Hussain, Afreen A. "Crimes Against Persons." In *Victimology: A Comprehensive Approach to Forensic, Psychosocial and Legal Perspectives*, edited by Rejani Thudalikunnil Gopalan. 253–282. Cham: Springer, 2022.

Hustvedt, Siri. *A Woman Looking at Men Looking at Women: Essays on Art, Sex and the Mind*. New York: Simon & Schuster, 2016.

Hyde, Walter Woodburn. "The Homicide Courts of Ancient Athens." *University of Pennsylvania Law Review and American Law Register* 66, no. 7/8 (1918): 319–362.

Idema, Wilt Lukas. "Introduction." In *Judge Bao and The Rule of Law: Eight Ballad-stories From the Period 1250–1450*. ix–xxxiv. Singapore: World Scientific Publishing Company, 2009.

"IPCC, 2021: Summary for Policymakers." In *Climate Change 2021: The Physical Science Basis. Contribution of Working Group I to the Sixth Assessment Report of the Intergovernmental Panel on Climate Change*, edited by Masson-Delmotte, et al. Cambridge: Cambridge University Press, 2021.

Jacobsen, Michael Hviid. "Towards the Poetics of Crime: Contours of a Cultural, Critical and Creative Criminology." In *The Poetics of Crime: Understanding and Researching Crime and Deviance Through Creative Sources*, edited by Michael Hviid Jacobsen. 1–25. Farnham: Ashgate, 2014.

Jameson, Fredric. *Raymond Chandler: The Detections of Totality*. London: Verso, 2016.

Jones, Mark and Peter Johnstone. *History of Criminal Justice*. 5th edition. Amsterdam: Elsevier, 2012.

Jones, Stephen. *Criminology*. 7th edition. Oxford: Oxford University Press, 2021.

Kabak, Amanda. "We Need More Victim-Focused Narratives." *Crime Reads*, July 19, 2021, https://crimereads.com/we-need-more-victim-focused-narratives/

Kaplan, Cora. " 'Queens of Crime': The 'Golden Age' of Crime Fiction." In *The History of British Women's Writing, 1920–1945*, edited by Maroula Joannou. 144–157. Houndmills: Palgrave Macmillan, 2013.

Keetley, Dawn. "Unruly Bodies: The Politics of Sex in Maj Sjöwall and Per Wahlöö's Martin Beck Series." *Clues* 30, no. 1 (2012): 54–64.

Kenley, Nicole. "Global Crime, Forensic Detective Fiction, and the Continuum of Containment." *Canadian Review of Comparative Literature* 46, no. 1 (2019): 96–114. https://doi.org/10.1353/crc.2019.0006

King, Stewart. "The Reader and World Crime Fiction: The (Private) Eye of the Beholder." In *Criminal Moves: Modes of Mobility in Crime Fiction*, edited by Jesper Gulddal, Stweart King, and Alistair Rolls. 195–210. Liverpool: Liverpool University Press, 2019.

Kirino, Natsuo. *Out*. Translated by Stephen Snyder. London: Vintage, 2004.

Knafla, Louis A. "Structure, Conjuncture, and Event in the Historiography of Modern Criminal Justice History." In *Crime History and Histories of Crime: Studies in the Historiography of Crime and Criminal Justice in Modern History*, edited by Clive Emsley and Louis A. Knafla. 33–44. Westport, CT: Greenwood Press, 1996.

Knepper, Paul. "Laughing at Lombroso: Positivism and Criminal Anthropology in Historical Perspective." In *The Handbook of the History and Philosophy of Criminology*, edited by Ruth Ann Triplett. 51–66. Chichester: Wiley-Blackwell, 2018.

Knepper, Paul. *Writing the History of Crime*. London: Bloomsbury, 2016.

Knight, Stephen. *Crime Fiction Since 1800: Detection, Death, Diversity*. 2nd edition. Houndmills: Palgrave Macmillan, 2010.

Knight, Stephen. *Form and Ideology in Crime Fiction*. London: MacMillan, 1980.

Kramer, S. N. "Ur-Nammu Law Code." *Orientalia* 23, no. 1 (1954): 40–51.

Kranioti, Elena F., Dan Grigorescu, and Katerina Harvati. "State of the Art Forensic Techniques Reveal Evidence of Interpersonal Violence ca. 30,000 Years Ago." *Plos One*, July 3, 2019. 1–16. https://doi.org/10.1371/journal.pone.0216718

Larsson, Stieg. *The Girl with the Dragon Tattoo*. Translated by Reg Keeland. New York: Alfred E. Knopf, 2010.

Leavis, Q. D. "The Case of Miss Dorothy Sayers." *Scrutiny* (December 1937): 334–340.

Le Jan, Régine. "Wergild." In *Encyclopedia of the Middle Ages*, edited by André Vauchez. Paris: James Clarke & Co, 2005. *Oxford Reference*.

Levay, Matthew. "Crime Fiction and Criminology." In *The Routledge Companion to Crime Fiction*, edited by Janice Allan, Jesper Gulddal, Stewart King, and Andrew Pepper. 273–281. London: Routledge, 2020.

Linnemann, Travis and Kyra A. Martinez. "Let Fury Have the Hour: The Radical Turn in British Criminology." In *The Handbook of the History and Philosophy of Criminology*, edited by Ruth All Triplett. 222–236. Chichester: Wiley-Blackwell, 2018.

Lock, Helen. "Invisible Detection: The Case of Walter Mosley." *Melus* 26, no. 1 (2001): 77–89. https://doi.org/10.2307/3185497.78

Lombroso, Cesare. *Criminal Man*. Translated by Mary Gibson and Nicole Hahn Rafter with assistance from Mark Seymour. Durham, NC: Duke University Press, 2006.Lyons, Kelan. "CT Supreme Court tosses 60-year term of man judge called 'superpredator' Keith Belcher to be resentenced." *The CT Mirror*. January 24, 2022. https://ctmirror.org/2022/01/24/ct-supreme-court-tosses-60-year-term-of-man-judge-called-superpredator/

Machado, Helena and Rafaela Granja. *Forensic Genetics in the Governance of Crime*. Singapore: Palgrave Pivot, 2020.

Maeder, Evelyn M. and Richard Corbett. "Beyond Frequency: Perceived Realism and the CSI Effect." *Canadian Journal of Criminology and Criminal Justice* 57, no. 1 (2015): 83–114.

Maida, Patricia D. *Mother of Detective Fiction: The Life and Works of Anna Katharine Green*. Bowling Green, OH: Bowling Green State University Popular Press, 1989.

Martin, Theodore. "War-on-Crime Fiction." *PMLA* 136, no. 2 (2021): 213–228.

Mayer, Ruth. "In the Nick of Time?: Detective Film Serials, Temporality, and Contingency Management, 1919–1926." *Velvet Light Trap* 79 (2017): 21–35. doi:10.7560/VLT7903.

Maynard, John R. "The Bildungsroman." In *A Companion to the Victorian Novel*, edited by Patrick Brantlinger and William Thesing. 279–301. Malden, MA: Blackwell Publishing, 2002.

McBratney, John. "Racial and Criminal Types: Indian Ethnography and Sir Arthur Conan Doyle's *The Sign of Four*." *Victorian Literature and Culture* 33, no. 1 (2005): 149–167.

McCaw, Neil. "Sherlock Holmes: Sir Arthur Conan Doyle (1859–1930)." In *100 Greatest Literary Detectives*, edited by Eric Sandberg. 90–92. Lanham, MD: Rowman & Littlefield Publishers, 2018.

McDermid, Val. *The Last Temptation*. New York: St Martin's Paperbacks, 2003.

McDermid, Val. *The Mermaids Singing*. London: HarperCollins, 2006.

McGarry, Ross and Sandra Walklate. *Victims: Trauma, Testimony and Justice*. London: Routledge, 2015.

McGregor, Rafe. *Critical Criminology and Literary Criticism*. Bristol: Bristol University Press, 2021.

McLuhan, Marshall. *The Mechanical Bride: The Folklore of Industrial Man*. London: Routledge & Kegan Paul, 1951.

McMahon, Richard. "Histories of Interpersonal Violence in Europe and North America, 1700-Present." In *The Oxford Handbook of Crime and Criminal Justice*, edited by Michael Tonry. 111–131. Oxford: Oxford University Press, 2019.

Merivale, Patricia and Susan Elizabeth Sweeney. "The Game's Afoot: On the Trail of the Metaphysical Detective Story." In *Detecting Texts: The Metaphysical Detective Story from Poe to Postmodernism*, edited by Patricia Merivale and Susan Elizabeth Sweeney. 1–24. Philadelphia: University of Pennsylvania Press, 1998.

Merton, Robert K. "Social Structure and Anomie." In *History of Criminology*, edited by Paul Rock. 389–399. Aldershot: Dartmouth, 1994.

Messent, Peter. *The Crime Fiction Handbook*. Chichester: Wiley-Blackwell, 2013.

Mills, Rebecca. "Victims." In *The Routledge Companion to Crime Fiction*, edited by Janice Allan, Jesper Gulddal, Stewart King, and Andrew Pepper. 149–158. London: Routledge, 2020.

Milne, A. A. "Introduction." In *The Red House Mystery*, by A. A. Milne. ix–xii. New York: Vintage, 2009.

Miron, Jeffrey A. "Violence and the U.S. Prohibitions of Drugs and Alcohol." *American Law and Economics Review* 1, no. ½ (1999): 78–114. https://doi.org/10.1093/aler/1.1.78

Monahan, John. "Slouching Toward Crime." *The Yale Law Journal* 95, no. 7 (1986): 1536–1551.

Moore, Michael. *Placing Blame: A General Theory of the Criminal Law*. Oxford: Clarendon Press, 1997.

Morris, Bob. "History of Criminal Investigation." In *Handbook of Criminal Investigation*, edited by Tim Newburn, Tom Williamson, and Alan Wright. 15–40. London: Routledge, 2007.

Mosely, Walter. *Devil in a Blue Dress*. New York: Washington Square Press, 2020.

Naremore, James. "Dashiell Hammett and the Poetics of Hard-Boiled Detection." In *Essays on Detective Fiction*, edited by Bernard Benstock. 49–71. London: Macmillan Press, 1983.

Neill, Anna. "The Savage Genius of Sherlock Holmes." *Victorian Literature and Culture* 37, no. 2 (2009): 611–626. doi:10.1017/S1060150309090378.613.

Newburn, Tim. *Criminology*. 3rd edition. London: Routledge, 2017.

The New Oxford Annotated Bible with Apocrypha: New Revised Standard Version. Edited by Michael D. Coogan, et al., Oxford: Oxford University Press, 2010.

"The New York Times Fiction Bestseller List 2022." *Booklistqueen*. 2023. www.booklistqueen.com/the-new-york-times-fiction-bestseller-list-2022/

Norris, James A. "Three-Strikes Laws." In *American Prisons and Jails: An Encyclopedia of Controversies and Trends*, Volume 2, edited by Vidisha Barua Worley and Robert M. Worley. 648–651. Santa Barbara, CA: ABC-CLIO, 2019.

Nyman, Jopi. *Hard-boiled Fiction and Dark Romanticism*. Frankfurt: Peter Lang, 1998.

O'Brien, James F. *The Scientific Sherlock Holmes: Cracking the Case with Science and Forensics*. Oxford: Oxford University Press, 2013.

O'Dell, Benjamin D. "Performing the Imperial Abject: The Ethics of Cocaine in Arthur Conan Doyle's *The Sign of Four*." *Journal of Popular Culture* 45, no. 5 (2012): 979–999.

O'Flaherty, Brendan and Rajiv Sethi. *Shadows of Doubt: Stereotypes, Crime, and the Pursuit of Justice*. Cambridge, MA: Harvard University Press, 2019.

Orcutt, James D. "Crime, Social Control Theory of." In *The Blackwell Encyclopedia of Sociology*, edited by George Ritzer. *Wiley Online Library*. 2016. https://doi.org/10.1002/9781405165518.wbeosc156.pub2

Panek, LeRoy L. *The Special Branch: The British Spy Novel, 1890–1980*. Bowling Green, OH: Bowling Green University Popular Press, 1981.

Park, Chan-wook. *Decision to Leave*. Moho Film, 2022.

Parsons, Joanne Ella. "Fosco's Fat: Transgressive Consumption and Bodily Control in Wilkie Collins' *The Woman in White*." In *The Victorian Male Body*, edited by Joanne Ella Parsons and Ruth Heholt. 215–233. Edinburgh: Edinburgh University Press, 2018.

Paternoster, Raymond and Ronet Bachman. "The Positive School of Criminology: Introduction." In *Explaining Criminals and Crime: Essays in Contemporary Criminological Theory*, edited by Raymond Paternoster and Ronet Bachman. 47–56. Los Angeles: Roxbury Publishing Company, 2001.

Paternoster, Ray and Daren Fisher. "The Foundation and Re-emergence of Classical Thought in Criminological Theory: A Brief Philosophical History." In *The Handbook of the History and Philosophy of Criminology*, edited by Ruth Ann Triplett. 173–188. Chichester: Wiley Blackwell, 2018.

Paternoster, Raymond and Daren Fisher. "Social Disorganisation and Crime: Introduction." In *Explaining Criminals and Crime: Essays in*

Contemporary Criminological Theory, edited by Raymond Paternoster and Ronet Bachman. 113–123. Los Angeles: Roxbury Publishing Company, 2001.

Pemberton, Antony and Inge Vanfraechem. "Victims' Victimization Experiences and their Need for Justice." In *Victims and Restorative Justice*, edited by Inge Vanfraechem, Daniela Bolívar, and Ivo Aertsen. 16–47. London: Routledge, 2015.

Pepper, Andrew. *Unwilling Executioner: Crime Fiction and the State.* Oxford: Oxford University Press, 2016.

Pezzotti, Barbara. "Transnationality." In *The Routledge Companion to Crime Fiction*, edited by Janice Allan, Jesper Gulddal, Stewart King, and Andrew Pepper. 94–101. London: Routledge, 2020.

Pinker, Steven. *The Better Angels of Our Nature: The Decline of Violence in History and Its Causes.* London: Allen Lane, 2011.

Piquero, Alex R., et al. "The Criminal Career Paradigm." *Crime and Justice* 30 (2003): 359–506. *JSTOR*, www.jstor.org/stable/1147702.

Plain, Gill. *Twentieth-Century Crime Fiction: Gender, Sexuality, and the Body.* Edinburgh: Edinburgh University Press, 2001.

Plato, *The Republic*, translated by Benjamin Jowett. Oxford: Clarenden Press, 1888. Retrieved from www.gutenberg.org/files/55201/55201-h/55201-h.htm#pref

"PLR Most Borrowed." *British Library.* n.d. www.bl.uk/plr/popular-loans.

Poe, Edgar A. "The Murder in the Rue Morgue," *Graham's Lady's and Gentleman's Magazine* 18 (1841): 166–179. *Hathi Trust.* https://babel.hathitrust.org/cgi/pt?id=osu.32435051465326&view=1up&seq=16

Polasek, Ashley D. "Surveying the Post-Millennial Sherlock Holmes: A Case for the Great Detective as a Man of Our Times." *Adaptation* 6, no. 3 (2013): 384–393. https://doi-org.ezproxy.cityu.edu.hk/10.1093/adaptation/apt006

Potter, Hillary. "Intersectional Criminology: Interrogating Identity and Power in Criminological Research and Theory." *Critical Criminology* 21, no. 3 (2013): 305–318.

Pratt, Travis C., Jacinta M. Gau, and Travis W. Franklin. *Key Ideas in Criminology and Criminal Justice.* Thousand Oaks, CA: Sage Publications, 2011.

Presdee, Mike. *Cultural Criminology and the Carnival of Crime.* London: Routledge, 2000.

Price, Richard. *Clockers.* London: Bloomsbury, 2009.

Priestman, Martin. *Crime Fiction from Poe to the Present.* Devon: Northcote House, 1998.

Proudhon, Pierre-Joseph. *What Is Property?: An Inquiry into the Principle of Right and of Government.* Translated by Benj. R. Tucker. New York: Dover, 1970.

Pyrhönen, Heta. *Murder from an Academic Angle.* Columbia, SC: Camden House, 1994.

Qiao, Mina. "Fifty Shades of Noir: Female Masochism and Evolving Male Characterization as Cultural Critique in Kirino Natsuo's Writing." *Japan Forum* 33, no. 4 (2021): 679–703.

Ramirez, Mary Kreiner and Steven A. Ramirez. *The Case for the Corporate Death Penalty: Restoring Law and Order on Wall Street.* New York: New York University Press, 2017.

Ramsland, Katherine. *The Mind of a Murderer: Privileged Access to the Demons That Drive Extreme Violence*. Santa Barbara: Praeger, 2011.

"Ranking of the Most Dangerous Cities in the World in 2023, by Murder Rate per 100,000 Inhabitants," *Statista*. February 2023, www.statista.com/statistics/243797/ranking-of-the-most-dangerous-cities-in-the-world-by-murder-rate-per-capita/

Rapezzi, Claudio, Roberto Ferrari, and Angelo Branzi. "White Coats and Fingerprints: Diagnostic Reasoning in Medicine and Investigative Methods of Fictional Detectives." *BMJ: British Medical Journal* 331, no. 7531 (2005): 1491–1494.

Reddy, Maureen T. *Traces, Codes, and Clues: Reading Race in Crime Fiction*. New Brunswick, NJ: Rutgers University Press, 2003.

Redfield, Robert. "Primitive Law." *University of Cinncinati Law Review* 33, no. 1 (1964): 1–22.

Reilly, John M. "Criticism, Literary." In *The Oxford Companion to Crime & Mystery Writing*, edited by Rosemary Herbert. 109–111. Oxford: Oxford University Press, 1999.

Reilly, John M. "History of Crime and Mystery Writing." In *The Oxford Companion to Crime & Mystery Writing*, edited by Rosemary Herbert. 210–222. Oxford: Oxford University Press, 1999.

Reilly, John M. "The Politics of Tough Guy Mysteries." *University of Dayton Review* 10 (1973): 25–31.

Reilly, Katie. "Here Are All the Times Donald Trump Insulted Mexico." *Time*, August 31, 2016. https://time.com/4473972/donald-trump-mexico-meeting-insult/

Reiner, Robert. *Crime: The Mystery of the Common-Sense Concept*. Cambridge: Polity, 2016.

Rendell, Ruth. *Road Rage*. London: Arrow Books, 1998.

Reuter, Timothy. *Medieval Polities and Modern Mentalities*, edited by Janet L. Nelson. Cambridge: Cambridge University Press, 2006.

Rich, Nathaniel. "American Dreams: 'Clockers' by Richard Price." *The Daily Beast*, July 14, 2017. www.thedailybeast.com/american-dreams-clockers-by-richard-price

Richardson, M. E. J. *Hammurabi's Laws: Text, Translation and Glossary*. London: Bloomsbury, 2005.

Roberts, Julian V. *Criminal Justice: A Very Short Introduction*. Oxford: Oxford University Press, 2015.

Roberts, Paul. "Thinking through Critical Criminology." In *Social Censure and Critical Criminology: After Sumner*, edited by Anthony Amatrudo. 1–45. London: Palgrave Macmillan, 2017.

Robinson, Matthew B. and Kevin M. Beaver. *Why Crime?: An Interdisciplinary Approach to Explaining Criminal Behavior*. 2nd edition. Durham, NC: Carolina Academic Press, 2009.

Rock, Paul. "Introduction: The Emergence of Criminological Theory." In *History of Criminology*, edited by Paul Rock. xi–xxix. Aldershot: Dartmouth, 1994.

Roth, Mitchel P. *An Eye for an Eye: A Global History of Crime and Punishment.* London: Reaktion Books, 2014.

Ruggiero, Vincenzo. *Crime in Literature: Sociology of Deviance and Fiction.* London: Verso, 2003.

Ruggiero, Vincenzo. *Power and Crime.* London: Routledge, 2015.

Rutigliano, Olivia. "Agatha Christie is the best-selling novelist in history." *Lithub*, April 3, 2020. https://lithub.com/agatha-christie-is-the-best-selling-novelist-in-history/

Ruyters, Michele, Greg Stratton, and Jarryd Bartle. "'They're making money off tragedy'—Netflix's Dahmer series shows the dangers of fictionalising real horrors." *The Conversation.* October 10, 2022, https://theconversation.com/the yre-making-money-off-tragedy-netflixs-dahmer-series-shows-the-dangers-of-fic tionalising-real-horrors-192006

Rzepka, Charles. *Detective Fiction.* Cambridge: Polity Press, 2005.

Sampson, Fraser. "Cyberspace: The New Frontier for Policing?." In *Cyber Crime and Cyber Terrorism Investigator's Handbook*, edited by Babak Akhgar, Andrew Staniforth, and Francesca Bosco. 1–10. Amsterdam: Elsevier, 2014.

Sandberg, Eric. "Contemporary Crime Fiction, Cultural Prestige, and the Literary Field." *Crime Fiction Studies* 1, no. 1 (2020): 5–22.

Sandberg, Eric. *Dorothy L. Sayers: A Companion to the Mystery Fiction.* Jefferson, NC: McFarland, 2022.

Sandberg, Eric "Peanut-butter-and-pickle-sandwiches: Sue Grafton's Alphabet Series and Everyday Life." *Mean Streets: A Journal of American Crime and Detective Fiction* 1, no. 1 (2020): 61–84.

Sayers, Dorothy L. "Aristotle on Detective Fiction." *English* 1, no. 1 (1936): 23–35.Sayers, Dorothy L. *Five Red Herrings.* Toronto: Signet, 1967.

Sayers, Dorothy L. *Gaudy Night.* New York: Avon, 1968.

Sayers, Dorothy L. "Introduction." In *The Omnibus of Crime*, edited by Dorothy L. Sayers. 9–47. New York: Garden City Publishing Company, 1929.

Sayers, Dorothy L. *Murder Must Advertise.* New York: Harper Paperbacks, 1995.

Sayers, Dorothy L. *Unpleasantness at the Bellona Club.* New York: HarperPaperbacks, 1995.

Sayers, Dorothy L. *Whose Body?* London: New English Library, 1977.

Sayers, Dorothy L. and Robert Eustace. *The Documents in the Case.* London: New English Library, 1978.

Scaggs, John. *Crime Fiction.* London: Routledge, 2005.

Scaggs, John. "Double Identity: Hard-Boiled Detective Fiction and the Divided 'I'." In *Investigating Identities: Questions of Identity in Contemporary International Crime Fiction*, edited by Marieke Krajenbrink and Kate M. Quinn. 131–143. Amsterdam: Rodopi, 2009.

Scholfield, Karin. "Collisions of Culture and Commodification of Crime: Media Sexual Abuse." In *Cultural Criminology Unleashed*, edited by Jeff Ferrell, Keith Hayward, Wayne Morrison, and Mike Presdee. 121–131. London: Glasshouse Press, 2004.

Schwartz, Martin D. and Henry H. Brownstein. "Critical Criminology." In *The Handbook of Criminological Theory*, edited by Alex R. Piquero. 301–317. Chichester: Wiley Blackwell, 2016.

Scribner, Amy. "Kate Atkinson: Scandal in Scotland." *BookPage*. October 2006. https://bookpage.com/interviews/8372-kate-atkinson#.YYi_h-mQyUk

Sheehan, Jason. " 'The Force' Is Basically 'Game of Thrones' With Cops—And That's Pretty Great." June 24, 2017. *NPR*. www.npr.org/2017/06/24/532976 297/the-force-is-basically-game-of-thrones-with-cops-and-thats-pretty-great

Shepard, Jim. "Clockers." *The New York Times*. June 21, 1992. www.nytimes. com/1992/06/21/books/clockers.html

Shklovksy, Viktor. *Theory of Prose*. Translated by Benjamin Sher. Normal, IL: Dalkey Archive Press, 1991.

Shpayer-Makov, Haia. *The Ascent of the Detective: Police Sleuths in Victorian and Edwardian England*. Oxford: Oxford University Press, 2011.

Shpayer-Makov, Haia. "Detectives and Forensic Science: The Professionalization of Police Detection." In *The Oxford Handbook of the History of Crime and Criminal Justice*, edited by Paul Knepper and Anja Johansen. 474–496. Oxford: Oxford University Press, 2016.

Sim, Stuart. *Justice and Revenge in Contemporary American Crime Fiction*. Basingstoke: Palgrave Pivot, 2015.

Simpson, Christine R. "Marple, Miss Jane." In *The Oxford Companion to Crime & Mystery Writing*, edited by Rosemary Herbert. 278–279. Oxford: Oxford University Press, 1999.

Sjöwall, Maj and Per Wahlöö. *Cop Killer*. Translated by Thomas Teal. London: 4th Estate, 2016.

Sjöwall, Maj and Per Wahlöö. *The Man on the Balcony*. Translated by Alan Blair. New York: Harper Perennial, 2007.

Sjöwall, Maj and Per Wahlöö. *The Man Who Went Up in Smoke*. Translated by Joan Tate. New York: Harper Perennial, 2006.

Sjöwall, Maj and Per Wahlöö. *The Murder at the Savoy*. Translated by Joan Tate. London: 4th Estate, 2016.

Sjöwall, Maj and Per Wahlöö. *Roseanna*. Translated by Lois Roth. London: 4th Estate, 2016.

Sjöwall, Maj and Per Wahlöö. *The Terrorists*. Translated by Joan Tate. London: 4th Estate, 2016.

Smith, Erin. *Hard-Boiled: Working-Class Readers and Pulp Magazines*. Philadelphia: Temple University Press, 2000.

Smith, Wendy Serbin. *Victimless Crime: A Selected Bibliography*. n.p.: National Institute of Law Enforcement and Criminal Justice, 1977.

Snyder, Robert Lance. "Entropic Disintegration: Jim Thompson's *The Killer Inside Me*, *Savage Night*, and *A Hell of a Woman*." *Journal of American Culture* 44, no. 3 (2021): 177–193.

Sova, Dawn B. *Critical Companion to Edgar Allan Poe: A Literary Reference to His Life and Work*. New York: Facts on File, 2007.

Spencer, Nicholas P. "Ecological Struggle in Neal Stephenson's *Zodiac*." In *Tomorrow Through the Past: Neal Stephenson and the Project of Global*

Modernization, edited by Jonathan P. Lewis. 39–56. Newcastle-upon-Tyne: Cambridge Scholars Press, 2006.

Spierenburg, Pieter. "The Rise of Criminology in its Historical Context." In *The Oxford Handbook of the History of Crime and Criminal Justice*, edited by Paul Knepper and Anja Johansen. 373–395. Oxford: Oxford University Press, 2016.

Starr, Douglas. *The Killer of Little Shepherds: A True Crime Story and the Birth of Forensic Science*. New York: Knopf, 2010.

Steiner, Franz. *Taboo*. Harmondsworth: Penguin, 1962.

Stephenson, Neal. "Acknowledgements." *Zodiac*. London: Arrow Books, 2001.

Stephenson, Neal. *Zodiac*. London: Arrow Books, 2001.

"Stephenson, Neal 1959-." *Concise Major 21st Century Writers*, Volume 5, edited by Tracey L. Matthews. 3422–3425. Detroit, MI: Gale, 2006.

Stone, Lawrence. "Interpersonal Violence in English Society 1300–1980." *Past & Present* 101, no. 1 (1983): 22–33.

Stone, Lawrence. "A Rejoinder." *Past & Present* 108, no. 1 (1985): 216–224.

Symons, Julian. *Bloody Murder: From the Detective Story to the Crime Novel*. 3rd edition. New York: Mysterious Press, 1992.

"Table 16: Number of Crimes per 100,000 Inhabitants by Population Group, 2019." In *2019 Crime in the United States*, FBI: UCR, https://ucr.fbi.gov/crime-in-the-u.s/2019/crime-in-the-u.s.-2019/tables/table-16.

Taylor, Ralph B. "The Ecology of Crime, Fear, and Delinquency: Social Disorganisation Versus Social Efficacy." In *Explaining Criminals and Crime: Essays in Contemporary Criminological Theory*, edited by Raymond Paternoster and Ronet Bachman. 124–139. Los Angeles: Roxbury Publishing Company, 2001.

Thomas, Ronald R. "The Fingerprint of the Foreigner: Colonizing the Criminal Body in 1890s Detective Fiction and Criminal Anthropology." *ELH* 61, no. 3 (1994): 655–683.

Todorov, Tzvetan. "The Typology of Detective Fiction." *The Poetics of Prose*. Translated by Richard Howard. 42–52. Oxford: Basil Blackwell, 1977.

Tremblay, Richard E., and Moshe Szyf. "Developmental Origins of Chronic Physical Aggression and Epigenetics." *Epigenomics* 2, no. 4 (2010): 495–499.

Triplett, Ruth. "Crime, Social Learning Theory of." In *The Blackwell Encyclopedia of Sociology*, edited by George Ritzer. *Wiley Online Library*, 2015. https://doi.org/10.1002/9781405165518.wbeosc157.pub2.

Triplett, Ruth Ann. "Introduction." In *The Handbook of the History and Philosophy of Criminology*, edited by Ruth All Triplett. 1–11. Hoboken, NJ: Wiley-Blackwell, 2018.

"The Twelve Tables," *The Avalon Project: Documents in Law, History and Diplomacy*, Lillian Goldman Law Library, Yale Law School, 2008, https://avalon.law.yale.edu/ancient/twelve_tables.asp.

Verplaetse, Jan. *Localizing the Moral Sense: Neuroscience and the Search for the Cerebral Seat of Morality, 1800–1930*. Dordrecht: Springer, 2009.

Vervaele, John. "Forward." In *White Collar Crime: A Comparative Perspective*, edited by Katalin Ligeti and Stanislaw Tosza. v–vii. London: Bloomsbury, 2018.

Wacquant, Loïc. "Class, Race & Hyperincarceration in Revanchist America." *Daedalus* 139, no. 3 (2010): 74–90.

Walsh, Melanie. "Where is All the Book Data." *Public Books*, October 4, 2022, www.publicbooks.org/where-is-all-the-book-data/

Walters, Glenn D., and Thomas W. White. "Heredity and Crime: Bad Genes or Bad Research." *Criminology* 27, no. 3 (1989): 455–486.

Walters, Reece. "Green Criminology." In *Alternative Criminologies*, edited by Pat Carlen and Leandro Ayres França. 165–181. London: Routledge, 2018.

Walton, Paul, and Jock Young, J. "Preface." In *The New Criminology Revisited*, edited by Paul Walton and Jock Young. vii–viii. London: St. Martin's Press, 1998.

Wambaugh, Joseph. "Feeding the Force." *Joseph Wambaugh: Grandmaster of Police Stories*, www.josephwambaugh.net/Police_Novels.html

Welsh, Lucy, Layla Skinns, and Andrew Sanders. *Sanders and Young's Criminal Justice*. 5th edition. Oxford: Oxford University Press, 2021.

Westron, Carol. "The Golden Age: Authors and the Death Penalty Dilemma." *Promoting Crime Fiction by Lizzie Hayes*. December 16, 2018, https://promotingcrime.blogspot.com/2018/12/authors-and-death-penalty-dilemma.html

White, Ethan Doyle. *Wicca: History, Belief, and Community in Modern Pagan Witchcraft*. Eastbourne: Sussex Academic Press, 2022.

White, Rob. *Crimes Against Nature: Environmental Criminology and Ecological Justice*. Cullompton: Willan Publishing, 2012.

White, Rob. "Criminology." In *The Wiley-Blackwell Encyclopedia of Social Theory*, edited by Bryan S. Turner. 1–4. Oxford: Wiley Blackwell, 2017.

Whitlock, Tammy. "Forms of Crime: Crime and Retail Theft." In *The Oxford Handbook of Crime and Criminal Justice*, edited by Michael Tonry. 155–169. Oxford: Oxford University Press, 2019.

Willbern, David. *The American Popular Novel after World War II: A Study of 25 Best Sellers, 1947–2000*. Jefferson, NC: McFarland, 2013.

Williams, Andy. *Forensic Criminology*. London: Routledge, 2015.

Wilson, Andrew. "Ruth Rendell: An Appreciation." *Contemporary Women's Writing* 11, no. 1 (2017): 121–125. https://doi.org/10.1093/cww/vpw038.

Wilson, Ann. "The Female Dick and the Crisis of Heterosexuality." In *Feminism in Women's Detective Fiction*, edited by Glenwood Irons. 148–156. Toronto: University of Toronto Press, 1995.

Wilson, Edmund. "Who Cares Who Killed Roger Ackroyd: A Second Report on Detective Fiction." *New Yorker*, June 20 (1945): 59–66.

Wilson, Edmund. "Why Do People Read Detective Stories?" *New Yorker*, October 14, 1944, www.newyorker.com/magazine/1944/10/14/why-do-people-read-detective-stories

Winslow, Don. *The Force*. London: HarperCollins, 2018.

"Witchcraft." *UK Parliament*, 2022. www.parliament.uk/about/living-heritage/transformingsociety/private-lives/religion/overview/witchcraft/

Wolfgang, Martin E. "Victim Precipitated Criminal Homicide." *Journal of Criminal Law, Criminology & Police Science* 48, no. 1 (1957): 1–11.

Worthington, Heather. *Key Concepts in Crime Fiction*. Houndmills: Palgrave Macmillan, 2011.

Wrong, E. M. "Introduction to Crime and Detection (1926) by E. M. Wrong." *Golden Age of Detection Wiki*, edited by Juergen Lull. November 28, 2008,

http://gadetection.pbworks.com/w/page/7930836/Introduction%20to%20Cr
ime%20and%20Detection

Zappe, Florian, and Andrew Gross. "Introduction." In *Surveillance I Society
I Culture*, edited by Florian Zappe and Andrew Grosse. 9–23. Berlin: Peter
Lang, 2019.

Zola, Émile. *Thérèse Raquin*. Translated by Andrew Rothwell. Oxford: Oxford
University Press, 2008.

Index

For Product Safety Concerns and Information please contact our EU
representative GPSR@taylorandfrancis.com
Taylor & Francis Verlag GmbH, Kaufingerstraße 24, 80331 München, Germany